Entangled

By Florence St. John

Based on a true story, some names, places, and details have been changed to protect the innocent. The author does not claim to be qualified to diagnose personality disorders. All events are based on actual experiences.

Knowledge of narcissistic abuse isn't limited to licensed therapists. As a victim of this abuse, I have firsthand experience not limited to clinical diagnosis. The victim isn't always able to "just walk away."

Please excuse any typos. Between the auto spell, my cats running across the keyboard, and an occasional glass of wine, it happens.

La Maison Publishing, Inc.
Vero Beach Florida
The Hibiscus City
lamaisonpublishing@gmail.com

Table of Contents

Eye of the Hurricane 9

Charm and Wit 13

Une Merveilleuse Nuit 21

Fantasy Land 26

Hypnotized 30

Love Bomb 35

Under the Stars 43

A World of Frogs 50

In the Clouds 55

Leap of Faith 63

Rockin Eve 67

Sugaroo 75

Complicated 81

Cool Touch 84

Sweets 91

On the River 97

Valentine Massacre 101

Roller Coaster 106

Just Florence 110

Charlatan 116

Georgia 120

The Promise of Love 124

Pauper 128

Deep Water 133

Betrayed 136

The Five C's..141

Wildlife 146

Pickin 151

Control Freak..157

Coffee Talk...161

Homeward Bound 166

Escape in the Night..172

Up in Smoke 178

Fishin 184

Good Babe...189

Rebel..194

Comfy 198

License to Drive 202

A Home for Mack 206

Overboard 210

Smooth Operator 213

Ten/Love..216

Father Figure 221

Floating...226

Right Mind 231

The Abyss 235

Teddy Bear 238

Celebrate 244

The Wrong Tool 247

Untouchable 250

Bitter Honey 254

House on Wheels 260

Surrender 264

Skype 269

Head Games 274

Super Sleeper 278

Time 284

Scociopath 289

Scarred 294

Guilty as Charged 298

Sinking Ships 305

Turning the Table 311

Smell the Roses 316

Road Trip 323

Worm 328

Gambling Man 335

Fighting Words 340

Mashed Potatoes 345

Salesman 349

Time and Money 354

Blackout...360

Purgatory...364

Holy Grail...370

Behind the Mask 377

Toxic 381

I'm Done 385

No Contact 389

Words of Wisdom 394

Replaced..403

Plenty of Fish..408

Post-Traumatic..412

Cognitive Behavior 417

Stages of Anger 423

Joe Dial 429

Gypsy..435

Survivor 440

Codependency: Don't Dance..454

Arlington Heights, IL 60004 459

Suggested Reading 460

Eye of the Hurricane

I want to hear the thunder shake
The ground beneath my feet
The earth around me rumble
And cracks in the concrete

The bus to Manhattan pulls in right on schedule, sparing me the agony of waiting. As I step out of LaGuardia's terminal, the cold bites sharper than expected. Florida's sunny embrace is a ghost I've already forgotten. Overhead, black clouds churn and twist, foretelling chaos. I clutch my jacket tighter, steeling myself against the approaching storm.

"We're heading into rough weather," the driver warns as I board and snag a seat near the heater. The words hang heavy, but I have no idea how prophetic they'll become. Outside, the rain begins as an impatient patter, but it escalates quickly, hammering down by the time we reach Grand Central Station.

I step off the bus and hug close to the buildings, futilely dodging streams of water cascading from awnings. By the time I enter the station, my hair clings to my scalp, my shoes squelch. Grand Central's rhythmic chaos envelopes me. Commuters swarm in relentless waves, their hurried steps echoing in a tempo that defies the grandeur of the gold-trimmed arches above. They don't notice the beauty here. They're too busy chasing time.

I follow the signs toward the downtown subway, swept along by the tide. The roar of an approaching train beckons me. With a final push, I slip aboard just as the doors snap shut.

"Mind if I sit?" I ask the man beside me, whose newspaper spills over half the bench.

"Not at all," he replies, gathering the rogue pages. His eyes flicker with mild amusement as he folds the paper away. "Business or pleasure?"

I hesitate, but his easy demeanor lowers my guard. "I'm meeting an old friend. Haven't seen him in thirty-six years."

His eyebrows rise. "An old flame, perhaps?"

"Not exactly." The truth stings. "He wasn't interested in me that way back then."

"Maybe he's changed his mind." He smiles—a teasing, knowing grin—before returning to his paper. The train jolts to a stop at a central station. A mass of humanity surges off before the car begins its next journey. The space left behind is sparse but breathable.

At Whitehall Station, I ascend into a world drowning in gray. Rain streams down in relentless sheets, cascading off skyscrapers, collecting in turbulent rivers along the curbs. A street vendor's cart fills the damp air with the sweet, nutty scent of roasted almonds, teasing my empty stomach.

"Thanks for the directions," I tell the man as he leads me toward my hotel. He hands me a business card with a playful wink.

"If your friend flakes, I know a great spot for dinner."

I slip the card into my pocket, a polite afterthought. But there's no room in my mind for anyone but Daniel.

Back in high school, He was a sliver of a boy with long, dirty blonde hair in high school. He wasn't conventionally handsome, but he did make me laugh, quick with a joke that left you laughing despite yourself. I remember his eyes, smiling and mischievous. It's been so long. I wonder if he'll be disappointed when he sees me.

The hotel lobby offers sanctuary from the weather, and I check in quickly, my fingers trembling more from nerves than cold. Upstairs, I try calling Daniel. No answer. Anxiety pricks at me until my phone buzzes, his name flashing on the screen.

"You thought I'd stand you up, didn't you?" His voice comes through warm and familiar, laced with teasing humor.

"I was starting to wonder," I admit. "Are you still coming tomorrow?"

"Absolutely. Just need to drop the girls off at their mother's first."

"Girls?" My curiosity flares.

"My daughters. Four and ten. Didn't I mention them?"

"No," I say, startled. "I thought your kids were older."

"I'll explain everything tomorrow. It's a long story."

Long story indeed. My mind churns with questions I tamp down for now. Instead, I head out to hunt for dinner. The hotel provides an umbrella, though it's a feeble shield against the monsoon outside. My steps lead me into the first open Chinese restaurant I spot. Inside, I find solace in a steaming bowl of wonton soup, the warm broth thawing my bones.

I linger, hoping the rain will subside, but nature offers no reprieve. Resigned, I dodge puddles and passing cars as I trudge back toward the hotel. Each droplet feels heavier, weighted with an anticipation I can't shake. By the time I collapse into my room, the city's usual spark has dimmed.

As the storm thrashes outside, I curl up on the stiff hotel bed, the anticipation of seeing Daniel brewing within me. What if he's fat and bald? What if he smells bad. What if I don't like him? My pulse quickens with thoughts of tomorrow's reunion, the answers hovering just out of reach.

Charm and Wit

Collided back in high school
For only a brief second
Our future life together
We could never reckon

My heart is pumping with exhilaration as I search in my suitcase for something special to wear. I must have been in a fog when I packed because nothing seemed good enough. Going shopping is a great excuse, so I jump on the subway and head toward Times Square.

This time, it's a beautiful sunny day, and I'm walking on air as I stroll along Broadway. No one pays attention—just another reason to love New York. People rush to work with coffee in one hand and their briefcases in the other while the tourists cram into local eateries. I stop at a corner deli to get a bacon and egg sandwich on a roll. Then make my way to Bryant Park, where I join the masses sitting under the trees, leisurely reading their newspapers and books.

Horns blaring and cabbies yelling in the background, the grittiness of the city envelopes me as I walk each block. Feeling one with the city, I sip my coffee and eat my deliciously greasy breakfast. Then stroll down Fifth Avenue toward 32nd Street and Macy's and stop in small boutiques, searching the racks for a perfect outfit.

Keeping an eye on the time, I return to the hotel, so I'll be ready when Daniel arrives. Along the way, the aroma of food from street vendors drifts through the air, sausage and peppers, gyros, and hot dogs. It's tempting, but I'm too nervous to eat.

I go downstairs to wait in the guest lounge, but I begin to lose my nerve. *Maybe I should leave a note at the desk and return to my room.*

Before I act on the impulse — my phone chimes with a text from Daniel.

"I'm in the cab."

Another text. *"I'm here."*

My insides twist into a knot, and I rush into the lobby, passing right by him.

"He-y-y!" I hear a smooth and sultry voice say.

I spin around, and our eyes lock — instant attraction. Daniel Weaver is every bit what I'd imagined, older but good-looking in a bad-boy way. His arms fold around me for a hug, and the fragrance of his cologne entices me to linger a second or two more in his embrace. We stand in the lobby, neither of us knowing what to do next.

"Okay," he says, breaking the spell. "Let's do coffee."

"Or pizza," I say, changing the itinerary.

His face lights up like a child. "I love pizza!"

"I know of a great place near the Brooklyn Bridge. It's kind of far, but we can take the subway."

"Great, but first, I need a cigarette. Do you mind?"

"No, not at all," I lie.

Outside, the rain has subsided. Warm air escapes the grates that line the street. It turns to steam as it hits the chilly evening air and hugs the ground like a fog.

As I clip-clop in my heels, he lights his cigarette, and I try to stay out of his smoky trail. From the corner of my eye, I stare at him. *He's very handsome.*

"I almost fainted when I saw your profile picture on our class website," he says. You haven't changed a bit. Remember when we cut English class, and you tried to kiss me under the stairway?"

"I did not!" I object. "It was *you* that tried to kiss me."

I look up at Daniel, who has a devilish smile. Thank goodness he can't see me blush in the dim light of the subway station. We buy two tokens and go through the turnstile.

"We should have met in Vegas," he gripes.

"I was there once," I say, "and after three days, I couldn't wait to leave."

"That's because you weren't there with me!"

"You're a tease. Why didn't you ever ask me out?"

"I thought you were going out with my friend Robert."

"Who?"

"You know, Robert Adams… tall, brown hair?"

"I was never going out with anyone named Robert. I never dated in high school. I wasn't part of the popular crowd like you."

"That's not true. Everyone knew you."

"Everyone made fun of me, especially Brenda and Josette. Do you remember them?"

"They were catty little bitches, weren't they? I wonder whatever happened to them."

"I hope they're fat and wrinkled with lots of gray hair."

"Be nice," he says with a smile.

"Are you still friends with Robert?" I ask.

"He died in a car crash a few years ago."

"I'm sorry to hear that."

We exit the train and ascend the station stairs to the streets of Brooklyn. I'm more at ease but still have difficulty keeping up with him in my heels.

"I'm glad you agreed to meet me," he says.

"I have to confess — I was nervous. You're the first date I've had since my divorce."

"How long were you married?"

"Thirty years."

He whistles. "Wow, that's a long time. What happened?"

"We just went in different directions. I went to college, and Edward smoked pot!"

Daniel laughs. "You should have married me."

I look up and notice that his eyes are sparkling. He flashes a smile that almost stops my heart.

"Oh, sure!" I tease and abruptly stop walking.

"What's wrong?" he asks.

"I think we're lost."

"I thought you knew where we were going?"

"The concierge gave me directions. Maybe we missed a turn. We'll have to ask someone."

"I'm not asking. *You* ask."

"What a sissy!" I walk toward a group of men. "Excuse me. Do you know how to get to the Brooklyn Bridge?"

They look at me as if I just came from Mars. "Six blocks that way and make a left. You can't miss it."

We backtrack and continue our conversation.

"Do you have children?" he asks.

"Yes, two, but they're grown now. My daughter Annmarie lives in Florida, and my son Joseph lives in Georgia. We used to be close before my divorce, but lately, we're just cordial."

"I know what you mean," he says. "My son is nineteen now. After I divorced his mother, he and his sister stopped talking to me."

"Ahh! Children can be so judgmental."

"At least I have two daughters from Lisa."

"Your second wife?"

"No, we were never married."

"Oh! Why didn't you marry their mother?"

"She's twenty years younger than me. After our first child, things fell apart."

A confused look crosses my face. "Yet, you had a second?"

"She said her biological clock was ticking, and I figured it would be better if the children had the same father."

"How did you meet her?"

"It's a long story."

I get the feeling he doesn't want to share, so my imagination fills in the blanks. He must have flashed that beautiful smile of his. If so, Lisa didn't have a chance.

Again, I notice we're no closer to the bridge. I walk up to a couple waiting for the bus. "Is the bridge up this way?"

"No, you have to go back a few blocks, make a right, then go a few blocks more and make a left."

"Ask ten people, and you get ten different answers," he jokes, and we laugh.

By the time we find Grimaldi's Pizzeria, my feet are killing me, and I look forward to sitting for a while, but the line is long. We get behind a group of young people. Daniel has no filter as he jokes with the other people in line. He reminds me of my father—very amusing.

At the table, he turns to talk to the couple next to us, two men. "You guys are gay, right?"

I cringe, expecting they'll be offended. Instead, the couple smiles and makes polite conversation.

After our pizza, we get up to leave.

"Let's walk over the bridge," I suggest, forgetting about my heels.

We finish our pizza, and he takes my arm as we leave. Walking over the bridge is so romantic. Other couples are holding hands. By the time we reach the other side, Daniel is holding mine.

"Hey, let's go to Rockefeller Center and check out the Christmas tree."

"It's kind of far," I say, thinking of my aching feet. "Maybe we should take the train."

As we walk to the subway station, he brushes against me, and I get a shiver.

I dig through my coat pocket for the metro map I took from the hotel lobby. Daniel stares at it for a long time.

"The print is small," I say. "Do you need my reading glasses?"

"No, I have some." He reaches into his jacket pocket and smiles. "We must be getting old."

"It's not so bad," I say. Actually, at this moment, I feel like my life is just beginning. After years of an unhappy marriage, I'm single, and now I have a second chance for love.

"We have to take the G-train," he says, quickly removing his glasses.

We hear the train coming down the track as we descend the stairs. It approaches with a screeching halt, and we run to catch it, jumping on it before the doors close.

We're so busy talking and learning about each other that we miss our stop. Instead of taking another train, we exit and walk to Rockefeller Center.

The night has a gothic feel to it. Sparse clouds drift past the moon and over the tops of high-rise buildings. Tourists congest the streets, but wrapped up in our little world, they don't exist.

We arrive at the famous Christmas tree, but it's naked. "Oh, no! I forgot! They don't decorate the tree until after Thanksgiving."

"Bummer," he says and flashes that smile again. "I don't want the night to end just yet. Let's find a bar and have a drink or two."

"Okay." I squirm in my uncomfortable shoes.

He puts his arm around my shoulder, and I try to keep in step with him as we walk. We come to a bar that is overflowing with people. The thumping bass of the club music is loud, even before he opens the door.

"Find us a table, and I'll get some drinks," he shouts over a blaring Jennifer Lopez song.

Through the smoky haze, I look around. *Daniel would have to choose one of the last places in New York that allow smoking.*

There's no empty table, so I find a spot at a small counter and put my coat on the stool next to me to reserve his seat. Two girls are dancing in the center of the floor. I wish I could dance, but my body never falls in sync with the music. Back in school, I've always been the typical wallflower. I was invisible, but tonight, I feel like I'm about to blossom.

Daniel returns with two drinks, but a conversation is impossible over the noise. He looks at his watch. "It's after midnight!" he shouts. "I think I missed the last train out of Penn Station."

"Oh, no! What are you going to do?"

He shrugs. "I'll just catch some zzz's while I wait for the morning train."

Somehow, I hadn't thought about how we would end the evening.

"That's crazy! You can come back to my hotel."

"Great! Let's get out of here."

Une Merveilleuse Nuit

I want to feel the blood
Pulsing through my veins
To feel alive once more
Be free of all my chains

Daniel and I step into the elevator at the hotel, and I try my best to avoid looking into those sultry eyes which peer into my soul.

"Don't worry, Daniel says, "no stress, no pressure," as if he could read my mind.

The doors open on the fourteenth floor, and he follows me down the corridor. With every step closer to the room, my mind is racing.

There's one bed, and I sit on the edge. The hems of my pants are wet from walking through the puddles on the street.

"I need to get out of these clothes," I say, embarrassed at what that suggests.

Daniel settles into a nearby chair, staring with a mischievous grin. "Go ahead. You don't have to feel uncomfortable around me."

I emerge from the bathroom wearing a camisole and panties. Somehow, it feels natural because I know we'll make love.

"Don't you look cute?" He says and strips down to his boxers.

Control Freak is written on the front in big, bold letters. I giggle.

"What's so funny?" he asks.

"Nothing." I smile.

"I want you," he whispers and strokes my shoulder.

As Daniel leans in to kiss me, my heart thumps like a rabbit caught in a trap. I haven't kissed anyone in years. Should I keep my mouth closed or open? He decides for me. His tongue searches for mine. The faint taste of tobacco is on his breath, even though he's been chewing gum, but my desire for him is stronger than my disgust for cigarettes.

My body quivers under his touch, and I struggle to catch my breath.

"I'm sorry," he says. "Am I coming on too strong?"

"No, I'm fine. It's been so long since I've had…."

"Relax," he whispers.

Locked in heated passion, I soon melt into the moment and slip into ecstasy. I can't stop shaking. I'd forgotten how good it feels to be loved.

"Are you all right?"

"Yes," I say.

He kisses my forehead. "I'm glad I have that effect on you." He wraps his arms around me and closes his eyes. It's confining but comforting at the same time. I note the small alarm clock on the night table. It reads two-thirty. My body yearns for sleep, too, but instead, I stare out the window at the New York Skyline, listening to him as he breathes.

The horizon outside the hotel window lightens, and we lie entwined in each other's arms. I turn toward Daniel and study his face. He's very handsome, but there's something more compelling about him.

Daniel's eyes remain closed, but he cradles my head and plants a gentle kiss on my forehead. "What time is your flight?" he asks.

"It's not until 1 o'clock, but I have to catch the bus to the airport."

"Then I guess we should get dressed. Do we have time to grab a cup of coffee?"

"I think so," I reply. I'm anxious about the time, but I don't want this to end.

We walk out of the hotel and across the street to a coffee shop on the corner.

"Let's sit on the bench outside," Daniel suggests.

He wants to smoke. I had forgotten about that.

He takes a long drag on his cigarette and spits the smoke out in short puffs that encircle his head like a storm cloud.

We're both silent as we sip our coffee, and he puffs his cigarette.

"So, what are your plans when you get home?" he asks.

"I'll be packing up and heading to Florida for the winter."

Daniel's eyes widen. "Do you have a place there?"

"Yes. My ex-husband, Edward, got our family business. I got the house in Georgia, and he agreed to pay for the townhouse in Florida until I could take over the mortgage."

After our coffee, we walk towards the subway station. Daniel lights another cigarette, so we stand at the top of the stairs until he's finished.

Struggling with my suitcase as it thumps down the stairs, I wonder why he doesn't offer to help, but I don't ask. Instead, I carry the bag down the stairs by myself.

We reach the bottom, and a crooked smile crosses his lips. "I don't do helpless," he says, brushing the hair away from my eyes.

"Hmm, very funny!"

We sit among the morning commuters on the subway going uptown in silence. Daniel is going to Port Authority, and I'm going to Grand Central to take the shuttle to La Guardia.

The train slows as it enters the station, and he gives me a quick kiss on the cheek. "I'll talk to you soon," he promises and hops off the train. The doors close, and he walks away from the platform. As the train rolls on, I try to keep sight of him, but he disappears into the crowd. I wonder if I'll ever see him again, but then, I assumed it was a one-night stand.

I realize I'm on the wrong train and snap out of my trance. Now, I have to exit Times Square and take the shuttle to Pershing Square on the city's east side.

At the bus station, my cell phone chimes with an incoming text.

"Do you miss me? Lol."

Strangely, I do.

When I get home, I post a picture of the Brooklyn Bridge on Facebook.

Une Merveilleuse Nuit, A marvelous night.

I can't seem to get him out of my mind. Every time I hear my phone ring, my heart leaps.

"You're back," my daughter Annmarie cries. "How was it? Did you like him? Tell me everything. Did you sleep with him?"

"Annmarie! I can't believe you're asking me that."

"I hope you used protection. You don't know how many women he's slept with."

Just what I need. A safe-sex lecture from my daughter!

My phone chimes.

"I have an incoming text, Annmarie. I'll call you later."

"Is it *himm?*" she says.

"Yes… and his name is Daniel."

Fantasy Land

I want to be in Love
Tumble into space
And feel every emotion
My heart will keep the pace

In the distance, I see the Fuller Warren Bridge in Jacksonville. My Florida townhouse is beckoning. Usually, I can spend only a week or two there. Now that I have two tenants occupying my house, I can afford to stay in Florida until I sell it in the summer.

I'm in control of my life for the first time in years. I'm free to go anywhere, do anything, and be anybody. The sense of liberation exhilarates and scares at the same time. I've always been afraid to be alone. It kept me in my marriage longer than I should have stayed.

My cat Ripley is asleep in his crate, which I strapped into the backseat. Unlike other cats that meow and hyperventilate, Ripley adapts to anything. He's such a good traveler.

A warm breeze swirls through my car from the open windows, and a vision of Daniel flashes through my mind. Where does he fit into my life? I didn't plan to jump into another relationship this soon after my divorce. But I never expected to meet anyone like him.

I arrive at my townhouse at three in the afternoon and enter my code. The *Iron Gate* opens to welcome me.

My place is across from the pool. I click the remote on my visor and drive into the garage.

The door closes, leaving me in darkness. It's eerily quiet as I grope for the doorway to the kitchen. Flipping on the light illuminates the peach-colored cabinets. I'm home. It's what I've been waiting for, but I can't shake the feeling that something is missing. The air is hot and stifling. I turn on the air conditioner before unloading the car. All I want to do is sleep.

After setting the automatic coffee maker, I check my phone, a little disappointed that Daniel hasn't called. A surge of loneliness sweeps over me as I climb the stairs to bed.

The phone wakes me up. "He-y-y," Daniel sings. "What are you doing?"

"It's two a.m. in the morning. I'm sleeping, silly."

"Well, wake up. We have a lot to discover about each other."

"Can't we do it in the morning?"

"You're not going to hang up on me, are you?"

"Not a chance." I giggle.

"I have this intense feeling about us, Florence. Come to New York, right now!"

"I don't have winter clothes."

"I'll be your winter clothes."

"Ahh, but I love the sun."

"Love me...it's better."

"Why don't you come and visit me in Florida."

"Maybe, I will. You can go back to sleep now."

Like a symphony, his melodic voice is in my head as I drift to sleep.

The coffeemaker whines and belches, and the smell of fresh coffee wafts upstairs. I open my eyes and think about Daniel before getting out of bed.

With my coffee and my cell phone, I head to the pool. The water soothes me, and I relish every moment as the sun climbs higher in the sky.

My phone rings.

"Mom. When did you get in?"

"Yesterday afternoon."

"Why didn't you call me?" she complains.

"I'm sorry. I was tired, and I went to bed early."

"Well, I'm glad you got in alright, but I was worried."

"Annmarie, do you remember that guy I met in New York?"

"What about him?"

"He may come to visit."

"Really? You just met him." I can imagine her eyes narrowing. "Doesn't he have a job?"

"He's in construction."

"That means he doesn't work," she quips. "Does he have children?"

"Yes, three daughters and a son, but he doesn't talk to the older ones since he divorced their mother."

"He must have done something awful if his children won't talk to him."

My phone chimes. "I have to go, Annmarie. I'm getting a text."

"All right, I'll talk to you later. Be careful."

We hang up, and I read Daniel's message, "We'll be together soon."

Excited, I dial his number.

"He-y-y...." he sings. "I'm flying into Orlando on Tuesday evening. Can you pick me up?"

"Orlando? That's almost three hours away. There's a closer airport in Melbourne."

"This one was cheaper."

Hypnotized

Falling slowly into sleep
Your arms around me snug
I feel your breath upon my neck
Your sweet and tender hug

Daniel books a hotel on the edge of town where the buildings are older. My stomach is doing a summersault, and I feel giddy as I enter the lobby. "Welcome to the Hilton," the girl at the counter asks, "Do you have a reservation?"

"Yes, but I believe it's under the name Weaver, Daniel Weaver." She clicks some keys on her computer. "You must be Florence," she says in a conspiratorial tone as she gives me two keys. "The Honeymoon Suite is on the ninth floor. Just follow the signs."

Honeymoon Suite? There must be some mistake. As the elevator ascends, my heartbeat is so hard that I feel lightheaded. I drag my suitcase down the long hall to the end room and let myself in.

"Wow!" I murmur and run to the window. I kick off my shoes and gaze out the windows, watching the sunset in shades of honey. Lakes on each side glisten under the setting sun, and a flock of birds flies across the landscape. I absorb the surrounding beauty. It's incredible and almost too good to be true.

High on the ninth floor, I feel like a princess in a tower, waiting for my Prince Charming.

The starry sky opens up before me. Snapping out of my daydreams, I slip on my shoes. Daniel's flight is due to land at seven-thirty. Soon, I'll be in his arms again. The excitement is building inside me, and I feel I will burst. My stomach muscles clench, and I feel queasy.

The phone rings, making my heart race.

"He-y-y, my plane just landed. I'm in front of the terminal. Take your time. I'm smoking a cigarette." Daniel's leaning against the wall in a cloud of smoke as I drive up to the arrival area. He sees my car, takes one more drag, and then flicks the lit cigarette into the gutter.

Hiding my frown, I pop my trunk so he can load his small duffel bag. He slides into the passenger seat, just as relaxed as the last time we met. We banter back and forth, laughing so hard that I can't find my way out of the terminal.

"You're distracting me," I giggle.

"I can't help it if you can't drive and talk at the same time," he teases.

Finally, we exit the airport and head toward the downtown district. Since it's a Friday night, parking spaces are scarce, and we have to park further away from the venues.

The wind picks up, and there's a chill in the air, but I feel safe and warm with Daniel's arm draped across my shoulder. Following the sound of loud music from one of the restaurants, we walk toward the crowd.

"Look, it's the House of Blues," he says. "I've always wanted to go there."

His boyish excitement amuses me, and I follow him inside. The music blares from the stage as the hostess leads us to a booth. Under the low lights of the restaurant, my eyes drift from the menu to look at him. I study his face and try to figure out what it is that captivates me.

The waitress rushes over and intrudes, ready to take our order with pen in hand. Her nametag says, Amy.

I order the Buffalo wings, forgetting how messy they are to eat, and she turns to Daniel.

"Nothing for me, Amy," he says, making me feel self-conscious.

Amy trots off toward the kitchen, and the band takes a break, enabling us to talk. I'm in awe as he tells me about things he has achieved in his life, including training horses.

"Really? I love horses."

"Maybe I'll teach you how to ride."

"I'd love that. How many horses do you have?"

"I had three, but I'm down to one. It belongs to my daughter."

"Do you ever regret getting divorced?" I ask.

"Nah, I was never happy. I kept a packed suitcase by the front door."

"That's strange. What did your wife think about that?"

"She probably thought I was bluffing. When I left, she poisoned my kids against me." Daniel hangs his head.

He tugs at my heartstrings. Before I can speak, the waitress returns and sets a platter of wings in front of us.

"I brought two plates, in case you want to share," she says.

"Thank you." Daniel flashes her a flirty smile.

I have a pang of jealousy.

When she's gone, I stare at the red, barbeque-sauced wings, and my appetite disappears.

"I think you have to eat them with your hands," Daniel says.

Picking one up, I take a bite, feeling the smear of sauce around my lips. Daniel's stare makes me uncomfortable, and I reach for a napkin.

"Would you like one?" I ask.

"Yuck, I hate chicken, but I will take a piece of celery." He grabs a stalk from my plate and dips it in the small cup of blue cheese dressing.

We share the celery until it's gone, and Daniel flags down the waitress.

"More celery," I say.

"No problem," she says to *him*.

"So, what were you doing in California?" I ask.

"I was renovating a house. It's on the market for a million dollars. The woman who invested with me is filthy rich. Yep. I'm just waiting for my money." He looks away.

"Would you mind if I come and sit on your side?"

"Not at all." I scoot over to make room.

He slides next to me, and his thigh is pressing against mine. It sends a thrill through me like a jolt of adrenaline.

"Let's go to the hotel?"

The waitress returns with our celery, but he pays no attention this time.

Daniel pays the bill, and we leave.

I hand him the key, and we pass the front desk and enter the elevator. He pretends to open other people's doors as we walk down the hall. He's so funny. We're laughing so hard that he drops the key when we get to our room. He tries again and opens the door.

I want him to kiss me, but he's making me wait. We gaze at the night sky, and I search for the moon. It's a crescent shape with a star alongside it.

After a few awkward moments, he nibbles my earlobe. I look into his soulful eyes, and his lips invade my mouth in search of my tongue. I've never kissed like this — it feels weird, forbidden.

Love Bomb

I've never had this joy
Romantic interludes
That is why I treasure
Your words and loving coos

Sunlight filters through the large windows in the morning. Daniel's legs entwine with mine like an octopus. I'm entangled. There's no way out. His strong arms around me make me realize how lonely I've been. I stare out the window and breathe in his scent. It's hard for me to stay still. Gently freeing his arm, I try to escape his silken web and move toward the edge of the bed. "Five more minutes." He murmurs and pulls me back. We cuddle for a little longer. Then I feel him get out of bed. Damn! I had to go to the bathroom, but he beat me to it. He's in there a long time, so I knock. The door flies open, and a cloud of cigarette smoke drifts out.

"I think this is a non-smoking room."

"It's no big deal. I do it all the time."

Smoke circles me, but I close the bathroom door and take a quick shower. When I come out, Daniel is dressed and ready to go. He kisses me with his cigarette breath.

"Hurry up. I want to get some coffee and have another cigarette."

After one cup of coffee in the hotel restaurant, he pays the check, and we go outside so he can smoke. At least now, the breeze blows the smoke away, but he reeks when we get in the car, and I wrinkle my nose.

"Is everything all right?"

"Yes," I fib. "Have you been to Florida before?"

"When I was seventeen, I drove down to the Keys with two buddies, but I didn't see much. I like California. I have a house there."

"You mean the one you renovated?"

"No, I have another. I'm planning to move my construction business out West."

Now, I'm impressed. Daniel has two houses and a successful business.

He flicks his lighter on and off, focusing on the flame, and tells me about his family. "I have an older sister and brother. I'm the youngest. We have different fathers. I'm the black sheep of the family. My sister, Sheri, and I drifted apart when our mother died, but Sal and I stayed together. He wasn't right in the head after an accident. Before my mother died, she made me promise to take care of him. I did for a while, and he came to stay with me until my sister called DCF. She accused me of using him for his social security check and made him move in with her."

"Wow! What about your real father?"

"I've never met him, but I'm sure I didn't miss much. My stepfather treated me like one of his own."

"I'm the oldest in my family," I say.

"So, that's why you're always so serious!"

"No, I'm not."

He gives me a devious smile, and I laugh.

The gate for my townhouse opens, and we drive past the pool. As we pull into the driveway, I hit the remote for the garage.

Daniel whistles. "Wow, this is nice."

"I'm trying to hold on to this place," I say. "The mortgage is high, but I'm hoping to sell my house in Georgia next spring so I can pay for this one."

Daniel follows me into the kitchen, his eyes landing on the coffeemaker. "I sure can use some coffee," he says. "I love coffee."

"Make yourself comfortable, and I'll brew some."

From the serving window, I see him sitting on my couch.

"Here you go," I say, handing him the cup and sitting beside him.

He puts the cup on the coffee table and presses his lips against mine. "I want you," he murmurs.

Forgetting the coffee, I lead him upstairs to the bedroom and pull down the comforter while he strips down his boxer shorts. This time, they have little sharks on them. I giggle. "Where do you find these shorts?"

"They were gifts," he replies, pulling me to him. "They won't bite."

Daniel lowers me on the bed and invades my mouth with his tongue. We make love until the sun goes down. He has unusual stamina. Viagra crosses my mind, but not my lips.

"I'm so tired," I whimper.

"No sleeping," he says sternly. "It's not two-thirty yet."

"Why do we have to stay up 'til two-thirty?"

"That was what time it was when we first made love in the city."

"I can't believe you remembered that!"

"Do you have something to tell me?" he whispers.

I'm unsure what he means, but his reflective tone makes me laugh. "Yeah, I need to sleep. Is it two-thirty yet?"

He snuggles up next to me, swinging his right leg over mine, and sighs. "Ah… comfy."

❧

The coffeemaker gurgles, and I slide out from Daniel's arms.

"Where are you going?" he says with a hint of alarm in his voice.

"Downstairs to make us some breakfast."

"I'd rather stay in bed." He wriggles his eyebrows. "Come back here," he says as if talking to an insubordinate child.

Torn between my desire for caffeine and his sultry appeal, he wins.

"Can you rub my chest?" he asks.

I comply, savoring the sensation as my fingers glide over his muscles.

Daniel gets up to go to the bathroom. When he comes out, he's brushing his teeth.

"Is that mine?"

"Yeah, I forgot to pack one," he answers with my toothbrush dangling from his mouth.

Gross! I never let anyone borrow my toothbrush. It's right up there with my hairbrush and pillow, but then, *I did let him put his tongue in my mouth.* I make a mental note to buy a new one.

"I'll make coffee," I say.

The aroma lures him downstairs. Daniel comes behind me and kisses my neck while I set up a tray with two cups of coffee, cream, and muffins.

"Corn muffins! He shouts. "They're my favorite. How did you know?"

"You told me one night when we were on the phone."

"Incredible!" He sets the tray on the counter and gives me a long, passionate kiss. "Let's go upstairs."

"I was hoping we could have coffee by the pool. Besides, we have all day."

I pick up the tray again, and he follows me, where we sit on lounge chairs under the warm morning sun.

"Do you spend a lot of time with your daughters?" I ask.

"I try. Lisa's getting better about letting them visit me, but it wasn't always like that." He looks hesitant but continues, "When our first daughter, Colleen, was five, I tried to get custody. Lisa is very promiscuous. Whenever she meets a new man, she drags the kids along or leaves them with a stranger. It pissed me off, and I took her to court, but she held the upper hand since we weren't married. I had to do something."

"What did you do?" My curiosity peaks.

"I'd rather not talk about it."

My brow furrows. "If you didn't get along, why did you have another baby with her five years later?"

"We reconciled, and she wanted Colleen to have a sibling. I figured at least they would have the same father. Nothing's changed," he continues. "She's still jumping from one man to another, and I worry about my kids."

❧

We hang out at the pool all day and relax. Then I pop the lasagna I made for him in the oven. Impressed by my cooking skills, he sits back with a full stomach.

"I can get used to this."

By the end of the evening, it doesn't take much persuasion for him to talk me into bed. It's warm and cozy. Daniel calls it *comfy*. He's a beautiful man and a devious child, all wrapped into one. Lying in his arms, I wonder what his childhood was like. "Were you mischievous when you were young?"

"I only got into real trouble once," he says. "My mom had to go somewhere, and she left us, kids, with my grandmother. Her name was Edith. Boy, was she strict! I was jumping on the bed with my brother and sister. They stopped, but I kept going. I didn't know Grandma was watching. She left the room and came back with a belt. She whipped me good!"

"That's horrible!" My heart aches at the thought of Daniel getting beat with a strap.

"I never liked her after that."

My compassion leads me to the deepest parts of his soul as he sucks me into his childhood stories.

Daniel gazes intently into my eyes. "Do you have something to tell me?" he whispers, with a voice as smooth as velvet. This is the second time he's asked that question. *Is he serious or playing?*

Before, I had no desire to kiss another man. It's different now that I've met Daniel. His kisses are addicting. I crave them—his lips' taste, smell, and feel, but I'm not sure I like the tongue thing.

"I'm going to miss you when you leave," I say.

"Smile. At least we have two more nights."

I give him a wistful grin.

"You call that smiling? You look like a grouper fish. Hey, I know what will cheer you up. Let's take a bubble bath."

"A bubble bath?"

"Come on. It'll be fun."

My insecurities are screaming, but I run the water in the tub and pour in almost the whole bottle of soap, hoping I can hide under the bubbles.

"Yum—watermelon! It smells delicious."

"I think we need wine!" I run downstairs to grab a bottle, two glasses, and a couple of candles. Daniel uncorks the bottle, and I admire his powerful shoulders and muscular arms.

"What's that?" I say, noticing a dark spot on his skin.

"That's my tattoo."

I take a closer look. "It's the size of a pea."

"I wanted it to be bigger, but it hurt too much, and I chickened out."

"You're such a baby!"

"I am!" he agrees.

The glow of the flame softly frames his face as he takes a swig from the bottle.

"Don't you want a glass?"

"We don't need them," he says, taking another sip and handing me the bottle.

It's hard to stay afloat after drinking half of the bottle, and we laugh as we slide beneath the water.

"Is this water going down, or is it my imagination?" I ask.

"I accidentally hit the drain. My hands are shriveling up anyway. Let's get out."

Grabbing a towel, I rush to put my panties on and slip into bed.

"I'll take those," he says.

Daniel kisses me and stares fixedly into my eyes. "Do you have something to tell me?"

There's that question again. Is Daniel trying to get me to say I love him? There's no denying the connection between us, but love? Is it possible to know such a thing in three days?

"Je ne sais pas quoi dire." I wonder if he knows French.

He wraps his arms around me. Caught in his wonderful web, the warmth of his body next to mine feels good, and I fall asleep.

under the Stars

My heart was closed
There was no key
But you reached out
And came to me

Daniel agrees to leave the house for a few hours, and we eat breakfast at my favorite beachside restaurant. The waitress leads us to a prime table on the veranda with a view of the ocean. The staff know me on sight and smile as I walk in on Daniel's arm.

"I'm sure you had women after you all the time. You're a good-looking man. So, tell me. Why didn't some California blonde snatch you up when you were there?"

"Oh, they came close." He smirks. "But they were all wackadoos! I don't know why they got the wrong idea and thought I was interested in a long-term commitment. I've never met the right one—until now. The woman I worked for in California was the worst. Terry was rich, used to getting whatever she wanted, and she wanted me—*bad*."

"Is she pretty?" I ask as a spark of jealousy surfaces.

"Yes, but she drank too much. One time, we were at a bar, and Terry was drunk. She kept asking me if she was my girlfriend. When I refused to say yes, she made a scene. I couldn't get out of there fast enough. I hate when a woman makes a fool of herself."

"I never get drunk," I say, eager to look good in his eyes.

The server interrupts us with the check, and Daniel pulls out his wallet.

"It's such a beautiful day," I say, gazing out at the ocean. "Let's go for a walk on the beach?"

As we walk arm in arm along the shore, other couples are walking too.

"We're so lucky we found each other, Florence, but I should be mad at you."

"Mad at me? Why?"

"You never knocked on my door when we were back in high school."

"I didn't realize you lived only five blocks away. Besides, you could have found me."

"Well, I guess I'll forgive you for not being in my life *all* of my life," he says, "but you could have saved us a lot of pain and suffering."

"We're together now." I sigh. "I wish you didn't have to leave so soon. Maybe we can come back tonight," I say, craving the romance of a star-filled sky.

He runs his nose along my cheek and bites my ear.

"That tickles," I squeal. "I think you have an ear fetish."

"I do!"

⁓⁓⁓

Under a full moon, we return to the beach with a bottle of wine and a blanket. The parking lot is empty, but the gate is closed to the entrance, so we park the car across the street and sneak across. Daniel looks apprehensive.

"Watch for security guards," I tease as we cross the parking lot to the beach.

"Guards?" He looks around nervously."

I feel adventurous and drink in the beauty and serenity of the sea. It is the first time I've been to the beach at night. It's mysterious and scary, but I feel safe with Daniel. It's a clear night, and a balmy breeze drifts off the ocean. Although the moon shines on the waves' crests, the shoreline is dark.

He spreads the blanket, and we lie down, pulling it around us. It's a perfect cocoon.

Under the dome of the endless night sky, it feels like we've left the planet. Our breathing and the waves crashing upon an invisible shore are the only sounds. The ocean mist is intoxicating as we peel off our clothes and make love without restraint.

"Don't you want to tell me something?" he whispers.

My heart pounds. "Look at all those stars," I say to avoid the question.

"Look at me." His eyes search mine in the dim moonlight. They hold me captive, possessing me.

"I love you," he whispers and presses his lips to mine.

Devouring me with kisses, he implores, "Tell me!"

"Je t'aime!" I say, and the wall I had carefully built around my life crumbles into a million pieces.

❧

I wake with Daniel curled around me and his left leg flung over mine as if he's afraid I'll escape. How cute! *Did he tell me he loved me last night? Did I say I loved him too?* My inner voice says to take it slow, but as much as I'm determined to distance myself and control my emotions, I am drawn to him. He's different from any man I've ever known, not that I've known that many. Being married for thirty years put me out of the dating circuit.

Daniel is funny, sexy, and appealing in a boyish way. Before, I had no passion in my life. Now I know what I've missed. Being in love is amazing. What is it about him that makes me feel this way? Is it his eyes, bright and jovial? Or could it be his sultry voice, low and sensual?

Breathing in his scent, I sigh. In a few short hours, I'll take him to the airport, and he'll be gone.

"Good morning, Babe," he says. "How did you sleep?"

"No one's ever asked me that."

He lifts me onto his chest. "Let's stay in bed a little longer."

"I don't want you to leave," I whine.

"It's too bad we live so far apart. Maybe I should move to Florida."

"I thought you were moving to California."

"Now that I met you, I may have to rethink that. Or maybe you can move to New York."

"No, thank you. It took a long time to get to Florida. I love the warm climate."

"Why does it have to be Florida? Why can't we live someplace like the Bahamas or Aruba?"

"Aruba?" I smile at his reckless way of looking at life.

"Why not? We're free to live wherever we want. Just think. We'd lie on the beach all day drinking margaritas, and every night we would make wild and passionate love to each other."

"That sounds like a dream," I say.

"It's in our power to make our dreams a reality."

"You're crazy," I say, but he planted an intriguing thought.

Checking the time, I jump up. "If we don't get dressed, you'll miss your flight."

When he comes downstairs, we take our coffee on the patio, and he lights a cigarette. He must feel more comfortable around me because he's smoking more. At least he's chewing gum and brushing his teeth...*with my toothbrush!*

୧ৡৄৡ৩

I'm dressed and ready to drive to the airport — well, one out of two, anyway, I'm not prepared to let him go. Four days have flown by, but I think I've learned *everything* I need to know about this man. We are soul mates, and destiny has brought us together.

"I guess I should go upstairs and pack," he says, tossing his cigarette out onto the grass.

"You can't do that, silly. You'll start a brush fire." I grimace.

He picks up the lit cigarette then mashes it on the cobblestone patio. "It's out, okay?" He goes upstairs to gather his clothes.

Five minutes later, he comes downstairs, looking like the proverbial cat that swallowed the canary.

"I guess we'd better go," he says.

"I need to get my purse upstairs."

When I come down, I hand him a shirt. "You forgot this. It was on the doorknob."

"I left it for you," he says.

"Thanks." I'm not sure what he wants me to do with it. Wear it? Smell it? Miss him?

The ride to the airport is sober. "Just drop me in front of the terminal. If you come inside, it'll make it harder to leave."

Daniel exits my car. Frozen, I stay until he disappears into the terminal. The driver behind me honks his horn, and I drive away. As I get farther away, emptiness overtakes me. I feel a part of me is missing.

Jordan Sparks is singing "No Air" on the radio. *Tell me how I'm supposed to breathe with no air, no air, no air.*

Just like Jordan, I can't breathe. The sad songs on the radio and thinking about Daniel make me feel empty and alone.

My phone rings when I open my front door. "Are you on the plane?"

He laughs. "I missed the flight!"

"How did you do that?"

"We were so engulfed in passion. I lost track of the dates. The flight was yesterday."

"Do you want me to come back to the airport?"

"Relax. The airline booked me on another flight. We're getting ready to board."

"Oh," I say, disappointed.

"I'll call you when I get home, Babe. Remember, I love you."

The thought of us living in Florida together is enticing. I love the way he says, "Let's get *comfy*." I could sleep in his arms every night.

⁕

As the sun is going down, Daniel calls.

"He-y-y!" He says in his smooth, velvety voice. "What are you doing?"

"Missing you."

"I'm starving," he says. "I think I'll eat a Snickers bar."

"Is that your dinner?"

"That's my favorite dinner. You better make sure there are plenty of Snickers when I move down there."

"I don't eat junk food."

"We'll seeeee!"

"Are you trying to corrupt me?"

He laughs. "It's been a long day. I'm aching all over."

"That's because you're old."

"We're both old. I'll talk to you in the morning."

"Good night, my love."

"Good night Florence."

I fall asleep with visions of his sweet face. I can't believe how lucky we are to have found each other. He says it was our destiny.

A World of Frogs

I am yours and yours alone
Never far away, I'll roam
There is no one else for me
Of my heart, you hold the key

In a world full of frogs, I cringed at the thought of kissing a few to find my Prince. I had forgotten that silly notion long ago, but here he is, sweet, romantic, funny, and confident. I'm giddy like a schoolgirl and want to share my happiness. I call my mother.

"Mom, remember the man I told you about—the one I went to school with?"

"David, right?"

"No, Mom. Daniel, Daniel Weaver. He's wonderful."

"Did he come for a visit?"

"Yes, four days. Daniel had to get back home to his children."

"Children?"

"He has two daughters, one four-year-old and the other ten."

"What in heaven's name are you thinking, Florence? You've already been through the motherhood stage. Why would you want to waste your time with a man who hasn't finished his responsibilities?"

"I'm not their mother," I point out. "They're *his* children, not mine!"

"I'm sure he has to support them. Where do you fit into the picture?"

"I don't know, Mom, I just wanted to tell you I'm happy, that's all."

"Well, you had more in common with Edward."

"Edward and I lost whatever love we had."

"And you love this, Daniel?"

"Maybe." My voice softens.

"You're going to get hurt."

I roll my eyes. "I'm a big girl, Mother."

"Florence, I love you. I'm only saying I think you should be careful, that's all."

"I love you, too. Try not to worry."

My mother thinks of Edward as a son, even though I divorced him over a year ago. She, of all people, knows how miserable I had been in my marriage. After my divorce, I had hoped we could be civil for our children's sake, but he couldn't forgive me for leaving. He simply amputated me from his life and turned my children against me.

I cried in my mother's lap one night. A grown woman, but I felt so wounded that I needed the solace of her arms. I thought I would end up alone, but Daniel came into my life and changed everything. He makes me happy, something Edward stopped doing years ago. Despite my fear of intimacy, there's something strangely electric about him. I can't resist the urge to let my emotions flow. I've known him for two months, but I feel like I've known him forever. Still, my mother's words magnify my niggling doubts. Could she be right? I start a mental list of why we're not compatible. He smokes, lives far away, and has young children. Yes, they concern me, but not as much as the fact that he didn't marry their mother. Although I loved Edward, at one time, I was never *in love* with him, not the way I am with Daniel. As I whitewash his negative attributes, everything seems tolerable. Needing validation, I call my brother Patrick and tell him about Daniel.

"He sounds just like your ex-husband."

"No, he doesn't."

"Does he have a pension?"

"I don't know. Daniel is self-employed. He just finished renovating a house. Once it sells, he's coming into money."

"Oh, Florence. Don't be naïve. The economy is bad. He'll be lucky to get what he put into it."

"Doesn't anyone want to see me happy?"

"Sorry, Sis. I didn't mean to bring you down. If this guy makes you smile, there must be something good about him."

We hang up, and I feel deflated.

※

The receptionist is a young Asian woman with shoulder-length black hair. Her desk is neat and clean. There's nothing out of place except for a romance novel. She buzzes someone on the intercom. "Ms. St. John is here! Have a seat," she tells me. "Someone will be with you in a moment."

A man with silver hair comes into the receptionist area. He's wearing a blue shirt, black pants, and no tie, but very stylish. "Ms. St. John?" He extends his hand. "I'm Ben Grant. Please, come to my office so we can talk."

We pass a row of cubicles with employees on the phones or typing away on computer keyboards. He stops at the end of the hall, and we enter a corner office with large windows. The walls are golden, accented with brown woodwork, which gives the office a warm feel.

Mr. Grant sits behind his desk and shuffles through my three-page résumé. He has the bluest eyes I've ever seen. They light up like a hundred-watt bulb.

"How long have you lived in Florida?" he asks.

"I moved here from Georgia last month after my divorce. I'm trying to rebuild my life."

"I know the feeling." He stares at me intently. It's awkward.

"Are you familiar with Excel?"

"Yes, I use it all the time," I lie. I'm really at the primary level.

"You have an impressive résumé. If I hire you, when would you be able to start?"

"Tomorrow."

"It probably won't be until after the holidays, but I'll be in touch. Ben Grant stands and shakes my hand again.

I'll get the job, but I hope I can concentrate. Since I met Daniel, I've been so distracted.

The phone rings again. I jump to answer it.

"Hi, Florence. Are you all right?"

"Of course, Mom. Why do you ask?"

"It's been a while since you've come to visit. Carol and I hoped to see more of you since you moved to Florida."

It's true. Since Daniel, I rarely think of anything else. A day with my family is long overdue.

With my cat Ripley and my phone, I snuggle into bed and wait for Daniel to call. Like a drug surging through my veins, I can't get enough of his sexy voice. It transports me to another realm.

"Hello, woman-of-mine."

Daniel's *woman!* I like the sound of that. "I wish you were here," I sigh. "Maybe we should retire like you suggested and move to Aruba."

He huffs. "Retire? Not me. I have to work."

Hmm. I wonder why Daniel enticed me with living on an island. Maybe it was wishful thinking.

In the Clouds

Don't know just where you came from
I did not seek you out
You have made me love you
Escape…there is no route

In the morning, I wake up to a text on my phone. It's a poem.

"Embers burning from a past…who would know how long they last? She was young, and so was he. What the future held; they could not see."

I snuggle under the covers, and my thoughts float to English class. I try to picture him back then. As if my thoughts summon him, the phone rings. I love Daniel's ringtone—it's like Christmas.

"Good morning," he chirps. "Did you enjoy my poem?"

"I've already read it four times. You are full of surprises. I love the way you express your feelings."

He laughs. "That's funny. Women usually complain I'm untouchable."

"Unfortunately, that's true since you're in New York, and I'm in Florida."

"I wish I was there basking in the sun with you. So, what's on your agenda today?"

"I'm going to visit my mom."

"Well, you have yourself a fantastic day, and make sure you text me every hour," he demands.

"Yes, sir!"

There's a permanent smile on my face as I pull out a pair of jean shorts and a white tank top, then head to the bathroom for a quick shower.

❦

As I drive south, the sun is beating through my sunroof. I point the vent toward my face to cool off. Thinking about Daniel, the phone rings, and my pulse races.

"Ms. St. John?"

"Yes, this is Florence St. John."

"This is Ben from LCN."

"Oh, yes!" I say, recalling the job interview.

"The position is yours if you can start on Monday morning."

"I have the job?" I squeal and quickly retrieve my conservative voice. "That's wonderful. I'll be there."

"We'll see you at nine then?"

"Nine. Yes, I'll see you then."

I hang up and stare into space. All I wanted was a part-time job, but this is a full-time commitment, something I must adjust to since I was a homemaker for almost thirty years. Excited but nervous, I need reassurance, so I call Daniel.

Expecting to hear his cheery voice, I'm taken aback. "Hello!" he says gruffly.

"Daniel? Is everything all right?"

"No. Someone reported me to animal control because I left my horse in the yard while I was out of town."

"He was out in the snow? Wasn't it too cold?"

"He's a horse. Horses love the snow. Anyway, he's taken a turn for the worse. I can't put it off any longer. I need to put him down. I've been searching for my gun all morning. I think it's in the attic somewhere."

"You're going to shoot your horse?" My stomach twists into a knot. "You don't want to have that memory burned into your brain. Why don't you call the humane society?"

"Because they're all assholes. They have strict rules about euthanasia, and they want to charge me to remove the carcass. I'm going to bury the horse on my land. Screw 'em!"

"I don't want to talk about it anymore."

A shiver runs through me. I don't know if my heart aches for Daniel or the horse.

My Mom's waiting outside in the parking lot with my niece, Sophie, when I arrive.

"I'm sorry I didn't get here sooner," I say.

Sophie is hugging a stuffed white cat.

"Oh, what a nice kitty you have, Sophie. What's her name?"

"Ari."

"Ari?"

"She's obsessed with the Aristrocats from Disney lately. Believe it or not, this cat used to be white."

"Really? How would you like it if I take you to the Magic Kingdom, Sophie?"

"Yessss." She squeals and jumps up and down.

"Where's Carol?" I ask my mother.

"She's inside searching for a job on the computer."

Carol lives with my mother. She's twelve years younger than I am and has never married. Carol is beautiful, but she's carrying a few extra pounds, and just like the character from the book *Jemima J*, she has no confidence.

We walk through the front door, and my sister jumps up. "I can't believe you're finally here! You've been in Florida for almost a month, and we haven't seen you."

"I've been a little preoccupied."

Carol smiles and settles her daughter in front of a Disney video on her laptop. "So, tell me about this man you're head-over-heels with."

"His name is Daniel Weaver. He's sooo cute. On a scale of one to ten, Daniel's a nine. His eyes are sexy and playful. When he laughs, they laugh with him."

"Sounds like you're quite taken with him."

I give my mother a side look and whisper, "He told me he loves me."

"It's too soon to be in love," my mother says.

God! For eighty years old, she sure has excellent hearing.

Carol rolls her eyes. "Don't listen to her. She doesn't believe in love." We laugh, and my mother tries to hide a smile.

"What did *you* say?" Carol asks.

"I told him I love him, too." My voice lowers. "I melt when he takes me in his arms.

"Oh, Florence!" my mother sighs. "Sex isn't everything."

"Who's talking about sex?" For me, it's the feeling of being in love. That's all that matters.

"Maybe sex is all he's after!" She's relentless.

"Mom! This man could have any woman he wants. I'm sure he's not with me for the sex." I turn my attention back to Carol, who is eager to hear all the details, and we go up to her room.

"It was so romantic," I continue. "We made love at the beach, under the stars. I thought things like that only happened in the movies. We were so engrossed with each other that he missed his flight home. He didn't realize it until he checked in, and they informed him his flight was the day before."

"Wow...that *is* love!"

"Read this." I pull up the poem he sent that morning.

"You're so lucky," she says. "I wish I could find a man like that."

Back downstairs, Mom is watching FOX News.

"Mom! Why do you have to watch this stuff?" I ask. "It's so depressing."

My cell phone chimes. I smile at Carol. "It's a text from Daniel."

"What does it say?"

"You are a treasure. I'm the luckiest man on the planet."

"Wow! What a charmer," she says.

"He seems too good to be true," my mother jeers. "Are we going out for lunch or not?"

I smile and put my phone away to focus on the rest of my visit.

After lunch, we go back to the house for coffee. Sitting in the living room, I noticed the walls needed some paint. Little Sophie had her way with a crayon, and the entryway was dinghy and gray.

"Mom. You need to have their walls painted."

"I know. The painters want so much money. I don't have it right now."

"Maybe I can do it," I say. "I've always been handy with a paintbrush."

"Oh, would you? That would be so nice, Florence."

"It's not a problem, Mom. I'll just run to Home Depot and pick up some paint and supplies. You and Carol can clear the room and get everything off the walls while I'm gone. It won't take long. The hardest part is cutting in the ceiling and baseboards. After that, the rolling is a breeze."

Forgetting about Daniel, I spent the day painting my mother's living room walls and continued into the hall.

"It looks so much better, Florence. Thank you. You're the only one I can rely on to help me."

Next time, I'll tackle the kitchen," I said. "Maybe we can find a nice border design."

At the end of the day, Carol, Sophie, and my mom walk me out to my car. I promise to visit again soon, and they wave as I drive off.

When I'm on the road back home, my mind returns to Daniel. This remarkable man is in love with me. My life feels surreal, and I'm floating on a cloud.

When I get home, I kick off my shoes, pour a glass of wine, and flick on my computer to check my e-mail.

The sun goddess is staring at me. She's a reminder of the wonderful man in my life—a man who knows so much about beauty and art and can teach me to appreciate the finer things in life. I found such a perfect man and love being in love. It's all very new for me, but I wonder if I should trust the feeling.

Even though it's light outside, I crawl into bed and wait for him to call. Finally, my phone rings like a sweet lullaby.

"Oh, Daniel. The Sun Goddess is beautiful."

"I knew you'd like it," he says. "I collect miniature paintings. Some of them are quite valuable. The Goddess is one of my favorites."

"Daniel! Why did you send it *to me?*"

"I want to share everything I have with you."

"You're so sweet! But most men send flowers or candy," I tease.

"I'm not most men."
"I'll find a special place for her."

We talk long into the night, neither of us wanting to hang up. My neck hurts from holding the phone.

"I guess we should get some sleep," I reluctantly say.

"Yeah, we both have to work in the morning. I'll let you go, but you better dream of me tonight!"

"You're all I dream about, Daniel. Good night!"

I wait for the phone to go dead, but it doesn't. "Aren't you hanging up?" I ask.

"You hang up first," he teases. "On the count of three, we both hang up. One, two, three!"

I wait for the line to go dead. "Daniel! You didn't hang up."

"I don't want to let you go yet."

"Neither do I."

There's nothing better than being in love, and it's been so long since I had the intoxicating feeling. I don't want to miss one moment of bliss.

"Do you remember the reservoir in the woods when we were growing up? He asks.

"Yes," I murmur, with slumber in my voice. "I used to love walking through the woods."

"It's changed a lot since then. They've cleared it out and made biking trails. It looks more like a park now."

"That's a shame."

"I spent a lot of time there when I was a boy."

"Me too…when I was a girl, that is," I laugh. "I wonder why we never ran into each other."

"It's your fault," he banters.

"No, I think it's yours," I yawn. Drowsiness filling my eyes, I hug my pillow, pretending it's Daniel, and I fall asleep with the phone still on my ear.

Leap of Faith

Come dance, my love with me
But only if it's right
I want to be your woman
To be there in the night

The phone wakes me. "Heyyyy sleepy head. You fell asleep while we were talking last night."

"You should have called back," I say, feeling gypped. "I miss you."

"We're going to have to do something about that," he says. "We can't just have a relationship over the phone."

"I'll visit you for one month. Then you visit me."

"We need to do something more permanent," he says. "Maybe we need to sell our houses and make a fresh start."

"My house needs a lot of repairs before I can put it up for sale."

"What kind of work? I'm a contractor, remember?"

"I know, silly, but you're in New York, and I'm here in Florida. The house is in Georgia."

"I can drive there and work on it. We're in this together. We need to make a move toward our future."

Future? "No, I couldn't let you do that."

"I'll send you pictures of my progress," he promises. "I can come to see you afterward, and we can spend the holiday together."

"Don't you want to spend it with your kids?" I ask.

"I'd much rather be with you. Maybe I can talk you into coming back to New York with me."

I laugh. "Remember, I'm a snowbird. I need to be where it's warm. Can't we figure it out in the spring?"

"I can't wait that long."

"As long as we love each other, it doesn't matter how long it takes."

"How do you feel about marriage?" he says.

I gasp. *Marriage? Did he say marriage?* It took thirty years for me to break free from my previous marriage. I don't plan to tie a knot—either with Daniel nor anyone else. If I discourage him, there's a chance I'll lose him, and I don't want that to happen.

"I haven't given it much thought," I say, "but if I were to get married again, you'd be the one."

"Just wondering," he says and laughs. "We'll talk about it later. I have to go to work."

Before leaving for work, I put the sun goddess replica in a small frame and set her on my desk. It's an appropriate gift since Daniel knows how much I love Florida. There's a permanent grin on my face. My daughter says I'm dizzy like a schoolgirl, and it's annoying, but I'm happy for the first time in a long time. With my phone on vibrate, I keep it on my lap in case he tries to send me a text. I shouldn't be texting at work, but I'm addicted. I'm trying to concentrate on the report I'm working on, but my phone vibrates. It's a text from Daniel.

"We belong together."

"I'm working," I reply.

"Okay, I'll stop texting."

"Don't you dare!"

I look up from my text to see Ben walking toward me, and I tuck my phone next to me on the chair.

"Maybe we can have lunch together one day, Florence."

"Maybe," I say. I'm not sure it's a good idea, but I don't want to get on bad terms.

My cell phone vibrates again, causing me to jump. Before I can grab it, the phone falls, rattling on the floor. A look of dismay washes over Ben's face, and he turns to leave. As he strolls back to his office, I check my phone and smile at the text from Daniel. *"You should know... I love you more than anyone or thing in my life,"* he texts. *"You rock my world."*

"You're wonderful," I text back. *"I can't believe you're real."*

"I'm real...we're real. Life floats by fast, Florence. We don't want to miss the boat. Take a leap of faith."

❧

If faith were rational, I'd have an easy time leaping, but it's something I cannot see or touch. Still, I'm dancing on a cloud, but things are changing so fast that I barely have enough time to absorb it all. I want him to move to Florida, but it took so long to gain my independence. I'm not sure I want to live with someone again. Still, I don't want to be alone for the rest of my life. Besides, if Daniel moves in with me, I'll have help with the expenses.

I need to keep one foot on the ground — just in case. But really, it isn't possible. Either I'm in it, or I'm not.

Tired, I slip into bed early and close my eyes, but I can't sleep. I give up and go to the bathroom to rearrange my toiletries to make room for Daniel. Then I empty one side of my dresser for his clothes. I clean out half the closet on a mission to make room for him. I even divide my computer hard drive into two users.

Rockin Eve

It's fun to talk and plan
Of things, we want to do
Were at a crossroad now
To somewhere good and true

Daniel is en route to Georgia in one of his work vans with the three thousand dollars I sent him for travel and materials. I had planned to deal with the house in the spring, but he assured me he could fix anything. It makes me nervous. I don't want him to feel obligated. It could distract from the happiness that we share.

He fixed the wood floor in the den that flooded during a heavy rainstorm and hired workers to landscape the yard. He even secured the loose siding on the house. I'm amazed at what he accomplished in a few short days.

Winter holidays have always been melancholy, but now that Daniel is in my life, Christmas is bearable — even enjoyable. As the yuletide rushes upon me, I have a reason to celebrate. Music is streaming through the stereo. *I Only Have Eyes for You* by the Flamingos. I've listened to it countless times this month while I daydreamed about him.

His van pulls up, and I rush to open the front door to greet him. He looks tired, but his eyes burn with desire as he pulls me to him. We kiss, connecting once more.

"I smell cinnamon," he says, scanning the kitchen.

"Yep, I've been baking Christmas cookies all week."

Like a child, Daniel's eyes widen. He spots the dish of cookies, opens the Saran wrap, and pops one in his mouth. "That's so good." He reaches for two more.

"I made dinner." I laugh.

"This *is* dinner," he says. "Oh, I forgot something in my van." He runs out to retrieve it. When he comes back, he's holding a CD. "You have to hear this. The man is phenomenal." He ejects my CD and inserts his.

"Dean Martin!" I gush. "My father used to listen to him all the time. Art, music, what else are you hiding?"

He gives me a cocky smile. "My tastes are wide-ranging."

"Oh, one more thing for you," he says and rummages through his case. Daniel pulls out a small picture similar to what he had sent me in the mail. This time it's an image of a woman lying on her side. She has red ribbons around her wrists. "It's a replica from a famous artist, Dion Hamill," he boasts, "and part of her red ribbon series."

"Thank you, Daniel. You're so thoughtful." I place it next to the picture of the sun goddess.

"Oh, and this is my mother," he says, proudly showing me her picture.

I study the old black and white photo, and her smiling face stares back at me.

"I wish you could have met her before she died," he says. "She would have loved you."

"I'm sure I would have loved her, too," I say, wrapping my arms around him and gazing into his amber eyes.

"Speaking of family," I say, taking the opportunity, "We were invited to my mother's house for New Year's Eve."

It seems to go over his head. Before he closes his case, he removes some paperwork. "Here's the contract for the real estate agent listing your house. You need to sign and have it notarized. Bob Morrissey's fax number is at the top."

"Does Bob think the house will sell right away?" I ask.

"I'm sure," he says with optimism in his voice. "I did a lot of work to clean it up. It looks great. I have to follow up with the carpenter that I hired to fix the floor, but that can wait until tomorrow."

"When are you putting *your* house up for sale?" I ask.

"I have a lot of work to do on mine," he says, "but I don't want to talk about it now." His eyes come alive with wicked amusement as he pulls me toward him and kisses me. "Let's go to bed."

Forgetting dinner and the houses, I follow him up the stairs to my bedroom, and we get undressed. I cross my arms over my bare breasts, and he pulls them away.

"Don't be shy. We've been here before."

As we make love, I close my eyes and let him take me to places I've never been.

"Open your eyes," he says. "I want you to look at me."

I tend to close them when I make love. Now I'm self-conscious, but I succumb.

I'm soaring through the clouds and land softly against his chest. His rib cage rises and falls beneath my head. Content, I sigh. Everything about this man fascinates me, yet there's much more to learn.

⚜

What a beautiful sight! Daniel is beside me in the morning. My head is on his chest, and his legs thread through mine. His hair is tousled, and he looks like a little boy, except for his chin, which is stubbly with tiny gray hairs. I run my fingers across his face, and he moans.

"Who's your man?" he murmurs and opens his eyes.

"You are!" I sigh.

"Don't you forget it!" he says and wraps me in his arms. We fall back asleep.

When I wake up, the bed is empty, and I hear him downstairs, talking to someone on the phone. His tone is serious and authoritative.

"The floor has to be dry before the new surface gets installed," he barks. "If I have to go back there, I won't be a happy camper." He's in charge — Master of his expertise and my hero.

While brushing my teeth, I notice a sore developing on my lip. It's swollen and angry. Alarmed, I cry out.

Daniel rushes into the bathroom. "What's wrong?"

"What is *this*?"

"You have herpes," he says, scrunching his face in disgust.

A trip to the drug store confirms it. "You have Herpes Simplex Type 1," the pharmacist says. "It's a cold sore, very common."

Speechless, I stare at the pharmacist, feeling embarrassed and ashamed. *How did I get this?*

As we're walking toward the exit of the drugstore, Daniel calls from behind me. I turn around to look at him. He's leaning on a walker and inching his way up the aisle.

"I wouldn't fool around if I were you." I laugh. "You may end up with one of those things someday."

Leaving it in the aisle, he catches up to me. "One day, we'll both be in one of them, Babe." He smiles that brilliant smile, and I forget about my affliction for a moment. The pharmacist says it's a common affliction, and millions of people have them.

I dab on some medicine and a little lipstick at home, then join Daniel in the living room. He hugs me, and I move to kiss him, but he avoids my mouth. His reaction makes me feel dirty. I try to understand, but I miss his lips. I'm hoping it goes away before Christmas. Days go by, and it reduces, but it remains evident. Merry Christmas!

❧

New Year's Eve is my least favorite holiday. It's been years since I've stayed awake until midnight. I've never seen the point. But this year is different. Daniel and I have so much to look forward to, and I want to do it right.

"Flo, what time are we supposed to go to your mother's house tonight?"

"I guess we should get there by six," I say. "I want to get there before dinner."

Daniel grabs me in a bear hug. "I have a better idea. Let's stay at home. We can watch the ball drop in bed."

"What about my family?"

"They won't miss us. Besides, I'm leaving in the morning. It's our last night together. We can open a bottle of wine and get *comfy*—just the two of us." His eyes plead.

How can I say no?

Now I have to break the news to my family. Hesitantly, I pick up the phone and dial.

"Mom," I say. "I'm going to have to cancel."

"What's wrong?" she sounds alarmed.

"I'm not feeling too good. I think I may be getting the flu or something."

"It's all right," she says, but I can hear the disappointment in her voice.

"I'll come next week, and we can celebrate then," I promise.

"Okay. Have some tea and go to bed early."

"I will. Happy New Year, Mom. I love you."

"I love you too," she says.

When I hang up, Daniel is yawning. "I think I'll take a little nap," he says, laying his head on my lap.

As he sleeps by my side on the couch, I listen to him breathe and watch Dick Clark's Rocking' New Year's Eve on the television. Five minutes before midnight, I gently shake him. "Wake up, sleepyhead. The ball is about to drop."

He grins and reaches up for me, but no kiss. *Damn cold sore!* "Happy New Year!"

⌘

"Daniel, I can't believe you're leaving today. It's not a good way to start a new year. I can't bear to be without you," I whimper, tears escaping my eyes.

"No tears," he says and caresses my cheek. "You could come back to New York with me," he tempts.

"I Can't. I have to work, but maybe I can get some time off around Valentine's Day next month."

Daniel laughs. "My birthday is on Valentine's Day."

"Perfect," I say. "I'll fly to New York for the weekend, and we can meet in the city and go to a show."

"I would love to see West Side Story," he says.

"That would be great. We can go on your birthday. I'm so excited. I can hardly breathe."

"Florence, we'll both be gasping for air."

"We'll lock ourselves in the hotel room the whole time," he purrs.

"I won't argue with that, as long as we have plenty of wine and food."

"You sure do love to eat," he jokes.

I watch him drive off in his van, and I have an empty feeling in the pit of my stomach.

Daniel doesn't even make it to the highway when he texts. "He-y-y, Babe. Do you still miss me?"

"I miss you so much. I can't breathe."

The house is quiet without Daniel. Although my bed is empty, my heart is elated at the thought of being in his arms again. I fall asleep with the tune *I Feel Pretty* in my head.

Sugaroo

Should have kissed you one more time
Or lingered in your hug
Looked so deep into your eyes
Your love is like a drug

When I open my eyes in the morning, all I see is my cat, Ripley. It's only been twenty-four hours, but the realization that he isn't here makes me feel lonely, like part of me is missing. How will I get through a whole month without him?

In the drawer, I find one of Daniel's shirts. I know that he put it there on purpose. Every time we're together, he leaves something for me to find. I know he's doing it on purpose. I breathe in the scent.

I search for traces of him and discover the picture of his mother is still on my desk. Somehow, I feel close to this woman and thank her for giving birth to such a wonderful man. Her reassuring smile comforts me. I put her picture in a frame next to the sun goddess and lady with the red ribbons.

My cell phone chimes, and my heart sings along with the tone. I stare at Daniel's text. *"With a love so strong...In your heart is where I belong; Don't keep us apart for too long. In that area, I can't be strong; If you love me as you say, don't make me wait another day; I need to have you to love and hold; In the north where it's really cold."*

I'm lost in a daydream at work and can't wipe the silly grin off my face. I look up to see Ben standing in front of my desk. I don't know how long he's been there, and I quickly stash my phone in the drawer. Usually, when faced with a task, I'm like a laser beam, but my heart keeps getting in the way of my brain. I am unable to concentrate on my job. All I can think about is Daniel.

"I should have the revenue report on your desk by the end of the day," I tell Ben.

"We have time," he says with a smile. "Hey, would you like to grab a sandwich at the corner deli with me?"

"I brought my lunch, but thanks for asking."

Ben looks deflated, as if someone let the air out of his tires.

"Maybe next time," he says and turns to leave. He steps onto the elevator, and I sigh with relief when he's gone. Lunch is short enough. I want to spend it talking with Daniel.

The phone rings.

"Hey, baby," I say in a sexy voice.

"Florence, I need a favor." Daniel sounds different. There's urgency in his voice.

"What kind of favor?"

"I need to make a payment to someone in Florida. I was hoping you could pay it for me. I'll give it to you back as soon as possible."

"Payment? How much?"

"Six hundred and forty dollars."

"I don't have that kind of money."

"Oh."

He sounds disappointed, but no one has ever asked me for money. I feel terrible, but for the first time since my divorce and the real estate collapse, my money situation is under control, and I want to keep it that way.

"I'm sorry. I haven't even received my first paycheck. My ex-husband has decided to stop paying the mortgage, and I may lose the townhouse."

"Don't worry about it," he says. "I'll find another way."

"Lunch is almost over, Daniel. I had better get back to work. I'll talk to you later."

"My phone is running out of minutes," he says, "but I'll try to call."

For the rest of the day, my phone doesn't chime. I stare at it, willing it to ring, but it's ominously silent. I keep checking for messages, in case I didn't hear it, but there's nothing.

I wonder if he's mad. *Maybe I should have given him the money.*

⁊⚭⚮

I've never suffered from anxiety attacks, but I have one now. It's been three days since I've heard Daniel's voice, but it feels like three weeks. My emotions are spinning out of control, overwhelming me. If he loves me, why doesn't he call?

Instead of stopping at my usual one glass of wine during dinner, I pour another. I don't want to think. By the third glass, I have to crawl to my bed and close my eyes. The bed spins. Instead of hugging the man I love, I spend the night hugging the toilet and wake up with my first hangover.

Daniel's ringtone bounces off the walls, and I jump to answer it.

"Hey," Daniel says. Not, "He-y-y," in his usual playful manner.

"Are you all right?"

"I'm sorry I haven't called Babe. I've been dealing with a lot of crap lately."

"Is there anything I can do to help?"

"You can jump on a plane and come to New York."

"I thought you were coming here."

"What's the use? You said you were losing the townhouse. Besides, it's winter—not the best time to sell a house up north, and the way this economy is, I don't know how long it'll take. I could rent it, but I hate having another renter in my house. I may have no choice. I'll put an ad in the paper and see who answers it."

"At least you have your phone back."

"Yeah, I've missed our evening chats."

"You're so far away, Daniel. I'm afraid I'll lose you."

"There's no risk of that. Our love is strong! I'll call you again tonight. I'm on my way to see my accountant."

"Are you having financial problems?"

"No worries, Florence. I have it under control."

"I'm here if you need to talk."

"Thanks. You're my Sugaroo."

I laugh at his silly, made-up word.

☙❧

There's a note on my desk from Ben, telling me to come into his office in the morning. I've avoided his passes, pretending I don't notice. He must think I'm dense. Age aside, I suspect he's not used to women ignoring him.

Ben is on the phone when I enter his office. He winks and motions for me to take a seat. I sit in the chair across from him and wait for him to hang up the phone.

"You did a good job on that report," Ben says. "How would you feel if I put you in charge of coordinating the next advertising campaign?"

"Really?" I try not to sound too eager, but it's my chance to advance in the company.

He hands me a thick folder. "I'll include you in the next department meeting. In the meantime, look over this file and get yourself up to speed."

I take the file and grin. "I'll read it during lunch."

"Hey, you owe me lunch," he says with a wry smile. "Read it now, and we can discuss it over a sandwich."

"All right," I say, but the smile on Ben's face makes me nervous. We could never be anything more than friends. *I hope he's not getting ideas.*

At lunch, we walk across to the deli. Ben stares at me from across the table as I take small bites of my sandwich. Just in case he thinks he has a chance, I shift the conversation to Daniel.

"He lost everything in the divorce, and his ex-wife turned their son against him."

"I thought he had two young daughters?"

"Yes, but he also has two children from his ex-wife."

"So, he's been divorced twice?"

"No, he didn't marry the second girl."

"The *second girl* gave him two children," he points out. "They might as well have been married. It sounds like he's playing you."

"Daniel's a sweet guy," I defend. "He's just going through a rough patch."

Ben smiles, but his eyes aren't joining in. "For your sake, I hope he's sincere."

He's struck a nerve. I've lost all sense of perspective when it comes to Daniel.

Complicated

Life is complicated
This much we know is true
But love should be so simple
And worthwhile to pursue

As the blades of the ceiling fan swirl above my bed, the humming of the motor is a lonely sound.

Daniel will take away my loneliness — if he ever gets here. Nostalgia washes over me. I have an urge to read some of Daniel's early e-mails and messages. I open the computer, log on to my Facebook page, and then click on Daniel's profile. His relationship status says "complicated." *Complicated? What does that mean?* I also notice that Daniel has six new friends. They're all women, added recently. One of them is Josette. I gasp.

A few minutes later, my phone rings.

"He-y-y, whatch ya doin?"

"Nothing," I say, trying to sound cool, but it's hard to hide the distress in my voice.

"What's wrong?"

"Nothing."

"Come on! I can tell something's bothering you."

"Well, I was looking at your Facebook page. I noticed that you've added some women."

Daniel laughs. "They're just girls I knew growing up. Besides, you have plenty of guys on your page."

"Yeah, but they were there before I knew you. I haven't added anyone since."

"You have nothing to worry about, Florence. I love you."

"I know that, but do *they*?"

"Don't be silly."

"Daniel, are they why your status doesn't say you're in a relationship?"

"It's complicated." He laughs.

"What is? It's not every day people connect from high school. I think you'd be proud to say we found each other."

"I am proud! I'm just a very private person. I don't like people knowing my business."

When we hang up, my chest feels heavy. Except for the Facebook status incident, I have no reason to doubt Daniel or perhaps I don't want to.

꧁꧂

Daniel's tenant moves in, and he moves out. I expect him to be in Florida very soon, but he says he has some things to take care of and needs to stay a little longer. He moves in with a friend but doesn't tell me whether it's a woman or a man. I'm guessing it's a woman, but I keep my suspicions to myself.

"He-y-y woman," he sings. "I'm sorry I haven't called, but I've been busy packing."

"Packing? Are you still coming to Florida? I thought you might have changed your mind."

"I found a renter. I'm sorry if I bummed you out last week. I was going through a bad time. It has nothing to do with us. We're solid. I should be wrapped up here in a few weeks."

"Good," I tease. "I'm having trouble paying the mortgage, and I can use the help."

"Help?"

"Yeah, I figured we would split the bills."

He doesn't respond. His mind seems to be drifting to another place.

"Have you heard from the real estate agent about selling your house in Georgia?" he asks.

"So far, no one's interested."

"Keep on top of that."

"I wish you could come to Florida now."

"I've been boxing my stuff, and it's bringing me down. I don't want to lose any of it. Would it be all right if I bring some of my artwork?"

"Sure, you can be in charge of decorating the walls."

"I'll be in charge of everything, Florence."

"Really?" I ask.

He laughs. "I don't know if you can handle my personality," he teases.

"Are you trying to warn me off?"

"No, but I'm very bossy."

"I've noticed!" I add.

Daniel's never been stingy with his thoughts and feelings, but he's changed. Although he says sweet things to make me feel we belong together, he's vague about his intentions. Our conversations have become one-dimensional. Maybe I imagined it all, or maybe the distance is making his feelings fade. *I need to find out.*

Cool Touch

Gravity has lost me
I struggle to keep hold
Whenever you are near me
I spin out of control

In the past, my heart fluttered with anticipation at seeing Daniel, but this time, I feel less confident about our relationship. Deep down, I'm feeling insecure and don't know why. I don't want to lose him. I'm not sure why my mind goes there. Flipping through my itinerary, I locate my e-ticket and inch my way up to the gate. The attendant glances at my license and boarding pass before feeding it through the machine. In a few short hours, I'll be face-to-face with Daniel and able to assess the situation.

Soon, the plane's tires are screaming down the runway at LaGuardia Airport, and the air hostess announces we can turn on our cell phones. I check to see if I have a message from Daniel, but I don't. After we disembark, I ride the elevator from the terminal, searching for the waiting faces at the top. People are hugging and kissing as they reunite. The crowd thins, but there's no sign of Daniel. *Hmm!*

I follow the signs to ground transportation. The wheels on my suitcase keep seizing whenever I make a sharp turn. It slows me down. Cars, buses, and taxis line up to pick up passengers outside. Searching for

Daniel, I spot his van double-parked at the curb. He's inside, puffing on a cigarette.

He jumps out when he sees me, wearing a sexy black V-necked tee shirt under a sports coat with jeans. I approach him, hoping he'll sweep me into his arms, but he looks tense. Daniel gives me a peck on the cheek as if I'm his long-lost sister, then lifts my bag and puts it in the back.

"For a moment, I worried you wouldn't be here," I say.

"I didn't want to park. It's too expensive, so I drove around the terminal until I saw you."

As we pull away from the curb, we exchange smiles, but there's tension in the air. With each separation, the gap between us seems to widen.

"Are you all right, Daniel?"

His mouth opens as if he's about to tell me something, but he hesitates. "I'm fine. I just have a lot on my mind."

"You're not sorry that I came, are you?"

"No, not at all," he says, but I'm not convinced.

For over a month, I've anticipated our reunion. And the love that has swept me out of my reality. *Something is wrong.*

There's a cool breeze coming in from the open window. I have so many questions, but I'm afraid to ask. Instead, I watch the world outside rush past me.

"Hey, let's stop and get some wine."

My eyes widen. "And drink it in the van?"

"Sure, why not?" He gives me an impish smile that makes the dimple on his chin reappear. He's such a handsome devil.

"But we don't have glasses."

"Then, we'll buy some!"

We stop at *Pier 1*. He walks around the store, picking up small glasses and turning them over to look at the price.

"This is crazy! I'm not paying this much for a glass. Let's check the clearance aisle."

I follow him to a display, and he picks up a beautiful stained glass. "I like this one, but it's expensive," he says.

"They're only five dollars each," I say. "I'll put it on my charge card if you buy the wine."

"Deal."

We leave in search of a liquor store, and I wait in the van while Daniel buys a bottle of wine. There's a huge smile on his face as he heads back to the van. He must have been flirting with some young thing behind the counter. It doesn't make me jealous because I know he enjoys the attention.

"Do you have a corkscrew?" I ask when he gets into the van.

He looks around in the back and picks up a screwdriver. Putting the bottle between his legs, he twists it into the cork pulls the screwdriver out, along with the cork. "Voila!"

The van rolls over bumps in the road as I pour the wine into our new glasses.

"Here's to us." He raises his glass and clinks mine.

"To *us*, I like the sound of that."

"I like these glasses. I think I'll keep them."

"No, they are mine," I banter.

"We'll see!" His voice goes up five decibels.

We tease along the way. I love this man and fall back on the memories of when we first met in the city.

Already, the wine is making me relax. "Where are we staying tonight?" I ask.

"I thought we could stay in a bed and breakfast. Have you ever stayed at one?"

"No, I've always preferred a hotel. I kind of like the privacy."

"Well, there aren't many hotels here in the boonies, and the ones they have are seedy. Here, see if any of those look good." He pulls out a tattered piece of paper.

I look at the list and read the amenities.

"This one sounds nice. It's right on the river."

I dial the number, and a woman answers.

"Hi, do you have any vacancies?"

"Yes, I have a beautiful room available," she says softly. "It overlooks the river."

Rummaging for a pen in my purse, I write the directions on the back of the crumpled paper.

"I know where that is," Daniel says.

Pulling into a long dirt driveway, two large dogs come running into the front yard, followed by a woman in her late fifties whose appearance screams hippie—long flowing skirt, make-up-free face, and long brown hair tucked behind her ears.

We step out of the van, and the dogs circle me.

"Don't worry, they don't bite," she says and turns to Daniel.

"Hi. I'm Tricia Gielding. Welcome to *mi casa*," she says.

Her home! Already I wish we were staying at a motel. I reach down to pet one of the dogs.

"I'm Daniel, and this is Florence."

"I'm so pleased to meet you," she says. "Have you ever stayed at a bed and breakfast?"

"Yes, plenty," he says.

"Then you know how it works." she smiles at him and leads us into a blue and white country kitchen. It's small. The appliances are old, but it's clean. There's a large bowl of fruit and a bottle of white wine beside two glasses on the counter.

"Would you like a glass of wine?" she asks.

"I'll have some," Daniel says. He hates white wine, but he's smiling like a Cheshire cat.

She's quite taken with Daniel. I can tell by the way she looks at him — all dewy-eyed. Some men have that effect on women. He is one of them, handsome, flirty, and can charm a snake. He's too good-looking, that's the problem.

"How about you, Florence?"

"Yes, thank you."

Tricia pours two glasses of wine. "Breakfast is at seven o'clock," she informs us, "but you can use the kitchen anytime. There's a computer available down the hall if you need to get online. Come on. I'll show you to your room."

We climb a flight of wooden stairs located off the kitchen. I have to catch my breath as we enter the room. Large picture windows line the full length of the wall, and I can hear the river flowing below us.

"It's beautiful!" I say and run to check out the bathroom. It also has windows and a tub...an old-fashioned one with claw feet.

"Make yourselves comfortable," Tricia says. "I'll be downstairs if you need anything."

We kick off our shoes and finish our wine as the sunsets. The sound of the river is louder, and there's a chill in the air, clean and fresh. It reminds me of camping out in the mountains when I was young. The moon is full and bright. *It's so romantic.* Daniel kisses me for the first time since I arrived. My heart races as we climb into bed.

"Look at the moon," I say. "It's beautiful."

"If you've seen one moon, you've seen them all," he mumbles, keeping his eyes closed.

"I guess romance and stardust are a thing of the past," I tease. With a sigh, I roll onto my side, missing the way I used to feel like I was soaring through the clouds.

Daniel hugs my back. At least we still spoon.

"Don't move," he says. "If you do, I'll squish you like a tomato."

Soon Daniel is asleep. I can hear him snoring. I have to go to the bathroom in the middle of the night, so I gently pry myself from his grip and slip out of bed.

Not wanting to wake him, I leave the light off and make my way into the bathroom in the darkness. I cry as my butt hits the water and my feet lift off the floor.

"What's the matter?" he mumbles.

"You didn't put the seat down, and I fell in!"

"Next time, be more careful," he says.

Sweets

Things have changed
I don't know why
I can hear the Angels sigh

The sound of the river wakes me. I look over at Daniel, sleeping next to me. He's curled around me, making it difficult to move. Gentle puffs of air escape his mouth.

"Stay," he says.

"You're such a control freak."

"I'm the commander."

"Where's your spaceship?" I wriggle out from his leg trap.

We hear Tricia's car as she leaves for work.

"Come outside with me while I have a cigarette," Daniel says.

He chewed gum after a cigarette when we first met, but now he doesn't bother. "Can you please brush your teeth, Daniel? You smell like an ashtray."

"You need to find a non-smoker!" he says. The lines blur, but humor is lurking in his eyes this time. Sometimes, I'm not sure if he's serious or joking.

"Maybe *you* need a smoker," I retaliate, "someone with yellow teeth and nicotine-stained fingers."

"Funny!"

"I'd like to take you to where they held the Woodstock Festival," he says.

"That sounds like fun."

I pour us two cups of coffee and join him on the deck as he puffs on a cigarette. The sky is crystal blue, but there's a bite in the air, and I feel cold, so I go inside the house to get a blanket. I wrap it around my shoulders as we watch the river flow by the house.

After three cups of coffee and four cigarettes, which he tosses into the rushing water, Daniel says, "Okay, let's do this."

We jump into his van, and he takes me to the Performing Arts Museum down the block. Along the way, he tells me all about the concerts they have every summer. We tour the free exhibits and walk around the grassy field where thousands of people camped and took mind-trips forty years ago. Daniel stays at a safe distance and looks pensive.

"Do you have friends who live around here?" I ask.

"I have a few. Most people like me," he says. "That is until they get to know me."

I'm curious about the friend Daniel has been staying with, but he doesn't mention her. The thought flashes through my mind. It's a woman.

"Are you sorry I came?"

He looks off, avoiding my eyes. "No, but it isn't a good time."

"All you had to do was say so," I reply with a hint of irritation.

"When you get something in your head, there's no talking you out of it."

"That's not true!" I feel my eyes water. "If you're not happy I'm here, you can take me to the train station."

"You're not going to cry, are you? You're too sensitive." He puts his arm around me.

"No!" I pull away.

Seeing my anger, he pacifies me with a crooked smile. "You're so cute when you're mad."

"I'm not!"

"Tone is everything." He seems amused that he could push me to the edge and manage to make me laugh.

"Tricia won't be here until late this evening, so we have the entire house to ourselves," he says. "Let's go back and take a bath in that old-fashioned tub. I'll look at the moon tonight."

Playful Daniel is back. My anger abates. "All right," I recall the last time we bathed together.

Daniel fills the tub with bubbles and slips into the water. We can hear the river through the open window as it flows past the house.

"The house is empty. Why don't we go to bed?"

"Nah, it's too early. Let's watch a movie. Tricia has Netflix."

I wonder if he has the desire to have sex anymore. If he does, he sure has self-control. No, it can't be that — he's impetuous. He likes immediate satisfaction in all areas of his life — all areas except sex.

I find it hard to sit still for two hours and watch a movie, but Daniel is excited as he pulls up the listings. We get cozy on the recliner, and he puts his arm around me. The chair is too small for both of us, but I'm craving the closeness. The movie ends, and he starts another—and another. It's a movie marathon!

"Don't you want to make love?"

"I'm not in the mood," he says.

"What's wrong?"

"It's broke."

"Broke? What does that mean?"

"I don't want to talk about it."

"Are you sick? You can tell me."

"Stop!"

His sudden emotional withdrawal confused me. I never had to beg to be loved, and I wasn't about to start now.

Maybe it's erectile dysfunction!

"Let's watch another movie and get comfy. Dish us out some ice cream? I'll even promise not to steal yours," he says, giving me a devious smile.

He's so good at diverting me from anything he doesn't want to discuss. It works.

It's dark when Tricia returns home. We sit in the kitchen, and she tells me about her job in Manhattan. It sounds exciting. I'm a smidge envious. She has the best of both worlds, the country, and the city.

"He-y-y wench!" Daniel says. "Make me some coffee and join me on the deck," and he returns outside.

He requests coffee at least four times a day and insists that I sit outside with him while he smokes one cigarette after another.

"For the life of me, I can't understand why you put up with that," Tricia says.

I don't know why, either. I go out to the yard with two cups of coffee, where he's smoking another cigarette. It's all so pathetic.

The moon is already visible in the sky. I close my eyes and listen to the river as it rushes by. I shiver in the chilly air.

"Wait here," Daniel says and runs to his van. He comes back with a heavy blanket. It has a southwestern motif on the front and a fur lining on the other.

"I call this my man-blanket," he beams. "Sit in this chair." I sit, and he tucks it around me with a self-effacing grin.

"There — snug as a bug."

An hour later, we go to bed, and he snuggles against me. Locked in his embrace, I wonder, who is this man?

⌘

I'd like you to meet my kids. Lisa said I can pick them up this afternoon."

"I can't wait," I say, but I'm nervous about being around them. Kids can be very critical when it comes to relationships. I hope they don't see me as a threat to their mother.

When Lisa calls, his face lights up with joy. "All right," he says. "I'll be there in a few minutes." There's a pause. "Don't worry. I'll make sure they eat. Yes, I'll have them back at a reasonable hour. No candy! Got it!" He hangs up and grabs his keys. "I'll be back soon, Florence."

While he's gone, I take a walk. The country air smells fresh and clean. Spring is over, but the summer heat and humidity don't have a foothold.

Except for Daniel's lack of affection, I love it here. The air is easier to breathe and lulls me into a state of passivity.

He returns to the house, ushering in Emma, a girl who appears to be about four years old with long, curly hair, the color of a raven's wing, and her ten-year-old sister, Colleen, with lighter hair.

"Look what I have," Emma says, holding up a bag of treats.

I shake my head at him, and he smirks.

The girls are sweet, especially little Emma, who takes to me immediately. Colleen, more guarded, is polite, but I can tell she is possessive of her father by the way she gazes at him — with expectation and love. I don't want to seem like a threat, so I stand back and give her access to his attention.

Emma's sitting on my lap when her mother pulls up to get them. Emma drags me outside and announces, "This is Florence."

If Lisa has any jealousy, it doesn't show. She smiles and says that it's good to meet me. I like her right off. She looks like a strong woman. She has to be to deal with Daniel.

On the River

Over rocks and partial trees
The white foam rises high
To jump across all obstacles
With strength, none can deny

Sunlight angles through the window blinds. I take a moment to realize where I am. I try to get up, but he clamps his arm around me.

"Daniel. I have to go to the bathroom."

"Think of me as a vice-grip. The more you struggle, the more entangled you'll be."

"I wish you were more romantic, Daniel."

"I am romantic," he insists. "You just need to learn who the boss is." He puts me in a headlock. "Come on. Tell me. Who's the boss?"

"You seem to think you are." I try to wiggle free, but his leg tightens around me.

"Now tell me, who's the boss?"

"You are," I relent.

He releases his grip. "And don't you forget it."

"What are we going to do today?" I ask.

"We should relax and lie out in the sun. I love to tan."

"You already have a farmer's tan," I tease. "Only your face and lower arms have color."

He laughs. His happiness is contagious.

"First, I'm going to have my coffee and a cigarette."

I roll my eyes.

"Aren't you coming?" he asks.

"I'll be down in a minute."

"Don't be too long."

"Why? Are you going to miss me?"

"I'll miss your nagging."

"Ha, ha. You're such a funny guy."

I rarely sit out in the sun, but I put on a bathing suit and search for sunblock.

When I come downstairs, Daniel is on the deck, smoking a cigarette. He's tapping away on his laptop. I wonder if he's connecting with another woman. I tell myself that I don't care. Protected by my ego, I try not to let my composure slip and take a seat away from his smoke.

Cut off from the rest of the world, the river is hypnotizing, and my worries melt away.

Daniel appears to be sleeping, so I head toward the house.

"Where do you think you're going?"

"I need a pen," I say. "Don't worry. I'm coming back."

He has abandonment issues, but he doesn't talk much about his childhood.

"Bring me a Coke."

I cluck my tongue with exasperation. "Do I look like your servant?"

I must, because I come back with a pen and a Coke.

Daniel opens one eye. "Thanks, Babe." He pops the tab, takes a noisy sip.

My gaze returns to the river. Tricia is so lucky to have a house that overlooks this kind of beauty. After reading a few nature poems, I feel inspired.

I've never written poetry before, but my creativity is flowing.

"Look, Daniel. I wrote a poem about the river." I shove the paper in front of him.

"I can't see without my glasses."

"I'll get them." I jump up to run into the house. When I return, I hand him his glasses and wait for his critique.

"This is good," he says, then hands it back, giving the sun his full attention. As it sinks lower in the sky, our tanning session ends.

"I'm hungry," I say. "I'll go inside and whip us up something to eat."

"*Hmm.* You're going to get me fat, woman."

"Real food won't make you fat. It's all the junk you eat."

When it comes to snacks, he doesn't know when to stop.

"It's probably all those Hostess cupcakes you eat."

He smacks his lips. "Yum!"

"Should we have some wine?"

"Nah, just give me a big glass of milk."

"Moo!" I laugh and pat his stomach.

"I'm gonna pop you!"

"You have to catch me first." Laughing, I run from the deck to the yard.

Daniel is close behind, huffing and puffing. I turn to make sure he's not having a heart attack, being a smoker, and it slows me down. He catches me, and we both roll onto the grass, laughing.

"Let's find a movie and get *comfy*," he says.

Watching television, we eat our frozen treats and snuggle together in bed. It's become a nightly ritual.

Comfy. That's what Daniel calls it. I call it intimacy without sex. Most of the time, it suits me fine. I never had a strong libido, but sometimes I question if I still have what it takes to arouse a man. I do miss kissing. Daniel was a good kisser — until he stopped brushing his teeth.

Valentine Massacre

Our love was so red hot
We relished in the flames
Each knowing in our heart
It could not be sustained

I listen to the river while the sun climbs higher in the sky and shifts around the room.

"Happy Valentine's Day," Daniel says and produces a small box. Inside, a portrait of a woman wearing a gray hat with a large white flower. Her lips are deep red, and she looks fashionably French. The frame is worn and chipped, and I realize he must have taken it off his wall at his house. *It's the thought that counts.* I reach out to embrace him.

He stiffens. "We're in someone else's house. I hear Tricia downstairs, which means she can hear us."

The aroma of pancakes drifts up the stairs, making me hungry. Daniel wants a smoke, so we get dressed and go downstairs.

"What are you guys doing today?" Tricia asks.

"We're going into the city to see a show," he answers.

"Don't you want breakfast?" Tricia asks.

"No, we'll grab something when we get to the city," he says. "We have to buy tickets."

"I thought you bought them already," I say. "I hope it isn't sold out."

"Don't be so negative, Florence."

Negative? It's an unfair assessment, in my opinion, but I start to wonder. Am I negative?

The first thing Daniel wants to do when we're in the city is to get coffee. "Do you really want to see a show?"

"We've been talking about this play for months, Daniel."

"I'm just saying, maybe we can do something else today." He looks away. His face is impassive.

I abruptly put my coffee cup down with a clang. "Forget it." Resisting the urge to cry, I twirl small pieces of a napkin between my fingers. I can never tell what he's thinking. He's been moody ever since I arrived.

"Fine! We'll go."

We walk out onto the busy street. I try to hold his hand, but he pulls it out of my reach. "I don't like public displays of affection, Florence."

"I remember a time when you couldn't keep your hands, or lips, off me."

Stop!" he says and pushes me with his hip.

I'm indignant. I've never had to throw myself at a man, and I don't plan to start now. I'm not convinced that he loves me enough for a lifetime commitment, and I may be searching for a future that doesn't exist.

The rushing traffic and street noise makes talking harder, so we silently head to the theater. At the window, he asks for two tickets.

"We're sold out," the clerk says. "We do have two seats. They're just not together."

Daniel looks at me for approval.

"I don't want to sit in separate seats," I protest.

"Wait here," he says and scurries up to a man in a black hoodie with a knit cap on his head. I suspect he's a scalper.

Daniel's smiling when he comes back. "I have the tickets."

"Are they real?" I ask skeptically.

"See for yourself."

It looks authentic, but there's no way of knowing for sure until we try to use them. I check the time on my cell phone. "The show starts in less than a half-hour. We're not going to have time to eat."

"All you ever think about is food, Florence."

"You're never hungry, but I am!"

He shrugs. "We can grab a candy bar or something."

"I need real food, Daniel!"

"Do you want to skip the show and find a restaurant?" There's a twinge of sarcasm in his voice.

Part of me wants to put on my boxing gloves, but it would only make matters worse. "No," I say, my stomach aching with emptiness as we rush into the theater. I regretted not having a muffin or a piece of toast with my coffee when I had the chance. It's dark, except for the candlelight fixtures scattered on the walls and the grand chandelier hanging from the center of the ceiling. Daniel's phone vibrates.

Fifteen minutes pass before he returns. We watch the play without speaking.

"We've been planning this trip for months, Daniel. Where is the man I fell in love with? I want him back," I say, half-joking.

"Maybe I'm not the right man for you," he says, pushing me to the edge of tears.

"You've been mean ever since I arrived." I want to run outside where he can't see me cry, but it's too late.

"Ah, come on. I was joking! Let's get a pizza."

"I'm not hungry anymore."

"I find that hard to believe," he teases. "You're such a baby."

⁂

Daniel is brooding because he hasn't heard from Lisa. He thinks she's trying to cut him out of his children's lives, and he's upset. I can tell because he's sitting alone in the yard.

"I think I'm gonna kick those tenants out and build a swimming pool. The kids would love it."

It's a stupid idea, but I suspect he's looking for a way to make them want to be with him instead of their mother. It won't work. It doesn't matter what he buys them. The bond between a daughter and her mother isn't easily broken, even with constant brainwashing from their father.

"Do you plan to move back into your house?"

"I'm not sure. How would you feel about that?"

"I don't know. I thought you were coming to Florida."

He doesn't answer, so I leave him to his deep thoughts.

Daniel's in a bad mood. I bring him a cup of coffee and sit in the chair next to him. The burning tip of his cigarette glows brighter with each drag.

"Can you blow the smoke the other way?"

"You're a pain in the ass!" He says and jumps up, knocking over the chair.

"Why do you have to act this way?"

"Shut up! You're making a scene."

"And you're not?"

Before I can protest, he gets in his van and drives off.

In shock, I watch his taillights disappear into the night.

Two hours later, he's back. Without a word, he undresses and climbs into bed.

Leery, I crawl in beside him, but he moves away, careful not to touch me. I don't know of any time I have been this close to a man and so completely shut out. I scoot over to my side of the bed and pretend I'm asleep.

I should cut my losses now and run. *Who am I kidding? I'm so tangled up with this man it hurts.*

Roller Coaster

Emptiness has taken
Over my raw heart
I don't' want to lose you
Don't want you to depart

In the morning, Daniel's body presses against me. He puts his arm around me as if nothing had happened the previous night.

It's dark outside, but the smell of bacon and freshly brewed coffee causes me to open my eyes. I put on my clothes and go downstairs.

Tricia is sitting at the dining room table.

"You're up early, Florence. Would you like some breakfast?"

"Just coffee, thanks."

"I heard how he spoke to you last night. Are you all right?" There's a genuine look of concern on her face. "You look so sad."

"I'm sorry if we disturbed you."

Tricia seems like a nice woman. We must be around the same age, but she doesn't fuss much with her appearance. Her earth-mother demeanor makes me confide in her. I feel better sharing with another woman, so I tell her about Daniel's behavior.

"I don't think Daniel wanted me to come for a visit."

"I'm sorry," she consoles.

We sit in silence and watch the sun come up outside the large bay window.

Daniel comes downstairs, acting all happy. "Good morning, girls. Did you sleep well?"

After some small talk, he turns to me. "Pour me a cup of coffee, Babe. I'm going outside to have a cigarette."

Once he's gone, Tricia narrows her eyes. "He has you jumping at his every whim. Why do you do it?"

"It's just coffee."

She shakes her head and puts her coffee cup in the sink.

"I have to leave early today," Tricia says, "But the two of you are welcome to stay as long as you like. Just lock the door on your way out."

As her car backs out of the driveway, I'm glad she's gone. With two cups of coffee, I join Daniel.

Sitting on the deck, we watch the local bald eagle that flies over the river every morning, looking for breakfast. The river is so peaceful.

We banter back and forth, enjoying Tricia's backyard. I rub his arm, but he shrinks under my touch.

"What's wrong?"

"Nothing," he whispers. "I'm just under a lot of stress."

His eyes soften. "I haven't been feeling well."

"Have you seen a doctor?"

"I don't want to talk about it."

He's so fragile. I feel the need to take care of him. I'm willing to give up sex for a while — as long as he loves me.

In just a few short hours, we'll be twelve hundred miles apart again. My heart aches as I pack. I'll miss this place. Like a desperate passenger wanting to find a reason to stay on the train, I don't want to leave.

⁂

On the way to the airport, we drive to the lake. It's almost summertime, but the leaves aren't as green yet, and the last remnants of winter hang in the air.

"Every winter, they build a large ice sculpture when the lake freezes over. I think it's a lion. People will ice skate around it until spring. The ice weakens until it can't support the lion and plunges under the water. It's a warning to the skaters that they're on thin ice! Thin ice, get it?" He laughs without amusement. "Then, next year, we do it all over again."

Sensing that this could be the last time I see him, my throat tightens. I feel the same lump from yesterday. Stress! It does that to me.

Daniel pulls his van in front of the terminal and parks at the curb. I wish he would come inside with me, but he doesn't want to pay for parking. He carries my suitcase to the curb and kisses me on the cheek.

An empty feeling comes over me as he waves goodbye and drives off. I'm standing alone with my suitcase at the curb. My chest hurts, or is it my heart?

As I make my way to the gate, I replay the weekend. *Was it something I said?* No one could change that much in just a few months. *Could they?* I miss that loving feeling when we first met. I want it back.

Soon, the stewardess tells us to power down our cell phones. Before I do, Daniel sends pretty little words to my phone.

"Here's a reminder...I love you!"

And I'm back on the roller coaster.

As long as he calls me every day, we perpetuate the illusion that I'm not alone in the world.

At seven-thirty each morning, he rings to say hello and ask about the weather. He calls to say he's tired and ready for bed in the evening. When he doesn't call, I feel sick. My heart races, and I'm overwhelmed with anxiety.

It takes only a five-minute conversation, and, like a drug fix, it quiets my inner torment.

Just Florence

If you want me by your side
Then do not take your time
Show me that you want me
And make me feel sublime

One week turns to two and then three, and Daniel hasn't left New York. He makes one excuse after another to delay the move. My life is on hold, and I feel like I'm in limbo.

"When are you coming to Florida?" I ask.

"I've meant to talk to you about that. I've been doing some work for Tricia. You know, the lady at the B&B."

"Really? I didn't know that."

"She hired me to build a retaining wall, and I could use the money. The poor woman is in over her head with the business. She has a full-time job in the city and runs everything from there. She offered me a job running the place and said I could stay in one of the rooms."

Daniel doesn't intend to come to Florida, but I suspected it. He's so good at keeping his feelings to himself. He hasn't said it's over between us, though.

"She asked me about you. I told her that you're a good egg." *Gee, thanks!* Maybe I should feel flattered by his remark, but somehow, it makes me feel like a casual friend.

I mix a batch of oatmeal cookie dough, pop it into the oven then log on to Facebook. A private message pops up. It's Josette.

"How are you involved with Daniel Weaver?"

"He's my boyfriend," I reply.

"Really! I went to visit him last month," she says. "I asked if you were his girlfriend. He said you were just Florence."

I swallow the lump in my throat and glance at the photo of Daniel's mother on my desk. She looks as if she has a secret.

"I think he's playing us both," she says. "Daniel likes to control women, you know."

Josette knows him, and not just from high school either. How else would she know that he's controlling? I can smell the cookies burning in the oven, but I ignore it.

"He's a dog and deserves to be alone for the rest of his life!" She logs off.

Paralyzed, I stare at the screen. The smoke alarm goes off, jolting me out of my trance. I run into the kitchen and pull the pan out of the oven. After opening the windows, the piercing sound shuts off, but I'm still fumbling with my internal alarm.

Josette appeared on Daniel's Facebook page shortly after we first met in the city. I suspect he might have contacted her once he returned home. Maybe that's why he's stalling about the move. I wince as pain radiates through my heart. It's my fault for bringing her name up that night.

The alarm clock is screaming at me in the morning. After tossing and turning all night, my mind is chaotic. Standing under the warm stream of water in my shower, I close my eyes. My phone rings, but I let it go to voicemail instead of jumping out to answer. There are two missed calls. I stare at Daniel's name, and my finger hovers over the speed dial button. Tears well up in my eyes, but I'm determined not to cry. I won't stand in his way if he wants to be with another woman. I push him out of my mind and leave for work.

As I'm slipping into a pity party, Ben strolls out of his office. He pauses in front of my desk. "Are you all right, Florence?"

I nod and try to hide the tears in my eyes, but he notices.

"Daniel?"

Usually, I try not to mention him. Today, however, all logic and reason are gone. I need someone to talk to; maybe a man's perspective would help.

"I don't understand him," I say. "He came on so strong when we first met. Now he's pulling away."

Ben shrugs. "Maybe he's met another woman."

"You may be right. A woman named Josette contacted me last night. She claims she's seeing him."

The floodgates open, and hot tears roll down my cheeks.

Ben reaches into his pocket and pulls out a clean handkerchief. "What does he say?"

"I haven't asked him. I almost feel guilty that I know."

"He's the one who should feel guilty."

"Do you think I should confront him?"

"How else will you know the truth? He's not a child. Surely, he has the maturity to be honest with you."

"Maybe I don't want to know the truth," I murmur.

Ben looks disgusted. I'm not sure if it's because he doesn't like Daniel or if he thinks I'm stupid for putting up with his cruelty.

"Maybe it's for the best," he says, trying to comfort me, but I suspect it's wishful thinking on his part. "Now, you can put Daniel behind you and move on."

❧

The afternoon drags on, and neither my mind nor my eyes want to focus. Eager to leave the office, I keep checking the clock.

At five, I slip past Ben's office without him seeing me. I want to go home and bury my head in a pillow.

I turn on the car radio and set the volume higher than usual. Natalie Merchant's voice is streaming from my stereo with the song, *Seven Years*. I'm in tears as I sing along with her.

So warm and insightful…Were you in my eyes…I was sure the rightful …Guardian of my life …Damn you, betrayer …How you lied.

Tears stream down my face. I cling to my pillow as if it's a lifesaver. Daniel's scent lingers from the last time we were together, and I inhale deeply. How can he be seeing Josette? He said he loves me.

⋙⋘

Every time I hear his ringtone, my blood pressure increases. My pulse pounds in my ears. I think about shutting the phone, but I don't. Part of me derives comfort because he is trying.

I pull the pillow over my head until the ringing stops. Persistent, he calls again. *Don't do it. Don't answer the phone.* But I can't help myself.

"Where've you been, Babe?" he asks. "I've been calling you all night."

"Why don't you ask Josette?"

"Josette?"

"She told me all about your relationship."

"What relationship? We're just friends."

"That's not what she said."

Daniel sighs. "We grew up in the same neighborhood. We connected on Facebook. She came to visit me. Maybe she thinks there's something between us, but I never promised her anything. I can't believe you listen to idle gossip!"

"How can you turn this around on me?" I ask. "It's not my fault!"

"Like I said, we're just friends. If you don't believe me, there's nothing I can do," he huffs. "I've had it with you, women."

"You, women?"

"Josette is just jealous and trying to start trouble."

Josette is envious. His explanation is plausible. "So, nothing is going on between you?" *I wish I could hide the neediness in my voice.*

"Of course not. I have to go to work. Can we talk about this later?"

"All right," I say, but there's a little voice screaming inside of me. I ignore it. If I rip off the Band-Aid now, I don't know if I'll be able to stop the bleeding. I never could stand the sight of blood, especially my own. Besides, if he didn't love me, why would he insist that he did? I give him the benefit of the doubt.

"Make sure you answer the phone," he warns.

Charlatan

Must ignite the ember
Smoldered back to flame
Breath in new life
Be in love again

Josette's picture is no longer on Daniel's Facebook page. Neither are the other women. For the moment, I fool myself into thinking all is well. It's as if nothing ever happened. Yesterday, I was devastated—a heap of ashes on the floor. But today, my soul is renewed. Surely, Ben will disapprove when he finds out I've forgiven Daniel. He doesn't mention that I'm twenty minutes late, but he notes the improvement in my mood.

"I take it you and your boyfriend made up."

"Daniel says nothing is going on between him and Josette. They're just friends. We're still together, kind of."

Ben rolls his eyes. "What does that mean?"

"I guess we have a phone relationship."

"It sounds like you're fanaticizing this long-distance encounter."

"I'm in love with him."

"That doesn't sound like love, Florence. Are you in love with Daniel, or are you in love with the *idea* of being in love?"

I shrug my shoulders. I don't want to have this discussion.

Ben shakes his head in disapproval. "He's a charlatan," he mutters under his breath. Even though I'm not sure what a charlatan is, his accusation makes me defensive. Besides, I can't imagine the worst in Daniel. Unsure how to spell it, I google the word charlatan, but the computer pulls up the correction.

1) A charlatan, also called swindler or mountebank, is a person practicing quackery or some similar confidence trick in order to obtain money, fame or other advantages. 2) A person who makes elaborate, fraudulent, and often voluble claims to skill or knowledge, a quack or fraud.

My phone chimes with a text from Daniel. *"I love you, Babe."*

I haven't heard those words in a long time. Long-distance relationships can be so tricky, and texting could be misleading! I tuck my phone into my desk drawer, but I'm distracted the rest of the day, thinking about love. Love…that elusive feeling makes one feel wanted, needed, and alive. Anyone who stumbles across it is lucky, especially if it's mutual. I want to be in love with a man who values me — a man who loves me and isn't afraid to show it. *Is that man Daniel? What does Ben know!* I call my friend Sharon to get her opinion. During our conversation, I tell her about Josette and instantly wish I hadn't.

"Daniel insists he wants a future with me," I add.

"Maybe he just *thinks* he wants a future with you."

"He's constantly calling or texting, wanting to know what I'm doing."

"Oh? So, he's a control freak."

"Daniel's just one of those alpha males. Besides, you know I would never let someone run my life."

"Love can make us do crazy things."

"Do you think he's a charlatan?"

"A what?" Sharon laughs.

"You know, a con artist, a pretender, a phony. My boss thinks he is."

"You know him better than I do, but it sounds like he's not sure what he wants."

∽∽⊶∾∾

Daniel once said we had the power to make our dreams a reality, but lately, I can't get a grip on my emotions, much less make my dreams come true.

The phone jolts me out of my reverie. It's my real estate agent, Bob Morrissey. I'm hoping he has a buyer for my house in Georgia. I need the money if I want to hold on to the condo in Florida.

"Hi, Florence. I have a potential buyer, but I'm afraid we may lose him unless we fix some problems. The railing that Daniel built is not up to code, and he never applied for a permit. You'll have to fix it before we can sell the house."

"I guess I have to come back to Georgia."

"Sorry, Florence. There doesn't seem to be any other way."

I call Daniel to tell him there's been a change in plans.

"Bob says the railing you built is too low, and you didn't apply for a building permit."

"Bob doesn't know what he's talking about," he says.

"Whatever, it has to be fixed," I insist.

"Why don't you ask your son?"

"My son isn't a carpenter."

"I can't leave New York for that long," he says. "I'm in the middle of a job."

Before I make the trip to Georgia, I want to see my mother. Lately, I'm reaching out to her more often, but I'm careful not to mention Daniel. Even after her stroke, she sees right through me.

"You look tired," she says.

"I'm fine, Mom." I don't want her to worry, so I keep up the illusion that things are okay, but I'm over my head. The more I struggle, the more I'm caught in an emotional web.

I haven't heard from Daniel at all in two days. Whenever I call his phone, it goes directly to voicemail.

I try again, and this time, he answers.

"Where've you been?" I ask, trying my best to sound unaffected by his lack of communication.

"Oh, you know…the usual. It's summer. I've been swimming at the lake and its concert season. I see the kids, and we go to music festivals. There was one last night. You should have seen little Emma dancing. She's so cute. All the women fell in love with her."

Yeah, sure, and they ignored you!

Georgia

I Could walk away
Or just stand my ground
Hoping that one day
You will come around

After ten hours of driving, I arrive in Georgia. My house looks run-down from the outside. Weeds and yellow forsythia bushes have reclaimed my yard, and the property wears an air of neglect. Part of me wishes I didn't have to sell it. I can't help feeling sad, but the house reminds me of my failed marriage, and it's a page best turned. Grateful to stretch my legs, I get out of the car and walk around the back to see Daniel's handy work. He's done many repairs, but I don't think it adds up to three thousand dollars, so I call him.

"What did you do with the receipts from working on the house?"

"They're somewhere in my van. I'll look for them later." He's impatient. "Don't worry! I'm sure they add up to two thousand dollars."

"I gave you three."

"No, you didn't," he says condescendingly.

"I know I gave you three," I say under my breath. It bothers me for the rest of the morning, but I have to let it go. What good would it do to argue? I have no proof.

At the county clerk's office, they tell me that the railing needs an inspection before they'll sign off on it.

"Ask Bob to meet the inspectors," Daniel says. "That's what he's getting paid for."

"What if he says no?"

"You're so negative, Florence."

"I'm not negative! Stop pressuring me."

His demeanor changes. "Me? Pressure?"

Bob calls and asks me to come to his office and sign some paperwork. I'm tired, but I agree.

"You must be Florence." He says and shakes my hand. He grabs a file from the front desk, and I follow him into his office, where he gestures for us to sit.

"Did you repair the railing and get the seal?"

"Yes, I had the railing fixed. The county signed off on the permit, but the inspectors are coming this week."

"That's not a problem," Bob says. "I can meet with them." He shuffles through some papers and then looks up. "But I have some bad news."

"Bad news?" I hold my breath. *What now?*

"I had to reduce the selling price of the house by five-thousand dollars."

I can't hide the disappointment on my face.

"You're lucky to be selling it. The market is plummeting, and there's no end in sight."

"That's all right. I know you did the best you could."

As I leave his office, I have doubts. I call Daniel.

"Maybe I should wait until the market goes back up before I sell my house," I say.

"Don't be silly," he says peevishly. "I'm sure it'll go up someday, but we won't see it in our lifetime. You're better off getting rid of it. You should drive up here once you ditch your house. Just put the money in the bank and don't look back."

⌘

My friend Sharon is waiting for me with a Chinese take-out and a bottle of wine. I drag my suitcase up to her front steps. Surrounded by her five cats — no, *six!* We sit on the floor and eat from white containers.

"So, how are things going with Daniel?"

"He's so vague. I have no idea what he has in mind. It's annoying, but I'm afraid to pressure him."

"You deserve better. The right man is out there, but how will you find him if you're with Daniel?"

Promising Sharon that I'll keep my options open, I hug her goodbye and drive to the closing.

Bob Morrissey meets me at the title company, where I'll sign over my house. My price has gone down so much I won't have enough to pay off the townhouse as I'd planned. After signing and initialing a zillion pages and paying the balance on the mortgage, I'll have a little money to put in the bank. I should invest it once I'm settled. That is if I ever do settle. For the past few months, I've felt like a pinball, bumping from state to state.

After the closing, I look at my yellow bi-level house on the hill and try to force back a sob, but it's useless.

Daniel hasn't called since I left. A sudden urge to call him has me picking up the phone. There's no answer, so I call Tricia's home phone. The housekeeper answers.

"Hi, Rhonda, is Daniel there?"

She hesitates. "I think he's upstairs. He went to a concert last night and didn't get home until late."

My stomach is coming up to my throat as insecurity creeps in.

The Promise of Love

Don't know if I'll come back
You may have sealed our fate
Now you're not so sure
May be too late

Feeling down, I pour myself a glass of wine and call Daniel.

"Did you have the closing?" he asks.

"Yeah, it's over."

"How much did you walk away with?"

"Not enough," I skirt the question. "I'm leaving for Florida tomorrow. I need to figure out a way to hold onto the townhouse."

"Bob thinks I should apply for a loan modification."

"Bob? What does he know? That place isn't worth it. The market's down. Just turn in the keys."

"You mean to let it go into foreclosure?"

"Why not? Plenty of people are doing it. You can't afford that place," he points out. "You'll be sinking good money into an inflated mortgage."

"I'm not plenty of people. Besides, I love it there."

When we hang up, Daniel sends a text.

"If you want TLC, call Bob!"

"Very funny!"

I go over why we shouldn't be together, but my resilience disappears when I hear his ringtone.

"He-y-y woman," he says in that lyrical tone that hooked me in the first place. "Don't you miss me yet?"

"Of course, I do. *I love you* wants to sneak out of my mouth, but Daniel doesn't say those words anymore. Lately, I'm holding back, too.

"How long are you planning to stay at Tricia's house?"

"Not long. Those dogs of hers wake me up every morning, barking their fool heads off. I've decided to give my tenant notice and move back into my house."

"I guess we weren't meant to be together, Daniel."

"Stop!" he says. "Winter is over, and it's beautiful here."

"Are you asking me to move up north again?"

"Why not? Now that you're losing the townhouse, there isn't any point in me coming to Florida. You should come to New York. I gave my tenant notice. He's out in ten days." Daniel sounds triumphant.

"I love this place," I say. "I can't just leave."

"Then keep it — I don't care."

His voice turns gruff. Even though he's hundreds of miles away, I am intimidated.

"Hey! Did I tell you I bought a dog?"

"Daniel! Why did you do that? You said you hated Tricia's dogs."

"The kids wanted a puppy, and I couldn't say no. He's a Chocolate Lab, and I named him Mack."

He's such a child, never thinking of the consequences of his actions. Having a dog comes with responsibilities, something he avoids.

"You've got to see him, Florence. Pack up your stuff and hire a moving van—right now.

"You're pushy."

"Come *home,* Babe. I miss you."

"If I come, and I'm not promising that I will…. I need time to think about it."

"All right, but I won't ask again."

Just what I need—pressure!

We hang up, and I stare out my back window. I won't be able to hold onto the townhouse much longer. The memory of the river slowly floods back. I recall how wonderful it was watching the water flow past with Daniel. "It sounds tempting, but…"

"We'll be together-r-r." He drags the word in an enticing tone.

"Are you sure you want me there? Things haven't been the same between us lately."

"I told you. I'm having some problems. It has nothing to do with us. Come on, Babe! Once the renter is out, I'll get in there and clean it up for us. Then you can pack your stuff and drive up here."

"I don't know… I'd have to break it to my mom. I'm going to visit her next week."

"Tell your mom I said hello."

Hello from Daniel is the last thing my mother wants to hear.

Thinking in circles with no clear solution, I'm unsure. I need to go to the ocean and walk along the shore. I drive to the beach. It's a luxury to live only a few blocks away from paradise. I only wish that Daniel could have appreciated the lifestyle. After an exhilarating dip in the ocean, I lay on my towel. The sun is soothing, and I doze off to the sound of the seagulls. If I leave Florida, I'll miss the beach most of all. It's a high price to pay. Staring out at the horizon, I mull over the situation. It didn't feel right when we were together, but Daniel promises this time it will be different.

Couples hold hands and smile at each other. Love comes easy to some women, while others struggle for love. That's all I want—to be in love! I'm feeling fragile. There's no room for mistakes.

Pauper

I will follow you, my love
We fit together hand in glove
I see a light; it's in your eyes
Lighting up my earthly skies

My phone rings. "Hi, Mom," Annmarie chirps. I haven't heard from you lately. Is everything all right?"

"I'm sorry. I've been feeling a little blue about selling the Georgia house."

"At least you have the townhouse."

"Uh...not really. I didn't make enough to pay the mortgage. I can't afford to stay here."

The phone seems to go dead. "Annmarie? Are you there?"

"Where are you going to live?"

"Daniel wants me to move to New York."

"I was afraid of that. Wasn't he supposed to come to Florida?"

"He thinks it would be better if I go to New York."

"It's not like you, letting some guy dictate your life."

"He's not dictating," I hedge. "He's just a little bossy.

"What are you going to do with all your furniture?"

"Daniel wanted me to hire a moving truck, but I told him no. I'm planning to return to Florida, so I'm having my stuff put in storage."

"Have you told Grandma?"

"No, I'm visiting her tomorrow. Do you want to come with me?"

"No, thanks. I don't want to be there when she freaks out. Grandma hates Daniel."

"You're exaggerating, don't you think?"

"If you say so." She snickers. "Let me know how that goes."

It's true! My mother disapproves of Daniel. She thinks he's the reason I don't visit as much. Although my brain is yelling, don't go, my heart doesn't want to release him.

❦

When I get there, my mother is sitting in her recliner in the living room.

"Mom? You look so frail."

"It's the stroke. I can't bounce back."

"Have you been going to physical therapy?"

"No," she says with the flip of her hand. "My life is over. I'm just waiting to die."

"Don't say that!"

"Florence, how are you? You haven't been yourself lately. I've been so worried. Are you still with that, Daniel? I wish you'd get rid of him."

Good grief! Annmarie was right. Why does she have to weigh me down with all this guilt?

"Can we not talk about him right now?"

Her eyes soften, and she hugs me. "I'm sorry. I don't want to see you get hurt."

"I'm not going to get hurt," I reassure her.

Who am I kidding? I'll be a soggy mass of tears if I lose him.

My sister, Carol, is the only one I can confide in. I tell her about my sex life — or lack thereof.

"It's not fair. We were in love. I thought this was it!"

"Maybe Mom is right," she says. "There's something off about Daniel."

Oh no, not her too!

"Let's go out for lunch," I suggest. Maybe my news about moving to New York will be less dramatic if we're in a public place.

"Okay, but I have to pick Sophie up from school at two. I'll get dressed."

I leave her to it and go downstairs, where Mom watches FOX News. Ten minutes go by, and Carol isn't ready, so I yell to her.

"In a minute," she shouts from her room. There's frustration in her voice. "I can't find anything that fits."

"She's been gaining so much weight," my mother whispers. "I don't know what to do. If I say anything, she eats more."

I frown. When I was younger and living with my mother, I also carried a few extra pounds. It's all the stress. Mom has always been a nagger. The funny thing is that she's usually right, but it's hard to hear it all the time. Carol comes downstairs in a flowing skirt and a long-sleeved blouse. Even though it's summer, she doesn't like to show her arms. She must be hot, and I could tell she was crying.

"You look beautiful," I say. "Give me a hug."

She grimaces, then smiles. "I shouldn't eat. I'm on a diet."

"Then, we'll get salads."

We drive to the restaurant with Carol by my side and our mother in the back seat. I want to tell them about my plans to move to New York but bite my tongue until we're sitting around the table.

"Mom's birthday is coming up soon," Carol says. "Maybe we can plan something special for her."

"I don't think I'll be here," I say.

"Are you going out of town?" my mom asks.

"You've been acting weird all day," Carol says. "What's up?"

"I'm moving to New York," I blurt.

"New York? What's in New...," My mother's brow wrinkles. "How did he talk you into that?"

"He didn't have to. I want to go."

"You need to get rid of him," she says under her breath, but loud enough for me to hear. "He's not the right man for you."

"Mom, I know you don't like Daniel, but you don't know him.

"I hope you're taking your car!"

"Of course."

"Good. That way, you can make a quick getaway when you wake up out of this love-fog."

I roll my eyes.

"I don't trust him," she says.

Carol rolls her eyes. *We're a family of eye-rollers!*

"You're wasting your time," my mother says. "He has nothing to offer you."

"I love him," I mutter.

"Love?" She chuckles. "It's just as easy to love a man with money. You picked a pauper."

My cell phone chimes. It's Daniel.

"What are you doing?"

"I'm trying to figure out my future," I reply.

"I am your future."

Deep Water

I search among the embers
Looking for a sign
That I am still your sweetie
Your love, it is still mine

Daniel hasn't called all day. I try to resist the urge to call him. It's late in the afternoon — not a good sign. My radar is on alert. I break down and pick up the phone.

"Daniel! Where have you been?"

"I'm sorry, Babe. I've been busy cleaning the house. That tenant was a real pig. It took hours to bleach out the tub and mop the floors."

"At least I'll come to a clean house next week."

"Florence? Do you feel secure in our relationship?"

"Of course," I say, but my confidence is shaky.

"I want to make sure you know that I love you."

"I love you, too." *There! I said it — but he said it first.*

"Flo, I have to tell you something."

"What?"

"A friend wants me to pick her up from the airport."

"Her? Who is she?"

He hesitates. "Josette."

"Josette? She's the one who tried to break us up. And now she's coming to visit?" My insides are twisting, and I want to scream.

"She's a friend, Florence. Don't be jealous."

"I'm not jealous!" I say, but I'm struggling to keep my voice calm. "Where is she staying?"

"She's spending the week at the B&B with Tricia."

The thought of it makes me cringe.

"I didn't know she was coming," he says. "She just called yesterday. I'm telling you because I want to be upfront... no secrets."

"You're going out with your old girlfriend, and you want my blessing?" My voice goes up in volume.

"I thought you would understand. Now I wish I hadn't said anything."

He's trying to make me feel irrational, and I waver. "I appreciate that your telling me, but why do you have to pick her up? Doesn't she have a family?"

"It's complicated."

There's that word again.

"You have nothing to worry about," he says. "You know I love you."

"That's the problem...I *don't* know."

"You're overacting. Trust me. You are my future. Josette is my past. I'll call you tonight," he says in a soothing tone that lulls my fears.

"All right." The words squeeze past my tight lips.

"You're the best, Babe."

The whole situation is confusing. Daniel claims he and Josette are just friends and that he loves me. My heart wants to believe him, but there's a voice inside my head saying, fool.

The night drags on, and Daniel doesn't call. My mind goes into overdrive, and I feel an anxiety attack coming on. She has her claws in him. *I know it.*

I call Daniel's cell phone in the morning, but there's no answer. Although I don't savor the idea of talking with Tricia, I try her number.

"Hello, Tricia, it's Florence. Is Daniel there?"

"Yes, he's down at the river swimming with the kids."

I want to ask where Josette is, but why bother. She must be with him.

"Daniel says that you sold your house in Georgia. Congratulations."

"Yes, he's convinced me to move in with him."

"That's great. I'm glad things are working out. I'll tell him you called when he comes in. Take care of yourself, Florence." The phone goes dead.

Thirty minutes later, I get a text. *I love my Florence.*

Great! He's on his phone. I dial his number.

"You didn't call me last night," I say in a cool tone. "Daniel? Are you there?"

Women's voices laugh in the background, muffled as if his hand is covering the receiver.

"I told you I'd try," he says. "Don't be mad."

"Tricia told me you couldn't come to the phone."

"Emma wanted to go swimming. I have to drop her back off at Lisa's. Then I'm going for a bite to eat. I'll call you later, Babe."

Before I can ask him about Josette, he cuts me off.

Betrayed

Afraid to tell the truth
I might be left alone
Need to find the courage
Honest, on my own

Once more, I feel a tug on my heart. There's been a definite shift in his attitude. Lately, his texts have been shorter. The romantic bantering between us is limited to a few lines of *I love you*, and *I can't wait to see you*. I try to convince myself that things will be fine once we're together again, but I'm unsure. I find myself constantly looking for signs of dishonesty. I can't sleep, so I call the B&B again.

"Hi, Tricia. Is Daniel there?"

"No, he and Josette are at his house."

"His house? He told me she's staying with *you*." I feel my chest cave in as the oxygen drains from my lungs. Shame washes over me. I know what she thinks of me for taking his crap.

"My heart goes out to you, Florence. I once was in a relationship like this, and it damaged me."

"What does he want from me?" I let out a defeated sob.

"He knows that you sold your house. Maybe he's after the money."

Her words are like a slap in the face. My mind swirls.

"Daniel has a way of picking sweet, kind women and then screwing with their heads," she continues. "Josette claims he's a pathological liar, but she's still with him."

Don't cry, don't cry, don't cry.

"Florence, I believe whatever doesn't kill you makes you stronger."

I always hated that saying, and I hate it more from her.

When we hang up, I call Daniel's cell phone and leave a message on his voicemail. "Tricia told me everything!" I say and hang up. It doesn't take long for Daniel to call back.

"What going on, Florence?"

"Tricia says that Josette is staying at your house!"

"She's just trying to start trouble. She hates that you're coming back to New York."

"You're a liar, Daniel. You told me Josette was staying at the B&B."

"I didn't tell you because I knew you would overreact."

"Overreact? Hell yeah! What woman wouldn't?"

"Do you love her?"

"Don't be silly. If that were the case, why would I ask you to move in with me?"

I try to collect my composure. "Josette told her...."

"Stop!" He says. "Consider the source. Tricia is angry because I wouldn't be her partner at the B&B, and Josette is jealous because she wants to be with me.

Tricia and Josette are spiteful bitches, and you've played right into their hands."

He's trying to push my *us against them* button.

"I don't want to hear it," I yell, my temper stoked by his cavalier attitude. My body betrays me, and I start to hyperventilate.

"Well, if that's how you feel, I guess it's over between us. Have a nice life." He hangs up, getting in the last word.

A brand-new bottle of wine is beckoning to me. I open it with the intent to get rip-roaring drunk.

Mission accomplished. I crawl upstairs and slip into my bed. The sun is like a sleepless eye that remains open, watching me. I want it to be dark—as dark as the hole in my heart. The room spins, and soon I'm sitting by the toilet, worshipping the porcelain god.

My phone rings. I cover my ears to silence his ringtone. With my head buried in the pillow, I cry over my loss; I cry because the dream is shattered; I cry because he's gone.

∽∘⚓∘∾

My eyes feel glued shut by my tears. What day is it? The concept of time is gone from my world, which has collapsed under my feet. God, it hurts. There are two messages from Daniel on my phone.

I listen to the first one. "Florence, I've been trying to reach you. I'm getting worried. Please call me back so I know you're all right."

I play the second message. "I guess you have no intention of talking to me. If you don't want to answer,

I'll stop calling. Good-bye and good luck." His words are so final. I feel so alone. *Alone*—it's such an empty word. I gasp for air.

A few hours later, the phone rings, and I'm compelled to hear his voice.

"I thought you would be halfway to California by now," I say.

"Florence, I love you."

"If you love me, why did you ask Josette to stay at your house?"

"I don't know. Maybe I was mad at you."

"For what?"

"For not being here with me."

"I told you I was coming."

"You can still come. I want you, not Josette. I need you," he says in desperation. "Can't we get past this?"

Struck by his audacity, I'm not sure what to say. "You put me through hell and back. Now you want to know if I can get past it?"

"Florence, be reasonable. I've been telling you how much I love you. I've asked you to come and live with me. What more do you want?"

"I don't know. How can I ever trust you?"

If you're not happy, I'll give you the money to go back—no questions asked."

"Daniel, it's a long way to travel. I'm not sure I have the energy."

"Ah, come on, Babe."

Every time I move toward independence, it feels like the weight of the world is crushing the air out of me. I can't breathe. My body trembles with pain. I'll do anything to make it go away.

Should I forgive him? Even as I ask myself this question, I know that I will. I can't let go of the dream — the dream of being happy with Daniel.

My plans to break away evaporate as I slip back under his spell.

∼✕∽

The trip is on again. Daniel calls every day to make sure I don't change my mind.

"If I take a plane, I won't be able to bring my cat."

"Get rid of that cat!"

"That's not nice. Besides, I need my car."

"You can use mine."

"What if I want to come back to Florida? I'll be stuck."

"Exactly! I'm not letting you leave again."

The Five C's

If we only had the chance
To tear down all the walls
Could we go back to
A place where lovers call

My car is packed, and I'm ready to go to New York. Everything I need to survive is in my Honda. I call it my five C's, my car, my computer, my clothes, my cell phone, and my cat — the sum of my life.

Fueled with four hours of sleep, I lock my front door under the dim porch light and drive off. As I head north on the highway, the sun is rising on my right. I'm feeling scared, but I don't know why. I've driven many times between Georgia and Florida. I'm used to traveling long distances. I'm finding it hard to breathe. I feel an anxiety attack coming on. I've never had anxiety until I met Daniel. At first, I thought it was just that he took my breath away, but maybe it's something more serious.

Too bad I'm not as calm as my cat. Ripley is already asleep in his crate. He travels better than me. Stressed out, I'm getting a cold sore on my lip. *Damn!* I turn up the music and listen to John Mayer sing. *"Back to you! It always comes around, back to you. I tried to forget you, I tried to stay away, but it's tooo late."*

My cell phone chimes. *"Relax,"* he texts. *"It's all good."* Is he reading my mind again? Taking a deep breath and loosening my grip on the wheel, I turn up the radio, so I won't have to think. Keane is playing a song called *Looking Back*. The lyrics make me sad. Maybe Daniel's stuck in the past, and that's why he can't be with me.

As the sun sinks low in the sky, I decide to stop for the night and check into a hotel. They allow pets but require a one-hundred-dollar deposit. I leave Ripley in the car with food and water and wait until dark. I'll have to sneak him in. I exit through the side door, which locks once I'm outside. This may be a problem because I have to walk by the front desk to get to the elevator. Surely, someone will spot my large pet carrier.

Then I have an idea. I empty the contents of my suitcase and stuff Ripley inside. He isn't happy, but he has no choice. Moving quickly, I re-enter the hotel and walk toward the elevator.

Before the doors open, I look down to see his little head working through an opening in the zipper and close it, but he's smart. Now he knows the way out and will not give up easily. Luckily, no one else is on the elevator with me.

Once inside the room, I let him out. He's content to smell the unfamiliar scents while I shower off the road grime. I call the restaurant downstairs to order a burger.

"We can have it sent to your room within thirty minutes," the clerk says.

"No! That's all right. I'll come down and order," I reply hastily. *Whew! That was close.*

I slip out of the room, hoping Ripley won't see me leave and cry while I'm gone.

The restaurant was closed for the night, but I could order food at the bar. It's cavernous and dark, with a few soft lights on the ceiling and candles on the tables. There's a big-screen television set to a sports channel, with a group of men watching intently. They don't acknowledge my presence as I take a seat on the barstool, but there's another man across from me. He smiles, and I turn away to break eye contact. I'm not looking to meet someone. I just want to eat.

I order a hamburger to-go and a glass of merlot while I wait.

The man across the bar is gone.

"Do you mind if I sit here?" a voice says.

Startled, I look up to see him next to me.

"Not at all," I say and move my purse from the stool next to mine.

"I'm Phil," he says and takes a seat.

"I'm Florence."

The other men let out a loud cheer when their team makes a touchdown.

"Do you like football, Florence?"

"No, not really."

"Neither do I. So, what brings you to Atlanta?"

"I'm on my way to New York."

"Is that where you're from?"

"Yes, I grew up on Long Island."

"I love Long Island. I played guitar in a band and used to perform there. Now I live in Virginia and write music lyrics and poetry."

We chitchat until the bartender comes with my food, neatly packed in a brown shopping bag with the hotel logo printed on the front.

Phil reaches into his pocket and pulls out a business card. "If you contact me, I'll send you some of my poems."

"Thanks," I say and put his card in my purse.

I pay the tab and take the food to my room. *Why couldn't Daniel be like Phil?*

Ripley's using the makeshift kitty litter pan under the bathroom sink when I enter. Litter is flying everywhere, and the odor is unbearable. I guess he has travel stress. I can't blame him. After cleaning up, I'm more tired than hungry. I crawl into bed and turn off the light, falling into a deep slumber.

I'm awakened by a low, guttural sound from Ripley. He can't sleep and starts meowing.

"Psst! Get over here," I whisper.

He jumps onto the bed and lies next to me, but as soon as I'm asleep, he meows again. I put my arm around him to soothe him.

With just four hours of sleep, I pack up to leave. Now I have to sneak Ripley back out of the hotel. Thank goodness I paid for the room already. I shove him back into the suitcase, but he won't have it this time. He paws and scratches the inside with fury. I leave the keys on the dresser and pray there is no one in the elevator.

The doors open, and my stomach sinks. There's an elderly couple inside. I hold my breath as we descend.

Luckily, they must be hard of hearing.

Welcome to New York State, the sign says. I pull off the Interstate. As the landscape changes, I pass under a canopy of spruce, the soft, fragrant trees indigenous to this area, not the scrub pines of the south. The windows are open, allowing the scent to waft through my car, and I breathe in. There's something different about the air in the north. It's thinner—crisper. Maybe it has to do with the altitude. I'm glad to be back upstate. My cell phone chimes with a text. *"Where are you?"*

I'm tempted to call him, but it's against the law to drive and talk on a cellphone in New York. I don't need to start my new life with a ticket.

"Hurry …My heart is waiting," he texts.

"I was born a house cat. By the slight of my mother's hand." I smile and turn up the music to sing along with John Mayer.

Wildlife

We sometimes take for granted
A touch or a small kiss
Until it is removed
And then so sorely missed

Daniel is waiting for me on his front deck when I pull into the dirt driveway. Shaky, I step out of the car and stretch my legs from driving.

"I should kick your ass," he says.

"I missed you too, Daniel," I say mockingly.

Before I can get the pet carrier unstrapped, Daniel's new dog, bounds toward us. Mack is big, brown, clumsy pup with sweet brown eyes.

Ripley's eyes are wide with anxiety. He hisses, and I have to hold his carrier out of reach.

"I thought you said he was a puppy."

"He was!" Daniel laughs. After wiping the sweat from his face, he gives me a quick hug.

"I mowed my neighbor's yard for him today, and you know how he paid me?" He holds up a small white pouch.

"What's that?"

"Heroin! Do you believe it?" He laughs again. "Come inside. I'll give you the grand tour. You can put Ripley in the bathroom."

He grabs my case and leads me through the living room to a small bathroom in the back of the house.

"He'll be scared in here," I argue.

"Just give him some food. He'll be fine."

The food is in the car. As I cross the living room, I observe the pictures on Daniel's wall. Watercolors, oils, abstract and traditional — some are partially nude women, others are random designs, each image executed in a completely different style. Somehow it works. There's a large oil painting of a bison and another of a clown. Clowns give me the creeps. "You sure have a lot of art."

"Eye candy," he says. "I know what I like." He's so cocky — but cute. Shaking my head, I retrieve the cat food and litter from the trunk. It's six p.m., and already the sky is darkening. A sudden breeze blows in from the lake a mile away, raising goose flesh on my arms.

Once Ripley's settled, Daniel shows me around upstairs. There's only one room with an air mattress on the floor and a small bathroom in the corner. The room overlooks the front yard, and the main highway is three hundred feet away. Semi-trucks whiz by every few minutes. The bathroom is small and in need of a makeover. The vinyl tiles are old and worn, and the shower doors don't slide easily. The lighting is dim, and I decide to use the downstairs bathroom. Daniel pours us some wine and loads some CDs into the disk player. He wraps his arms around me and amorously bites my ear. I'm so tired, but I'm not about to ignore his passion.

"Let's take a bath in my Jacuzzi. You'll love it," he says, leading me into the bathroom. His voice is soft and seductive.

He sets his glass of wine down and turns on the faucet.

"Do you like honeysuckle?" He pours the bath oil into the water, filling the room with a sweet aroma. Then he lights some candles. For a brief moment, I wonder how many women he's entertained in his tub. Perhaps Josette was one of them. *No! I won't go there, not now.*

Daniel drops his boxers and slips into the hot steamy water. "Get in," he coaxes.

"It's too hot!"

"Just get in," he orders.

"You're so bossy." Wincing from the heat, I ease into the bubbly liquid. Daniel lays back and closes his eyes. The candles flicker in the corners of the room, and soft music from the stereo sets the mood. It's very romantic, even with Ripley staring at us from his carrier. The cold air hits me when we step out of the bath and zaps the rest of my energy.

"Let's jump under the covers and get *comfy*." Daniel races me up the stairs to his bedroom. I gaze at the mattress in the corner of the room. Our eyes lock, and it's as if he reads my mind.

"Stop," he says dismissively and kisses my shoulder. A smile flits across his face. He turns down the covers and climbs into bed. "Come over here." He pats his side of the bed.

Daniel tries to steal my pillow, and we banter back and forth. Picking up the water bottle, I give him a devious smile.

His eyes open wide in a warning. "You better not pour that on me."

"Would I do that?" I feign innocence.

He grabs the bottle, puts it on the table next to the bed, then pulls me to him and nuzzles my neck with his mouth.

"What are you doing?" I ask.

The pressure increases as his lips suck harder. His full weight is on my chest. We make love on his blow-up bed. I get the distinct feeling he'd rather be smoking a cigarette. He doesn't ask me to look into his eyes like before. Sex is more and more difficult, and I don't know why. His pace is too rapid. He's trying too hard. I can't give him what he wants, so I pretend. I know it's wrong, but I feel his need to be in control. Satisfied, he positions me, so we're spooning.

Daniel wraps his arms around me. His body is warm and comforting. Feeling safe, cherished, and loved, I drift off to sleep with a false sense of security.

A few hours later, the sound of semi-trucks traveling past the house wakes me. It's a lonely sound. Their headlights peer into the window, moving up the wall and fading away. It's hard to sleep. I slip out of his arms and wander downstairs to check on Ripley.

Daniel says there are coyotes and bears on his property. Pressing my head against the frosty glass doors, I search for wildlife. It's dark outside, except for the porch light. I stare at my car in the driveway feeling another anxiety attack. *Isn't there a pill for this?*

Mack is lying on the leather couch and wags his tail when he sees me. He's a nice dog, but he should sleep on the floor. I search for Daniel's man-blanket in the chest and then notice Mack lying on it. Taking his place on the couch, I enjoy the calm serenity of the darkness. The porch light creates shadows on the walls, and I can barely make out the beautiful works of art. Daniel must have spent a lot of money. The irony strikes me. Such expensive art, and yet he has the cheapest windows and doors. It reminds me of a trailer.

My place in Florida didn't have many furnishings, but the walls, lighting, and trim were perfect. Maybe I should leave. Just pack my bags and escape while he's asleep.

"Leave Daniel," I say aloud, testing the words, sounding them out. They feel strange on my tongue. Unable to breathe, the thought of not being with him is unbearable. The needy little child inside me doesn't want to be alone. She's well aware that I may get hurt, but she doesn't care, and I'm too weak to fight her. Besides, Josette would swoop in, and I'd be out in the cold. I push her out of my mind and go back upstairs to slip into comfy with Daniel.

Pickin

I feed upon the crumbs
You often throw my way
As soon as I am strong to leave
You throw some more, I stay

In the morning, Mack is by the bed to greet me. I stretch to pet him and then think of Ripley, locked away in the bathroom. I go downstairs with Mack at my heels and open the sliding doors. He darts off and runs at full speed around the yard. This is my chance to rescue Ripley. I open the bathroom door. He looks sad. "Don't worry, sweetie. I'll find a place for you."

While in the bathroom, I check myself in the mirror and gasp when I see the red mark on my neck. That bastard! He gave me a hickey. I pick up the pet carrier and bring Ripley upstairs.

"What are you doing with that?" Daniel nods at the pet carrier with a cautious smile on his face.

"I'm keeping Ripley up here. From now on, the upstairs is off-limits for Mack."

"I don't know how he'll feel about that. Where'd you go last night?"

"I couldn't sleep."

"You can't just leave without telling me."

"Why not?"

"Because I'm the boss of you." He gives me a wolfish grin. "Do you feel like making us some coffee?" Now he gives me his little boy, innocent look. I go back downstairs, wondering if he has milk in the fridge. There's just enough, but after seeing little else in the refrigerator, I know what we'll be doing today — food shopping. The aroma brings him downstairs.

"What did you do to my neck?"

"I branded you. You're mine."

"You're a devil!"

"Let's take our coffee outside," he suggests.

"Isn't it chilly out there?"

"We'll bring the man-blanket," he says.

There's no backdoor, so I follow him outside and around the house. We take a seat at the picnic table on the patio, and he wraps the blanket around us. It smells like dog. Although it's nice to sit and watch Mack tear around Daniel's enormous grassy yard, something is missing. It's the river. His house doesn't have a view like Tricia's does. What a shame. I loved that river!

"Let's get dressed and go *pickin*," he says.

"What's *pickin*?"

"You'll see." He smiles.

After my shower, the hickey appears to be redder. Feeling like a teenager, I try to cover it with makeup.

We spend the afternoon going from one garage sale to another. Sometimes we stop at antique stores. He looks at everything, deciding if it's a hidden treasure. It all looks like junk! That is until we find a store with millions of old books. I'm in heaven and decide *pickin's* kind of fun. At the last antique store, an elderly couple greets us when we walk in. They tell us it's their sixtieth wedding anniversary.

"How long have you two been married?" the woman asks.

"Thirty years," Daniel says. "Only we didn't live together."

Everyone laughs, and Joe shows Daniel his watch collection. Daniel tries on each one in the case.

"I love old watches. I have to buy this." He holds a jeweled watch up to the light. "I once had one like this, but someone stole it."

He digs in his pocket for his wallet and discovers that he has left his wallet on the kitchen counter.

"Florence, can I borrow two hundred dollars? I'll give it back when we get home," he assures me with puppy-dog eyes.

When we get home, I start dinner while Daniel admires his new watch, a shit-eating grin on his face.

"Do you have the money I loaned you?"

His expression changes as he grabs up his wallet. "Here's your money!" he snaps and slams it on the counter.

Dinner is solemn as he picks at his plate. I sip on my wine. Things aren't turning out the way I expected. I wonder if this is how things will always be with us. I feel as if someone hit the pause button on my life.

Without turning on the light, I go to the bathroom, careful to feel for the toilet seat. Ever since I fell into the toilet, I check before I sit.

❧

Mack decides it's time to get up. He's dancing around the room like a nut.

"Can you take the dog out and make us some coffee-to-go, Babe. I have a side job, and I'm late."

After being dragged around the grass lot by Mack, I brew some coffee and look for a disposable cup to put it in. Daniel only has a few coffee mugs. None of them matches, and they're all chipped, but it probably won't come back if I send him off with one. I notice an empty water bottle on the counter and shrug. *Good enough.*

Outside the window, a bird sitting high on the branch of a tree mesmerizes me. He appears to be looking at me. Perhaps he knows that I don't belong here. He flies off, and I drop back into reality. *Without a parachute!*

Daniel leaves for work. I should use the time to search the house, but I go to the store instead.

He's home when I return.

"You look so serious, Daniel. What's going on?"

"Did you send Josette a text?"

"Why would I do something like that?"

"I don't knooow?" He emphasizes the "o" and gives me a look like I'm lying. "Josette says you're taunting her by sending her text messages."

"That's ridiculous, Daniel. If you don't believe me, check my phone." I hand it to him.

"No, if you say you didn't do it, you didn't do it, but if you did, please stop."

He cares about her enough to think the worst of me. I can't wrap my head around their relationship.

"Why didn't you stay with Josette? It seems like you still want her in your life, or maybe you're not sure which one of us you want to be with."

"I told you. We had business."

Yeah, monkey business.

"It's going to be cold tonight," he says. "I'll go cut some wood."

"I bet Josette could keep you warm."

"Be nice," he teases and smacks my butt.

One minute, Daniel is secretive and moody, and the next, he's upbeat and full of humor — very erratic. It's difficult to keep up. Part of me wants to know what he's thinking. The other part prefers to be in the dark.

While Daniel chops wood for the burner, I start dinner. I cook steak, salad, and mashed potatoes, Daniel's favorites.

We sit on the couch and use the storage chest as a table. Daniel devours everything on his plate and then stabs a piece of my steak with his fork.

"Hey, I was eating that!" I say, retrieving it before he puts it in his mouth. He can't keep his fork out of other people's plates.

After cleaning the dishes, we watch a movie on the couch. Daniel curls around me like a vine.

"Do you love me, Daniel?"

"Love?" He scrunches up his nose. "Ewe."

Babe, he sometimes calls me that or sweetie. For a moment, the endearment makes me feel like he cares, but these days, I call it crumbs.

"What are we doing tomorrow?" I ask.

"I'll probably finish a job because I need to get paid this week." His expression is weighty but quickly changes, and he smiles. "Then, I'll clean up around here. You're so messy!"

"Me? Messy? Mack's fur is all over the floor and rolls around in clumps like dust bunnies. Then there's your smoking. It leaves a film on everything. Dust sticks to it and...." I'm riled up until I see the smile in his eyes.

He stares at me for a moment, then his smile disappears. "I have a business proposition for you."

"Business?"

"Yeah, what do you think about making this place into a B&B like Tricia's?"

"I don't know," I say and shrug my shoulders. "It's kind of small."

"We can add an extension. Think about it — we're only five miles from the concert center. Besides, I can run it better than Tricia does hers."

"Yeah, but Tricia has an advantage."

"What's that?"

"The river!"

"We'll build a pool."

"I don't know. Running a business is hard work."

Daniel puts his arm around my shoulder. "We're getting old, Babe. We need an income."

It's comforting to think we can grow old together, but Daniel wants me to use my money to go into business with him. *Maybe he asked Josette, and she said no.*

I have a lot to lose and try to avoid the discussion. I promise him we can talk about it in the spring. By then, I should know if our relationship *has teeth.*

Control Freak

Retreat to a place
That's easy and free
The heart does not care
Where that would be

In the morning, Daniel has his legs draped around mine. I try to get up, but Daniel tightens his grip. "Think of me like a Venus flytrap."

"I'm going to take a shower," I say.

"Make sure you come back," he says.

"I intend to stay far away from that bed."

"He jumps up. "I get the shower first."

I inch toward the bathroom, but he runs in, locking the door. He can be a bastard for sure, but most of the time, he's funny. I find it amazing he can be that way with all his problems. Even damaged, I love him. After all, being mentally sound is not a choice. He steps out of the bathroom, and I retaliate.

"Stinger!" I say and give him a wicked smile.

Daniel's lip twitches, and his eyes dance with laughter.

I get ready to run, but a call saves me on his cell phone. He says he has to go out for a while and leaves.

An eternity passes until I hear his van pulling into the driveway. He slams the door when he comes into the house, along with the heavy smell of cigarettes.

"What's wrong?"

"Lisa's moving in with her boyfriend."

"So, what's wrong with that?"

"She screws every Tom, Dick, and Harry and claims she's in love. This is the third time she's dragging my kids into a situation."

"You can't stop her from living her life," I point out.

Daniel ignores my comment. He's so far away in his thoughts—I don't even think he heard me.

"The last time, I had to bail her out. It cost me over ten thousand dollars to move her into an apartment and get her a new car. After all that, what did she do? She wouldn't let me see my kids."

"Why?" The thought flashes through my mind. *Daniel is so bossy.* He might have tried to control her after that.

"She claimed that I hit her. I had the police knocking at my door at two in the morning."

"Did she file charges?"

"No, they were dropped, but I had to pick up my girls at the police station when I wanted to see them."

"It must have been very traumatic for your daughters."

Daniel looks off in the distance. "Lisa brainwashed the kids. They were scared to be alone with me," he continues. "It pissed me off. I'm not proud of what I did, but I had no choice at the time."

"What did you do?" My eyebrows rise.

"Let's just say there were enough drugs in her car to put her away for life. It scared the shit out of her."

"That's awful!" I try to absorb how any man could be so malicious as to have the mother of his children sent away on drug charges.

"She cheated on me! The first time, she was boinking the landscaper while I was out of town on a job."

"Maybe she didn't feel loved."

"Love! Is that all you women think about?"

"Women like to feel secure in a relationship. Maybe Lisa didn't."

"Anyway," he continues. "I found a good lawyer and fought her for custody. I could have won, too. He dug up a lot of shit on her, and we went to court."

"So, what happened?"

"When it came down to it, I dropped the case and settled for joint custody."

"Is that why you moved to California?"

"I don't want to talk about it," he says, shaking his head. "The bottom line is she's doing the same thing all over again with another man."

I suspect there's more to the story and wonder if maybe he's just jealous. If Lisa moves on with her life, she'll be out of his control.

The phone rings. It's my daughter, Annmarie. The last time we talked was two weeks ago.

"Hi, Mom, I haven't heard from you. Have you been busy?"

"Nah! One day is the same as the next here. I miss Florida."

"Then come home. What are you doing there?"

"I came to be with Daniel, but...,"

"You're getting too dependent on him."

"I can't leave. Not yet."

"You sound needy. It's not like you. It's as if you've disappeared off the face of the earth. What kind of power does this man have over you?"

"It's not him," I defend.

"Daniel is calling me. I have to go, Annmarie. I'll call you next week."

"You need to come home. The sooner you realize that, the better."

She's right. I left everything to be with Daniel. He was supposed to bend — not me. I'm waiting, but for what — I'm not exactly sure.

Coffee Talk

I want to say I love you
Don't know if you will hear
Now you don't seem ready
Intentions are not clear

The smell of coffee lures Daniel downstairs, and I pour him a cup. He coughs and lights up a cigarette.

"You really should quit, or you're going to get cancer."

"You're always trying to control my life." He takes a sip of his coffee. "Ewe! What's in this?"

"It's powdered milk. I have to go shopping."

He pours his coffee down the drain. "Just buy some potato chips." He grabs his keys and sticks the pack of cigarettes in his pocket. "I have to go to work. Pick up a six-pack of coke, too!" He calls over his shoulder.

Daniel's laptop is on the counter, and his e-mail is open. My curiosity is piqued, and insecurities compel me to click on a message. *He-y-y Woman!* It's *his* standard greeting in the subject line. I have a bad feeling in the pit of my stomach. The e-mail is addressed to someone named Susan. *"Susan. Let's do coffee and see where it goes. You'll find I'm a very romantic man. No stress…no pressure."*

Romantic? I feel the blood draining from my face. I check the date and time. It was yesterday. My throat tightens, and I feel an anxiety attack coming on. I forward the e-mail to myself. Sobbing, I pick up the phone to call my friend Sharon.

"Are you okay?" she asks.

"No. I think Daniel's looking to replace me."

"What makes you think that?"

"I found an e-mail he sent to some girl named Susan." I swallow hard. "He asked her if she wanted to *do coffee*."

"Did she respond?"

"Yes. Susan said she would love to meet with him."

"Florence, you don't have to put up with his shit, you know. He doesn't deserve you."

"Should I tell him, I know?"

"No, not unless you're prepared to walk away, and from the sound of it, you're not."

"Walk away!" That's what everyone says, including my brain, but every time I get close to the edge, my body betrays me, and I feel like I'm going to have a heart attack.

Outside, the wind is howling. It's stripped the trees bare, and the fallow breath of winter is upon me. It sends a shiver down my spine. My mistake was coming here during a season of gradual endings, falling leaves, and the fading glow of summer.

Daniel keeps insisting that he loves me, but he sends mixed signals. Why can't he be honest and tell me he's changed his mind about having a future with me? I twirl the ends of my hair between my fingers—a bad habit whenever I get nervous.

The crunch of his wheels on the gravel driveway warns me of his return. Keeping my anger under control, I suck up the pain and smile.

"I'm beat," he says and flops down on the couch. I slide next to him and search his eyes. He doesn't look at me with love or hate. There is nothing—only a tolerance that feels excruciatingly hurtful.

"Do you love me, Daniel?" The words tumble from my mouth. I know that once you have to ask, the answer is clear, but I can't stop myself.

He stares at me with a questioning expression. "Why are you asking me that?"

"If you're not happy, I'm willing to let you go."

Taken aback, Daniel squints and then gives me a wry smile. "But I'm not willing to let *you* go."

"You never tell me you love me anymore."

"Oh, Florence," he says impatiently, "You know I do."

"Sometimes, I need to hear it."

The warmth disappears from his eyes as if a door has slammed shut. "If I don't give you what you need, maybe you should go back to Florida."

My legs weaken.

"You sound like you're having second thoughts about us," he continues, turning the blame onto me.

"It's *you* that may have second thoughts," I retort. I'm tempted to mention Susan, but knowing it would be the point of no return.

He could either be with me or not. It doesn't matter to him. Anger washes over me.

"Fine!" I scream. "I'll leave." Driven by adrenaline, I bound up the stairs to get my suitcase, then run around the room, shoving my stuff in the bag. My heart is pounding like a drum.

Daniel watches as I spin out of control, his eyes wide with surprise and amusement.

With my suitcase overstuffed, all I need is the next flight out. Avoiding his gaze, I open my laptop and comb the airfares. Nothing is less than a thousand dollars. There has to be a mistake. I check another date, hoping it will be cheaper. Instead, the price goes up. I can't think straight. Then it dawns on me. Christmas is in two weeks. I'll never get a flight out.

"Calm yourself down, Babe." Daniel grips my arms and stares into my eyes. *If he tells me I'm cute when I'm mad, I'll pop him!*

I do love you," he says, with words dripping with sweetness.

"I need to get out of here."

"Okay, but it's a long walk to the train station. You'd better borrow my sneakers."

My eyes soften, and I resist the urge to laugh.

"Ah, come on," he says, seeing the anger leave my face. Damn! There's that twinkle in his eyes. He kisses the top of my head. "Let's forget about this and have a nice dinner. I know how you love to eat."

Within minutes, things are back to normal. Normal? What is that? We're an old married couple who have learned to tolerate each other. We banter back and forth, neither giving an inch.

"We're eating chicken," I say defiantly.

His eyes light up with humor. "I hate chicken!"

"I know. That's why I'm making it."

"I'll go chop some wood. It's going to be cold tonight," he says, leaving me alone in the kitchen.

Susan is yelling inside my head.

In the middle of the night, I wake in a cold sweat. Daniel has his arms around me, and I feel like I'm in a straitjacket. I disentangle myself and slip from his grasp to go downstairs. A fire rages in the woodstove, and the crackle of flames grabs my attention. Mack looks comfortable, so I don't move him off the couch. Instead, I shove him over and curl up next to him, wrapping myself in Daniel's man-blanket to keep warm. Mesmerized by the logs hissing as the flames lick and consume them, I'm lost in a world of blazing orange and cobalt blue.

Homeward Bound

The winds of winter are upon us
I feel his cold caress
The birds fly high above us
It brings me to confess

After a restless night, I stare at the man sleeping next to me. He looks so sweet, so innocent. Daniel stirs as if he senses I'm staring at him.

"Are you all right, Florence?"

"No... I... I want to go back home," I blurt. "To Florida. I'm not happy here."

"You haven't given it a chance, Florence. Don't leave."

"I have to."

"You sold your townhouse. Where would you go?"

"I'll find an apartment."

"You'll miss me."

My insides turn to jelly. I already feel my resolve caving in and find it hard to breathe.

"You can come with me. We could be nice and warm in Florida."

"I want to," he murmurs, "but...." Daniel stares out the window. "I've been under a lot of pressure."

"You're always saying that. What's wrong?"

"The IRS has seized all my accounts. I've lost everything!"

"What about your house in California?"

He doesn't answer. Hmm. I wonder if there really is a house. If there is, it's certainly not his. Daniel has a knack for taking a kernel of truth and wrapping it in a lie. Even though I'm aware of his tall tales, I'm learning to keep my curiosities to myself. Questioning is the button that sets him into spin mode.

"Believe me," he says. "I don't want to spend another winter in this town, but I don't have any money."

"How much do you need?"

"Five thousand should do it."

"Five thousand dollars?"

"I'll pay you back when I get there and find a job."

My mind is racing. I have money in the bank, but it won't last forever.

"What if something happens to you?" the logical part of my brain speaks out. "What if we break up?"

"That's not going to happen," he says. "If it makes you feel better, I'll give you the title to my van. If that's not enough, I'll sell my Rolex. I'll even give you my artwork."

"Don't be insulted," I say, "but I think I'd feel better if it was on paper."

He shrugs. "Write out an agreement. I'll sign it."

My eyes narrow. "I want to get it notarized. It's not that I don't trust you," I add, trying to soothe his injured pride. "I need to protect myself... just in case."

"Fine." His tone is daunting.

"Where's the title for your van?"

"I think I lost it," he says with the flip of his hand. I wonder if the van is really his, and my anxiety level increases.

"Relax," he says. "I'll apply for a new one."

I convince him to let me go to Florida first. This way, I can find us a nice apartment — that allows dogs.

Daniel is moody all week, but I'm on a mission to get back to where I belong.

❧

It's been over a week since I found the email to Susan. I don't think he's contacted her, but he could be deleting his messages. Maybe I'll catch one of hers. I click on the e-mail, keeping an ear out for Daniel, who should be home soon.

"He-y-y," Susan writes in the subject line." I scroll down to the message. "That coffee is getting cold." Obviously, she hasn't been on his mind. I wonder if he would've gone through with the date if I hadn't come.

First, I had to deal with Josette, and now, this. The only way I can win is to pretend it doesn't bother me.

It's just an e-mail. If Daniel wanted Susan, he wouldn't be coming to Florida. Do I *really* want him to come back with me? I may be wasting my time and the opportunity to meet someone else — someone who truly loves me. I'm in so deep now. I might as well see where this goes. I know I'm playing a dangerous game.

My finger moves to the delete button, and, like magic, Susan's gone.

It's still dark when I wake in the morning.

"You're not going anywhere today," Daniel mumbles. "There's a snowstorm outside."

"Snow?" I jump out of bed and run to the window. It looks cold, but there's no snow. "Nice try." I laugh.

"Once I find an apartment, you can drive down."

"No. You fly back to New York, and we can drive there together."

"Are you afraid you'll get lost?"

"Don't be a wise-ass," he warns.

The cold air hits my face as I carry my suitcase to the car. I strap Ripley's carrier into the back seat with the seatbelt. For the past few weeks, he was free to roam around the woods. I'm not sure he wants to leave.

⟊

There are plenty of apartments in Florida, but I'm having a problem. Most of them won't accept dogs.

He isn't thrilled about apartment living. Whenever I ask for his advice, he says, "Get one that floats." *Cute*! He says he prefers a houseboat, but I assure him I can find us a great place, close to the ocean, on firm ground.

On the second day of my search, I find a luxury apartment that allows pets. It has a pool, tennis courts, and clubhouse, and they have a barbecue with live music every month. It was a typical cookie-cutter development where all the units were the same. I've lived in places like this, and the result was never good. Before I put down a deposit, I want to check one more place, two hours north, in the same town where I had my townhouse.

The apartment is downtown in Vero Beach. It might be enjoyable to live among restaurants and small boutiques. There's even a park within walking distance. The complex is small and has no pool, but there's a field next to the building, perfect for Mack to exercise and do his business. The property owner shows me the available unit on the second floor. The kitchen is small and adjoined to the living area, but large windows stretch across the room. Sunshine pours in, and it's very cheery. We walk down the hall to the first bedroom. I think it will make an excellent guestroom, although I'm not sure my king-sized bed will fit. The main bedroom is at the end. My mouth drops open when we enter. Like the living room, windows line the walls. It has a cathedral ceiling with more windows and a walk-in closet. The best part is — Dogs are allowed. I second-guess my decisions most of the time, but not this time. I love it. This apartment is unique.

The property owner is friendly, and there's no annoying management team like in other developments. With the beach just two blocks away, who needs a pool?

He insists that our separation is only temporary, saying just enough to make me believe we have a future. He feigns love for me but keeps his single status to the world. The evidence is in the stupid things he says. For instance, last night, he called while he was out with his kids.

"Florence, you have to hear this. It was so funny. We were in the store, and the cashier said I was a chick magnet."

A chick magnet? Hilarious. *He couldn't get it up the whole time he lived with me, and now he's a chick magnet.*

"Sounds like you're flirting again," I say, knowing how he loves to puff himself up.

"Florence, you have no sense of humor," he snaps. "I don't know why I tell you anything."

Neither do I.

Escape in the Night

Settle for less
Don't think I could
Be happy in life
The way I should

A sudden urge to call Daniel has me picking up the phone. There's no answer, so I call Tricia's home phone. The housekeeper answers.

"Hi, Rhonda, is Daniel there?"

She hesitates. "I think he's still sleeping. He went to a concert last night and didn't get home until late."

My stomach is coming up to my throat as insecurity creeps in. Somewhere in the back of my mind, I suspect Daniel hasn't been faithful. The thought of losing him to someone else has me so worked up that I can't breathe.

An hour later, my phone rings. It's Daniel.

"Did Rhonda tell you I called?"

"No, when was this?"

"Early this morning. She said you were still sleeping because you went to a concert."

"Oh, that. One of the guests had an extra ticket and offered to take me along."

"Was she pretty?"

"S-t-o-p!" he says in a playful voice, but I know him. In his world, he can flirt with whomever he wants.

"Remember," I tease. "What's good for the goose is good for the gander."

"Oh, noooo, it isn't!"

I used to think he was my prince. If he is, he's a dark one. Now I almost wish I had kissed a frog.

Worse than losing him, I don't want to be his fool.

I think of the poet, Phil, whom I met last spring. Since I wrote my first poem, we've been exchanging e-mails. He's asked me to visit him in Virginia. I send him a message saying I will.

"I'm so excited that you want to come and visit me," he says. "How about next weekend? We can watch fireworks on the beach."

Now I did it. A huge lump swells in my throat. There's no way out.

"If I come to visit you, it's just as a *friend*."

"I would never force you to do anything you weren't comfortable with. You can stay in my guest room."

"Well, I suppose it'll be all right."

This is all Daniel's fault. I wouldn't be traveling to visit another man if I didn't suspect him of cheating on me. I turn on the stereo and pop in one of the CDs my sister, Carol, downloaded for me. I sing along with *Rusty Halo*, as I drive toward the Atlantic coast.

"*Now, I'm running for the light in the tunnel, but it's just the train. Yeah, I'm looking for the right type of pleasure, but all I find is pain, oh. Now there's no light to guide me on my way home. Now, there's no time to shine my rusty halo."*

Phil is waiting outside. With a full head of wavy gray hair and super-white teeth that gleam when he smiles, he's very handsome for his age. Feeling anxious, I follow him into a sunny kitchen, where he has a bottle of wine chilling. As he pours, I look around at the décor.

Ordinarily, I detest country, but now I'm grateful. It's very comforting. I expect to see his grandmother come out to greet us any minute and doubt that Phil is an ax murderer. Still, I took a risk, coming to his house only after getting to know him through e-mail.

After the grand tour of his house, he takes me to The Pier, a well-known tourist attraction with restaurants, stores, and live music. He chooses a casual seafood restaurant, and we settle onto wooden stools by the open window. Outside, throngs of people walk by, and watching them fills in awkward silences. I catch the scent of the sea with every breath. Taking a sip of wine, I let it swirl around my tongue, trying to think of something to say.

"You look like you're a million miles away," Phil says, grabbing my hand and staring at me with a big, silly grin on his face. He's nothing like Daniel, who's rough around the edges. Too, it's obvious Phil's looking for a permanent relationship. I wish I were attracted to him, but I'm not.

After dinner, we walk along the boardwalk. His hand brushes against mine and grasps it. *Maybe this is a mistake.*

When we get back to Phil's house, he pours us more wine and picks up his guitar. Sitting in his living room, he serenades me with songs he has written. It's a wonderful distraction because Daniel is rolling around my brain. Between each song, we talk. He tells me his first wife left him for another man. I tell him about my ex-husband and my divorce. I also tell him how Daniel seduced me and then dropped me. I say too much, as usual, and try to change the subject.

"You look tired," he says. "Maybe you should get some rest. I have a lot of things planned for tomorrow."

"Yeah, sleep sounds good," I say, grateful for the chance to escape.

He puts his guitar back on the stand and leads me to a large bedroom dressed in perfect shades of blue with large fluffy pillows on the bed.

"I think you'll be comfortable in this room," he says. "I'll take the guestroom."

"This is *your* bedroom? I don't want to...."

"It's fine. This room is bigger, and there's a private bathroom in the corner. If you need anything, I'm right next door." He leans forward to kiss me goodnight, but I lean back.

"I'll see you in the morning," he says.

I close the door and take a deep breath. In the dimly lit room, I notice pictures in small frames on the dresser. Most are of Phil's children, but there's a beautiful woman, too. I assume it's his ex-wife. It's nice that he displays her picture. Most men would be bitter if their wives left them for another man. That was his story, and, so far, I have no reason to question it.

I stare at myself in the bathroom mirror. A tear rolls down my cheek. I can't hold it in any longer and quietly sob so Phil won't hear me. I cry until there are no more tears, and my eyes are red and puffy. I climb into the king-sized bed and check my phone for any missed calls from Daniel, but there is none. It's two in the morning. Phil must be sleeping. He's so sweet, but my mind, heart, and soul are with Daniel. I shouldn't be here.

I'll find an excuse to go home early tomorrow. I just have to get through tonight. I close my eyes, but the street light shines into the window and illuminates my suitcase. I think of only one thing. I have to leave. Quickly getting dressed, I zip up my case and slowly turn the doorknob. Tiptoeing out of the room, I feel my way down the carpeted hallway.

Thank goodness the front door doesn't squeak as I close it behind me. I shove my suitcase into the passenger seat because I don't want to risk the sound of my trunk closing. I jump in the car. The motor starts, and I cringe at the sound. I tap the gas pedal with my lights off and let the car roll down the block. My hands are shaking as I turn on my lights and speed away. *I'm free!*

Rattled by the experience, I need to call someone, even though it's the middle of the night. Carol! She's always up late. I reach for my phone. Where's my phone? I search for my purse, but it isn't in the car. The blood drains from my face. My phone is in my pocketbook—*in Phil's house!*

I'm already on the highway. Maybe I should forget about the phone. No, Daniel may call. Besides, I need my purse. I turn off at the next exit and drive back to Phil's house. I'm sure God is punishing me.

My heart feels like it will leap from my chest. Luckily, the house is still dark inside.

My palms are sweaty as I slip back into the house like a cat burglar and feel my way down the dark hall. As I pass Phil's room, the floor creaks, and I bump into a small table. I catch the lamp before it falls. What will I say if he wakes?

I could say I was sleepwalking. *Yeah, right, he'd believe that!*

I retrieve my purse and rush out the front door. Safe in my car, I can breathe again, but as I pull away, I look in my rearview mirror. To my horror, the place is lit up like Times Square! Expecting Phil to come running out of the house any second, I floor the gas, making the tires screech as I speed off into the night.

My phone rings. It's Phil! I can't — *won't* answer, so I pull over and send him a text instead. *I'M SO SORRY!*

There's no response. I don't ever expect to hear from Phil again.

Up in Smoke

It doesn't matter where we've been
Now our lives can begin
We are here, you and me
The way it was supposed to be

With his van filled with tools, a bag of clothes, and the dog he bought for his kids, he sets out for Florida. Daniel promises his children they can come and visit. He had advertised for a tenant in his house again, but no one answered.

When Daniel arrives at our new apartment, he has to park his van at the curb because there's only one allotted spot, and it's mine. Before we go upstairs, we take Mack into the field to do his business.

"Let him off the leash," Daniel says.

I'm hesitant. "It's not a good idea. Mack doesn't have tags. You need to take him to a vet for his shots and a license. I think he has fleas, too."

"Mack doesn't have fleas."

"Haven't you noticed him scratching?"

"He's fine; it's your cat that needs a vet. Ripley has worms."

"No, he doesn't. He gets his shots and always gets a clean bill of health."

"All cats have worms!" Determined not to listen, he unleashes Mack. At first, the dog wanders a few feet away from us, smelling the dirt for the right spot.

Daniel moves toward him when he gets too far, and Mack bolts. He runs around the field two times, then takes off down the road with Daniel running after him, huffing and puffing. By the time he catches the dog, he's having difficulty breathing and has to climb the stairs to get to the apartment.

"I haven't hung any of my pictures," I say as we enter the apartment. "Since you're the artistic one, I thought you could find a place for them."

"Your pictures are ugly," he says. "But don't worry. I brought a few rare prints with us. All we need are frames. I need a cigarette. Where's the balcony?"

"There is none. You have to go downstairs when you want to smoke."

The sound of a train interrupts our conversation.

"What the hell is that?"

"There's a train track two blocks from here, but don't worry. In a few days, you won't even notice it."

"I hate this place already."

"You haven't given it a chance."

"I'll go outside if you come with me. Otherwise, I'm lighting up right here."

"Are you blackmailing me?"

Daniel waits with an annoying smirk. It's another losing battle for me. We head downstairs with Mack, much to Ripley's relief.

Although Mack likes my cat, the feeling isn't mutual. The only sanctuary he has is in the back bedroom. I need to buy a gate.

Daniel puffs away and then mashes the butt into the tiled walkway. "Let's go get *comfy*, Babe."

I love getting *comfy*. Exhausted, we both have one thing in mind—sleep.

⦿⦿⦿

At six o'clock the next morning, Mack is crying in the living room. I nudge Daniel. "You need to take the dog out."

"He can wait," he says in a sleepy voice.

"No, he has to go out."

"Ten more minutes," he drones.

I'm just as tired as he is, but I can't let Mack suffer. I slip out of bed and throw on some shorts and a tee shirt. Mack tugs at the leash, and it's more like he's walking me.

We come back inside when he's finished with his business, and I crawl between the sheets. Daniel moans and wraps himself around me like a kudzu vine, but I've learned how to get free when I want to. All I have to do is mention sex or money.

"Would you like some coffee?"

With his coffee and an unlit cigarette hanging from his mouth, he gets on the Internet and posts an ad for work. He uses my phone number because it has a local area code. While he's surfing the net, he pulls up eBay and looks at boats.

"Hey, Florence. Check this out."

I load the last dish into the dishwasher and stand behind him to look over his shoulder.

"Wouldn't you love to live on this beauty?"

I see the price, ten thousand dollars. "Wow, that's expensive," I say, shaking my head.

"Not really, if you compare it to buying a house."

"Boats are money suckers. There's docking and maintenance. And don't forget about gas. The news says it's going up to five dollars a gallon by the end of this summer."

"You're so negative, Florence."

"No, I'm not. I'm realistic."

His mood shifts, and he swats me on the butt. "Stinger!" Playful Daniel is back, and I retaliate. It's become our version of affection.

"Let's take Mack to the beach," he says.

"I'm not sure if they allow dogs on the beach."

"There must be someplace people take their dogs."

We load Mack in the van and drive to the beach. A man is walking his dog.

"Ask that guy," Daniel says and stops. I roll down the window. Mack sticks out his head, causing the man's dog to bark. "Excuse me, sir. Do you know if there is a canine beach in the area?

"No, I don't know of any beaches around here that allow dogs," he says, "but there is a boat ramp two miles down the road. I've seen dogs swimming down there."

"Thank you!" I pull Mack's head back in and roll the window up. The boat ramp is secluded at the end of a long dirt road. The minute we unleash Mack, he runs in circles, half-crazed with excitement over his freedom. Daniel throws a stick into the water. Without hesitation, Mack leaps in, his head breaking the surface as he paddles toward it. Amused, Daniel continues to throw sticks farther and farther out. "He's a water dog," he says with a proud smile.

"I hope so because it's going to rain," I say. At the first sign of drizzle, the fun is over. Now we have to catch Mack and put him back in the van, not an easy task. The dog senses he's about to lose his freedom and races into the woods. Daniel's huffing and puffing by the time we catch him. "I need to stop smoking," he says.

I agree, but not too strongly, because I've learned one thing about Daniel. He does the opposite of what I say and would only smoke more.

On the way back home, we stop at the supermarket to buy something for dinner. Daniel waits in the van. I'm not sure I want him with me anyway. He grabs everything off the shelves and questions the items I put in the cart.

It's a downpour when I exit the store. Daniel parked one hundred feet from the entrance. I wait for him to pull it in front of the store. The car remains frozen in place. Finally, I grab the bags and make a run for it.

"Why'd you have to park so far away? I'm soaking wet."

He smiles mischievously. "You're fast! I thought you'd be in there for hours."

My anger lessens with his praise. *It's a compliment, right?*

It's still raining when we get home, and Daniel wants to smoke a cigarette. While I grab an umbrella and take Mack for one more walk, he smokes under the ledge of the building and gripes. *What does he have to complain about?* At least he's dry.

Daniel stomps up the stairs like a child about to have a tantrum. He sulks through dinner and goes outside for another smoke. The rain is torrential now, and there's no end in sight. On his third trip out, he pleads, "Can't I open the window and smoke in here?"

I'm horrified at the idea and think about nicotine film on everything. "You want to smoke in the apartment?"

"It's your fault for renting an apartment that doesn't have a balcony," he complains. "Come on. I'll sit near the window and blow it outside."

His need for nicotine never entered my mind when I found this apartment. Grudgingly, I agree. "Just this once."

He grins and strikes a match.

"At least turn on the ceiling fan," I say, getting up to flip the switch. With no sign of the rain stopping, Daniel is in for the night. I give him one of Ripley's stainless-steel food bowls as an ashtray. Feeling inadequate for not standing up for my beliefs, I convince myself it's no big deal. It's easier to bury my doubts and hide from reality.

I'm as good at denial as he is at manipulation.

Fishin

When you open up your eyes
I'll make sure that you arise
With a sense of being loved
Safe and warm within my hug

Mack is quiet in the other room, so we remain in bed. Daniel runs his fingers over my skin. I savor the sensation, but his touch is fleeting, a wink of a bird, a rare summer breeze, a shooting star across the dark sky.

"Maybe you should see a doctor," I say.

"I don't want to talk about it," he mutters.

"You never want to talk about it. How are we ever going to resolve anything?"

Daniel wraps me in his arms and moans. Even though sex is out of the question, it's comforting. We have become cordial platonic friends. I guess there are worse things in life.

I slip out of bed, this time without a fight. Mack has his head down when I come into the kitchen, and he's not acting his usual self. He's jumping and clambering to go out. Strangely, neither of us heard him crying in the morning. The reason is sitting in the middle of the living room.

Daniel comes out just in time to witness the gift his dog has left for us. There's a look of disgust on his face. "You have to clean it," he says, holding his nose.

I roll my eyes, scoop up the poop, and flush it down the toilet. Daniel has Mack in a headlock when I come back, roughing him up. Mack seems relieved that he's not in trouble and wags his tail.

"Maybe you should take him out for a walk," I suggest.

"Why? He's already pooped."

I roll my eyes again and pour two cups of coffee.

"I might have a job," he says. "This guy is looking for a painter. He has a *Cuddy Cabin*. Nice boat! We should go and check it out. In Port St. Lucie."

"That's forty-five minutes away. Can't you find something closer?"

"Don't you want me to get a job?"

How can I argue with that?

"Be a good boy," I tell Mack before we leave.

He gives me a sidelong look, his head down as if he remembers doing something wrong. I don't blame him, though. We should have taken him out before we went to bed.

"Do you have your keys, Daniel?"

"No, I thought we would take your car. It's cheaper on gas."

Cheaper for who? We use my credit card to charge gas along the way because Daniel is broke.

"How did you go through five thousand dollars so fast?" I ask, annoyed that he has no money.

"I used it on bills."

"That money wasn't intended for your bills. It was for getting you settled in Florida. I can't believe you spent it all," I mutter.

His eyes glaze over. "Don't worry. I'll pay you back."

A good salesman, Daniel, gets the job. His experience has been painting cars, but he insists boats are the same.

"Let's go to the pawnshop. I need to get some tools."

"Did the guy give you money in advance?" I ask.

"No, I just want to look."

"All right, but let's go home first so I can walk the dog."

Mack has unleashed his revenge on us for leaving him home. This time, he chewed up my special computer pad. It had a picture of Ripley sitting in a birdbath.

"What did you do, Mack?" I reprimand.

He puts his head down and gives me a sheepish look. He's so cute—I can't stay mad at him.

While Daniel smokes a cigarette, I take Mack for a walk in the field. It's become my job to walk him. Daniel keeps saying he'll do it, but the poor dog's eyes are watering before he ever gets out the door. Mack is getting stronger every day, and I can't handle him.

"Maybe we should take him with us," I suggest.

"No, he's a pain in the ass. Just leave him in the apartment."

"We're always out," I argue. It's not good for a dog to spend its life in one room. He needs fresh air."

Daniel shakes his head. "We'll take him to the boat ramp tomorrow."

"Sorry, Mack!"

The dog tilts his head and whimpers.

At the pawnshop, I follow Daniel as he checks out the tools.

Easily distracted, he picks up a fishing rod. "Hey, Florence! These rods are only fifteen dollars. Why don't we go fishing?"

"Do you have fifteen dollars?" I ask, careful to keep humor in my voice.

"I'm sure I can bargain with them and get two for the price of one," he says, giving me a devilish grin. "Loan me the money, and I'll pay you back Friday."

He reels me in. I can't say no. Besides, I haven't been fishing in years, and it might be fun. Daniel says he's a born angler. *This should be interesting.*

Within the first half-hour, I catch a Pompano. Daniel sulks and decides it's time to leave.

Mack is nowhere in sight when we walk through the apartment door, and I sense something is wrong. He usually greets us when we come in.

I find him in the back bedroom. Ripley is hiding under the bed and doesn't look happy.

"He must have jumped the gate," Daniel says.

"I drag Mack to the living room. White foam covers the floor. It looks like snow.

"He ate the couch." Daniel laughs.

"It's not funny!"

He smiles and puts his arm around me. "If you make me some coffee, I'll take you to the movies."

"Okay, but you buy the popcorn."

"First, I want to finish my coffee and have a cigarette."

I roll my eyes and go to the bedroom to change into pants.

"Where are you?" he yells five minutes later.

"I thought you were having a cigarette?"

"Well, I'm done, and I'm waiting for you."

"I'll be right there." I grab my sweater and purse.

"Sure, when you're the one that has to do something, it's fine. God forbid I have something to do."

After the movie, we leave the theater, and a homeless man approaches us in the parking lot. "Do you have any spare change?"

Daniel skims through his wallet and pulls out two dollars. His generosity surprises me. He'll give his money to a bum, but his wallet is closed when it comes to helping me pay the bills. I want to say something, but we fight about money too much. Why ruin a good evening?

Good Babe

Our love is very beautiful
I want to keep it such
It doesn't take too much, dear
Only a gentle touch

Something is up with Daniel. Despite his denials, he's been moping around all morning, chain-smoking. Even though the window is open, it bothers me, but I'm too much of a coward to stand up to him. Besides, my daughter hasn't met Daniel yet, and I've invited her and her husband for dinner. I don't want to fight before she gets here. It would be awkward for everyone.

"Are you nervous about meeting Annmarie?" I ask as I spray air freshener around the room.

"No, not at all," he says, but he looks tense.

"Relax," I say, using his favorite word against him. "My daughter's going to love you."

"It's not that," he insists.

"What is it then?"

Daniel hesitates for a moment. "I've been trying to get hold of that woman, Terry, in California, but she won't answer my phone calls."

"Terry? The woman who was mad that she couldn't be your girlfriend?"

He frowns. "Yeah." He's annoyed at my observation. "Anyway, I've been searching on the internet and found out she put the house up for sale. You know—the one I helped to renovate."

I'm still waiting for some proof he owns part of the house, but he gets irritated whenever I mention it.

"Do you think she'll give you your share of the money?" I ask.

"No! It's listed way below what it's worth. I know how much money went into that house. There's no way the sale price will cover it." Lost in his world, Daniel stares out the window. "She won't get away with this. If I have to fly to California…."

"Maybe you should e-mail her or write a letter."

"I don't want to talk about it," he says and shuts off the computer.

Now I'm curious, but I dare not ask, not when he's in this mood. Before I can think about it any further, he walks to the sink with puppy dog eyes. "Will you scratch my back, Babe?"

I gently run my nails across his bare shoulders.

"No," he says. "Scratch it like I got fleas."

"You're such a dog!" I laugh, forgetting about the house in California.

Mack barks to alert us that there's someone at the door. Daniel rushes to the bedroom to put on a shirt while I let Annmarie and her husband inside. They pet the dog because he's jumping up and down for attention.

"What happened to your couch?" Annmarie asks.

I point to Mack. "Sit in the leather chairs. They're more comfortable."

Mack has taken a liking to Annmarie and jumps up onto her lap. "Get down, Mack," I reprimand.

Annmarie enjoys the attention, but Mack is as big as she is. He looks funny, playing lapdog. "He's fine," she says as he licks her face.

Daniel comes out and flashes his trademark smile. "I see you've met Mack," he says and shakes Paul's hand.

"Do you guys want a drink?" He doesn't wait for a response. Instead, he pours four glasses of Sambuca and hands one to each of us.

Annmarie takes a sip. "aww, this is sweet!"

"Just drink it down fast," Daniel suggests, his eyes sparkling. He loves to get people drunk.

She chugs it and makes a face. Paul has no problem with the sweet liqueur, and Daniel fills his glass again.

"You need to buy a crate for this dog," Paul says. "That's the only way you'll train him."

"I can't put my Macky-boy in a *crate*!"

"We have to do something," I insist, "or soon, we may not have any furniture."

There's silence as everyone stares at Mack.

"Something smells good," Paul says. "What are you cooking?"

"It's lasagna," I say. "Oh no, I forgot to pick up the Italian bread."

"Let's take a run to the store, Mom. That way, Daniel and Paul can get to know each other."

They already have their heads together, talking about boats, so we leave.

"What do you think of Daniel?"

"I like him. He's cute and funny, too."

"Tomorrow is Valentine's Day. Do you and Paul have anything special planned?"

"Paul will most likely give me roses. We're going out to dinner, and then we'll kanoodle."

"Kanoodle?" I laugh. "Is that what it's called nowadays?"

She laughs. "What about you and Daniel? Do you have any plans?"

"I'm not sure. Daniel never buys me flowers. I don't expect he will now, especially since he has no money, and kanoodling is out of the question."

When we get back, Daniel and Paul have bonded. I don't know if it's the Sambuca or if they actually like each other.

"Paul's going to work on the boat with me," Daniel announces.

I'm sure it's not a good idea to get my son-in-law involved, but they're excited, so I keep it to myself.

After dinner, Daniel pulls me aside. "Florence, I have to ask you for a big favor."

"What is it?"

"I need you to lend me two-hundred and fifty dollars," he whispers.

"What for?"

"To pay my storage in California. If I don't pay, they'll auction off my stuff. There's over twenty thousand dollars worth of beautiful furniture and electronics in that warehouse. We don't want to lose it." *We?*

"Daniel, I don't have that much cash lying around. You'll have to wait until I go to the bank."

"Maybe you can write a check. It won't get there until next week. By the time it arrives, I'll have it, and you'll have the money back in your account. I promise!"

"I don't know."

"Don't you trust me?"

"I do. It's just, well, all right," I say with some hesitation.

"You're such a good Babe," he teases.

Good Babe. I smile at his verbal reward.

Rebel

We have lived apart so long
Our ways are set in stone
We will surely find a way
To overcome alone

Daniel is up early for work, so I get up with him. There are no signs of love—not that I expected anything. I think Valentine's Day is overrated. Still, I'm a little disappointed.

"I have to go," he says. "Paul is meeting me at the boat."

"Are you sure it's a good idea to work with your family?" I ask.

"Don't be ridiculous." He kisses me on the cheek and turns to leave. "Don't forget to mail the storage payment. It needs to be postmarked today, or I lose everything."

After taking Mack for a walk, I get dressed and head to the post office. While I'm out, I shop for a crate. When I set it up in the living room, Mack sticks his head in the cage and then bolts. I'm not crazy about the idea, but Mack gets into mischief every time we leave him alone.

"Sorry, boy, but this is where you're going to stay from now on when we're not home."

The water is boiling for the pasta when Daniel walks through the door. I throw in the linguini.

"That smells good," he says. Picking up a spoon, he scoops out clams from the pot.

"Stop that! Save some for dinner."

He puts down the spoon and opens the refrigerator. With the door wide open, he drinks from the milk container.

"That's disgusting," I say. "Use a glass."

He smiles and licks the rim of the milk container. I make a mental note not to use milk in my coffee and buy creamer the next time I'm at the store.

"What did you bring me for Valentine's Day?"

"I wasn't sure what you'd like."

"Chocolate! Everyone should have chocolate on Valentine's Day."

Daniel notices the crate and scoffs. "You're never going to get him in there."

"He'll have no choice," I say, but I know I'll have a problem.

We sit down for dinner. "So, how did it go working with Paul?"

"It was horrible. He didn't know anything. He was on the phone with your daughter more than he worked. I told him he didn't have to come back tomorrow. I can't work with people who don't know what they're doing."

"I hope you weren't an ass."

"Me? An ass? Of course not."

Daniel is eyeing my dish. "Oh, no, you don't," I say, moving my plate out of his reach.

He hasn't mentioned the two-hundred and fifty dollars he borrowed from me. I'm concerned.

"Did you get paid today?" I ask.

"Yes, but I have to pay the mortgage on my house. It's late."

I could have sworn he once told me he had no mortgage on his house in New York. I narrow my eyes.

"Don't worry," he says. I'll have your money before next Friday."

His financial irresponsibility appalls me. He pays all his bills late. Fees and interest add up, but it doesn't bother him. I wonder if he's been like this his whole life. Daniel hasn't filed a tax return since we've been together. I know he owes the IRS money. They'll have to find him first, which may be near impossible. He has no credit card or bank account, and he gets paid on a cash basis. *I could be harboring a fugitive.*

"Don't you have to pay Lisa child support?" I ask.

"No. We have an agreement. Let's go and get you some chocolate," he says to avoid any further discussion of money.

She's been crying to him about how she has no money, no home, and no chance of getting married. On one level, I understand. I'd feel the same way if I was in her shoes. She gave him two children.

He buys me chocolate turtles at the Candy Factory but complains it's his last twenty bucks. We go home to eat them in bed and watch the Food Network on television. Our favorite show is *Chopped*, but sometimes he likes *Cupcake Wars*. Millions of other couples are probably making love, but not us. He snuggles against me, but I sense it's out of need, not passion. He doesn't even kiss me anymore. Sometimes

I wonder if I'll ever be kissed again. The thought makes me sad. I used to yearn for his kiss. I hear Mack whimpering by the gate and realize that he hasn't been out all evening.

"Can you take him, Babe?"

"He's your dog. You take him out."

Daniel grabs my pillow, and I yank it back.

"Lately, you're a little rebel," he says.

"I have to be, or you'll walk all over me."

"Is that what you think I do?" He looks injured.

"Ahhh! Did I hurt your *feeling*?" I tease, emphasizing the singular.

We both laugh, but I end up taking Mack out.

Comfy

In your dreams, I want to be
A comforting embrace
Free of stress from daily woes
Your cares I will erase

"How was your Valentine's Day?" my daughter asks. "Did you get some?" she teases.

"Nah! Daniel had to work late, and we were both tired."

It's easier to make excuses for him than to confront the problem. His inability to have sex is disturbing, though. Maybe it's stress. I hear that it can play a big part in erectile dysfunction. He also has financial problems, and I'm finding out they're bigger than he lets on. Aside from his mortgage, there's his cell phone bill and the storage facility in California. Weighed down with debt, no wonder he can't perform in bed. He owes me five thousand dollars — no, five thousand two hundred and fifty. I don't feel right pressuring him for living expenses. I'd have to pay the rent even if he wasn't here, and, as the saying goes, two can live as cheap as one.

Daniel is a burden, but he promises that things will change once he's on his feet.

He walks through the door, and Mack jumps up to get his attention.

"You're home early," I say. "Did you finish the job?"

"That guy is a jerk," he sneers. "I have more knowledge in my little finger than he will ever have."

"Did you have a fight?"

"No, but I'm not going back."

"What are you going to do for money?"

"Actually, I got a call today. Someone answered my rental ad for the house in New York."

"A little too late, wouldn't you say?"

"No, I told them I'll fly back and open the house if they're interested."

"That costs money. How are you going to...?"

"I was hoping you would lend me the money for a flight."

"You still owe me for the storage."

"If I rent the place, they'll pay me for one-month security and first and last month's rent. It would cover my mortgage, and I'll have the money to pay you back."

"We won't be able to go back next summer."

"You don't understand. I need the rental money *now*," he says impatiently. "Besides, I have to renew my driver's license."

Feeling like I have no choice, I lend him the money, and he returns to New York.

⁓

Even with Mack and Ripley to keep me company, it's lonely without Daniel. I'm anxious about his return, but he calls the night before his scheduled flight to fly back home.

"The pipes froze, and I have to delay my flight."

I have to charge another fifty dollars on my credit card to change the departure date. I don't like spending more money, but I'm eager for Daniel to come home. He now owes me an additional six hundred and eighty-five dollars. However, I expect him to pay me once he has the rental money.

Waiting at the airport terminal, I see him striding toward me.

"He-y-y Babe," Daniel says. "I've missed you."

"I've missed you too," I say, giving him a huge hug.

"Well, I'm back, and everything will be great. The new tenants love my house and promised to take good care of it." Daniel puts his arm around me. "Let's stop off for a cup of coffee."

We drive to McDonald's. He stands on ling to put in his orders while I find a clean table. Smiling, he reaches into his pocket and pulls out his wallet. He gives me two-hundred and fifty for his storage in California, one-hundred and eighty-five for his flight, and two hundred for travel expenses.

"What about the fifty dollars to change your flight?" I ask.

"You'll have to put that on my tab. You need to trust me, Babe. How's Mack?" he asks, changing the subject of money.

"Not too good. Mack is biting himself raw. I bought a flea killer, but it isn't working. Maybe it's stress. I don't think he likes living in the apartment."

Daniel waves his hands.

"We should find him a good home," I continue.

"How can you say that? Mack's part of our family."

"I know, and I'd miss him, but truthfully, Daniel, he's cooped up in the apartment. Besides, it's my job to walk him, and he drags me all over the place like a rag doll. He needs to be trained."

"We'll talk about it later." The conversation is over.

"Did you renew your driver's license in New York?"

"The Department of Motor Vehicles was closed for Presidents Day. I couldn't do it. I guess I'll have to get a Florida license."

It's typical of Daniel to wait until the last minute.

"Let's go home and get *comfy*," he says.

Comfy! I've missed *comfy!*

License to Drive

We may be very different
And sometimes we're the same
It doesn't really matter
Our love we must sustain

The coffeemaker beeps, and I move to get up. Daniel grumbles and wraps his legs around mine so I can't move.

"I'm a python," he says. "You're not going anywhere."

"Daniel! I need to walk the dog."

"He's fine!"

"No, he's been whimpering since the sun came up."

He lets me up, and I let Mack drag me around the field. Daniel's chugging milk from the gallon carton when I return, wearing only boxers. "You're making me fat."

"Don't blame me! You were in New York for over a week. I bet all you ate were donuts and Snickers bars. You probably washed them down with Coke."

"I'm going on a diet," he says, taking another gulp of milk.

I shake my head and pour coffee, adding milk from the reserve bottle I hid in the bottom drawer.

"You're so funny, hiding milk all over the place."

"I have to with you around."

Unable to resist the opportunity, I smack him on the butt. "Stinger!"

Daniel's eyes widen. He springs toward me to retaliate, chasing me around the desk. Mack runs with us. I hear a crash.

"Oh, no! The dog knocked over the hard drive for my computer!"

I pick it up off the floor and check for damage.

"Shut it down and restart it," Daniel suggests.

"All right," I say apprehensively. The error message that pops up says it can't reboot.

"What am I going to do? I need a computer."

"Relax. We'll take it to the shop. I'm sure they can fix it. If not, I'll buy you a new one."

With what?

"Are you going to look for another job today?"

"Sit down, Florence. I want to talk to you about that."

I get a sick feeling in the pit of my stomach.

"I owe you a lot of money," he says, his eyes meeting mine briefly before he turns away. "At the rate I'm going. I don't know when I'll be able to pay you back."

"I need money to help with food and expenses right now."

"That's my point. Florence, I'll never make enough money working for someone else.

"What do you suggest?"

"I want to flip a boat."

"Flip? What's that?"

"It's when you buy something that's damaged, fix it, and then sell it for twice what you paid."

"It's much harder to sell something than buy it."

"I know what I'm doing. I found a Sea Ray for three thousand dollars, and I need you to lend me the money."

"Where would you keep it?" I scramble for a reason to refuse. "What if no one wants to buy it?"

Daniel's eyes darken. "Do you have to be so negative?"

I feel my blood pressure rising at his accusation. Damn! He knows what buttons to push to exploit my insecurities. In reality, it's my optimism that feeds this one-way relationship.

"I want to see you get on your feet, but...."

"Never mind." He gives me the cold shoulder for the rest of the morning.

"It's obvious you don't trust me," he says.

"I *do* trust you, but...."

Even though he shorted me, he *did* pay back most of the money for his trip to New York.

"All right," I say. "I'll lend you the money."

Happy Daniel is back. "We can swing by the bank on the way to get my license. He kisses the top of my head. "You're a difficult woman."

Difficult? I'm a pushover.

⚓

Daniel waits in the car while I run into the bank to access my safe deposit box and the secret cash. I'm sure he'd burn through it like a pine forest on fire if he knew.

I hand Daniel the envelope with the money when I get in the car.

The next stop is the DMV for his license. After waiting in a long line, it's his turn, but we hit a snafu. Homeland Security requires all applicants to prove their American citizenship with a birth certificate or passport. Daniel has neither, so we leave empty-handed.

"I can't drive without a license," he says in a panic. "I got caught once, and they revoked my driving privileges. It took five years. I had to hire a lawyer to get it back."

"You were without a license for five years?"

"I didn't want to deal with the hassle."

"I couldn't go one week without driving."

He shrugs, and we go home to apply for another birth certificate online. It costs twenty dollars, and I have to use my credit card.

"Just put it on my tab." He laughs, but I don't think it's funny. It will cost me more if he gets a ticket for driving without a license.

A Home for Mack

Heart in pain and stomach knots
Desire not to eat
Body yearns for rest
But doesn't welcome sleep

"We need to find Mack a home, Daniel. Look at him. He's not a happy dog.

He gets the dog in a headlock and wrestles him to the floor.

"It was different when we lived in New York. He had all that land to run free on. It's not fair."

"I guess you're right. We don't have the time for Mack. I'll consider it if you can find a nice family, but only if they have a house and a yard."

While Daniel is on the phone working out the details to buy the Sea Ray, I put an ad on Craigslist to find Mack a home.

He hangs up and walks over to me. "I'm going out for a while," he says. "I'm having the boat delivered to a marina."

Shortly after he leaves, the phone rings.

"Hi. Do you still have the Chocolate Lab?"

"Uh, yes, I have him."

"I'm very interested," the woman says.

"Great, but I need to ask you some questions," I say.

"Sure."

"Do you have children?"

"Yes, four. The oldest is fifteen, and the youngest is eighteen months."

"Good. One more question. Do you own a house?"

"Yes! We have a fenced yard and plenty of room for a dog. We even have a pool."

"You sound perfect. Mack is a good dog. We're only trying to find him another home because he needs space, and our apartment is too small."

"Do you think I can come over and see him?"

"I'd prefer that you wait until after dinner."

"That's fine," she says. "My husband doesn't get home until six."

I give her the address and hang up the phone. That was fast—too fast. I dread telling Daniel. Just as I suspect, he isn't happy.

"You're really going to give Mack away?"

"We discussed this, and you agreed. They're coming tonight. Should I tell them you changed your mind?"

"No. Do what you have to do."

Throughout dinner, he uses guilt like a weapon. He pets Mack and tells him I want to get rid of him. It tugs at my heart.

"Don't make me feel guilty, Daniel. You had no business getting a dog if you didn't intend to take care of it."

He retreats to the bedroom, and I take Mack for a walk one last time. I'm too old for this, but it's not Mack's fault. I blame Daniel.

When the family arrives, they love Mack. I take his leash off, and the older kids run around the field with him. This time he doesn't run away. He jumps into the back of their Jeep, and I watch them drive away. Sadness washes over me as I climb the stairs without Mack.

Daniel is lying in bed when I enter the apartment, and I join him, hoping for some comfort.

"You got rid of my dog," he says accusingly.

I'm stunned. "You told me to find a home for him."

"I didn't think you'd go through with it," he says. "He was part of our family. Wait till I tell my kids you got rid of their dog."

"You've got to be kidding! You're going to blame *me*?"

Anger replaces my sadness.

"You never took care of him. *I* had to feed and walk him. *I* had to pick up his poop whenever he shit all over the apartment. All you ever did was play with him."

I don't like going to bed with bad feelings unresolved, but he turns on his side. He's keeping far enough away from me so our bodies don't touch — *no comfy tonight!*

I stare at the ceiling. Maybe it was a mistake for Daniel to come to Florida.

A few hours later, I fall asleep but wake up when I hear Daniel yell. "What the fuck!" And a thud.

"Was that Ripley?" I ask. "Did you just throw him off the bed?"

"The little bastard bit me."

Outraged, I grab my pillow and my cat and leave to sleep in the guestroom.

Maybe I should have found a good home for Daniel and kept Mack!

Daniel's up before me in the morning. He had better not ask me how I slept, or I may lose it. I pour myself a cup of coffee.

"Hey Babe, pour me some, too," he says.

"Get it yourself!"

"What's eating you?"

"You were so mean to my cat last night."

"No, I wasn't. I like Ripley." He reaches down and rubs his head. "He's my buddy."

"You threw him off the bed!"

"Ah, Babe, don't be mad. At least I didn't give him away."

"Shut up! You didn't care about that dog."

"Calm down. I'm just trying to ruffle your feathers."

"At least he's with people who have time for him. It was the right thing to do."

"All right, all right," he says, sensing that I'm on the edge and he and leaves to work on the boat.

Overboard

Passion, joy, and love
I want to change my life
Crystal seas and sunny skies
Lay before our very eyes

Without Mack around, Ripley must sense he has the run of the place because he's out of the bedroom. He meows at my feet and follows me as I get dressed.

It's been a week since I dropped off my computer and I haven't heard from them, so I ride to the shop. With my fingers crossed, I approach the counter and give the clerk my repair ticket. He's not smiling when he returns.

"I wasn't able to fix your computer, Ma'am," he says. "The hard drive is broken."

"Were you able to get the data?"

"I'm sorry. There's no way we can retrieve it. Did you back it up?"

"Periodically. I forget."

"I suggest you get yourself an external hard drive. That way, you'll never lose your work."

I nod and pull out my credit card to pay for the computer service. Lately, I'm charging more and more. Most of the charges are for food and gas.

I text Daniel and tell him the bad news.

"Don't be sad, Babe. We'll buy you another."

He's so generous with the money he hasn't earned yet, but once the Sea Ray is fixed, he'll sell it, and I'll get my money back. So far, I've put out forty-five hundred dollars, which isn't counting the original five thousand Daniel borrowed to come to Florida.

"Maybe you should reduce the price," I suggest.

"Don't pressure me. That Sea Ray is beautiful, and I've done a great job restoring it," he boasts. "If I didn't need the money, I'd keep it."

There he goes again. He wants a boat so bad. The thought intrigues me, but.... What is it they say? "Buying a boat was the best day of my life, and selling it was the second best." Or something like that.

After dinner, Daniel gets on the new computer, and I read a book in the bedroom.

"Florence! Come in here for a minute? I want to show you something."

I walk into the living room.

"Sit on my lap." He pulls me onto his knee so I can look at the computer screen. "Look at this boat."

"It's beautiful," I say, furrowing my brow. I'm getting uncomfortable, and not just because his leg is bony.

"They're asking eight thousand for it but haven't gotten any bids so far."

"How do you know?"

"I've been keeping track of it."

"What happens if they don't get any bids?"

"The bidding will stop, and the listing will disappear," he says. "I think we should bid on it."

"Are you crazy?"

"Think about it, Babe. We can sail around on the ocean, traveling to tropical places. We can even live on it."

"Live on it?"

"Yeah, why not. Don't you want to do something different during our golden years? Let's bid for five thousand. We have nothing to lose."

Yeah, *he* has nothing to lose.

"They won't reduce the price by three thousand dollars," I scoff.

"It depends on how long they've been trying to sell it. Maybe they're desperate."

"It's on the opposite side of Florida."

"So what? We can move it over to this coast. Think about the adventure."

"I don't know." I'm starting to squirm. "Let's not rush into it."

"This boat will be gone. Come on, Florence. Just hit the button."

"I don't knooow!"

"It will be in your name," he says. "Think of it as an investment in our future."

Daniel is a master when it comes to playing on my dreams.

In my heart, I know this is wrong. But there's something exciting about it, too. Despite my better judgment, I'm about to jump off the edge of a cliff. I hit the button.

His bid is low. It most likely won't go through. We close the computer and go to bed. *Ahhh…comfy*!

Smooth Operator

As tears fill up my eyes
I cry for passion lost
I want it back; it will not be
So, this is what it costs

We are now the proud owners of a thirty-three-foot Carver Mariner. It's really mine because it's in my name, but Daniel promises he'll pay half when he gets the money.

Daniel stops to gas up and buys cigarettes on the way to check it out, and I wait in the car. His cell phone chimes with an incoming text. I can't help myself. I read it.

"He-y-y... baby boy. Let's buy an RV. I'll pack us some sammies, and we can hit the road."

Baby boy? RV? Sammies? Who is this?

I call the number on my phone. Flustered, I hang up. *Josette!*

He's still in contact with her! I realize he's keeping his options open. Why else would he be keeping her in his life?

I can't understand why she would want him. She thinks he's in New York and doesn't know he's living with me in Florida.

My phone rings. *Oh no! She has my number.*

Daniel walks toward the car, so I silence the ringer and tuck the phone in my purse. I'm burning to ask him about the text, but the fear he'll confirm that he's cheating on me keeps me from confronting him.

ↄ◦✧◦ↄ

The boat is wonderful except for the old furniture that clutters the cabin. We discard it, and it seems to float higher. Together we rip out the carpet and the dining seats.

Daniel checks out the engines while I clean the kitchen and bathroom. I like the idea of living on the water. It's unconventional, and I'm looking forward to the adventure. He pops his head in occasionally.

"Looking good," he says.

I already forget about Josette and her text. Submerged in the joy of décor, I'm thinking of a very nautical blue and gold color scheme.

"Make a list of everything we need," Daniel yells something from the flybridge.

"Aye, aye, Captain," I say.

My cell phone chimes. It's Josette. I stare at the message. *"The truth will set you free!"*

My chest is heavy as I feel the boat closing in to suffocate me.

Daniel comes into the cabin, smiling as if he doesn't have a care in the world.

"You told me you weren't involved with Josette anymore," I accuse.

His smile disintegrates when he sees the look on my face. He gapes at me for a second. "What did she say?"

"She sent me a cryptic message... something about the truth." I shove the phone into his hand.

Daniel reads the text. His jaw tenses. "That bitch! What does this mean?"

"You tell me," I shriek like a furious child. My fists clench so hard that my nails dig into my skin. "She doesn't know you're living with me, does she? Why are you hiding our relationship? Or am I the one who's being left in the dark? Are you still involved with her?"

"Don't be ridiculous," he rumbles. "I told her it was over between us."

"Evidently, she didn't get the message. What truth does she know that would set me free? Why is she telling me these things? I want her to stop."

"I told you. She's jealous. Next time she tries to contact you, don't answer. I'll deal with her."

Irritated, he packs up his tools. "Let's call it a day."

Neither of us has much to say as we drive home. I think he still cares for Josette, but he continues to deny it.

Exhausted, we climb into bed and watch the moonrise outside the large picture window. It's one of the benefits of this apartment.

"Florence, we have a good future ahead of us, living on the boat."

Living on the boat is the carrot he dangles in front of me. I don't have the strength to resist. My emotions are being stretched from one extreme to the other.

He's a smooth operator.

Ten/Love

Remembering all the times
your love was good and pure
And suddenly, I find
I'm craving so much more

There are no more texts from Josette. Part of me is pleased, but her words haunt me. What does she know about Daniel and me? Maybe she knows I'm supporting him. My mind floods with so many questions. If he weren't broke, would he want her instead? Broke! Maybe I'm the one who's broke—emotionally and soon financially.

Strangely, the boat has brought us closer together. Since we bought it, we now have a project to focus on. It gives me the illusion we're partners. We'll be living on the water, experiencing an exciting way of life. The boat is coming along, but I'm spending money like a drunken sailor between the materials to work on it, the gas to get to the other side of Florida, and the monthly docking fee.

I call my mother. I need to hear her voice. She's so close, yet so far. Daniel never wants to make the trip. Whenever I plan to drive down and see her, he thinks up some engaging activity for us to do together, like go to the beach or drive across the state to work on the boat.

"I was thinking of coming for Easter," I say. "Maybe we can get a table and eat by the pool."

"That's a good idea. This place is too small, and I know how you get fidgety. Carol can cook a turkey or something. You're welcome to bring Daniel," she adds.

"I'll ask Annmarie and her husband Paul if they want to come, but I'm not sure about Daniel. We'll see."

Maybe this time, he'll agree to come with me. After all—it is a holiday. I'll buy some Sambuca. Then he can hang out at the pool and drink.

∽∽∽

A constant struggle plays out in the middle of the night. The stress is tormenting me. Uncertain about my future, I fight with my subconscious. I wake to the sound of someone whimpering. It's me! Daniel pets my head.

In the morning, I feel his arousal beneath my leg, but it's just a mirage in the desert that disappears when you approach. All we ever do is lie in bed and cuddle. Any other man would have sought help by now. I roll over and stare into his eyes.

"Can I ask you something?"

"Sure."

"Why don't you want to have sex anymore?"

My question puts him on the spot, and panic washes over his face. His eyes frost over. "I, eh…I have a problem."

No shit, Sherlock. "Maybe you need to see a doctor."

"I don't have the money."

"I'll lend it to you."

I've lent him so much already, but this is important.

"Let it go! Hey, you said you would teach me how to play tennis," he says.

"Tennis? Today?"

"Why not? Are you afraid I'll whip your ass?"

"No, but I only have one racket."

"I'm sure we can find a cheap one somewhere," he says.

The idea of playing tennis is appealing, but that means I'll be buying him a racket.

Since he's in a good mood, I use the opportunity to mention visiting my family for Easter.

"You go see your mother. I'll just sleep all day," he says. "Maybe I'll even go to the beach."

"Without me?" Here he goes again, tempting me with a good time. "Please, Daniel. You'll have fun, I promise. Paul is coming, and there'll be plenty of food. You can swim in the pool or layout in the sun. Besides, my mother and sister want to meet you."

He sighs. "All right, Babe, but you owe me." He picks up a fifty-dollar racket, and I quickly find him one for fifteen.

"This is a piece of junk!" He puts the expensive racket back on the shelf and picks up a can of tennis balls. My mouth turns up in a cool twitch of a smile. "Yes, we *do* need balls," I say, but I'm the one who lacks them.

"How are you going to play in sandals?"

"Don't worry. I'll still kick your butt, even against you and your snazzy sneakers."

At least he didn't expect me to buy him sneakers.

Daniel goes to one side of the net with two balls in his pocket and one in his hand. I wait for him to get the first ball over the net. The ball shoots off into orbit and sails over the fence.

I laugh. "Let me show you how to serve."

Although unwilling, he gives up the balls. I fire a volley at his feet. He swings and misses. "Ha! Take that," I shout.

He tries again until the ball whizzes past my ear. "I think I'm getting the hang of it," he says, breathing hard and dancing around the court.

Daniel is so comical. There's a smug, competitive smile on his face. He's actually pretty good and soon has me chasing the ball around the court.

It's a beautiful sunny day, and I forget about my credit card balance for a while, but I can feel a cloud of desperation forming over my head.

He serves one hard and to my left. With a surge of competitive adrenaline, I trip over myself, trying to reach it, landing on the side of my ankle.

The pain is excruciating. Rocking back and forth, I remain on the ground, watching my ankle swell.

"What's wrong?" he yells. When he realizes I'm not getting up, he comes to my side of the net.

"I'm going to be sick," I whimper.

"You're fine. Just breathe." He helps me up and supports me as we walk to the car. I don't think I'll be playing tennis for a while.

Daniel props my leg up on a pillow with a bag of ice when we get home and orders me to stay off my feet. I'm too restless to stay in one place for long, so I hobble into the kitchen to make dinner while he takes a nap.

The smell of tomato sauce simmering on the stove lures him out of the bedroom.

"Dinner's almost ready," I say, but he's impatient. He grabs a fork and stabs a meatball from the pot.

"These meatballs are terrible," he says, spitting them in the trashcan.

"No, they aren't," I say defensively.

"You're not Italian!"

"Oh, and now you're going to tell me what I am? There's nothing wrong with my meatballs!" I retort. "In the future, you can have grilled cheese."

Father Figure

We may be very different
And sometimes we're the same
It doesn't really matter
Our love we must sustain

"Are you going to drag me to your mother's house today?" Daniel asks. "Why can't you go, and I'll wait here?"

"Because it's Easter, and everyone is expecting us."

"I don't want to stay late."

I was afraid he would do this. Whenever I want to do something, he limits my time and squeezes all the enjoyment out of it.

"We won't," I promise, hoping he'll have a good time and change his mind once we're there.

It takes us an hour to get there with Daniel at the wheel. As we approach, I'm not sure this is a good idea. Maybe I should have come alone. My mother is in the house when we arrive.

"Where is everyone?" I ask.

"Annmarie and Paul are at the pool with Carol. I stayed behind to wait for you."

For a moment, I'm at a loss for words. Then I find my tongue. "Mom, this is Daniel."

She smiles, but I'm not sure it's sincere.

"It's nice to meet you, Daniel. I've heard so much about you."

"I hope it wasn't all bad," he teases, making her giggle like a young girl.

Already, he has my mother eating out of his hand. Women can't resist him, no matter their age.

Daniel pulls out the Sambuca I bought at the pool and pours one shot after another, trying to get everyone drunk. I can't figure out why this pleases him. While he's busy, Carol and I go for a walk.

"How's everything going with you and Daniel?"

"It could be better," I say, unsure if I should confide in her.

"What's going on?"

"It's as if we're two old married people. The problem is, we're not married—we're not boyfriend and girlfriend, and we're certainly not roommates because he doesn't pay his half of the bills."

"Florence, are you lending him money?"

"He says he'll pay me back when he gets on his feet."

"I hope so."

We rejoin the family. Daniel is refilling Annmarie's glass, and she's slurring her words.

"Daniel! Stop trying to get my daughter drunk," I say, moving her glass out of her reach.

"Your mom is always telling me what to do," he says.

"She can be a little bossy," Annmarie says and laughs.

I roll my eyes. "I'm not looking to tell you or anyone else what to do."

"Haven't you learned by now? I'm the boss!" He chuckles. "Relax! Have a drink."

He's happy and carefree. Why not? He doesn't have to worry about living expenses.

This isn't the time to stress out, so I smile and grab a glass of Sambuca. Annmarie leans over and whispers in my ear.

"Mom, I *really* like him."

Wow, he's good!

※

Daniel moans and turns my body, so we're spooning. It's too warm after a few minutes, and I struggle to get free. I wait until he tires of the game and then slip from his grip, tiptoeing into the kitchen to make coffee.

He's right behind me, and I pour him a cup.

"What's on your agenda today?"

"I'm not sure," I say. "Why?"

"I'd like to borrow the car."

"My car?"

I can't hide the look of apprehension on my face.

"I don't know. It's going to rain all day. Maybe I'll stay in and work on the computer."

"Let me borrow your car then."

Panic washes over me. Even though I don't plan to go out, the thought of him leaving me stranded makes me nervous.

"There's an auto shop that needs a painter. I'll be right back," he promises.

Being stranded unnerves me, but I'll get some financial relief if Daniel gets a real job.

Grudgingly I hand him the keys. As he promised, he doesn't go for long and smiles from ear to ear when he returns. "I have a surprise for you," he says.

"What is it?"

He produces a candy bar and waits for my response.

Although I'm slightly disappointed, I have to smile. Daniel never goes out of his way to buy me a gift. Even though it isn't a diamond ring or tickets to a show, the effect is the same.

"Did you get the job?"

"The guy loves me." His mouth curls in an ironic smile.

Daniel is confident and at ease with himself, although some might call it arrogance.

"He wants me to paint parts, like fenders and such. I told him I have a shop."

My eyes open in surprise. "But you don't!"

"Relax. I'll farm it out. He'll never know someone else is painting them."

Hmm. It sounds like just another shady deal.

"Is that moral?"

"Don't be ridiculous. I don't want to talk about it anymore."

His phone rings, and he takes it to the bedroom. I hear him talking in a whisper.

"Who was that?" I ask when he comes back.

"Lisa. She had a fight with her boyfriend. Sometimes she needs a pep talk. I told her she should dump the guy."

He seems happy. Maybe he wishes that she'd dump him.

I wonder why they broke up. All he gives me are bits and pieces of the truth. He says she wanted more, but I suspect *more* to it.

She's twenty years younger than I am. She's also the mother of his two children. It's hard to believe she fell for Daniel. He's so much older than she is. Perhaps she was looking for a father figure.

Floating

If I feast off the emotions
Lying on the floor
Will I have regrets?
Before I close the door

Daniel is busy on the computer, and I'm impatient for him to finish so we can go to St. James Island and work on the boat. He looks serious.

"I've listed my house," he says.

A glimmer of hope ignites. "Really?"

"Yes. I think we should put the money into the boat and retire."

"That would be great. We can live in it and eat fish for dinner every night."

"I hate fish."

"You like shrimp and lobster! We can get some nets and lobster traps."

"Now you're talking, but don't forget, I'm the captain."

"Fine... I'll buy you a captain's hat," I joke. He's such a control freak.

"We have a lot of work to do," he says. "I have to go over every inch of those engines."

"All right! You stick to the engines and leave the decorating to me."

Before we leave to work on our boat, I check my e-mail.

"Congratulations on your eBay purchase."

Daniel is the ultimate consumer. "What have you bought now?" I ask.

"It's a rare vintage picture of Elizabeth Taylor, signed and authenticated."

I feel my blood heat. He's already burned through seven hundred dollars on my e-bay credit account, claiming he will make money re-selling celebrity photos.

"Relax. I'll make all the money back and then some," he says confidently.

I know he's a good salesman, but why do I have to finance his hare-brained ideas?

Daniel owes me over ten thousand dollars, not to mention I've been paying for everything, gas, food, rent, and utilities. Trapped by his cavalier spending, I tighten my purchases. I swore I wouldn't go below twenty-five thousand dollars in the bank, but I'm losing my grip.

His phone rings. He stares at the number and puts it down.

"Aren't you going to get that?" I ask.

"Nah, they'll leave a message."

"What if someone wants to buy the boat? Check to see if they left a message."

"Don't tell me what to do. His arrogance infuriates me.

"Daniel! This is important. Call them back, *please!*"

"Jesus Christ! I thought we were leaving."

"If someone is interested in the Sea Ray, we can show it to them before we go to work on our boat."

He glowers at me and picks up his phone. I cross my fingers.

Although I tell myself I'm in control, I'm not. *Daniel is.*

Holding my breath, I listen intently to the conversation.

"I've already reduced it to seven," he says. "I'm on my way out of town."

Oh no, we're going to lose him.

"Yes, it's in the boatyard on Seaway Drive. If you are a serious buyer, I can meet you there in an hour."

Whew! He hangs up, and I can breathe again. Whatever profit we make on the Sea Ray will go right back into my bank account.

❦

The man is waiting for us when we arrive, and Daniel takes him out on the boat while I wait in the car with Ripley. His carrier is strapped in, and he's ready to travel.

Soon, they return. My heart is racing as they approach the dock. They're smiling. That's a good sign. A novice fisherman, he loves the boat. I sign over the title, and he gives Daniel cash. Whew! He counts out the three thousand for the original investment and another eight hundred I spent on materials to fix the boat. *That was stressful.*

Presented with cash, my doubts about him evaporate. Along the way to *our boat*, my mood elevates. I have money in my pocket, and we're heading toward our boat.

"We should think about flipping another boat," Daniel says, shaking a cigarette loose from his pack.

"Jeez, give me a chance to enjoy selling the Sea Ray. It took so long. For a while, I thought we'd have two boats."

"Florence, you're so negative."

"Don't say that!" I object, feeling my blood heat. "I hate it when you say that."

His eyes blaze, but he cools down and says, "We can't move forward unless I make money."

Forward — full steam ahead. Our fight is over, but nothing gets resolved. With Daniel, there is no compromise.

Along the way, we talk about being out in the open seas once the boat is in prime shape. The project keeps me focused on the future, and I feel connected to him.

After working like beavers all day, we reflect on our progress. The sun sinks low, bathing the skyline in the fiery orange light.

"This is the life," Daniel says as we sit on the flybridge and sip Sambuca. We give the boat a name — *Call it a Day*!

At the first signs of darkness, I light a candle. The stars shine against an ink-black sky, and Ripley investigates something in the bushes. He's getting used to jumping on and off the boat and will prove to be a good second mate.

Daniel stares at the horizon as if something heavy is on his mind.

"What's wrong?" I ask.

"The bank will foreclose on my mortgage if I don't send them money this month. I may have to borrow some money."

For some illogical reason, I feel compelled to help Daniel.

"Let's go inside and get *comfy*," he says.

It's always the same, one step forward and two steps back.

Daniel's arm is around me, and I'm lulled by the boat, gently rocking back and forth against the dock.

"We should bring *Call it a Day* to the east coast," I say. "It's costing so much to go back and forth every week."

"I want to replace the carburetors first, and maybe even the distributors. I'll look for the parts on eBay."

I cringe. My credit card debt keeps creeping up. I'm carrying a balance for the first time in my life. However, I know nothing about boats, and I don't want to sink in the middle of the ocean. Still, I fear that I may not keep my financial boat floating.

Right Mind

When I pull away
You draw me back to you
I hesitate but follow
Seeking to construe

I try to get out of bed, and he pulls me back. "Today is Sunday. Relax!" *Relax?* It's his favorite thing to do, but I find it impossible with so much on my mind.

"Let's go to the beach today."

"That's a great idea," I say, thinking I could dive into a book and soak up some sun.

I entice him with coffee, and he lets me escape.

He plops into the chair and turns on the computer while I pack towels, sunscreen, and water.

"Are you ready, Daniel?"

"I don't feel like going anymore. You took too long."

"Don't be ridiculous! Let's go."

"Don't tell me what to do. I'm the boss."

"You're not the boss of me."

His brow creases. "Yes, I am. If you're not good, we won't go."

"I'll go without you."

He lights another cigarette, crosses his legs, and delicately takes a puff. "Go."

"You look so feminine," I tease. "Are you sure you're not gay?"

He laughs. "Maybe I am."

It works. He mashes the cigarette in the ashtray, grabs his keys, and we're *off.*

"Can you grab the umbrella?"

"I'm not taking that thing!"

"We can't sit in the sun all day without protection."

"I don't want to be embarrassed."

"Why would you be embarrassed? Plenty of people bring umbrellas to the beach."

"All right, but *you* carry it. I'm not putting it up."

"Fine, I'll do it myself."

"And, I'm not chasing it down the beach when the wind picks it up."

"You're such an ass, Daniel!"

"I am, aren't I?"

I pull out the umbrella and balance it with the bags and the towels.

"I can't believe you have to take this thing," he says, grabbing it from me and clucking his tongue.

"I'll laugh my ass off when you're chasing it down the beach."

Along the way, he pulls into 7-Eleven for a pack of cigarettes and a Big Gulp. "Do you want anything?"

"No, I'm good."

Two minutes later, he's walking out of the store with his drink in one hand and two bananas in the other.

"Here, I bought you a banana."

"I don't want a banana."

"You should eat it. It's good for you."

Daniel won't give me a cent for food shopping, but he'll buy me a banana, a chocolate bar, or an overpriced beverage. It's infuriating, but I guess his intentions are good.

"We should stop at the liquor store and buy a bottle of Sambuca," he says.

"Okay. I think we have glasses in the trunk from last time."

After a quick stop at the liquor store, we drive to the beach.

Daniel smirks as he watches me struggle to set up the umbrella in the sand. Determined, I get the pole deep enough, so it doesn't blow away, denying him the satisfaction of seeing me chase it down the beach.

"Look at that guy, Florence." He points to a fat, hairy guy walking on the beach. "I think you like him!"

I laugh.

"You do. I know you do," he teases.

Daniel sets up the chairs and pours us some Sambuca. I sip the sweet liquor, letting it flow through my body and into my brain. It's a beautiful sunny day, and I inhale the salty air. My worries melt away as I close my eyes and drift into oblivion.

"Come on, Babe, let's take a dip," he says.

"I'm comfortable right here. I toward the sun. "You go."

"Come with me," he insists.

"I don't want to swim right now."

"I wasn't asking." Daniel has a mischievous look in his eyes. Before I can react, he picks up the edge of my towel and drags me toward the water. Exasperated, I get up and return to the umbrella.

"Give me ten minutes." I spread my towel out again.

"You're so bossy," he says.

My eyebrows rise in disbelief. "*You're* the dictator around here."

He laughs and lights a cigarette. "You're my fudge-muffin." He keeps me laughing with his quirky humor, but everything has to be his way. *Hmm. I guess he never got the women's lib memo.*

Smoke is wafting into my eyes, and there's no way I will rest.

"All right, let's go for a swim," I say, giving him his way.

There's a smug grin on his face, and I have to laugh.

The ocean water is chilly but refreshing. We romp around in the waves, laughing and teasing each other as if we don't have a care in the world.

Soon, the warmth of the sun melts away my stress. I drink in the warm salty air and gaze out at the ocean. Rich or poor, this is *the life*.

"Daniel. Do you think we'll ever be intimate again?" I ask.

His eyes turn away from me, and he stares at the horizon. I wonder what he's thinking. His silence widens the gap between us.

What woman in her right mind would give up sex for the rest of her life? Then again, maybe I'm not in my right mind.

The Abyss

Lips of stone could cause abate
I'm blinded by the sun
I could break if it's too late
Trapped in a bleak outcome

"Florence, sit down for a minute. I want to talk to you."

"I'm washing the dishes. Can't you talk while I'm standing?"

"Sit down!" he repeats. "I want you to listen to me."

"What is it?" I prepare for the worst.

"I found a car I can flip. It's a 2006 Monte Carlo."

"Oh, no! After the Sea Ray deal, I thought you were finished."

"It's a salvage car. If I fix it, I'll double my money."

"Daniel, people will know the car was in a wreck."

"I'm good at what I do. No one will ever know it's been in a crash."

"The title will say it's salvage... they'll know!"

His eyes flare, and he throws up his hands. "I guess we have different ideas on how to earn money."

"It's my money. I should have a say in how it's spent," I say, raising my voice.

"Keep your voice down," he growls. "The window is open, and everyone can hear you."

"I don't care!" My voice is unexpectedly harsh. It even sounds unfamiliar to me.

"Forget it," he snaps. "I've had it with Florida anyway. I'm going back to New York."

His threat makes me feel sick, and I force myself to breathe.

"What about the boat?"

"I'll help you sell it," he says as if it's his decision. "I'm sick of depending on you for money."

"It's too risky."

"Stop," he says and flicks his hand.

"Stop, what?"

"Don't make me laugh, Florence. Your money isn't making you any interest in the bank. I can make more and faster.

"You don't know that for sure."

"There you go again—always negative. That's why your ex-husband wasn't happy."

My insides twist, and I have a moment of self-doubt. His tactic is effective…for a split second.

"Stop criticizing *me!* You do it all the time. If I don't do what you want—something's wrong with me. You're a control freak!" The words come out of my mouth, and the room turns arctic.

"No one wants a gas-guzzling automobile that's been in a major accident."

"I'm done!" he hisses. His eyes glitter with savage anger, and a moment of rage brings his glass of Sambuca crashing onto the counter.

Stepping back, I watch him unravel. He's mad, but I am too.

"Done? What's that supposed to mean?"

"I'm going back home."

"What are you going to do there to make money?"

"I'll find something. I don't give a fuck!"

The finality of his words fills me with terror. My anger morphs to fear — fear of abandonment — fear of being alone. He sucks all the air out of a room, and I flinch for a moment.

"I don't want to have this discussion with you," he snipes. "If nobody buys the car, I'll sell my van and pay you back. If I have to, I'll go back to New York and sell my Rolex."

"What, Rolex?"

"I have a watch that's worth over ten thousand dollars. You'll get the money back, I promise."

My stomach quivers with panic as he backs me into a corner. "Why are you always mad at me, Daniel?"

"I can't get ahead. No matter what I do, everything turns to shit." He turns away and puts his head in his hands. "I'm not mad at you — I'm mad at myself. Don't you think that I know I'm a burden? I feel like such a loser."

For the first time, I get a glimpse of his self-loathing. A twinge of pity stirs inside me. Daniel may just be a wounded soul who can't get a break.

"Things will get better." Already, I feel myself backing down. If I don't lend him the money, he might leave. If I do, he may earn enough money to pay me back. It's a gamble, but one I have to take.

"Okay, I'll lend you the money."

"Forget it. I don't want it."

"Don't be silly! I said I would lend it to you."

Teddy Bear

My heart is numb
Don't like the feeling
Emotions hijacked
My head is reeling

Daniel is surfing the net, so I leave him at the computer and drive to the supermarket. My phone rings, but I don't recognize the caller.

"My name is Ed. I'm looking for Daniel Weaver. Are you his girlfriend?"

"Yes, but this isn't his number."

"Well, he took some car parts to his shop to be painted, and I haven't heard from him since."

"Daniel doesn't have a .... You need to speak to him."

"He won't answer my calls. You tell him that I'm pressing charges. I may even come after you!" he threatens. "For all I know, you are in this together." The phone goes dead.

Pulling into the parking lot, I look up at our apartment window. I'm sure he's home. Where else would he be? He's still sitting at the computer when I come through the door, but he doesn't acknowledge my presence.

"Daniel! I just received a disturbing phone call from Ed, the guy you worked for last month. He's looking for his car parts."

He looks through me as if I'm speaking a foreign language.

"Oh, him!" The light of recognition illuminates his face. "They're in the back of my van." He shrugs as if it's no big deal. "I haven't had time to get them back to him."

"The guy is furious. He threatened to call the police."

He holds his hand up as if he's directing traffic. "I'll take care of it!"

My brow is in a knot. "Please do! I don't need more problems."

Daniel puts his arm around my shoulder. "You're stressing out, Babe."

"We're going to get in trouble," I say, pulling away. "He threatened to go after *us both*."

ཙ❀ঙ

Daniel still doesn't have his own car. I chauffeur him to and from work. It's either that or let him use my car, and that's not happening. When I go over fifty, the steering wheel shakes, and I ask if he'll check it.

"I'm not touching this car until you clean it," he says.

"I've been driving you all over the place. The least you can do is to fix the car."

"Stop!" he says and glares at me.

I glare back. "Don't tell me to stop. I'm sick of it, Daniel. You need to buy a car or find someone else to drive you around."

"You're a nasty bitch," he sneers.

Stunned by his venom, I stare at this man who claimed to love me once.

"I hate you, too." The words force themselves out of my mouth.

Daniel remains in the living room for most of the evening, leaving me to wonder. *What do I get from this relationship?* There's no romance, love, money, or security. *So why am I with him?*

Eventually, he enters the bedroom and crawls beside me with his clothes on. I roll over to sleep and feel him barricade the space between us with the sheets. *What kind of cold-hearted snake is this lying next to me?*

❧

Daniel's working again and no longer borrowing money, but I don't get much help with the bills. Down to five thousand dollars in my savings account, my money's disappearing fast. Besides the credit card balance, I'm barely scraping by. As I try to navigate the situation, I'm teetering on the verge of a nervous breakdown. Like a rubber band strained to its limit, I know I'm going to snap. It's not as if I didn't know the risk.

He jumps into the car, but I wait until we get home to ask him for money.

"Did you get paid?"

"Yes." He grudgingly opens his wallet and pulls fifty dollars. "That's all I have. I'm going to take a shower."

I follow him down the hall. "Daniel, I just spent seventy-five dollars for groceries and gas for the car."

"Stop hounding me!" he says. "I just got home."

"Hounding you? Is that what I'm doing? It feels more like I'm begging."

"Everything with you is about money," he says, pushing past me. "Money, money, money…that's all you think about." He slips into the bathroom and slams the door.

Furious, I swallow the knot in my throat. "That's not true!" I say from the other side. But he's right. *That's all I think about lately.* We wouldn't have a problem if he didn't feel entitled to my money. He's just using this tactic to get me off his back.

"I'm going to the store," I shout, but he doesn't respond.

As the veil of disillusionment falls, I'm less trusting — even resentful. From now on, I'll think about myself first. I won't care what he eats and will no longer cater to him. Our relationship is a dead end.

When I return home, the music is blasting from my apartment. Daniel is listening to *X-Factor* on my computer again. It annoys me because I know he's smoking one cigarette after another at my desk.

I'm not sure what I'll find on the other side of the door, but I enter, ready for a fight.

His face lights up. "Hey Babe, come here. I want to show you something."

Hesitantly, I walk over and stand behind him.

"Sit on my lap," He says, grabbing my wrist. "I want you to hear this."

Oh no! He's going to make me listen to a video clip. After enduring six talent videos, I beg him to let me get up.

"One more!" He's such a child!

"Only one," I warn.

"Or two." He smiles. "Then we'll get *comfy.*"

Ahhh, comfy! The magic words. I'm not sure I'm in love with him anymore, but I'm addicted to *comfy*. He's like a soft and warm teddy bear, albeit an expensive one.

Sensing my anxiety, Daniel nuzzles my ear.

"Stop," I murmur. "I'm trying to sleep."

He clicks on the light, temporarily blinding me. "Wake up and play with me, Flo." He licks the tip of my nose.

"Eww!" I shout. "Now, I have to get up and wash my face."

"No!" His eyes sparkle with wicked delight. "You can't leave. I didn't give you permission."

Daniel thinks I'm a horse, and he can break me.

"I want to make you laugh," he cajoles, delicately tracing his thumb over my forehead.

"You do, but can you do it in the daytime?"

"If you want me to let you sleep, you need to rub me."

"What is it with you?" I huff. "Why do you want to be rubbed?"

"Because it makes me feel loved." He gives me a little boy smile, and I'm compelled to comply.

"Scratch my head too," he says.

"I wish I could scratch your brain," I say and cuddle into his chest.

We're both needy in our own way.

Within a few minutes, he's snoring, but now I'm wide-awake.

Finally, I fall asleep but wake up again to go to the bathroom. If I turn on the light, I'll never get back to sleep, so I don't. Groping in the dark, I make my way to the toilet. My butt hits the cold water, and I scream.

"You bastard! Why can't you put the damn seat down?"

Celebrate

Day by day, I spent my time
Dependent on your love
I could not leave I could not fly
Away or high above

There's a buyer interested in the Monte Carlo. Daniel has reduced the price because of the salvage title, but it's enough to get my five thousand dollars back.

"We should use this money to flip another car," he says.

"I don't want to buy any more cars or boats."

"I have to flip something," he argues. "It's the only way I'll be able to pay you back."

"Find a job."

"There's a body shop a few blocks away looking for help. Either lend me your car or drive me there."

"I'll drive."

While Daniel talks with the shop owner, I look around the outdoor shop. The place is a mess. Old parts and rusty metal are scattered all over. There's an awning with so many holes that I can't imagine it would keep any rain out.

Ten minutes go by, and he's smiling as he walks toward the car. I sigh with relief because I can't afford to support him any longer and because I need space. Daniel tries to control everything I do when he's around. Ironically, I had more freedom during my thirty-year marriage to Edward.

"When do you start?" I'm smiling so hard my face hurts.

"After the holidays," he says. "Let's go celebrate, Babe. Buy us a bottle of Sambuca, and I'll pay you back when I get my first paycheck."

Hmm! Even if something positive happens, my bank account goes down. At least now, he has a job! It's five o'clock by the time we get home. He pours liquor into two shot glasses and hands one to me. Sambuca is Daniel's favorite. It's a little too sweet for me, but I like the buzz I get from it.

"Hey, Florence!" He grabs my arm and pulls me toward the bedroom. "Come with me. I have to show you something."

"Oh, no!" I protest. "I know what you're up to."

"Just twenty minutes," he pleads.

Unable to resist, I'm feeling the Sambuca's effects.

"Do you know what a toll is, Florence?"

"Of course," I say and cluck my tongue.

"Well, you rub my back, and your toll is paid."

"You're hilarious."

"I had a weird dream last night," he mumbles. "I dreamed that you were getting married to someone else. I rushed to the church to stop the wedding."

"And?"

"I was too late."

"Oh! I dreamed of you, too, but it was a nightmare."

Hmm. "You're a funny girl."

I lie on my side with my head propped on my elbow and caress his shoulder.

"*Comfy*," he murmurs.

My mind is somewhere else.

"We're spending Christmas at my mom's house," I remind him.

"I don't want to hang out with your family," he groans.

"They're expecting us. Besides, we can't spend it here, alone in this apartment."

Truth be told, I dread sitting in my mother's living room, watching the colored lights blinking on her artificial tree, but it's a holiday. I'm not in the Christmas mood, and Daniel does nothing to spark my spirit.

The Wrong Tool

I hear your voice and darkness goes
But it is short, I know
The clouds will reassemble
And it will be as so

Now that the holidays are over with the promise of change in the New Year, I try to get back on my economic feet. However, this man, who I once thought was the love of my life or soul mate, is a man with serious financial problems, dragging me down. I wonder if he has plowed through life, leaving a trail of empty bank accounts in his wake, or if he's having a run of bad luck.

The week drags on forever, until Friday. Daniel receives his first paycheck. The anticipation of financial relief keeps me optimistic all day, but by the look on his face when he jumps in the car, I realize it won't happen.

"I can only give you two hundred dollars this week," he says. "I have to buy tools."

"Maybe you can get a few every week."

"I need them now. If I don't show up with my tools, they'll fire me."

"No, they won't!" I smirk. "Don't be ridiculous."

"Just take me to the store."

Everything is urgent when he wants to buy something. Realizing there's no arguing with him, I drive to the nearest Home Depot.

I have a terrible feeling when we pull into the parking lot. "I'll wait in the car," I say.

"No, I want you to come in with me," he insists.

I roll my eyes and follow him up and down the aisles. Like a little boy in a toy store, it's clear he gets pleasure from these things. He picks up a wrench, examines it, then puts it down and picks up a spray gun. I stand impatiently by his side, listening to the beeping of the forklifts going up and down the aisles.

Finally, we head toward the checkout counter with three items in the cart. Thank goodness, we're finished. Before we get there, Daniel stops to examine a large, two-piece tool cabinet on wheels.

"Wow," he says. "I need this."

I look at the price tag and huff. The top is three hundred and fifty dollars, and the bottom is another five hundred and fifty.

"You said that you need tools, not a toolbox."

"I can't buy tools and have them all over the place. That's how things get lost."

"It's better to have tools with no box to put them in than an empty toolbox," I point out, but he's too far gone.

What kind of man does something like this?

It defies all logic.

The clerk rings up the merchandise, and Daniel counts out his cash.

"Florence, lend me fifty dollars. I'm short."

Disgusted, I stare at him. The money he gave me hasn't even settled at the bottom of my purse yet, and he wants some of it back.

"Come on," he says peevishly.

Under the curious gaze of the checkout clerk, I give him fifty dollars.

At the risk of ruining our weekend, I mention it again on the way home.

"You have no idea what it takes to do a job, Florence."

"What does *that* have to do with all the stuff you bought?"

He makes an abrupt turn, and we're now heading in the direction we just left.

"What are you doing, Daniel?"

"I'm taking the toolbox back. I can't deal with you."

"That's dumb. You already bought it."

"I don't want to talk about it anymore," he says, and the conversation is over.

The silence is maddening. Daniel's depleting my confidence, and I'm afraid to say anything because I sense that he's about to blow a fuse.

When we're almost at Home Depot, he changes his mind again and turns around to drive home.

Lately, we're arguing more, and it's always about money. It's the bane of our existence.

Daniel refuses to talk all night. We don't eat ice cream, and we don't get *comfy*.

Wide awake, I lie in bed, taking deep breaths. My chest feels like it's caving in. The feeling is overwhelming, as if I'm about to have a heart attack, but I know it's just anxiety.

untouchable

I flourished in the bounty
Of love that was expressed
Until it stopped abruptly
Left me heartsick and depressed

The weekend has gotten off to a bad start. Daniel is on the other side of the bed when I open my eyes in the morning. There's no danger of him holding me down, so I slip out of bed. I enjoy the solitude, check my e-mail, and watch the morning news.

Two hours later, I hear him thumping down the hallway. He nudges me playfully. "I know I'm hard to deal with," he says. "Sometimes, I'm untouchable."

"Don't make yourself sound mysterious," I say. "You're autocratic and cold."

"I'm used to getting my own way." He gives me that little boy smile. At least he acknowledges that he's demanding. I think about something funny my sister said about men. *"You don't know what kind of nut you have until you crack it open."* I laugh and forgive him — *again.*

"Why don't we go back to bed?"

"We just woke up, Daniel."

"Yeah, but I'm so tired. I had a shitty night's sleep because of you, your cat, and the train."

"You sure do sleep a lot," I say.

"I'm just feeling down," he mumbles.

What does he have to be down about? He's in sunny Florida, living off me.

"Is it depression? Maybe you should see a doctor. You might need medication."

He ignores my comment. "I'm just stressed out."

Daniel plops down at the computer and lights up a cigarette, blowing the smoke at me with no regard.

"The fan," I say, pointing to the ceiling. "You're smoking me out."

"Maybe if you stop smoking, you'd feel better."

"No, it's too late for that."

"It's never too late to get healthy."

"It's too late for me. I'm going to die soon." He opens the window but makes no move to switch on the fan.

"It's beautiful outside. Why do you have to smoke in the apartment," but I'm talking to the wind. Clucking my tongue, I get up and flip the switch. I wish it weren't Saturday. At least during the week, I have peace.

"Babe! You look so stressed out. The next time I get paid, I'm going to buy you something nice."

"You don't have to buy me anything. Just help me with rent and food."

"Okay, let me go to my secret bank account, and I'll get you the money," he jokes.

"You're crazy, Daniel, but I may be crazier for putting up with you. At least go smoke outside from now on."

"All right." He undoubtedly thinks he'll get around that, but from now on, I'm putting my foot down — no more smoking in the apartment!

⁓✦⁓

On Monday morning, Daniel rubs his neck. "I can't believe I have to work this hard at my age. I should have planned better for retirement."

"Next weekend will be here before you know it."

"That's easy for you to say. You sit around doing nothing all day."

"I don't have to work." *Not yet, anyway.* After selling my house, working full time wasn't on the menu, but if I keep using my money, I'll have no choice soon.

"If you sell your house, you can retire."

Daniel shrugs and looks away. "I'll never get what it's worth in today's market. Besides, I'm not sure what I want to do anymore."

"Are you saying you want to go back to New York?"

"No, but it's *our* house. We should hold onto it for our future. Once we improve our financial situation, we'll be fine. I promise."

I want to believe his promise that we'll have a good life together and cling to that illogical prospect to keep from having a mental meltdown, but all the pieces lay before me. He's continuously reminding me how his kids love the place and how he would love to hold onto it for them. I'm sure he promised Lisa the house, too.

It's a bargaining chip to control her, his daughters, and me.

Hmm! I think I've uncovered the root of his deception.

I never wanted his house anyway—just his love. But I'm not sure he's capable of real love.

Turning his attention to the computer, he stops talking to me and logs onto eBay.

"You have to stop buying things," I state emphatically. "You're using my account, and the bill is up to eleven hundred dollars."

"Don't worry about it."

"I have to worry about it. You promised to resell all those celebrity pictures. What's going on?"

Daniel stares right through me. His eyes darken. "Every time I have an idea to make money, you shoot me down. Because of you, I've lost interest."

"Don't use me as an excuse," I say, jumping up and pacing the floor. My eyes flash with anger. "You never do what you say you're going to do. You never follow through with anything. Now, you want to blame me. Why did you buy all that stuff in the first place?"

"I'm not justifying myself to anyone," he says, his response just as heated. "I'll pay you for the pictures."

I'd like to believe him, but I don't. It's my fault, too. I let him drag me by the nose, only to end up in debt.

Bitter Honey

I flourished in the bounty
Of love that was expressed
Until it stopped abruptly
Left me naked and obsessed

Daniel wants me to come with him outside to have a cigarette. I don't want to, but I'm trying to enforce the *no smoking in the house rule*.

While we're out there, a neighbor comes outside to walk her dog.

"What a beautiful dog," he says and sighs. "I had a dog like that once."

"Oh! What happened to him?"

"Florence got rid of him."

My mouth drops open, and I stare at him in disbelief. "Because he didn't take care of him," I explain. "He wouldn't even take him to the vet. The dog had no shots but plenty of fleas. He never took him outside, either. The poor dog was so stressed out in the apartment, and he bit himself raw."

"Oh! Well, eh, maybe someday you'll get another dog," she says.

"I hope not!" I rant. "Daniel shouldn't be allowed to have pets." I know it's cruel, but he started it. I want to add children, too, but I don't dare.

If Daniel is upset, he shows no sign. He looks amused. I think he loves confrontation.

Daniel's phone is blinking an alert that there's a text message from Lisa. *Call me.*" Lisa has been texting him more often lately. I try to be understanding. She *is* the mother of *his* children, but I get the feeling that he's up to something.

"Florence, do you realize I haven't seen my kids in eight months?"

"Why don't you go to New York and visit them?"

"Actually, I was hoping they could come to Florida."

"What are they going to do here? Our apartment is small, and we don't have a pool. Besides, you have to work. Who'll watch them while you're at work nine hours a day?"

"We'll talk about it later."

What's there to talk about? If we buy airline tickets for them, they will have to be on my credit card.

After dinner, Daniel picks up his phone. "He-y-y, my little honey, do you miss me?" he coos and turns on the phone speaker.

"Yes, Daddy," his eleven-year-old daughter chants.

"How would you like to come to Florida for the summer?"

My eyes dart up at him. *The whole summer?*

"Can we go to Disney World?"

"Of course, we can. You'll love Florida. In fact, you're going to want to live here."

Live here?

Forced to wait until the conversation ends, I hold my tongue until he hangs up.

"Why did you promise Colleen she could come for the whole summer? Anything longer than a week or two is unreasonable."

"This doesn't concern you, Florence. They're my kids. I want to see them."

"Them? You mean you want Emma to come, too?"

"They're sisters. I can't separate them. Don't worry about it." He grimaces. "It's none of your business anyway."

"None of my business? You want to saddle me with two children all summer. That is my business."

"What do you do all day anyway?"

"It's none of *your* business." I shoot back.

"If you won't help me, I'll make other arrangements."

Watching a small child for an extended time terrifies me, although I was a good mother to my two children. That was over twenty years ago. Nowadays, I have less patience for children. I'm too old for this, but it's apparent. He doesn't care about me. Retreating to the bedroom, I slam the door.

Daniel sits in the living room watching *Criminal Minds*, making me feel guilty. Perhaps I'm unreasonable. They *are* his children.

"All right," I tell him. "The kids can come, but you have to promise to find a summer camp they can attend."

He looks up and gives me a heady smile. "You're the best, Florence. We can check on flights in the morning. Let's go get *comfy*."

Sleep comes slowly, but soon I fall into an uneasy slumber. A soft moan escapes from the back of my throat. My subconscious is crying again. I'm *free falling*. Strangely, I don't fight it, accepting my fate as I speed toward the ground.

ⅇⅈⅈⅈⅇ

Daniel has promised to give me two hundred dollars a week, one hundred for living expenses, and one to go toward the money he owes me. At that rate, it'll take forever for him to pay me back, but at least he intends to try.

Before I met him, I had a house in Georgia, a townhouse in Florida, a nice car, and money in the bank. I've lost so much and strayed so far from where I wanted to be. I don't know how to get back. Hit with a psychological stun gun, I can't do anything to change my course. At least we have the dream of living on our boat, the one thing that binds us. We pack up food and tools and then head to our boat's west coast.

"I have a lot of work to do on those engines," he warns, "so I don't want you bothering me with silly-ass questions or stopping me so I can help you."

"I won't need your help," I say. "I'm planning to sand the cabin doors."

"Those doors are too far gone, Florence. It'll take hours to get that glue and varnish off. It's not worth it. Throw them in the trash."

"I think I can save them," I insist.

Daniel shakes his head. "Don't come crying to me when it doesn't work."

"Don't worry. I won't."

I'm not afraid to work. Already, I've stripped almost fifty pounds of laminate off the cabinets and interior doors. I want to restore it to the original natural wood finish. It's hot on the boat, even with two fans blowing at me. By the end of the day, I'm soaking with sweat, my nostrils are full of sawdust, and my body aches.

"Let's call it a day," Daniel says. He, too, is sweaty, his face and arms coated in grease from the engines.

"Can't we get another hour in?"

"Maybe you can because you've been sitting around all day, but I'm tired."

"I haven't been sitting all day. I've been sanding and hauling trash to the curb."

"Relax. I'm kidding. We'll come back in two weeks."

"We can't," I remind him. "The children will be here."

"They can come with us."

"We wouldn't get anything done. Emma is five years old. If we don't keep an eye on her, she can fall into the canal. Besides, they'll be bored to death."

"Fine, then we'll wait until they go home. Let's go home and get *comfy*, Babe."

No matter how much stress he puts me under, it dissolves when he folds me in his arms and we pretend to be in love. With two bowls of ice cream, we snuggle into bed and watch *Chopped*. There was a time when I thought that watching endless no-brainer shows on television was a waste of time, but I'm learning to accept it. These mundane things give our relationship a sense of normalcy and make it easy for me to stay in denial.

Our sex life is officially dead, but he coils his body around me like a second skin. I feel like I'm in a cocoon, stifled. "Isn't this *comfy*?" He has a knack for homing in on my neediness.

Maybe I'm naïve, but I often convince myself that it's more than the money that keeps him with me. He must love me — on some level. It twists my mind into a knot. My mind goes back to the night we first met.

"Remember when we got lost in the city trying to find that pizza place under the Brooklyn Bridge, and we ended up…."

"Yeah!" he says. "You had me walking for hours."

House on Wheels

We were lucky to find love
A whirlwind of emotion
It is gone… it disappeared
Like waves upon the ocean

I read the latest e-mail from eBay and gasp. RV? Feeling nauseated, I stand up and grab my desk to brace myself.

"You bought an RV?"

"Relax. I'm planning to flip it."

"How are you going to get it? It's in Chicago."

"I'll get a one-way ticket and drive it back here," he says. "Don't worry about it."

My puzzlement shows on my face.

"What now?" he asks in a cagey tone.

"How do you intend to pay for it?"

"If you must know, I plan to pawn my van."

I shake my head. "Just last week, someone offered to buy it for three hundred less than your selling price, and you said no. Now, you'll pay hundreds of dollars in interest until the loan is paid off. You're unbelievable."

"I have no choice."

"But...,"

"Stop!" he snaps, his eyes blazing. "I don't want to talk about it."

"Why do you have to be so gruff?"

His mood shifts, throwing my anger off balance. "I don't mean to be. That's just the way I talk."

"You're such a gangster, Daniel." The fight has gone out of me, and he knows it. "Why don't you ever include me in your plans?"

"You're just like every other woman I've known, trying to run my life."

"I'm just a spectator."

Since I met him, my emotions have been on a high-speed train powered — with no planned destination.

"You're so frustrating. I don't know why I put up with you."

A smile crosses his lips. "It's because you love me and want to marry me."

"No, I don't. You're not the marrying kind!"

"Babe! Relax. Everything is going to be fine." His tone is soothing and works to soften my attitude.

Daniel drains my energy, but I can't walk away. He has my money — and something else, but I'm not sure what it is. The more I struggle to get free from his web, the more entangled I become. My mind is racing.

"When are you leaving for Chicago to pick up that RV?"

"I'm not sure," he mumbles.

"You need to leave this week if you want to get back before your kids arrive."

"There you go again, trying to control my life."

I can't tell if he's serious. He continuously banters with New York sarcasm; I get it, but I tire of the game.

"I never know if you're coming or going," I press.

"Today is Sunday. We should have fun. Let's go to the beach."

Does it matter? I can use a little downtime. Just give me a few minutes to pack some stuff."

❦

With four hundred dollars on a pre-paid credit card in his pocket, I drop Daniel off at the airport so he can claim his RV in Chicago and drive it back to Florida.

Relief washes over me as he disappears through the security gate. I know he'll be back, but my sense of freedom is exhilarating. Lately, he weighs me down, and he's getting heavier. I wish our relationship would get better, but deep down, I realize it might be too late.

Daniel's absence has a calming effect on me. When I get home, my first impulse is to clean. I even rearrange the furniture. It somehow helps me organize my thoughts. I'm not eager for his return.

It takes him all day to reach the outskirts of Chicago, and he calls to let me know he's arrived
. "I got the RV, and I'm heading home," he announces.

Geez! He's gone for one day, and he's rushing back. Maybe he misses me, or he senses my distance. He calls me from the road every few hours. For the first time in a long time, we talk. He's relaxed and lets his guard down.

"I haven't been myself since I came to Florida," he says, "but all that's going to change."

There was a time when I believed him, but now I'm skeptical. Daniel's a manipulator, and he is very good at it. He uses humor, and I can't stay mad when he makes me laugh. His sense of humor lulls me to forget I'm dealing with a snake. Admittedly, he is a funny guy — very entertaining.

Fifty miles from home, Daniel calls. "Babe, I need you. I'm running out of gas."

"What do you want me to do?" A familiar sick feeling forms in the pit of my stomach.

"Either you drive here with some money, or let me use your credit card to gas up."

I'm tempted to leave him stranded, but I'm not about to drive this late at night, so I give him my credit card number.

Surrender

I want to fly... I want to flee...
Into the open sky
Trapped on earth... I cannot leave
A tear is in my eye

Daniel is standing in front of the thirty-four-foot house on wheels, beaming from ear to ear as if he's scored a personal victory.

"What do you think?" he asks.

You may end up living in it! I open my mouth to voice my thoughts and decide against it.

"It's big!"

"My boss said I could park it at the shop."

Thank God.

"She's a beauty, isn't she?" He pats the door and then turns his attention to me. "So, did you miss me, Babe?"

I nod, happy he's leaving for work and taking the monstrosity with him.

Once he's gone, I brew a fresh pot of coffee and fire up my computer to do some writing. Not even an hour has gone by before the phone rings.

"Florence, can you bring me a cup of coffee?"

I can hear the whooshing of a match and the sudden intake of air as Daniel inhales.

"I'm busy."

"You're not coming to visit me for lunch?"

"I can't keep running back and forth to your workplace. I have things to do."

"What's more important than seeing me?"

I roll my eyes. "I'm going to lunch with my daughter."

"Can't you swing by here first?"

"All right." *Why can't I say no?*

"And bring me a cup of coffee."

As usual, the other employees stare at me when I arrive. I wonder what they're thinking—that I'm a lovesick fool who can't stay away from her man even while he's at work.

I cringe. They don't know Daniel—*or maybe they do*.

"Ah, there's my Babe," he says, putting down his paint gun and walking toward me.

"Here you go," I say, handing him the coffee. "I'll pick you up at five."

"Stay for a minute," he says sweetly. "I'll take my break."

Suspicious, I wonder what he's up to, but I follow him to his workbench.

"So, what's on your agenda today, little woman?"

"I told you. I'm having lunch with Annmarie. You have a terrible memory."

"I'm old." His eyes twinkle. "We're old." He gazes at me with comradely admiration. Is it sincere? Maybe I'm paranoid, but I'm always looking for a crack in his armor.

"I have something to tell you," he says, "but you're not going to like it."

"What now?"

"I've decided not to flip the RV yet. I want to keep it while the kids are here so we can go camping. I want them to have a good time, and I don't care what it costs."

"I hope you didn't promise them more than you can deliver!"

He raises his hand to quiet my questions. "Stop! I'm going to sell my van."

My ears perk up. I've been begging Daniel to sell it. It's sitting in the pawnshop parking lot for over a month now.

"There's more."

"What?" My heart starts to pound.

"Now, don't have a conniption."

I shudder to think about what he needs now.

"I'm buying the kids a Sea-Doo."

"Really? Are you nuts? They're too young for that."

"This guy is selling it and wants four hundred dollars."

Four hundred dollars?" my voice rises.

"Be quiet. Do you want everyone to hear you?"

"You know how hard it's been for me to pay the bills. Your children are coming, and I don't even have enough money for groceries."

"Relax. I'll give you money for food."

"You better!"

"We'll talk about it later. I have to get back to work."

I drive away, trying to make sense of him. Daniel feels guilty about not seeing his children. I get that, but I suspect he's trying to buy their love.

Annmarie is sipping a glass of wine when I get to the restaurant.

"What took you so long?"

"Daniel," I sigh.

She nods. "Let's go shopping after lunch."

"I'd love that," I say, "but I have to pick Daniel up at five."

"You can be a little late, can't you?"

"No, he gets crabby if I'm not outside the gate at quitting time. I don't want to hear him, bitch."

After lunch, we walk around the mall, just like old times.

"I enjoyed having lunch and shopping," she says. "We should do this more often."

I nod.

Annmarie drives away, and I feel a little melancholy. She's right. We should get together more often. I need to break out of my Daniel bubble more often.

On the way to pick up Daniel, I receive a phone call for a potential job.

He jumps in the car when I pull up. "Did you have a good time with your daughter?" *Hmm!* He's in a good mood.

"Yes. We had lunch, then went shopping. I think I got that job I applied for last month."

"Job?" His face drops, and he stares at me with an expression of horror on his face. "You can't work! My kids are coming."

"I told you, Daniel. You need to find a daycare or summer camp for them. Either that or take off from work."

"I can't do that," he mumbles. "I need the money."

"Well, I can't watch your children *all* summer."

"I thought you were going to help me watch them."

"I will help... sometimes. But I can't do it every day. I have to work. I need money too."

"You don't need to work. I'll pay you."

"Really?"

"I sold the van," he says, pulling out a wad of cash from his pocket. This should be good news, but technically, I hold the title.

I suddenly yearn for my mother but resist the urge to call and burden her. She'll only tell me to send him packing, anyway. As if it's that easy.

No, I don't want to get my family tangled up in this mess.

Trapped between my insecurities and fears about the future, I drift off to sleep, but my inner voice gives me a wake-up call. It's happening more often. Unresolved concerns I ignore during the day roll around in my head at night.

Skype

The sun was bright around me
But now it is snuffed out
Hidden by the clouds
Darkness all about

Daniel's eyes come alive when his daughters run into his arms. It's been over a year since he's seen them. They missed him, I can tell, although he never spent much time with them. I'm surprised the little one even remembers him.

The next few weeks will be difficult. I've told Daniel there are two rules. They cannot sleep in my bed, and two, they cannot use my computer. With those boundaries in place, I hope I can handle anything.

Before we go home, we make a stop at the supermarket. I would have preferred that Daniel give me the money to shop, but he claims he can get everything we need for one hundred dollars. He buys an assortment of sugary cereal, hot dogs, cold cuts, and snacks, then we drive back to the apartment and get them settled.

The first thing he wants to do is take his daughters to the beach. Before we go, he makes a trip to the sporting goods store and comes out with two boogie boards, snorkel gear, and toys.

Daniel is happy when he has money, and his joy is contagious. I have to admit, the excitement on their faces when they see the ocean for the first time is delightful. What's so bad about relaxing on the beach while he swims with his children? I read a book and wave to them as they bob up and down in the waves.

By the time we get home, the salty air has tired us out.

"What's for dinner, Florence?" he asks.

"Hamburgers."

"I don't like hamburgers," Emma cries.

Daniel jumps up and grabs a pan.

"I'll make you a grilled cheese, honey."

It's the first time I've ever seen him lift a finger to cook. I have to hide my smirk.

"What about you, Colleen? Would you like me to make you one of my world-famous grilled cheese sandwiches?"

"No, I just want a salad, Daddy."

Even though she isn't fat by any means, I can relate to her preference.

While we crowd around the small coffee table to eat dinner, he jokes, and his children bask in his attention.

"Isn't Florence great?" he asks. "She'd be a good mommy. Do you think I should marry her?"

"Yes!" little Emma chirps.

My mouth freezes, and I stop chewing. What is Daniel up to now? They have a perfectly good mother back home. I can't help but wonder whether he's manipulating his girls or me.

Everything is fine until bedtime. Emma cries for her mother, and Daniel asks if I'll sleep with her. He's testing me. I have to think fast.

"I'll rock Emma on my lap until she's asleep, and then you can move her into the bed," I suggest, and it works. I've survived day one.

❧

While Daniel is at work, his children watch movies I've rented from the video store. It's not so bad. I log on to my Facebook page and discover that my cousins are taking another vacation. Usually, I'd go with them, but I'm not free. They don't ask anymore, and I'm sure it's because I'm tied up with Daniel. My mother's words of warning haunt me. I've already raised my children and earned my freedom.

The phone rings. "Hey Babe, do you think you can bring the kids to the shop at lunchtime so I can see them?"

"Daniel! That's no place to bring small children. There's rusty metal all over the place, and they could get a nail in their feet."

"They can stay in the car," he says. "I just want to say hello and show them what I bought for them."

"Bought? What did you buy?"

"I don't want to talk about it on the phone. You'll see when you get here. Oh, and can you bring me a cup of coffee?"

We pull into the parking lot, and Daniel is standing next to a Sea-Doo.

Oh no! I thought he had forgotten about that. I look at him with a question. He ignores me and speaks to his daughters in the back seat.

"Look what Daddy bought for you."

Excited, the girls unbuckle their seat belts and clamber to get out of the car. I can't stop them, so I watch as Daniel plays Daddy Warbucks. He's spending money as if he has no obligations. His extravagance depletes his budget. Soon he's asking me for cigarette money or a soda. I'm disgusted but powerless.

"What are you guys going to do today?" he asks.

"I'm not sure. Maybe I'll take the girls to the beach if it doesn't rain."

He looks up at the darkening clouds. "Here!" he pulls out a twenty-dollar bill from his wallet. "Take them to the movies."

"I want to see the new Katie Perry movie," Colleen squeals.

I want to go home!

The girls scramble into the back seat. "Bye, Daddy," they call out as we pull away.

The movie tickets cost eight dollars each because it's in 3D. Daniel gave me twenty, and there isn't enough for three movie tickets. I wonder if I can leave them here and pick them up when the movie ends. Colleen is old enough to watch her little sister Emma and says she can handle it. That leaves four dollars for candy. We have thirty-five minutes before the movie starts, so I run to the dollar shop and let them each choose two candies.

After dinner, I leave Daniel with the girls and sneak off to the bedroom with a book. Even though the place is a mess, and no one makes a move to help clean it, I don't plan to come out until he has them tucked in for the night.

Like the night before, at bedtime, Emma cries for her mother. My heart goes out to her when she begs to sleep — with me. I'm tempted to let her, but it's only the first week. I'll be sleeping with her for the rest of the month while Daniel sleeps with his eleven-year-old daughter.

"No!" I stand firm.

Emma's sobs soften him, and he lets her call Lisa to say goodnight. She suggests we buy a Skype camera.

Head Games

How long can I live this way?
A fragment of your love
My dignity is hanging
One thousand feet above

Daniel goes to Walmart the next day and comes home with the device. The girls communicate with their mother while we sit and watch, fascinated by the technology. It becomes a ritual. He took the next two weeks off work. Part of me is relieved, but I know he'll have money trouble without a paycheck. Since he sold his van, budgeting doesn't concern him. He has tons of plans. First, he reserves a resort in Miami with a giant pool, even though I suggest finding one closer to town.

What a waste of money! Unable to control the situation, I kick back and enjoy two days in the sun while he bends backward to amuse his kids. Before we unwind back home, Daniel is arranging a camping trip. Emma is excited about camping in the RV. I'm dreading it.

"I think it's going to rain," I say.

"You're so negative, Florence," he taunts.

I don't shoot back because I don't want to make a scene in front of the children.

"Daddy, I don't want you to sell the camper," Emma says. "I want you to save it for me when I grow up."

"All right, sweetheart," he says. "If you want it, it's yours."

Daniel is getting on my nerves. *He has no clue how to handle children.* The minute she whines, he's buying something to shut her up. He puts the Sea-Doo in the water but can't get it started. We head back to the RV. It's hot and muggy, so we have to stay in the air conditioning.

I hate camping.

"Let's go fishing," he decides.

"You take the girls, Daniel," I'll wait here."

"I want to stay here, too," Colleen says.

"Great, Florence! Now, look at what you did."

"What *I* did?"

"I want to go fishing." Emma insists.

He glares at me and leaves with his daughter. Within an hour, they're back, and he has a sour attitude.

"I was busted," he says. "I forgot to get my fishing license."

I kept telling him to get one, and he put it off.

Just as I think it can't get any worse, it rains, and water leaks into the back bedroom where the girls are supposed to sleep. We all have to cram into the front. The camping trip is a bust. The only one who isn't affected is Colleen. She watches videos on my laptop. It's making Daniel grumpy.

"What do *you* girls want to do?" he asks.

"I want to go to Disney World," Colleen says, looking up from her movie.

"Me too!" Emma shouts.

"All right," he says. "Since it's your birthday soon, I'll make the arrangements."

Oh great! Another trip to hell.

❦

We're on the way to Disneyworld. Since I can't do much about it, I'm starting to enjoy all the activities — as long as he's paying.

"What do you want me to buy you for your birthday, Sweetie?" Daniel asks Colleen.

"I want a charm bracelet."

"Okay."

We drive up and down International Drive, stopping at one jewelry boutique after another until he finds a charm bracelet. He'll buy anything for his little honeys, anything except food! Daniel supplies them with a steady diet of junk, with no mention of a real meal. On the way back to the hotel, we pass a famous restaurant known for chicken wings, and upon Colleen's urging, I convince Daniel to take us. Everything's fine until we leave to get her a cake. At the supermarket, he pulls me aside.

"Stop it, Florence! You made me spend thirty-five dollars at that restaurant, and you know I'm running out of money."

"It's your daughter's birthday. That's where she wanted to eat. Besides, you've been spending a lot *more* money on other things."

"It's none of your business," he sneers.

I refuse to talk to him for the rest of the night, but he doesn't care. Colleen blows out the candles on her cake.

"Do you remember our horse Nabisco?" he asks Emma.

"No." She looks puzzled.

"Yes, you do," he insists. "You used to ride on him."

"She was two years old," Colleen reminds him.

"Surely, *you* remember. Right, honey?"

"Yes, I remember Nabisco," Colleen says. "I remember the house too. You told Mommy we had to get out."

Daniel's eyes turn cold and menacing. "You've been brainwashed."

Colleen looks down.

"Look at me," he says. "Your mother had a new boyfriend every month. She used to drag you and your sister along with her. I tried to protect you."

"Stop, Daniel," I say.

"Stay out of it, Florence."

I shake my head in disgust. He's despicable, playing head games with a child.

"Can we go swimming now?" Emma whines.

Daniel snaps out of his lecture with a smile. "Of course, sweetie." They dive into the pool.

Soon, Colleen joins them, splashing and having a great time.

"Isn't Florida great?" he shouts. "Why don't you tell your mom you want to live here?"

Super Sleeper

I want to see the ocean
And sit upon the sand
I need to be in motion
It's what I always planned

Ever since his children went back home, Daniel's been depressed. It could be because he sent them back to Lisa and her boyfriend, Hank, a man who essentially is their *real father*. He acts all strong and overbearing, but he's a little boy in a man's body in reality.

Daniel refuses to go out, not even for a walk. He's throwing a pity party, crying about all the things he did wrong in his life. He complains about getting old, his body aches, or it's a gloomy, rainy day. All he wants to do is sleep. I call him a super-sleeper! Even the boat doesn't hold his interest anymore. We were excited about renovating it for a while, but lately, we've been arguing about how to decorate it.

Let him sleep his miserable life away; I don't care anymore.

In bed, he clings to me as if I were an inflatable life raft. I struggle to stay afloat. I want to help him, but he's too far out in the water. Besides, know what they say about helping a drowning man. He'll pull you under with him. Daniel's a heavy burden. He makes me feel like a log submerged in the water under his weight.

Terry, the woman from California, has sold the house he helped renovate. Unable to contact her, he's frustrated. He could kiss it goodbye if he had any money coming to him. I pack it neatly in my box of denials.

Daniel calls me from work. "I have to pay my storage, or they're auctioning off my stuff. Can you pick me up early so I can make a payment?"

"I'm in the middle of something right now. Can't it wait?"

"I have to make the payment before ten o'clock," he argues.

I don't want to pick him up, but he'll never forgive me if he loses that junk. Why did I have to answer the goddamned phone? "I'll be there in twenty minutes."

Daniel jumps into the car when I arrive. On the way to the Western Union, he counts his cash. "Shit!"

"What now?" *I shouldn't ask.*

"Babe... I need you to lend me sixty dollars."

"You have to be kidding. What happened to all your money from selling the van?"

"I spent it when the kids were here."

"I'm not surprised how you bought everything in sight for them. Now you want me to lend you money?"

His eyes darken. "Forget, I asked."

"Oh, stop!" I want to scream. If I give it to him, my boundaries will slip. Desperation and insanity — they're the only things driving me now.

"Here, take it, but I want it back when you get paid on Friday, plus the gas money to take you to the bank."

"Why do you have to be so petty?" he snipes.

"Petty? Here I am, bending over backward to help you, and you have the nerve to call me petty? By the way, do you plan to sell that RV?"

"I don't want to talk about it right now."

I get the feeling he's keeping something from me. I want to ask, but he'll never tell me the truth. Lies fall off his tongue like rainwater off a rooftop.

Whenever I catch Daniel in a lie, he says I'm irrational and insecure. I'll never get the truth out of him.

∽∽∽

My shitty day gets shittier. Daniel calls to tell me he was too late paying the storage, and everything was auctioned. In my mind, I watch the money I lent him flush down the drain.

He's feeling sorry for himself but has no empathy for the money I loaned him to keep it floating.

"If you had picked me up sooner, I would have made the payment on time."

"Don't you dare blame this on me. I've been helping you pay for that storage for almost two years."

The phone goes dead. Within an hour, Daniel walks through the door.

"What are you doing home so early?"

"I quit! My boss tried to tell me how to do my job. As if I don't know how to paint a car! I'm the best painter he ever had. He said, 'My way or the highway.' I took the highway. The old bastard didn't know what hit him. I'm an easy-going guy unless you fuck with me."

I feel bad for his boss. Daniel can be intimidating, especially with that gruff New York accent. The poor southern gentleman didn't stand a chance against someone like him. If he didn't hate Yankees before, I'm sure he does now.

"What are you going to do for money, Daniel?"

"I'll find another job!"

"Or sell something," I suggest. "What about the RV? You said you would sell it, but it's sitting in a parking lot. Unless you're planning to move into it, you don't need it."

Daniel doesn't answer. I suspect I've hit upon the truth. Maybe he's decided to travel around the country with Josette and her *sammies* after all.

I should be financially sound and would be if it weren't for Daniel. Before I met him, I paid my bills in full each month. Now, I agonize over the monthly payments. Apprehensive about his future abuses of my money, I withdraw two thousand dollars and stash it in my safe deposit box. Even going to the mailbox is a scary venture. I'm relieved when it's empty, but today there's an electric bill. I shudder and open the envelope. I show the statement to Daniel.

"How did we use this much energy?"

He rolls his eyes, and I can almost see his brain shutting down.

"I don't have enough to pay for it."

"Just pay the minimum."

"They'll charge interest. I'll never get the balance down. I'm on the verge of bankruptcy."

"Stop exaggerating, Florence." He glosses over the situation. Ordinarily, he takes me along for the ride, but not today.

"It's not fair. I have to carry the weight alone."

"Don't you think I know that I'm a burden? You're always rubbing my nose in it."

"I need you to help out."

"I don't think you're happy with me, Florence."

He knows how to push the panic button.

"It's not that I'm unhappy with you. I'm not happy with the situation. I'm almost broke, and you don't care."

Daniel's eyes soften. "You're a wackadoodle. Of course, I care. I'm in a bad way right now. You're the one who wanted me to come to Florida. I told you from day one I didn't have the money."

"You make me nervous. Every time we argue, you threaten to go back to New York."

Daniel stares out of the window. "I need to make a living, or *we* can't stay here."

"Daniel, once you sell your house, you'll have money."

"The market is bad. Only one couple came to see it. Besides, the listing expired."

"Are you going to list it again?"

"I don't think so. I want to hold onto it."

"Why? You keep saying you don't want to live there."

I can't help thinking he has a hidden agenda. Vague as ever, he intends to keep me in the dark.

"Besides, I thought you wanted to live on the boat."

"Plans can change. We have to think about our future."

"Florida is my future!"

"What good is it if you don't have money?"

"I would have money if...."

Anger emanates from Daniel's eyes, stopping my retort.

"Even if I weren't here, you would eventually run out of money."

"If you weren't mooching off me, I'd have a hell of a lot more."

"I don't want to talk about money anymore. Daniel heads to the bedroom to sleep his problems away.

Time

I gave you all; you did right back
We had a love that did not lack
The promise of true happiness
No longer in our grasp

There's another e-mail from eBay responding to his last bid for a car. *Here we go again.*

"Did you bid on another car, Daniel?"

"Yeah, I'm hoping I can find something to flip."

"Where are you going to get the money?"

There's an irreverent expression on his face. "I was hoping you'd lend it to me."

"Are you crazy?" He makes me squirm. I know that when it's time to pay me back, he'll tell me he can't because he has to buy a tool, pay a bill, or take his kids to Disney World.

"No... I can't use any more of my savings," I mutter defiantly.

"If it makes you feel better, you can have the title to my RV."

"Ha! If I remember correctly, you gave me the title to your van, and I didn't see one penny when you sold it."

"I should have kept it," he snaps.

"Don't even think about being angry at me. It's your fault. If you had sold the RV like you planned to, you wouldn't... *we* wouldn't be in this predicament!

"You don't understand, Babe. The only way I can make more money is by flipping things."

It's a clever ploy, but I'm not falling for it.

"What about all the other money you borrowed?" I ask. "I don't see you attempting to pay that back. I can't trust you. Find another way."

He doesn't answer. How I wish I could peek inside his head for one minute. Then, I would know what he's got planned.

❦

It's been a month since Daniel quit his job at the auto shop, but I'm afraid to push him. Like a pressure cooker, he could blow his stack.

"Let me use your card," he says. "I need cigarettes."

"You can't use my card to buy cigarettes."

"Then lend me some money. I promise I'll give it back."

"I don't want to spend money on cigarettes. That's why I quit twenty years ago. Why should I pay for your unhealthy habit?"

"Just let me use it," he says through clenched teeth."

Either I allow him to take advantage of me again or deal with his nicotine fit. If I don't let him use my card, he'll be miserable, thus making my life miserable too.

"You can have the money on one condition."

"What's that?"

"You need to find a job, Daniel."

"Deal," he says with a sly smile. "There's a body shop a few miles away. I want to check it out, but I need to borrow your car. It'll take me half an hour."

Begrudgingly, I let him have my debit card.

He grabs my keys with a quick hug and rushes out the door.

I check my bank account an hour later, looking for the four-dollar deduction. It says an eight dollars withdrawal is pending. *That little bastard! He bought himself two packs.*

It feels like hours, but in reality, he's only gone forty-five minutes. There's a smile on his face when he comes home.

"Did you get the job?"

"Yeah, but… It's twenty minutes away."

"That's far. How are you going to get there every day?"

"Relax." His voice is unbending. "I'll give you money for gas."

Defeated, I grab his keys and leave to go to the store.

"I left you a surprise in the car."

"What? No gas?"

"Very funny."

When I open my car door, there's a chocolate-covered cherry on the gear stick. It makes me smile. I'm tempted to go back inside and revel in his good mood, but I drive off.

⤸⟢⤷

Before I drive Daniel to work in the morning, I pack him a lunch and put coffee in an empty water bottle. At first, I was afraid it would melt the plastic. Relieved it didn't, I'm glad I won't lose any more cups. He takes them and never brings them back.

I hold Daniel to his promise on payday—every penny he borrowed during the week plus a few dollars toward the living expenses.

His expression is hard as he pulls out a hundred-dollar bill from his wallet.

"Here, take it!" He throws it at me. "You're a money-grubbing nag."

"You're kidding, right?" My heart is beating so hard. I think it will explode out of my chest.

"I'm going back to New York," he threatens.

"I don't care anymore!" I say, staring him down. "You're a vampire! You're sucking the life out of me."

Shocked by my brazenness, his lip curls. He pulls another fifty dollars from his wallet.

"Relax. I'll give you more money next week." He puts his arm around me. "You're so cheap!"

"I am not! What is it going to take to make you understand?"

"You know I have bills," he says.

"Yes, I do, too, and I've been patient, but… what about the Rolex? You promised if things got tight, you'd sell it."

Daniel's eyes glaze over.

"Where is it?"

"I left it back in the house."

"That was stupid. What if your tenant finds it? What if there's a fire?"

His eyes flash with anger, and the veins in his neck bulge. "Stop," he threatens. "You don't want to get me mad. It won't be pretty."

"Bring it on," I hiss, feeling antagonistic.

"You're such a little viper when you're mad."

Daniel fires me up with his anger and teases me back when I'm close to the edge.

"If something ever happens to you, I'll never get my money back."

"Relax… I'll put you in my will. Besides, I still have my watch. Are we going to eat or not?"

He has me on a rollercoaster of emotions. I nod, but my appetite is gone. *I wonder if Daniel really does have a Rolex.*

Scociopath

Meteorologists report hurricane winds in the Gulf of Mexico, and my boat is sitting in a canal beyond my reach, in danger of sinking. I'm trying to wrap my head around the possibility of losing a ten-thousand-dollar investment.

I had no business buying a boat. Everyone tried to warn me, but Daniel insisted we could float away and leave all our problems behind. He was supposed to be my second chance at happy-ever-after. The thought of sailing off into the sunset seemed like a dream within my reach but quickly became a nightmare.

"I can't take off from work," Daniel tells him. "We'll go there next weekend."

It's more like he *won't* take off from work, but I know better than to argue. Once Daniel has something in his head, there's no room for discussion.

He calls a neighbor who agrees to check on the boat. Bill reports that the lines were too tight, and he loosened them to give the vessel some slack.

"Shouldn't we go?" I gently ask when he hangs up, but I'm talking to a brick. I can never pin him down to specifics. I know from experience that what he says doesn't match what he does.

"Relax, Florence. The boat is fine." He smiles, and his amber eyes crinkle at the corners.

"We're going next weekend, though, right?"

His smile disappears. "I said we would, Florence. You sound like a broken record. Now stop asking, or we won't go."

"You said we were going two weeks ago. I'm at your mercy."

"No, you're not," he says. "Go without me."

"Maybe I will!" I say petulantly.

In reality, I need him, and he knows it. I don't know anything about boats. I've always said I'd never let anyone control me, but my words hold no conviction. I've already let Daniel dictate my life in so many ways.

I'm not happy with the direction my future is heading—but I lack the courage to make the hard decision to change it. The little bit of money I had in my bank account has dwindled, and my debts are mounting. Somehow, I feel removed. As if someone else is acting out my life. I can't let go.

Caught in a web of emotions, I can't divulge my problems to anyone. They wouldn't understand. Whenever I complain about Daniel, people offer their opinions. They get frustrated when I don't take their advice. Disapproval fills their eyes, making me feel ashamed. Strangely, women are more judgmental than men. I guess they don't think it could ever happen to them. My friend Sharon is the only one who understands because she's been through it herself. I take a deep breath and dial her number.

"Hi, Sharon."

"Hey, girl! How are you?"

"I'm... I'm.... "Oh, Sharon." I sob. "I'm so unhappy."

"What's wrong? Did you and Daniel split up?"

"No, we're still together, but I feel like I'm on a roller coaster. Daniel acts as if we're married, but there's no commitment. I've been going through all my money, and my credit card is maxed out."

"How much do you owe?"

"Twenty thousand dollars," I whisper as if saying it aloud would make things worse.

"You have to be kidding me."

"No, I wish I were. The interest is building every month, and my payments are like pebbles thrown into a lake."

"Well then, stop using the card."

"I already have, but I'm over my limit."

"I see. Are you able to pay the minimum?"

"Not lately. I've never had this problem before. It's Daniel. He thinks I can charge everything on my credit card, and I don't have the strength to say no. I don't know why I'm afraid to stand up to him. I must be stupid."

"You're not stupid! You just have no boundaries. He's playing you, and nothing will change until you learn how to say two little letters, n-o."

"I'm so embarrassed."

"Don't be! A lot of women find themselves in abusive relationships."

"Oh, no! It's not like that. Daniel is controlling and manipulative, but he would never hit me."

"Abuse is not always physical. Emotional and financial abuse is just as damaging. You need to ditch that man."

"I thought about leaving him so many times, but... Daniel owes me money, a lot of money. If I leave, he'll never pay me back!"

"Oh, Florence, whether you stay or go, you'll never see that money again. He doesn't care. He lacks empathy."

Empathy! The word rolls around in my head, and my mind peeks out from behind denial. Sharon's words squeeze at my heart. When we hang up, I look up the definition on the computer — lack of empathy. The term sociopath keeps coming up. I click on it and read the signs. My mouth drops open. Daniel!

Stages of a Sociopath

The first stage of a relationship with a Sociopath is known as love-bombing. You think you have met your soulmate. They'll bombard you with pretty words and convince you that they never met anyone like you before, and you're drowning in love and admiration. Vanity will be the convincing factor that traps you. It's hard to let go of such bliss, and you will find yourself on a merry-go-round, trying to catch the golden ring.

The second stage of a relationship with a Sociopath is referred to as "trauma bond." If only you behave the way he wants, you will be rewarded. You'll tolerate his outbursts and eagerly wait for the crumbs he scatters. They will string you along through manipulation as long as you have something they want. In that case, they will put you in limbo, giving only enough to make you believe there is a future for your relationship.

The third stage of a relationship with a Sociopath is devaluation. You know he's not treating you right, but you hold onto the hope that he really does love you and will come around. The dissonance between the memory of love and his uncaring demeanor will cause stress because your brain and heart are not on the same page. Fearful that you may lose him, denial is the only thing that can protect you from going insane.

Scarred

The middle of a road
Moving to one side
Traffic rushes by me
I stand by the wayside

Since my friend Sharon suggested that Daniel might be a sociopath, I've been reading about the dangers, and it's getting harder to pretend that nothing is wrong. I wanted to believe he needed my help, but my gut tells me I'm dealing with a ruthless conniver. He can control and charm me into submission because I fear the consequences. The truth rolls around my head to torture me.

It all makes sense. According to the article, sociopaths use their defense mechanisms to manipulate, control, and achieve dominance.

I have a hard time believing that Daniel is evil, but I struggle to find the good in the man. The evidence is indistinct, and I can't validate my feelings. If I pin him down, his explanations make enough sense to raise my doubt. It's easier to think he's a victim than to admit he's using me. Now that I'm aware of his psychological makeup, I'm one extra step ahead of him until I figure out what to do. I study his facial expressions and the tone of his voice, looking for a crack, but he's smooth.

Another characteristic of a sociopath is a short attention span. We've had the boat for over a year, and we're no closer to finishing it. Daniel jumps from one thing to another, and the engine is in pieces since he disassembled most of it.

The dream of living on the vessel is a distant memory. We should be cruising to the Bahamas by now. I doubt we'll ever realize that dream. I wonder if this is his way of getting back at me. He is the king of passive aggression. If he doesn't get his way, he goes into punishment mode.

The boat remains on the west coast of Florida and getting to it is a chore. If only he would bring it to this side. Then, maybe I could deal with the boat on my own.

"Maybe we can hire someone to drive the boat across Florida."

"I don't need to hire someone. I can do it myself."

Hidden behind his cocky exterior, I sense he's unsure. Perhaps Daniel's lying about his boating experience — or maybe he's scared? Why else would he be putting off the trip?

❧

I'm standing on the edge of a cliff. I think I'm going to fall. I can't stop pacing around my apartment. What's wrong with me? It shouldn't be a struggle to break away from Daniel, not now that I know he's a sociopath. *Why can't I cut the cord?*

Phycologists say that relationships with sociopaths are highly addictive. It must be true because that's how I feel — like an addict — and no one has sympathy for an addict.

The author of *Love Fraud* says the brain produces a hormone called dopamine, a chemical found in addictive drugs, and oxytocin, known as the "cuddle chemical."

Oxytocin is released into the bloodstream during intimacy and induces a feeling of calm, trust, and contentment. It also makes you want to stay with someone when you really should leave.

Toxic glue! That explains my craving for what Daniel calls "comfy." No matter how difficult he is during the day when he wraps his arms around me at night, I feel secure, and my bond deepens. However, sociopaths can't bond, unlike regular people—they merely pretend.

That's it! I'm addicted to dopamine! Daniel doles out the drug to manipulate me. He's like my old cigarette habit—hard to give up.

The sociopath and narcissist websites say "No Contact" is the only solution, but I'm not ready to lay my cards on the table. I need more time. Maybe my "No Tolerance Rule" will be enough. In theory, it sounds good, but as the light hits Daniel's shady character, it's getting harder to ignore his disorder. The battle of minds is draining me.

⌘

Trying to make everything look normal, I keep my suspicions secret until I can figure out what to do. Sometimes, I wish Daniel would disappear, but nothing is that easy. I know he can't go anywhere. How can he? Daniel has no money, no car, and a mortgage. I *did* convince him to come to Florida. He reminds me of that fact whenever things go badly for him. Then my guilt takes over. I can't just throw him out. Maybe he'll stay until something better comes along and then jump ship. I almost wish he would find someone else and leave me alone. No woman could resist him. It would be too late when they realize what's beneath the shiny wrapper. *They'd be trapped.*

I glance in the bathroom mirror and notice another gray hair. Daniel's aging me for sure. If he leaves, I'll cry, but I would endure the sting of humiliation. That's the only way I'll be free. Ordinarily, that would scare me, but in hindsight, I wish for another chance to make it on my own. I would wear it like a badge of honor and push past the pain. It's better than feeling stupid — stupid for trusting a man with my money.

There has to be a way to get through this unscarred.

Guilty as Charged

I think that I need more
For that, I must insist
But when I walk away
I will be sorely missed

Thank God it's Monday! Rain comes down in a lazy drizzle, but I don't care. I've made it through a touch-and-go weekend.

I hear his heavy footsteps in the hall. "It's already nine o'clock," he says in a panic. "Why didn't you wake me?" He grabs his cigarettes. "Let's go. I'm late for work." He doesn't appreciate what an inconvenience this is for me.

It takes fifteen minutes to drive him to work and another fifteen minutes to get home. I remind him that the rent is due this week on the way.

"It's not a good time to talk about this, Florence."

"It's never a good time. You either just woke up, you're tired, you're going to work, or you just got home. You always have an excuse." I can't hide the sarcastic tone in my voice. "I've been supporting you for years. It's not right."

"Yeah, and you keep throwing it up in my face," he snaps. "There's a hotel down the road. Maybe I'll move there."

"You would rather throw your money away at a hotel than help me pay the bills?" My voice rises as I pull in front of his shop.

"Stop yelling." He looks to see if anyone is around and jumps out of the passenger seat. "Now you've ruined my fucking day. Do me a favor. Pack all my stuff in a suitcase."

"Pack your own shit!" I yell.

A voice inside me screams *Run!* Adrenaline surging through my body, I slam on the gas pedal, the tires squealing as I race away.

When I get two blocks down the road, my phone rings, I know it's Daniel by the ringtone. No! I have nothing to say. I turn up the radio to drown out the tone and my thoughts.

When I get home, there's another credit card statement. A sense of impending doom envelops me. I'm afraid to open it, but I do. I have a gift for denial, but the truth is rearing its ugly head again. I toss it on the desk with all the other bills.

Whenever I complain about it to Daniel, he says, "Just default on your credit cards."

Default? Is that supposed to make me feel better?

After rejecting his calls all day, I break down and answer.

"He-y-y!" he says as if nothing happened. His ever-changing mood shifts once more. "I've been trying to call you all day. Where've you been? You're not mad at me, are you?"

"You *are* kidding, right?"

"Ah, Babe, you know I'm hard to deal with!"

"You make me crazy, Daniel."

Daniel is the devil, and I'm standing at the abyss, staring at the fire below, but he pulls me back from the edge of despair. With no more discussion of money, nothing gets resolved. I'm making friends with the devil.

༒

Hypnotized by the raindrops hitting the window, I twirl the ends of my hair and stare outside. I'm disappearing, a shadow of my old self. I think back to all the opportunities I had to leave Daniel. Maybe I could have met someone else, but I can't turn back the clock. I've wasted so many years of my life.

I've always thought of women who let their men control them as foolish simps. Now, I'm one of them. How does it feel? Humbling!

Despondent, I sit in front of my computer and debate whether to check his emails. Nagging insecurity gnaws at my brain like a hungry dog. I have to look. There's too much at stake, but I feel like a snoop, and I don't like it. I log on to his e-mail and scan his old messages. I stare at the name on my computer screen. JOSETTE! A wave of revulsion overtakes me. I feel as if someone has just kicked me in the stomach. He told me she was ancient history, and I believed him.

"Greetings, Woman: I'll be in New York this summer, and I have to talk to you. It's long overdue. Send me your phone number because I lost it."

The blood drains from my face. I suspected Daniel was e-mailing Josette and the other girls, but my ego got in the way. Warned numerous times, I thought I could handle it. I was wrong. He was always a cheater, but I quelled my fears as long as he was with me. What a fool I was to think I could control the situation! Jealousy is a strong shackle.

I check Josette's response.

"You really have some nerve. The time has come for you to pay me the money I lent you. I've been patient and have given you every chance to make good on the debt."

Money? Did he borrow money from her too? That must be what he meant when he told me it was *only business*. Josette trusted him, taking him as a man of his word. To him, their relationship was a business transaction. Perhaps, that's all I am. I read on:

"I also hope you've seen a doctor about your problem."

Problem? Josette knows about his erectile dysfunction.

"I wouldn't want some innocent woman to suffer, and when I say woman, I don't mean Florence. She's so naïve. She deserves everything she gets."

Her words sear my heart, and that feeling washes over me like in high school when I walked into a room and heard other girls talking and laughing about me. I can feel my guts drop. Josette doesn't know *me*. What did Daniel tell her? What does she mean by innocent women? I'm tempted to contact her, but what good would it do. She'd never sympathize with my plight, not after she tried to warn me about him. I didn't listen. Now I'm sure I'll never see a penny of the money I loaned him. I'll be broke while he moves on to his next victim.

Why should he be able to walk away and start fresh with someone else? I know that's not a good reason, but I can't help it. Even though I'd feel like a fool, it would bother me to know he was smiling at another woman with those amber eyes and teasing her with his sultry, sexy voice.

Stop it, Florence! It doesn't matter what he does with his life.

There's a hole in my bag of denial, and Daniel's lies are flying out, swirling around me, refusing to go back in. I've been thinking with my heart instead of my head, but I must face the sobering truth.

Daniel's a dirty rat bastard!

❧

My heart pounds wildly when I hear the front door open, and I try to pull myself together. There's a massive smile on his face as if all is right with the world. He tries to pull me to that place where it's easy to hide, but I refuse to fall for his manipulation. Should I hit Daniel with my discovery or wait until he settles down from work? The words are stuck in my throat.

"Dinner's almost ready."

"I'm not hungry."

"I made mashed potatoes and…,"

"You eat it," he cuts me off and runs his hand through his salt and pepper tousled hair splashed with silver paint from work. It's hard to tell where the real gray starts and the paint ends.

"Florence, I think our time together is coming to an end. Maybe I should move out."

My mouth is dry. My head is flooding with panic hormones. I pour a glass of wine to calm myself. "I'm sick of your threats, Daniel. If you're planning to move out, get out now!"

Taken aback, he stares blankly for a second.

"I read the e-mails from you and Josette."

Daniel inhales sharply. "You read my e-mail?"

"You told me she was just a friend." I bite my tongue hard, hard enough to taste blood.

"I'm not interested in Josette. How many times do I have to tell you that?"

"Then why are you planning to visit her? Oh, that's right. It's just business. I always suspected something was going on with you and her. You never told me you borrowed money from her—money you never paid back."

"That was over two years ago. I asked you then if you could help, but you refused. Remember?"

"You could have told me the truth."

"I didn't want to lose you." He tries to put his arm around me. "I'm sorry."

I fight to hold back my tears and pull away. "I don't want you to be sorry. I just wanted you to love me."

"Florence, I *do* love you."

He tells me sweet little lies to keep me frozen. I want to believe him, to melt into his arms and forget what I found on the computer, but I can't—not this time. Now, it's a matter of trust.

"You say you love me, but it doesn't feel like it. We don't even have sex like normal couples. You're a pathological liar! How can I believe a word that comes out of your mouth?" My eyes overflow with tears that trickle down my cheek. "It's been one thing after another. We're going nowhere. I refuse to beg for your love for the rest of my life."

He wipes my tears with his hand, and I pull back.

"I can't do this anymore, Daniel."

"What are you saying? Do you want me to leave?"

"I don't see how we can ever get past this."

Daniel's eyes turn cold. "Fine! Take me to my RV. I'll stay there."

When the car stops, he turns to me. "I guess we just don't get along," he says as if there is no one to blame and gets out. Before I drive off, he comes to the driver's side window.

"Can I borrow your phone charger? My phone is about to die."

I roll my eyes and hand him the charger. *Why can't I say no?*

I've always given him the benefit of the doubt, a broken soul I believed I could fix. There I go again, worried about his feelings and ignoring my own.

Why should I feel guilty?

Sinking Ships

Can't fix this problem
All on my own
If you still care
Don't leave me alone

The apartment is quiet. It feels strange. There's a quiver in the pit of my stomach, and my chest feels like it'll cave in. It hurts! Walking from room to room, I contemplate a life without Daniel. The feeling of loss is impossible to shake. I remind myself to breathe and ride through the anxiety attack. It's no use. I crumble to the floor in hysterical sobs. I have to find the strength to forget him. My heart remembers the plans we made together. Yet, my head reminds me of his lies and deceit. If I could only listen to my head instead of my heart, I'd be all right. Scraping myself up, I catch my ragged breath, determined to get back up and put on my big girl panties. What's the worst thing that can happen if I'm not with him? I won't die — It only feels like I'm going to die. Someone will help me through it. Of course, I'll have to endure a lot of "I told you so's!" I reach for the phone and dial my sister's number. It rings once, and I hang up.

Carol tries to call back, but I stare at the phone. We haven't spoken in a while. It's my fault. I let Daniel isolate me from my family. I don't have the strength to get through this on my own. I break down and call my mother.

"Florence? What's wrong?"

Fear wedges in my throat, and my tears gush in a cleansing release.

"You were right, Mom. Daniel is the worst thing that ever happened to me. I kicked him out."

"Don't cry," she soothes. "I know it's difficult, but I'm glad you've realized Daniel's not the man for you."

"I've known it for a long time, but I couldn't break away."

"Take one step at a time, Florence. I'm sure you'll figure it out. Remember, I love you...."

"Thanks, Mom. I feel a little better."

We hang up, and the phone rings again.

"Hi, Florence. It's Bill."

"Bill?"

"You know, Chuck's neighbor on the canal."

"Oh, yes. Bill. You're the man who checked on my boat during the storm."

"Right. Eh, I have some bad news." He hesitates. "Your boat is sinking."

"Sinking?" For a moment, the word sounds foreign as I try to understand what he's saying.

"We've had torrential rains this week. The bilge pump stopped. You need to come soon, or the boat will end up at the bottom of the canal."

"But I'm four hours away. There's no way I can get there in time."

"I don't have the equipment, but I could call my friend Chris at the boatyard. Maybe he can pump it out before it's too late."

"Please," I beg, "do what you can to keep it afloat."

"Okay, I'll try my best."

It can't sink! I need Daniel. I don't want to call him, but I can't deal with this problem alone.

There's no answer, so I leave a desperate message on his voicemail.

An hour later, Daniel returns my call. "What's going on?"

"The boat is sinking, and I don't know what to do."

"Are you sure?"

"Yes, I'm sure! I got a call from Bill." My voice cracks. "He's trying to get his friend to pump it out right now."

"Relax! Pick me up, and we'll drive there." He sounds annoyed, but at least he isn't leaving the problem to me for a change.

When I arrive, Daniel jumps into the passenger seat.

"Aren't you driving?"

"Isn't it enough that I'm doing you a favor?" There's humor in his voice, but for the first time since I've known him, I don't like him, even if he is kidding.

"Great," I snap. My hands are shaking. I want to scream, but I'm scared Daniel may change his mind and refuse to help me.

"All right, I'll drive," he snipes and gets out of the car for us to trade places.

As we drive across the state, I resist the urge to be negative, a trait that Daniel is quick to pin on me whenever I point out something that has the potential of going wrong. I grasp the remaining hope that maybe he'll fix this, but I know it's too late. My dream of living on the water is sinking along with the boat.

"I told you we should have bought insurance," I murmur.

"The boat is over twenty-five years old. It's uninsurable."

My phone rings. It's Bill's friend Chris. Frustrated, I hand the phone to Daniel.

"Thanks for trying, Chris," he says. "I appreciate it."

I sit up straight, and my eyes widen. Daniel hangs up and tosses me the phone but says nothing.

"What's going on?"

"The pump broke. We need to swing by the store and buy a pump."

"How did this happen?"

"I know exactly how it happened. Bill let the ropes out during the storm. The electrical cord must have disconnected from the dock, the battery went dead, and the bilge pump stopped working."

"We should have checked the boat two weeks ago. I told you…."

"Well, we didn't!" he cuts me off.

I want to point out that it's his fault for postponing the trip, but I didn't stand up to him. What did he have to lose? Nothing! After stopping at West Marine to charge a pump and a lantern on my credit card, we inch closer to my nightmare on the water, only ten more miles away.

We arrive at the boat, and I desperately scan the horizon. All I can see is the flybridge tilting to the side.

Both of us jump out of the car and race toward the boat. Daniel stares at the boat with an odd detachment, then sets up the pump. I look through the window. Everything is stacked on one side of the cabin, including the refrigerator and microwave. Faced with the reality of the situation, I think of all the hard work I put into this boat and recall the treasured items contained on it, all underwater. Thank God I never got around to hanging my father's painting of the lighthouse on the bulkhead.

Apprehensively, I wait, praying that this catastrophe is correctable, but nothing happens. The tide is too high, and the water is re-entering the side vents as fast as it's pumping.

"This pump is too small," Daniel says. "We need an industrial pump. We'll have to hire someone."

"I thought you said you knew about engines! Why can't you do it?"

"Even if I lifted the engine, it would have to be pickled, or it will rust."

I recall what my boss, Ben, had said about Daniel. Charlatan!

"What are we going to do?"

"Let's just walk away!"

I glare at Daniel, seeing him in the naked light of reality.

"Walk away? What do you mean?" I'm stunned at his audacity. "We can't leave the problem to Chuck and Nancy. They were nice enough to let us keep it in their canal."

He looks at me through devil eyes. "It's the easiest thing to do."

"It wouldn't be right."

"I'm trying to help you, Florence!"

"That's not helping. We can't walk away. I could never live with myself. Don't you have a conscience?"

The truth is plain to see. Daniel has no conscience.

"You never cared about me," I yell. "If you did, you wouldn't have let the boat sink."

"Are you trying to say it's my fault?"

"I wanted to come and check it after the storm, but you refused. You're the one who wanted this boat! How did I ever get involved with such a dishonorable man?"

He glowers at me but says nothing.

"I don't need you," I continue, no longer afraid. "What do I get out of this relationship anyway?"

"Fine." He packs up the pump and puts it in the trunk. "I'm done!" he says.

Taking one last look at the boat as he backs the car out of the driveway, the pain in my heart is excruciating. It's hard for me to understand there are people like him in the world.

Turning the Table

Don't know if I'll come back
You may have sealed our fate
Now you're not so sure
May be too late

After turning my life upside down and destroying my financial security, Daniel wants to pack up and leave without paying the last two months' rent on the warehouse—no compunction. I've come to realize he'd planned his departure months before he left. He lives in the moment, and when the moment doesn't suit him, he moves on. It's like that with everything... money, jobs, women, and the boat. I'm sure he'd want to stay here if I was willing to finance his moneymaking schemes.

"Daniel! You're going to leave me with the problem."

"You can come with me. I can find a job there. You won't have to worry about money. Things will get better, and we'll be on top again."

"Despite what you think, it's not all about the money. It's about trust. I don't trust you."

Daniel blinks as if I hit him. "I deserve that, but I wish you could understand. I screwed up my life financially, with my kids, and in my relationships. I don't want to lose you."

Great! Now he's working on my empathy.

The only way I'll have any decent future is to unhitch from his falling star. But if I want my money back, I must flex my mental agility and play the game. I'll go along with his little scheme for now, but I have to be careful. He'd devour my soul if he could, but I'll show him whose teeth are sharper.

I spend hours reading articles and blogs about narcissists and sociopaths, desperate for answers. Joining Internet support groups, I chat with other women who've gone through the same thing. They reach out to me with advice and understanding, but it doesn't lessen the pain. It's hard for me to admit that I was conned. All the warning signs were there, but I was blind.

He must think I'm a fool, and that bothers me. Ever since a friend suggested that he might be a sociopath, I've searched and read everything I could about the disorder.

ℝ

Most people are ruled by two primary emotions — love and fear. Daniel has neither. He plays a shell game, hiding his true feelings and feeding on my doubt. No matter which shell I choose, it comes up empty. I don't stand a chance.

I met Daniel shortly after my divorce. Thirty years of previous marriage assets must have been like catnip to him. He convinced me to sell the house claiming only then could we walk into our future life together. He played the moral argument that we were a 'couple,' and couples should 'support' each other. But when my money evaporated, so did he. Did he ever really love me? He sure put on a hell of a show. I reveled in his proclamations of a soul mate and the assertions that I was the first woman who touched his heart.

Whenever I complain about Daniel, people stare at me as if I'm stupid, but no one can make me feel worse than I do myself. I shouldn't look to him for comfort, but I trip and tell him I'm feeling down.

"Maybe you need Prozac!" he says.

Aha! Just like the narcissist website says, he's trying to make out that I'm the crazy one. They call it gaslighting.

"You say that about all women," I retort, "but if men like you took Prozac, women wouldn't need it."

He laughs. "That's funny!"

I'm not laughing.

Before I suspected Daniel was a sociopath, I realized something peculiar about him, but I ignored the gnawing doubts. Instead of walking away, I was trapped in a vicious cycle, reminiscing of a time when he showered me with affection, always seeking to revive the pleasure. Meanwhile, he faked the whole relationship. It's hard to believe someone would go to such lengths for a free ride and have no conscience about it.

I've passed pining over the honeymoon stage, but there is a longing and a need to understand. It's difficult to come to terms with the fact that he never was the man I fell in love with.

I made so many mistakes with my money, but the biggest mistake was letting him talk me into buying the boat. We could have had a good life living on the water. It was right there within our reach. Caught up in my fantasy, I trusted Daniel to navigate, but he ran us aground. When it sunk, he left me to deal with the mess.

Daniel says as soon as he finishes repairing his house in New York, he'll put it up for sale and come back to Florida, and we'll buy another.

"We're still going to live on a boat," he says, casting the bait.

Lies, lies, lies…. He thinks he can placate me with my dreams. I know his promises are empty, like the moon, close enough to see but too far to reach.

He makes no mention of the boat he manipulated me into buying—the boat that sank because he lost interest in it—ten thousand dollars—gone!

Little does he know, Chuck, the man who docked my boat, has agreed to help me retrieve it from beneath the water.

Daniel's invited me to come and stay with him in New York. He's in a great mood because he managed to sell the gas-guzzling RV the first day he listed it. Perhaps he's stringing me along, so I'll forget about the money he owes me… or maybe he wants to ensure that he can return to Florida if things don't work out in New York. It won't be because he loves me. Our breakup is inevitable, but it would bug me if he ends up in Florida. No, I have to deal with him on his own turf.

The experts say No Contact is the best way to handle a Sociopath. Just walk away and don't look back. But I can't! Why should I make it easy for him to escape without consequences?

Conventional wisdom says just walk away, but I can't! I feel used, and it's a bitter pill to swallow. I've given so much time, money, and emotion. It doesn't feel right to walk away without anything.

Maybe I *should* move in with him.

The thought of turning the tables and using him for once is intriguing. Besides, he has something I want. It's hidden somewhere in his house, and I'm determined to find it. A pang of guilt runs through me like a chill on a winter morning, but I remind myself I'm entitled to it.

Smell the Roses

I cannot blame you really
It is a choice you see
Consuming all you give
To fill the hole in me

Ordinarily, I would avoid any form of psychiatric care, but something's wrong. Although I don't need depression drugs, Anxiety is crippling me. This is too much for me to deal with alone. Desperate for relief, I find an anxiety group in town.

Looking around the table at the weathered faces, I wonder, *what the hell* am I doing here? Most people look like they just got out of a mental institution or wandered off the streets, looking for a place to land. Surely, there's no help for me here. By the time I move to leave, the counselor comes in and shuts the door. It's impossible to make a graceful exit. She introduces herself as a clinical psychologist, young and perky, with all her ducks in a row. We might have been friends if we had met in the outside world.

"My name is Karen. I'll be your group leader today," she says. "I'll pass this sign-in sheet around. Please print your name.

Oh great! Now there'll be a record of my attendance.

"Why don't we start by introducing ourselves and telling us why you're here today."

Thank God she starts on the opposite side of the table.

"My name is Ellie," the first woman says. "I am bipolar."

"No, you're *not* bipolar," Karen corrects. "You *have* bipolar."

The woman smiles and looks down.

A man wearing a well-worn black leather jacket strokes his long gray goatee before speaking. "My name is Tim, and I have anger issues."

Anger issues? I hope this place is safe.

Karen scribbles something on her notepad and nods to the next person.

"My name is Dave. I suffer from depression and anxiety, but I don't want to discuss it. I'm here because my doctor thought it would help."

"It's all right, Dave. No one is required to participate."

"My name is Leah, and I have depression. Everyone thinks I'm crazy. My own family won't talk to me."

I can tell she's a crier. Tears are already streaming down her face, her raw emotions on the surface.

"I'm Michael," the next guy says. "I just got released from the hospital after trying to commit suicide."

"Are you feeling suicidal now?" Karen asks.

"No, not today… but I think no one would care if I was dead or alive."

"Watch out, Mike," Tim warns. "She may Baker-Act your ass."

"There's no need to curse," Karen interjects. "We need to be mindful of other people in the group." Her eyes fall onto me, and it's my turn to divulge.

"My name is Florence. I, uh. I have anxiety attacks. I can't breathe."

Karen looks up from her notepad. "Do you know what's causing it?"

"Yes, I think so. I told my boyfriend I'd move to New York with him, but I'm not sure I want to go."

"Why don't you just say no?" Tim asks.

"It's complicated."

"If you loved him, you would want to be with him," Leah adds, dabbing her eyes with a tissue.

"I'm not sure…." Should I tell them my devious plan to get even with Daniel? No, they'd think I'm an awful person. *Maybe I am!*

"Then, it's your own damned fault!" Tim's eyes heat with anger. He makes me nervous.

"Tim!" Karen reprimands. "Don't yell!"

"Sorry."

"It sounds like you may be codependent, Florence," she continues. *There's that word, again.*

"Maybe that would be a good topic for today since I think everyone here has some form of codependency."

I had always rolled my eyes when someone used the term Codependent.

"I don't even know what it means," Dave says.

"Well, typically, codependency stems from growing up in a dysfunctional family. It occurs over a long period when a person seeks love from a source that cannot provide it. Maybe it was your mom or your dad, sometimes your siblings."

"My father was an alcoholic," I admit. "He preferred to spend his time at the bar. We rarely spoke to each other unless he was in a good mood. I felt like I was a disappointment to him, no matter how hard I tried to achieve."

"Did you ever discuss this with him?"

"No, I didn't talk about my feelings and thoughts with him because I was afraid he might get angry. It was better to ignore them."

"So fundamentally, you didn't feel entitled to your feelings and suppressed them. That may be why you have difficulty being direct about your needs." She smiles. "There's an old joke. What happens when a codependent is drowning?"

The group stares at Karen with blank expressions, waiting for the answer. "Someone else's life flashes before their eyes." No one laughs. Leah sniffles, and Dave slides a box of Kleenex to her along the table. "My sisters shun me. Even when I was on my deathbed in the hospital, they wouldn't come to visit me."

"I know how you feel," Mike says. "My family told me that if I tried to kill myself again, they hoped I succeeded. They say I'm just looking for attention and making the family look bad."

"Well, I *did* slap my older sister across the face last year," Leah says, "but she deserved it. I just want them to show me love."

"Perhaps you are expecting something from them that they can't give," Karen says.

"Is having codependency the reason I can't set boundaries?" I ask.

"Not necessarily. You might have a high tolerance for emotional abuse and inappropriate behavior. You can learn to set boundaries."

"Oh, I can set boundaries. It's enforcing them—that's the problem."

Maybe that's the problem. It made me the perfect victim. Now, I'm aware of his agenda, but I don't want to tip my hand and alert him that he's losing control. I'd better be careful.

"Things are going to be different when we get there, Flo. I even plan to stop smoking."

"Really?"

"Yeah. We'll walk and exercise—the whole thing."

There he goes again, making promises he has no intention of keeping. He must sense my indecisiveness because he's stepping it up.

Once I'm in submission, he'll go right back to his *usual* self.

Daniel's excited that I'm coming to New York. *Why?* I'm not sure yet, but I suspect it has something to do with my car accident settlement. He thinks I'm going to come into a lot of money. Whenever I want to get a rise out of him, I bait my hook and mention the financial settlement from my car accident. I wiggle the idea in front of his pea brain, and, voila, he bites.

"You're going to get at least $300,000," he says. I can almost see him salivating. I'm sure he's counting on the benefit, but he's wasting his time if he thinks he still has control over me and my money. This source has dried up!

Eventually, I'll have to face him, but not until I get what I'm after. Yikes! I'm getting the hang of this dishonesty routine. Guilt washes over me. This is not my nature. I don't know how long I can keep this up. I shake it off, but my soul feels the pain. When the truth comes out, I wonder if he'll hate me. Why should I care?

Wavering between heartache and revenge, I'm unsure about the journey. It's not too late. I could change my mind and cut my losses, but the minutes are ticking away. I have to land on one side of the fence or the other. I intuitively know my life would be much better without Daniel, but I'm not ready to let it go.

I need to establish better boundaries, but he has no regard for them. They challenge him. It's a battle of wills. Usually, I don't have a chance against Daniel. Too often, he throws me a curveball. I watch every move.

Mirroring his behavior, I try to take back my power. He's playing with me too, but he has more practice. I must throw him off track, but it's like climbing uphill with a heavy weight on my back.

I have to put up with his manipulation until the scales of justice tilt in my favor. Before I can even get there, though, I have to jump some hurdles.

∽∾

It's the last night in my comfortable bed and cozy apartment. My family and friends don't like the idea that I'm leaving. I guess they think that I'll get more entangled. *What if they're right?* I'll have to be strong and protect myself from further damage. I'll think of it as a vacation. I'm leaving everything intact for my return.

Someone once said, "If you can survive a road trip with a man without wanting to throw him out of the car, you know you're compatible."

I'm free—free to leave whenever I want. I always have that option. Throwing Daniel out of the car could be the second option.

Road Trip

Sadness will take me
Down roads best untread
Will I get through?
Tough time ahead

This is it—time for us to get on the road. Anxiety has me in a vice-like grip.

"Relax," Daniel says and pops a CD into the player. The smooth sound of Sade fills the air. "Buckle your seatbelt," he demands. The slightest trace of a smile crosses his lips.

"I'm thinking of getting another dog when we get back to New York."

"Why? You couldn't take care of the first one."

"Then, I'll get a horse."

"Haven't you learned your lesson?" Geez! He's pushing all my emotional buttons, but I know his game. This time, I'm not giving him power.

"Whatever!" I retort. He won't listen to me anyway.

"I want to have a moment of honesty," he says, "then I don't want to talk about it anymore."

Hmm! A moment of honesty. This should be interesting. "What's going on?"

"Well, you know how I've been grumpy and distant lately?"

"Yes." *How can I miss it?*

"My son won't talk to me. I've been a terrible father."

He claims his relationship with his son soured because he divorced the boy's mother. I feel there's more to it. Daniel would have made amends years ago if he were really bothered by the breach between them.

"Florence, help me reach out to him before it's too late."

"I'll do what I can, but he's a grown man."

He thinks this small confession will soften me up. Thinking he has my sympathy, his mood brightens. He wants to drive all the way to New York in one day, but I insist we stop one night at a motel.

After driving for ten hours, we pull into a motel. The entry door is in the parking lot, so I can sneak Ripley in without a problem.

"Florence! I lost my wallet. I lost everything — my license, credit card, and seven hundred dollars."

Ha… I knew he'd come up with an excuse not to pay, but I'm exhausted, so I pull out my credit card.

The clerk gives us two keys, and we ride the elevator to the fourth floor.

Daniel flops down on the bed. "Will you rub me?" he asks, giving me the puppy-dog eyes.

"If I rub you, will I get three wishes?" I joke.

"No, but if you do, I won't have to spank you," he says with a hint of a smile. Soon, he's asleep.

My stomach is growling because we haven't had dinner. I pry my legs out from under his and get dressed in the dark to go downstairs. I noticed a lounge in the hotel lobby on the way to the room. I'm sure they must have something to eat.

❧

I slip out of bed in the morning and go to the bathroom.

Daniel's waiting at the door with a cigarette in his hand.

"Oh, no, you don't," I say. "No smoking! You'll get us in trouble."

"They'll never know." He rushes into the bathroom, closing the door before I can argue further. Before we leave, I spray perfume, hoping to mask the smell of tobacco.

"We should stop for breakfast before we get on the road."

"I want to get back on the road. Why don't we pick up some donuts?"

Yuk. Daniel sure does love sugar. He goes outside to smoke another cigarette while I get to-go coffee at the complimentary breakfast buffet.

He's behind the wheel, tapping the dashboard impatiently. The window is open on the driver's side, and he has a lit cigarette. I raise my eyebrow.

"You're such a pain," he says and flicks it.

Before we get on the highway, he stops at 7-Eleven for snacks and cigarettes.

Daniel pulls out the *lost* wallet. Yep. It's his wallet, all right. My eyes narrow as anger bubbles to the surface again.

"You never lost your wallet."

Daniel stills, likely weighing the pros and cons of yet another lie.

"I thought that I did! It fell between the seat."

"Liar!"

"You're acting crazy," he says with annoyance. "Do you want anything?"

"No, I'm good."

"I have a surprise for you," He's smiling when he slides into the car.

"A surprise? What is it?"

He holds up a chocolate bar, and I have to laugh.

He starts the car, and the check engine light comes on."

"I hope we don't get stuck, Daniel."

"Relax. When we get to New York, I'll make it have an accident. You can collect from your insurance company."

"You're kidding, right?"

"No, I did it a few years ago and collected over three thousand dollars."

"I'm not crashing my car!" His Bonnie and Clyde attitude doesn't move me.

"What's the matter? Do you think you'll go to hell?"

"No, but I'm sure there's a reservation there for you!"

"You're hilarious!"

Within minutes, things are back to normal. What is normal? We're like an old married couple who have learned to tolerate each other. We banter back and forth, neither giving an inch.

Daniel pulls off the exit.

"Why are you stopping?"

"I thought you might be hungry."

"I'm famished, but whenever I mention food, you get crazy."

Daniel laughs and stops at a diner.

"I'll have the deluxe hamburger platter," I say.

"Would you like fries or coleslaw?" the waitress asks.

"Fries," Daniel decides for me.

I nod to the waitress, and she turns to him.

"Nothing for me, thanks."

"Aren't you hungry, Daniel?"

"Nah, I ate all those candy bars. I'll have a bite of yours."

"What if I'm not in a sharing mood?"

"If you're not, I'll eat it all." He smiles. "You know, I will!"

Worm

I will keep on dreaming
Although it is quite clear
I can read your mind
The end of us is near

I unload Ripley's carrier and let him out. He seems happy to be back and takes in the smells of wildlife.

"Why is the mattress in the living room?" I ask.

"I didn't want to put anything in the bedroom until we paint."

"We?" I laugh. *Good luck with that one.*

"We'll be sleeping down here?" I look around the room. *At least it's close to the bathroom.*

"Oh, we have to use the upstairs bathroom. There's a leak in the pipes. I haven't gotten around to fixing it."

I follow Daniel upstairs, and my eyes fall on the trap door to the attic. *Could the object I'm searching for be in there?*

"Did you hear what I said, Florence? The bathroom light isn't working. You have to use this lamp." He flips the switch, illuminating the small bathroom. The toilet and the linoleum floor tiles are filthy, and one of the sliding glass doors is missing from the shower.

"This place is a sty. You have dirty clothes in the corner and tools everywhere."

"Just shove everything in the closets. Maybe you can clean tomorrow while I look for work."

Hmm! My mother always said, "If you want to find something, just clean."

Daniel's phone rings, and he checks the number. "I have to run out for a while. Let me borrow the car."

"Why?"

"I just have to, that's all."

Ah, a challenge! "I'll come with you."

"No, wait here. I won't be very long."

"Why can't I come?"

"Wow," he says in a threatening tone of warning.

I'm treading on his personal space. "*The sociopath is always in your life, but you are never in theirs.*" Words of wisdom from one of the sociopath websites.

My amusement turns to anger. "Fine! Leave! But you better buy another vehicle before you go through all the money you made on the RV."

"Don't worry. I have something lined up."

I could strangle him with my bare hands. *I'd be doing all the previous women in his life a favor.*

Once he's gone, I use the opportunity to search the attic. The loft is crowded with lamps, furniture, art, and boxes. It reeks. I remove the screws that hold the trap door closed using a screwdriver.

I step along the beams and plywood with the flashlight app on my cell phone. If I'm not careful, I'll plummet through the sheetrock into the downstairs living room. That would be hard to explain. I point the light down at my feet and shriek. All I see are mouse droppings. Ripley darts past me in search of a mouse. Oh, shit!

Nothing I do can coax him out. I'm getting nervous. Daniel could be home at any moment. I can't close the trap door until I get my cat.

Just as I feared, he's home early. I hear his car as it crunches the gravel in the driveway. Before he enters the house, I run out to distract him. "Let's sit out here and enjoy the afternoon."

"I want to take a shower first," he says.

"Come on. You can do that later. I'll make us some coffee, and we can watch the sun go down. It's such a great view."

"Yeah, this property is *great*, isn't it?"

What would be great is to see Ripley.

I get my wish. Ripley comes slinking down the stairs with something in his mouth.

"Good boy, Ripley," he says. "I knew you were useful for something."

"He's got a dead mouse! Do something, Daniel."

Ripley drops the mouse at his feet. He scoops it up with a dustpan and moves to pitch it over the bushes.

"No!" I cry. "Ripley will eat it, or maybe a bear might smell it in the middle of the night. Take it to the back near the edge of the woods. Please!"

"You're a pain in the ass. You know that?" He heads to the backyard with Ripley at his heels, and I run upstairs to close the trap door. My hands are shaking as I turn the last screw. Whew! That was close. I join Daniel and Ripley out on the deck.

"Where'd you go?"

"Bathroom."

The sunset sends orange streaks across the sky, and the air is crisp and fresh. It *is* beautiful here.

⁂

Daniel takes a position at an auto shop, and they give him a deal on a van. He's always complaining that the other employees don't know what they're doing. Daniel's a troublemaker, and sometimes it pays off. Only two weeks into the job, he gets the supervisor fired and takes over the position.

My phone rings. It's Daniel. I'm sure he's calling because he wants something; a cup of coffee, a sandwich, or a bottle of water, geez. I ignore it.

He won't give up, and I give in.

"Florence! Why didn't you answer when I called?"

Excuse me, Mr. Sociopath. It's all right when you don't answer, but the minute I'm unavailable, the sky is falling.

I laugh. "Don't you think I've had enough of you all weekend?"

"Ha! He spits. "You're coming to see me at lunchtime, right?"

"No, I wasn't planning to leave the house today."

"I need a cup of coffee. Never mind. I'll get it myself."

He comes home before the end of the day.

"What's going on, Daniel? Did you quit your job?"

"I left work early... I couldn't deal with those assholes today. I took a hundred dollars and went to the casino — lost my shirt!"

Even though I shouldn't care, my anger shoots through me like a bullet. Daniel has money for the casino but doesn't have money for me.

"You never cease to amaze me, Daniel."

"Hey, let's go to the casino tonight, Florence."

"I'm not into gambling, but maybe I can sit at the bar and have a glass of wine while you play the slot machines."

"We won't be there for long—in and out."

The Indian-run casino is down the block. How convenient.

Even though it's twenty degrees outside, I roll down my window, letting a gush of cold air into the van.

Daniel hustles me toward his favorite machine and pumps in a hundred-dollar bill. Within fifteen minutes, it's gone.

"Florence, give me some of that cash I gave you the other day."

"That money's for food."

"I'll give it back when we get home."

He loses it. Although I didn't gamble, I feel like I lost my shirt.

꿍꿍꿍

The sound of his van rolling over the gravel gets louder. He comes through the door with a smile.

"How was your day, little woman?"

"Peachy!"

"I bought a new front door at Home Depot yesterday, but the opening is too small. I have to cover the doorway with plastic because it's going to rain tonight."

I marvel at his stupidity. "Why don't you just take the door back and get a smaller one?"

"This is the door I want. It was marked down from five hundred dollars. I got it for two hundred. I grabbed a young salesgirl and told her it was damaged, so she reduced the price on the tag. Now I have money to pick up a riding mower."

"I thought you hired a kid to mow your lawn for twenty bucks."

"He never came back."

I wonder why!

"I put a deposit on a riding mower. I'll do it myself."

Daniel's life is an endless quest for fulfillment through stuff! He's been on a spending spree for the past two weeks — trips to the city, a mattress, a satellite dish, the internet.

"Can I ask you something without you going all "psycho" on me, Daniel?"

"What?"

"You're spending a lot lately. What's going on?"

"Relax, Babe! Now that I'm working, there's plenty of money. I'll pay for everything. All you have to do is grovel — like I did when we were in Florida."

"When did you ever grovel?"

He ignores my comment and baits his hook. "I want to finish working on my house so I can sell it."

Daniel doesn't intend to sell his house. It's just a ploy to keep me believing there's a possibility of a future. I've finally realized it, but whenever he says something that confirms it, I get pissed.

"If you don't sell it, what will you do for money?"

"Relax. I've invested in something that will pay off in the future."

"Invested?"

"Yeah, but I can't tell you. You won't understand it."

"Try me!"

"Let's say I'm well equipped tool-wise.

They're not shitty tools either. I'll tell you that! They're top of the line."

"You have no priorities when it comes to money."

"You see! That's what I mean. You don't understand what it takes to work in this industry. I can work anywhere—Florida—California."

"California? Is that where you plan to move?"

"I'm just saying…"

Ahhh! Now I see. Daniel's hinted before how he could work anywhere with his arsenal of tools. He has a plan B… in case he doesn't weasel his way back to Florida next winter. Maybe he has another woman in the wings.

"I thought you wanted to buy another boat and retire."

"I do! But now I need to work."

I won't let him off the hook, although I feel like the worm.

Gambling Man

Love me as I need
Or please just let me go
I will be okay
Of that, I surely know

The alarm clock rings and Daniel rolls over. "I don't want to go to work," he whines and nuzzles my neck. I have to turn away because his morning breath smells downright evil. I think it's his teeth.

"How long has it been since you've had your teeth cleaned?" I ask.

"I don't know. I don't have money for that. I don't want to talk about it. Can you make us some coffee?"

Prying myself from his embrace, I go to the kitchen and peer into the refrigerator — eggs, bread, deli ham, and a rotisserie chicken carcass.

"There's no milk," I complain.

"Make a list. We can go shopping next time I get paid."

"What do you want for dinner tonight?"

"Surprise me," he says, getting out of bed to dress and shave.

Daniel hates chicken. I pull the chicken legs from the freezer to defrost. Such a small thing to bother my conscience, but I don't feel hungry for a hamburger.

"Maybe I'll take a sick day and help you clean the house today," he says.

"Don't be silly. You'll only be in the way. Besides, we'll have the whole weekend. I've got this."

"Be very careful with my stuff," he warns. "I have expensive knick-knacks and jewelry."

"I'll sort everything out and pack it neatly in storage."

"Yeah, but don't lose anything."

There's only one coffee mug, so I pour some coffee in a used McDonald's cup on the counter and hand it to him. "Now, get lost," *I mean it.*

Daniel goes off to work, and I have the house to myself to resume my search. I look around and shake my head. The place is a mess. I definitely have my work cut out for me. It amazes me how irresponsible he is. Not only did he buy himself a flat-screen television and a DVD player, but he also had to have a soundbar. He spares no expense for the things he wants. Still, it mystifies me that he has no regard for the stuff once he's acquired it.

The main water pipe to the house froze during the winter, and he hasn't fixed it. He's hooked up a garden hose. I have to go outside and turn it on if I need water. He makes his life so much harder than it has to be — just another indication of how disorganized he is.

Once the water's running, I start by cleaning out the cabinets. The bottom shelf contains bottles of pain relievers, their lids half-cocked. Daniel thinks ibuprofen can cure anything. Even in Florida, he ate them like Pez candies.

The next cabinet has two popcorn packets and a half-eaten bag of burnt kernels. I'm sure the mice are well fed.

Moving to the hall closet, I pull out a box. Mice have gotten into it, and all the paper inside is in shreds. The carton contains what Daniel calls knick-knacks. I call them dust collectors. It takes most of the morning to sort out the contents of the closet, but what I'm looking for isn't there, and I check it off my list.

In the living room, peel-and-stick wood flooring is piled arbitrarily in the corner. I gaze at the stacks of boxes, crushed and water-damaged from being stored in the shed before Daniel moved to Florida. The fact that he's taken them out of storage is another sign that he's home to stay. I should be relieved, but I fear it will lead to more head games to confuse me. There was a time I let him lead me around like a puppy, but nobody stays deceived forever. His power is waning.

Before starting the boxes, I take a break for lunch and sit in the yard. I stretch like a cat in the warm rays soaking up the sun. The daunting task ahead makes me linger outside a little too long. *I may enjoy being here for a while.*

As I'm about to continue the search, I hear Daniel's tires rolling up the driveway. It'll have to wait until Monday. I can't get anything done when he's around. He wants to know what I'm doing every minute. I walk around to the front and enter the sliding glass doors. He's in the kitchen.

"I bought you a present," he says.

There's a small square box on the counter. Could it be—a Kindle? Yes, I see the logo.

"That's not for you. I bought that for Emma. The other box is for you." He hands me a small case containing used sunglasses. He must have gone shopping at the pawnshop again.

"They're Coach!"

"I'd rather have the Kindle."

"You can't have that one. I'll buy another one."

"Did you get a raise or something?"

"I went to the casino in Monticello."

So that's where he's been hanging out.

"You complain that you have no money but blow it at the casino?"

"I've been winning."

"No one ever wins when they gamble."

"I do,' he says. "I know when to walk away. It just takes discipline."

Discipline! Something you don't have!

The only bad thing is if I win over six hundred dollars at one time, they make me pay taxes to the damn IRS. That reminds me, I need you to file my taxes. The government's been taking one-third of my paycheck every week."

"You know you won't see a dime of that tax refund, don't you? It's a shame! The IRS is going to get it all."

"Yeah, I'll have to win more money at the casino."

Actually, I'm starting to think like a gambler, but I'm on the wrong side of the table. If I play another hand, I might break even. However, a shrewd player knows the rules of the game—the stakes and when to quit. I don't have that instinct. I thought I was smart enough to beat him at his own game, but I'm wrong.

※

Daniel starts the barbecue for me, and after dinner, he clears the table and washes the dishes. He's on his best behavior.

I wonder. Could I be wrong about him?

No, it's all an act. Daniel's up to something. His brain is wired to manipulate and deceive. It gives him pleasure—like a drug. Unfortunately, there is no drug to counteract it. Even if I stay one-up on him, he finds a way to control me.

Like Jekyll and Hyde, he uses love and fear to keep me living in a state of anxiety, on edge, and waiting for the next drama to unfold. Emotionally wrung out, I go to bed, but my brain doesn't shut down. The many lies of Daniel skulk in my mind. I thought I had become immune. Now, they haunt me.

If you invite yourself into a snake's den, you need to keep both eyes on it, and that's what I plan to do.

Fighting Words

I need to find the road
That leads me far from you
I'm frozen in your love
My heart will see me through

On Saturday morning, we sit outside with our coffee. Daniel has a big yard. Most of it is lawn, and he takes care of it. He piles his garbage on the side of the house. The smell drifts in the breeze, and it's a feeding ground for animals at night. The tree line at the back and sides are abundant with adorable deer, which graze on the grass in the morning and evening, but deep in the woods lurk other animals that aren't so cuddly. That's why I keep Ripley in the house once it gets dark. I don't want him to get eaten by a bear.

"I saw a sign on the side of the road," I venture. "There's a festival in the next town this weekend."

"Nah! It's a beautiful day. Let's hang out here," he says.

I sigh. Daniel will be home for two days. All he ever wants to do is relax in the yard. All I want to do is hunt for the treasure he has hidden in the house.

"Put your shorts on," he says.

He even tries to tell me what to wear. But I might as well be comfortable, so I change into shorts. I join him in the yard, sporting the sunglasses he gave me and carrying a book.

"Oh no—you said you would rather have a Kindle."

"So what? I deserve both."

"I already promised them to my daughter Colleen."

"No, you didn't." His lies are as transparent as glass.

"What is a thirteen-year-old going to do with Coach Sunglasses?"

"I don't care what she does with them."

"Fine. Take them." I yank the sunglasses off my head.

Seeing my anger, he backs down and hands them back to me.

"Relax. We'll figure something out."

His phone rings. It's Lisa. Daniel puts it on the speaker.

"Did you want to take the girls today?" she asks.

"Yes, drop them off. Florence is here. She can't wait to see them."

Yep! I can't wait! Actually, they are lovely girls, but I'm a little nervous about seeing Lisa. She undoubtedly thinks I'm stupid for coming back here. I want to tell her the truth: I know all about him and that I have this under control. If she doesn't know, he's a sociopath. I won't be the one to tell her.

Daniel hangs up. "Make sure Colleen doesn't see you with those sunglasses."

"All right."

I will always come last in his eyes. That's why I don't feel guilty about keeping them. It feels good to stand my ground.

When Lisa pulls up with the girls, Daniel jumps up to give her a tour to show off his décor ideas.

I'm sure she doesn't care—not now, anyway. She might, once Daniel dies and leaves her the house. Usually, I wouldn't have a problem with this. It is his house, and he does have children, but he would have lost this place if I hadn't lent him all that money— money that should be handed down to *my children*. Still, it amazes me how he's so concerned about taking care of his children once he's dead but doesn't provide for them while he's alive.

Lisa tells Daniel about her boyfriend's brother, who just died of cancer.

"We're all on the list," he says.

Lisa laughs. "Don't worry, Daniel. Only the good die young." *She's funny.* "Do you want to be buried or cremated?"

"I'm going to burn his ass," I say.

Little Emma clamors for my attention while Daniel walks Lisa to her car. They have their heads together. I sense the tension.

"What are we going to do today?" Emma asks.

"We're going to a festival," Daniel says.

"Yay," she cries and jumps up and down. "Can I go on the rides?"

"Of course, sweetheart." He turns to me. "We'll take your car, Florence since you're the one who wanted to go."

"Fine!" At least we'll get out for a while. I go inside to retrieve my keys.

"Can you sit in the back with me?" Emma asks.

"No, honey," I say. "I'm going to sit next to Daddy. You can sit next to Colleen." I pull out the sunglasses.

"You better not get attached to those," Daniel whispers.

"I don't want to talk about it," I say, but he's like a dog with a bone. He won't let it go. "Colleen will eventually ask for them, and you'll have to give them up," he says under his breath.

I glare at him. "Stop! She doesn't even know they exist."

"You made your choice," he says.

I feel my blood heating up. "Don't you dare make this an issue, or I'll pack my bags—right now!"

"Calm down, Florence."

They're only a stupid pair of sunglasses, but it's the principle of the thing now. I refuse to back down so Daniel can play Daddy Warbucks. For once, I come first.

After the festival, the girls ask for pizza, but he suggests we go back to the house and barbecue.

"Everything's in the freezer," I say. "I don't know if we can put frozen meat on the grill."

"Sure, we can! Emma wants hotdogs anyway, and they don't take long to cook."

After dinner, Daniel and the girls lie on the bed and watch cartoons on TV while I clear the dishes.

Lisa rolls into the driveway, and Emma runs to her. Colleen goes straight to the van, ready to leave. *Teenagers!*

Before Lisa pulls out, Daniel flags her down.

"Wait! Colleen forgot something."

Here he goes, digging his own grave. If he asks for the sunglasses, I'll be pissed. It may even be the reason I give up this madness. Instead, he reaches into the back of his van and pulls out a tripod.

"She forgot this last time she was here. I bought it for her at a yard sale."

He gives me a smug look as if he was baiting me. I bite my bottom lip, so I don't burst out laughing.

I think I'm in stage three of detachment from Daniel. Emotionally stronger, the love and obsession I once felt are gone. I'm unaffected when he steps out of line because I don't care. I've been doing a lot of thinking and getting advice from my online support group.

As we walk back to the house, he turns to me. "You're really starting to get annoying, Florence."

He noticed!

The fourth and final stage of a relationship with a Sociopath is called **discard**. The sociopath probably won't get to this point until he meets someone else who can replace you and supply him with what he needs. Your only hope is to learn about this disorder, get strong, stop blaming yourself, accept it, and walk away first.

Mashed Potatoes

You had me in a place
Advantage to pursue
Then you turned your back
I slipped away from you

Finally, the weekend is over. I'm alone again. As I watch Daniel's taillights disappear, it's time to search the boxes. I flip on a lamp. Its shade is yellow with age, something he must have found this treasure at a garage sale. He gives value to the most mundane things.

Before I dive into the first box, I glance at a couple of sun-bleached photos scattered on the floor. I pick them up and enter Daniel's past. There's one of him standing next to an older boy and a girl. His stepsiblings? There's also one of him during the early '70s with his shoulder-length hair and pulling a stupid face. The elements damaged most of the photos. It's such a shame — a lifetime of memories without anyone to appreciate them.

A thunderous clatter rains down on the tin roof as the sky opens up. How depressing! I miss my cozy apartment in Florida, where storms pass quickly and everything is clean.

Daniel's getting the kids again next weekend and wants me to be here. He's trying to keep up the "good father" routine with his daughters — and their mother — pretending he has a stable life. Perhaps that's why he wants me around, but I have other plans. I'm going to the city to visit my cousin this weekend. Daniel promised to pay for the bus ticket, but I had no expectations.

Once I'm in Manhattan, I'll take the train to Chinatown, buy a replica of the item I'm searching for, and then I'll be ready to make a switch. I'll be long gone by the time he discovers it's a fake.

If I want to mimic a sociopath, I need to learn to be a thief like him. I still have the promissory note I made him sign when I had all my mental faculties, but I'll keep that as a backup.

◆

I'm going to Walmart, Florence. What kind of cereal do you like? Oh, and text me the name of the wine you want, too."

For a brief moment, I think he cares. My brain wants to go off track. I have to screech on the brakes and pull it back to reality. I'm not used to *the giving* Daniel. Suspicious me, there has to be a reason. He rarely pays for anything unless there's something in it for him. It's as if he's placing a bet. Daniel puts down a few bucks, so I feel obligated to pay a higher amount later. Typically, he wagers with words—words that I accept as reality. I've discovered the game is never fair. He never loses. The amount he invests is less than the reward.

He did say he was a lucky gambler.

He returns to the house whistling. "Look, I bought you salmon—a ton of it. You like fish, don't you?"

"Yes, but you don't."

"That's okay," he says. "I'm not eating it."

Great! Now I have something else to worry about—stinky fish!

He pulls out items one at a time and stacks them in my arms. There's some beef, the cut undeterminable, chicken legs, hot dogs, hamburger patties, and fish.

"Look, I even bought you a big bag of flounder; you like flounder, don't you?"

"I do!"

"Do you want some for dinner?"

"No, that's all right," I say. "I know you don't like fish. I'll save it for lunch. Why don't we have steak tonight? Do you have any vegetables?"

"Do you think you can rustle up some mashed potatoes?"

"Sure, if you start the barbecue."

Daniel's in high gear. Whenever I start romanticizing the relationship, I need to stop and remember how he pulled back his emotions, depleted my finances, and propositioned other women.

Once he knows I'm on to his tactics, he could get nasty. He'll paint himself as a victim and blame me for our demise. It's better if he's the victim, not me! At this point, I don't care.

After dinner, we sit outside with our coffee. Daniel's smoking, but at least the breeze is blowing it away from me. I get up to clear the table.

"You don't have to do that now," he says. "Wait till later, and I'll help."

The mattress he just bought is sitting in the middle of the living room.

"It's weird that the bed is down here."

"Look! I bought you a nice new pillow."

Great! Now I won't have to smell his head. I crawl between the sheets.

"Heyyy! That's my side."

I roll over to the other side of the bed.

"Comfy!" he says with a smile.

Salesman

I feel that I will lose
All sense of who I am
I need to step away
To shed and discard shame

Daniel is a Drama Queen. With a never-ending string of crises, he can drain the blood from a vampire. Just yesterday, he called from work in a panic to tell me Lisa, his baby mamma, is taking him back to court for child support. I'm surprised she hasn't done it sooner. He never sent anything to support his two young daughters. Now that he's working, Daniel does have money, but he still doesn't pull his parental weight.

"I'm a Florida resident," he says. "I still have my Florida license to prove it. They can't do anything."

I'm irritated that he's looking for a loophole. "You work in New York," I point out. "Did you forget that?"

"My boss will vouch for me. He'll say the position is temporary and has agreed to reduce my paycheck, so only part of it is taxable — the rest will be cash. This way, they'll settle on a lesser amount if I have to go to court."

What a sleazeball! His boss, too!

"If I have to pay, I'll sue for full custody."

Oh, my God! He means it, but he doesn't know the first thing about being a father. All he knows how to do is shower his girls with money and gifts. By now, I know how quickly he gets bored with stability. Daniel's need for an emotional stimulus would snuff the life out of his children.

I point out that he won't be retiring for another ten years if he takes custody. My comment goes over his head. I'm sure it's a control issue. He has no conscience about tearing them away from their mother, the only stable parent they've ever really known.

Daniel *is* a dark soul—dishonest to the core and unapologetic.

A few hours later, my phone rings again.

"What now, Daniel?"

"Are you all right, Florence? You're acting differently. What's going on?"

I laugh, amazed at how quickly a sociopath senses danger. I guess he can hear the monotone flatness of my voice.

"It sounds like you don't want to be in this relationship anymore."

I laugh. "You're imagining things. Maybe you better take your meds."

"Hmm!" he hums.

"Oh, stop. It's not as if we're in love. We're more like friends."

"That's crazy. I love you immensely. I'm just not good at expressing my feelings."

More like untouchable! That's what he claimed to be—until he met me. Now I know that untouchable means no feelings, no conscience, and no soul!

"I do love you."

His words are like candy. Something I crave even though it rots my self-worth. When Daniel says, I love you. He means I love — to use you.

"Daniel, you're what most women call a dead-end!"

"And you're a riot!"

My apprehensions are showing, and he's noticed them. I pretend all is well.

"I'm just stressed out today."

"Well, I'm not planning to fight for custody if that's what's bothering you. Lisa won't take the money even if the court awards it."

"How did you manage that?" I ask.

"We have an agreement. Lisa knows the kids will be taken care of when I die. I started a bank account for them while working in California."

"Bank account? You said you were penniless."

"I am!" he says. "That account is locked. I can't touch it."

"Not for nothing, but I hope you don't forget *me* in your will."

"Oh, don't worry. I haven't forgotten I owe you money. You'll be taken care of way before that!"

"What if you die in a crash — or more likely, what if someone shoots you in the head?"

"Hilarious, Florence."

He appears to have a plan for his future, and it doesn't matter to me if I'm included. Even with all his current income, he has never offered to pay the debt he owes me. At least now, I know where all *his* money is going.

I'm fuming about the savings he claims to have until I remember. He's a pathological liar! There probably isn't a bank account tucked away anywhere. He's just telling Lisa that; to keep the situation under control.

"I told the kids I'd take them on vacation. Lisa won't let me have them unless you come along."

My mind flashes to something I read about sociopaths and how they use other people to represent normality in their life. *Daniels's a good salesman, but he has no product.*

"I stopped at the bus station today," he says, holding up a roundtrip ticket to the city."

Just when I think he's the scum of the earth, he surprises me by doing something nice. It causes me to doubt, but only for a moment.

"What happened? Did you double your money at the casino?"

"You said you want to visit your cousin, didn't you?"

"Yes, my cousin is moving, and I agreed to help her pack. She's selling all her furniture cheap — too cheap. Even her Thomasville bedroom set from the early '60s."

"I want it!" His eyes widen. "Tell her we'll pick it up next week."

"Where would we put it?"

"We'll set some of it up in the living room. I'll store the rest upstairs. You'll have a place for your clothes instead of living out of your suitcase."

"I like living out of my suitcase…." *Ready to leave at a moment's notice.* "Besides, I thought you were selling the house." *Let's hear his excuse.*

"You're so stupid, Florence," he snips. "Don't you know anything about selling a house? You need to stage it."

The only thing you're staging is an act.

⁓

Before I go to visit my cousins, I remind Daniel to pay the electric bill. I feel like a nag, but I don't care.

"They're going to shut it off if we don't pay. They'll turn it on again." *It's not true, but there's no harm in putting a fire under him.*

Usually, I would feel guilty about being deceitful, but it's getting easier to act like a sociopath, which is scary.

I'm a bit worried about leaving my cat. I hope Daniel doesn't throw Ripley out of the house to fend for himself, but I suspect that's what he'll do. The poor little guy better not get eaten by a bear or a bobcat.

Time and Money

Trapped in memory of our love
I cannot turn away
Time has passed, and I am strong
My wings will not obey

When I return from a relaxing weekend in the city, there's a layer of dust on everything, and the fireplace is in pieces. Daniel had intended to brick the wall behind it. Only two or three feet are completed, and cement scraps litter the floor.

"Oh, did I tell you about the painter I hired last week to do the spackling and painting?"

"No, you didn't."

"I warned him that I was very fussy. It had better be perfect."

I see a problem already. "And…"

"The guy didn't know what the hell he was doing. I told him to pack his shit and leave."

"Did you pay him for his work?"

He laughs like a naughty child. "No, he's lucky I didn't give him a kick in the ass."

"The poor guy worked all day, Daniel."

"That's not my problem."

"You're such a bastard."

"Language." He shakes his finger at me as if he has morals.

Daniel thinks rules and laws don't apply to him. I'm amazed at how he gets away with it.

My plan for revenge is worth lagging behind a sociopath's trail of destruction. But once I find what I'm looking for, I'll make a quick getaway.

⌒⌒⌒

I shouldn't have mentioned my cousin's furniture. The price was a real bargain, and he jumped on it. She keeps asking why we haven't come yet. After three attempts to pick it up, she's probably sorry she offered it. Yet another humiliation, as I'm ready to cut my losses and bow out of the deal.

"If we don't pick up the stuff today," I tell him, "she has another person interested."

"The furniture won't fit in my van. I have to borrow my boss's truck. I'll be back soon."

"Maybe we can all go out for dinner later."

He tosses his cigarette on the lawn. "Okay."

That was too easy!

He'll tell me anything I want to hear. I know damn well he'll make an excuse to leave as soon as he gets what he wants.

Pacing the floor, I wait for him to come home. When he finally comes through the door, I'm livid.

"My cousin expected us to be there an hour ago. What took you so long?"

"I had to get this."

"What is it?"

"It's a toll pass. I found it in one of the wrecked cars they towed into the shop. Now we won't have to pay for tolls."

"That's messed up."

"I'll put it back tomorrow. The guy won't even know it was gone."

"I'm sure there's a way they can track those things."

"Relax."

He lives his life on the edge of the law, and he's dragging me with him. "Do you have the cash for the furniture?"

Daniel laughs. "I stopped off at the casino on the way home."

Here we go again! Why do I feel like I'm in a tug-of-war?

"How much did you lose? Do you have enough to pay my cousin?"

"I hope this stuff is worth it," he warns.

Already, he's prepared to blame me. "I told you the furniture is forty years old."

It's only the two of us, and I'm not sure how heavy the furniture will be.

Daniel lights up a cigarette.

"Open the window." I cough.

He takes his time. Even with the window open, the smoke gets in my eyes. He's holding it in his right hand and blowing it out in front of him on purpose. I narrow my eyes, resisting the urge to fight because it will be a disaster if we get to my family, and there's tension between us.

"Don't forget, Daniel. We're staying for dinner."

"We're going there for one reason. To pick up the furniture — in and out."

"We can't just swoop in, grab their furniture, and run. This is my family."

"It's getting late. As it is, we won't be home until midnight."

Whose fault is that, asshole?

My cousin is waiting outside when we arrive. After introductions, she leads us up to the bedroom. Daniel's face lights up when he sees the set. "Wow." He fingers the trim on the headboard. "You kept it in great condition."

I have to admit. The bedroom set is beautiful. Daniel doesn't deserve it, but at least I'll get to enjoy it — for a little while.

Even though Daniel already bought a mattress, he wants hers because it's the top of the line. He loads it on top of the van and covers it with plastic sheathing because there's a treat of rain.

My cousin has a lot more furniture, and he wants it all, but there's no room in the truck for everything. We'll have to make two trips. Once it's loaded, he promises we'll stay for dinner next time.

"What will you do with all that furniture when we move onto the boat?" I ask, knowing he doesn't really plan to sell the house. I'm starting to enjoy putting him on the spot.

"I'll give it to my kids."

Oh, here it is. The truth! Daniel's mentioned it a hundred times, how nice the house will look once it's furnished. I could almost read his mind. I know he's hoping they'll want to move in with him. He's still playing the game, and I'm losing it!

Whatever!

"Daniel, can we stop and get something to eat?"

"I'm not stopping. You can eat when we get home."

"That's two and a half hours from now! Why does everything have to be difficult with you? At least stop at a gas station so I can buy some chips or a candy bar, or I warn you, I'll blow."

He's derisive. "You'll blow?"

"Yeah!" I want to tell him what I think of him—moron! It's getting harder to hold my temper.

"Calm down, Babe. You're going to have a stroke!"

"This could have been a pleasant trip, but nooo. You have to make it a negative event." *Negative!* I'm happy to point that out to him.

"All right." He huffs. "We'll stop at the next exit."

Hmm... success! Not only do we stop, but there's a supermarket on the corner. "I'll run in and get us a sandwich," I say. "Give me a few bucks."

His face contorts as he shoves his hand in his pocket. I suppress a giggle. There was a time when I'd use my credit card, compelled to buy since it was my suggestion. But now I get great pleasure watching him open his wallet.

"Pick up a can of coffee while you're in there?"

"Okay," I say and suppress a smile, even though I bought coffee yesterday with my money.

Daniel is quiet the rest of the way home but smokes one cigarette after another. He's still puffing away when we get back and walks right into the house.

"What are you doing, Daniel?"

"What?" He's noticeably annoyed.

"The cigarette! Go outside with it."

"Can't I even smoke a cigarette in my own house?"

"Yeah, you can smoke a cigarette in your house, but I don't need to be here. Are you trying to get me to leave because all you have to do is, say so! I'll pack my shit and be out of here before you know it. Then you can smoke your brains out in your own house." I throw my purse on the bed in anger, feeling a sense of assertion.

He's excited when I'm confrontational, but I sense that he isn't happy with the situation when the dust settles.

"I think you need to start smoking, Florence." He opens the door. "Come and sit outside with me."

"You said you were going to stop smoking and go on a health kick, remember that, Daniel?"

"I will. Give me time."

Time? That's the third valuable commodity I've given you, after my love and my money.

Blackout

I cannot getaway
Addicted to the search
And you will not leave me
Remain upon your perch

The lights go out around noon, and my first thought is that we lost power because of the storm, but I can see lights at the neighbor's house. I check the breaker — nothing.

Hopeful that Daniel will answer his phone, I dial his number.

"Daniel, we lost power. I'm sitting here in the dark."

"Relax. It's probably due to the storm."

"No, I don't think so. We seem to be the only house without power."

"So, call the electric company."

"The power is in your name. They won't give me information about the account. You need to call."

"Shit," he snaps. "This isn't how I want to spend my lunch hour."

"If you don't call now, we won't have power tonight. We won't be able to cook or take a hot shower. Is that what you want?"

"Oh, all right. Text me the number."

He's such a pain in the ass. He could call information but has to make me work.

Expecting to hear from him shortly after I text the number, I call him back, but it goes to voicemail. I jump in my car and head to his shop.

Daniel is outside puffing on a cigarette—as if he doesn't have a care in the world.

"What's going on, Daniel? Did you talk to the power company?"

"Bad news," he says. "We may need to buy some candles."

"Didn't you pay the bill?"

"Yes, but they're claiming I owe them money from two years ago."

"Great."

Daniel opens his wallet—the one he claimed he lost. He pulls out a hundred-dollar bill.

"Switch the power in your name and use this as a deposit."

"No way! I'm not doing that!"

"Relax! I'm not asking you to pay for it. I'll give you the money when the bill is due."

"You don't have a good track record for paying bills. What if you're late? My credit will go bad."

What am I saying! My credit is already bad-- thanks to him.

"Do you want me to sign in blood?"

That's tempting.

"If I don't pay it, you can have the electric shut off again."

"I don't know…."

"Come on, Florence. We don't have a choice—unless you want to take cold showers."

I drive off, stop for a cup of coffee, and vow he's not going to rip me off again. I DON'T TRUST HIM!

Think like a sociopath.

After my coffee, I return to his shop.

"They want two hundred," I lie. It's the only way I can protect myself.

Daniel grudgingly peels off another hundred-dollar bill.

"I smell coffee. Did you bring me some?"

"No. It's just cold coffee from last night. I got desperate."

"Well, after you take care of the electricity, swing by here with a fresh cup for both of us." He hands me a few more dollars.

The electric company didn't require a deposit since I set up auto-pay, so I pocket the two hundred dollars and hold on to it as a cushion if Daniel doesn't pay the bill. I skip the coffee and go back home.

At least the rain has stopped, and the sun is shining. Although I should be looking through more boxes, I'm emotionally exhausted, so I sit outside for a while with my laptop. Connecting to the internet, I navigate to the sociopath website. Not that it makes things easier to accept, but I'm aware of his manipulations. They say that all sociopaths wear a mask. What you see is never what you get.

I hurry through a few more boxes. Among the fish sculptures and vases, I find a wooden jewelry box. My pulse quickens as I lift the lid. Jackpot!

On closer inspection, they appear to be knock-offs. I've searched all week, but there's still the shed outside. And that dreaded attic, but Daniel will be home soon.

After making a pot of coffee for Daniel, I sit outside with my laptop again. I'm so engrossed with my research that I don't hear his van until he drives up.

I shut off my laptop and make eye contact as he walks toward me.

He's a handsome man on the outside, but his chronic smoker's cough warns me that he's not healthy on the inside.

Purgatory

Tried to ignore it
Wait one more day
Things did not change
We drifted away

Daniel jumps on the riding mower. All he wants to do is roll around on that lawn. He's such a creature of habit—a hamster on a wheel. It's just like his life. Around and around he goes, never moving forward, never progressing. He's droning on and on about redecorating, unnecessary work since he claims to be putting the house up for sale. He's so full of his plans to build a brick wall behind his wood-burning stove. I smirk. He'll never finish the project, but he's happy living in a sociopathic euphoria.

"I don't see the point if you're planning to sell the house," I instigate. "Just clean it up and slap on a fresh coat of paint."

"This is why our relationship doesn't work," he snipes. "You're always telling me what to do."

I laugh. As far as Daniel's concerned, I'm just another dumb woman who wants to rule his life.

"Maybe we would get along better if we were partners, and you didn't think I was trying to control you."

"What I do with my house is none of your business."

"Nothing you do is my business," I snap.

"I think you need to drink the Kool-Aid."

I think he senses I'm pulling away. He'll double up on the sweet talk if all indicators are correct.

There's a chill in the air, so we find a movie and plan to snuggle in for the night. It's the only good thing about Daniel.

"Ahhh, you feed me too much," he complains.

I smirk, but he doesn't notice and climbs into bed.

"How can we get comfy if you keep your clothes on?"

"I'm cold," he insists.

"I don't get much from this relationship. Now you want to take away my comfy. Without that, I'll have nothing."

"All right. I'll take off my shorts, but I'm keeping my sweatshirt on."

Geez! What was I thinking? I need to suck it up and realize—there's no hope for us. Stiff and scratchy against my skin, I distance myself from him and fall into an uneasy slumber.

Comfy doesn't feel the same as before, but maybe that's a good thing. It was my downfall. If I fall into old habits, I might get entangled again. I can't let that happen.

I dream that we're in a basement. It's cold and dirty. All I want to do is go home. What am I doing here? I don't even care about the money anymore. How do I get out of this?

The following day, he moans. "You've given me an erection."

"You sound like that's a bad thing. Is that why you like to keep your clothes on?"

"Of course not!"

I laugh, but it's not funny. Does Daniel intend to avoid sex forever? I push the thought out of my mind because sex isn't why I came here.

            ❦

Since it's the weekend, Daniel asks Lisa if the kids can visit.

"I don't want to hang around the house," I warn him. "We need to take them out somewhere."

"We'll go to the lake, but first, I need to do some work around the house."

He still hasn't fixed the water pipes, and the bathrooms have no lights.

"Great!" I say. "You can start with the water pipe."

"Hell no! Do you know what a big job that is? What I need to do is take care of my yard."

We're outside when Lisa pulls up. Is it as awkward for Lisa as it is for me? After having two children with him, she knows how he operates. I like Lisa. If it weren't for Daniel, we'd probably be friends.

She's off to a childfree afternoon, and I almost wish I could go with her. Instead, I dutifully follow Daniel and the girls into the house.

He puts on a movie and leaves us alone so he can roll around on his mower.

We watch a movie and then another. Within a few hours, Colleen isn't enthusiastic about being here. Maybe she realizes that the attention her father has been lavishing is inconsistent. Someday, she'll figure out that her father is a sociopath, and it won't matter.

He leaves a trail of broken hearts. I'm not the only one who's his victim. Josette must have scars, too. Then there's the woman from California. I wonder what her story is. Maybe she's on Facebook. I type her name in the search engine.

Voila, she's active, but I can't see anything about her unless she accepts a friend request. I can send her a private message. I've thought about it before, but I was too scared that Daniel would find out. Now, it doesn't matter.

"What can you tell me about Daniel Weaver?" I type.

My finger hovers over the send button and clicks. My question is soaring through time and space on the internet.

Daniel comes inside. "Are you girls having fun with Florence?"

I roll my eyes. With the promise to go to the lake forgotten, I pull out the hot dogs, a box of macaroni and cheese, and discover a half head of broccoli. Dinner is covered.

We sit around the picnic table, surrounded by the smell of roasting franks on the grill. Daniel has no problem wolfing down three dogs, and the girls enjoy the mac and cheese—along with their father's full attention. I pick at the broccoli with no appetite.

"Can we go out for ice cream after dinner?" Emma asks.

"Yeah, let's go out," I chime in. I'm not in the mood for ice cream, but anything to get out of this house!

"All right, but you're buying," he whispers. "Since you're the one who instigated this.

I raise my eyebrows at him. He got me again.

Daniel revels in their appreciation as the girls lick on their ice cream cones.

"Father's Day is coming soon. How would you girls like to go to Hershey Park in Pennsylvania?"

"Yay!" Emma jumps up and down.

Colleen just smiles.

Smart girl!

She knows not to get too excited because he's disappointed her many times before.

"Ask your mom if you can spend the night," he instructs. "Tell her that Florence wants you to. Then we'll be able to leave early in the morning."

"I'm sleeping with you, Florence." Emma beams. I marvel at her innocence.

The headlights of Lisa's car illuminate the living room wall. The girls run around, packing their stuff, and Daniel walks them to their car. He probably promised them the world. I have to roll my eyes. I know him. They'll be lucky if he feeds them.

As the red taillights fade, Daniel comes back inside. I ask about his plans for Father's Day weekend.

"Where are they going to sleep?"

"Relax! We'll set up the old mattress here in the living room."

I'm starting to hate that word. I'm sure this will be uncomfortable. For me!

I'll remain in purgatory as long as I continue to play this game.

Against my better judgment, Daniel convinced me to put the electricity under my name. I figured if he didn't pay, I'd cut it off. It's funny how our minds can adapt to any circumstance.

I'm under more stress since it's in my name, but he has no empathy for me. I'm a constant emotional wreck, stuck in a crazy cycle of trying to make him understand. I'm tired of the endless conversations, all in vain.

He's in control—The glue that holds Daniel together. If he thinks he's losing it, I'll get a taste of his temper, but I'm fuming.

Get a grip, Florence! If he doesn't pay the electric bill, I'll have no other option than to shut off the power and go back home—without the object I seek. My breath hitches slightly, but I steady myself, determined to remain calm.

Holy Grail

My soul is scorched, but still alive
The pain reminds me so
I need to find a way to heal
Without feelings of woe

My sister is standing at the bus stop when we pull up. She insists we go to her boyfriend's house for a barbecue. I don't want to go, but she talks me into it somehow, so we're on our way.

Subjected to a long string of endearments, baby this and honey that, nausea whispers, and I'm feeling sick to my stomach but also a little jealous. As long as I stay connected to Daniel, I may never hear the words "I love you" again.

How sad!

Initially, he wooed me until I was sure he was my soul mate. He was open to affection, and words of love flowed on the phone and in texts. He sure had me fooled. I became addicted. Then his attention wavered. Like a junkie, I craved his attention with a hungry obsession. Whenever I pointed out his lack of passion, he'd roll his eyes and say, "You're not going to act like a wackadoo and talk about love, are you?" Well, that shut me up quick! The only thing real about Daniel and my relationship is that the end is near. I'm not eager to go home to him yet. Why would I be?

Daniel has dinner waiting for me when I get back. When I think he's rotten to the core, he does something to throw me off balance, but if the past is any indication, he has an agenda. I'm better at ignoring his manipulation tactics, but it's getting harder to focus on my main objective — the reason I'm here.

I miss my cozy apartment — and so does my cat. At least the sun is shining. I stare out at the garden. Weeds have overgrown the edges around the statues and rocks. I'm bored, so I change into my shorts and hunt for the rake. Losing track of time, I look up and wipe the sweat out of my eyes as Daniel's tires grate along the driveway.

He stares at my handiwork. "It looks great, but you missed a few spots."

"Yes, sir!" I mock salute.

I didn't expect a response. Even though I've weeded three-fourths of the garden, Daniel's unappreciative, minimizing my contributions, and always wants more. He's obsessed with petty details yet is blind to the big picture. What's that saying? Oh yeah. *The devil is in the details!*

My desire to please has evaporated. I throw down the rake and take off my gloves.

"Why don't we go out for dinner tonight, Daniel? We never go anywhere."

"I don't have money until payday. Besides, I'm tired." He puts his arm around me. "Let's just watch a movie and get comfy."

"We never do any of the fun things you promised. You said you would buy us bicycles, and we would go for walks when I got here."

"Ahhh, come on, babe. Don't be mad. Be a good girl, and make us a nice cup of coffee?"

"We're out of coffee," I say. "You drank the last of it this morning."

"I know I'm not perfect," he says, "but who is?"

He has a good point. I am certainly not innocent. Here to rob him, I may be no better. Is it really to get my money back or to hurt him? I'm starting to doubt my motives.

I've searched every drawer, cabinet, and closet and found nothing. It's time to go back into the attic. This time, armed with his high beam flashlight, I wait until Daniel leaves for work and make sure Ripley is outside.

After unscrewing the bolts, I open the trap door and enter. The flashlight illuminates all shadows. I hope I don't run across any more mice, but they'd most likely be dead if I do. I'm sure I've scared them into the crevices of the attic walls.

There are at least nine boxes to go through. The air is thick and stifling, but I have a job to do. I pull my hair up with a plastic clip and go through each carton.

It's all junk! He didn't want to part with old stuff from previous years and relationships.

I give up. As I turn to leave, I notice something at my feet and bend down, to pick it up. It's a crumpled piece of tissue paper and unfolds with little effort. A slow smile crosses my face. I found it! The Rolex!

Stepping out of the darkness, I hold the watch up to the light. It looks just like the replica I bought in Chinatown.

Finally, I stumbled upon the Holy Grail. There it was—ten-thousand dollars' worth of watch, stuffed between the beams and insulation, haphazardly wrapped in paper.

I had daydreamed about finding it, claiming what I believe is rightfully mine, and here it is.

Now that I've found it, my purpose for coming is fulfilled. I could stick it in my purse and leave. I should be ecstatic. Yet, there's no angel on my shoulder, whispering, "You win!"

Instead, sadness envelops me, and my pent-up anger evaporates. In retrospect, I have plotted as much as Daniel, rationalizing that he drove me to it.

Reality is crashing down on me. It can go one of two ways. The first is that I could take the watch and leave as planned. The second way is to leave the watch—and Daniel. Forget my plan for retribution, write off my losses, and move on.

If he discovers his precious Rolex is gone, he'll be devastated. I shouldn't care, but it doesn't feel right.

Daniel may not have a conscience, but I still do. Even after everything he did, can I justify stealing?

He drained my finances and ruined my credit. He convinced me to invest in his shoddy business deals, always vowing to pay me back.

Besides, he promised to sell his Rolex and reimburse me for all the money he borrowed. Then he changed his mind. He never plays fair.

Struggling with my conscience, I need time to think. I rewrap the Rolex and tuck it in the insulation. After securing the trap door, I go downstairs. You can't beat a sociopath at his own game without becoming one yourself. What now?

⌖

We sit at the picnic table, drinking our morning coffee, and watch the sun peek over the trees. Daniel gazes out at the horizon. Perhaps he's wondering how to get out of this relationship.

The question is--does he have the balls to admit he doesn't love me? Probably not — he'd have to face the fact that he owes me ten thousand dollars. Aside from that, he's most likely betting I'll get insurance money from my car accident and thinking he'll benefit.

Daniel had promised to take me out to lunch, but he's trying to back out. That is until he sees a spark of anger in my eyes.

At lunchtime, I drive to his shop, and we take his van to the deli, "Last Licks." It seems like a good time to break the news, but I won't tell him I'm leaving for good. He'll only dig his heels in and try to talk me out of it. I'm not ready for that. No, I'll give him the Dear John once I'm back in Florida.

Sitting on a bench in the sun, we share a sandwich. Although I forced him, we actually are having a pleasant time.

"Too bad, I have to go back to work,' he says. "I can't wait until we're living on a boat, Florence."

There he goes again, talking about the boat. A glimmer of hope ignites like an ember waiting to fan into a flame. Daniel insists he'll sell the house and buy another boat so we can retire. I have no reason to believe him, but he persists.

Trapped between two worlds, I thought I could navigate this relationship with the help of my support website, but he's sucking me under again. When we first got together, the target was Aruba, where we would live out the rest of our days in romantic adventure. Unfortunately, there was no link between his words and actions.

I've since learned that a sociopath thrives on words. Using his wit, he's able to hide behind lies — lies I gobbled up like a baby bird. My deliberate shortsightedness didn't mean I was blind. I know the difference between someone who treats me like a priority and someone who treats me as an option. Ignorance is bliss only if you remain ignorant, but I'm not so naïve anymore. His lies no longer affect me.

Three diamonds roll through my brain. Daniel told me he won a lot of money at the casino, but I didn't ask how much. Why? I don't know — another example of how he's trained me not to rock the boat. I have to keep reminding myself. He's in my life, but I'll never be in his.

"Can I ask you something? And don't get mad," I say as we sit on the picnic bench with our lunch.

"Sure."

"How much do three diamonds in the high roller room win you?"

"Eight thousand dollars." He beams. "I should have enough to buy the boat by the end of the summer."

"I won't be staying for the summer. I'm planning to leave this coming weekend." My words are toneless. Cool.

"You can't leave! Next week is Father's Day. The girls are spending the night. I promised we would take them to Hershey Park. They'll be disappointed."

Damn, he has to pull out the guilt card.

"At least wait until after the weekend," he pleads with puppy-dog eyes. He doesn't know I'm aware of his tactics, but confessing is no use. It's all part of the game. He'll never change.

Behind the Mask

You pulled my wings off one by one
Till our love was nearly done
Kept me grounded much too long
Now it's time I move along

It's Father's Day weekend, and he has his two daughters. I'm sure I'm the only reason Lisa agrees to let the girls spend the night. Daniel insists on takeout pizza and a movie. Oh, joy — a slumber party. The girls are excited about Hershey Park, but true to form, he changes his mind last minute.

"Wouldn't you rather go to New York City?" he asks.

Emma is skeptical, but Colleen lights up. "Can we go shopping?"

"Of course, honey. I'll give you money to bargain at the street markets."

"Lisa's going to kill you for disappointing them," I say.

"She'll get over it. I did the math. Hershey's is too expensive. Besides, they'll have a better time going into the city for the day."

Daniel is so predictable. He'll play Daddy Warbucks, and the girls will eat it up. It's sickening to see because what they truly need is something he can't give.

Losing the upper hand in the conversation, I let it go. At least we won't be hanging around the house. I'll enjoy the city, but he has no clue what he's doing. He thinks the street vendors are on Delaney Street. I follow his lead, all the while knowing we'll have to backtrack.

"Let's go to Little Italy," I say when he discovers Delaney Street is desolate.

"I want to go to Canal Street," he insists.

I roll my eyes. "We have to pass Little Italy to get there!"

Emma is whining that it's hot, and Colleen isn't thrilled about bargaining for what she wants to buy. Daniel won't let her buy anything unless she talks them down on the price, and she's getting discouraged.

"I'm bored," she says. That's when the fireworks start.

"You've ruined my Father's Day!" He barks and abruptly takes away her money. Then he gives it to her younger sister.

Emma is delighted to have the extra cash and looks for a store to spend it in.

Stunned, I hang back with Colleen, apologizing for her father's behavior. Colleen is fighting back the tears. It's heartbreaking.

I corner him in the first store that Emma drags him inside. "Daniel, why are you doing this?"

"Stay out of it, Florence. I don't have to take this shit from some spoiled little brat!"

Colleen is texting someone on her phone, probably her mom. I don't blame her. I try to distract Daniel, but it doesn't work. He sees her on the phone, and it inflames his anger.

"We're leaving!" he says, herding Emma out of the store.

We leave single-file.

Daniel grasps Emma's arm and practically drags her down the streets. Even I have a hard time keeping up with him. He is acting like he's a caveman. He thinks he could go around clubbing women and dragging them by their hair. He suddenly stops and gives Colleen an icy stare. His psychological manipulations — calculated for maximum effect.

"You ruined my day," he sneers. "Go home to your fake father." If he had a conscience, he would put a bullet in his brain.

"Don't tell her that, Daniel!"

He doesn't hear me or doesn't care. His mask is slipping, revealing the real Daniel. He can't hide the ugliness inside, but there's nothing I can do. I'm used to his asshole act, but his daughter doesn't know that her father is a sociopath. She must be confused. She's struggling between resentment and her need to be loved by him.

The ride home hurts like a toothache, and his vicious words hang heavy in the air. I conclude that Daniel doesn't like women — even his daughters. I've always known in my subconscious, but his abuse has been subtle until now. Before Colleen leaves the car, he tells her not to text him with an apology because "it won't fly!" Lisa looks confused as her daughters scurry into the back seat of her car. I want to tell her about the sociopath website, but it could backfire on me.

On the way home, I glare at him. "There's something wrong with you, Daniel! You don't know what love is."

I must have hit a nerve because when we get back to the house, Daniel texts an apology to his daughter and promises to buy her a new dress.

Even though I frown at his usual bribery tactic, at least he's put his mask back on. Colleen will forgive him until the next time, but our relationship is gasping with its last breath.

For years, I practiced denial, pretending he wasn't a fraud. All I ever wanted was to love him, but he made it impossible. There's nothing more degrading than jumping through hoops to prove one's worth.

Accepting that nothing has been real is the hardest part of letting go. The man I first met was an actor. He pulled the 'old bait and switch act,' and all that's left is the true man behind the mask.

"Tough Love!" I tell myself, but even as I prepare to leap, a nagging doubt held me in fear. *What if!*

Toxic

Driving down that road
The chill of emptiness
without you by my side
I do it with distress

It's our last night together, and Daniel puts on the old movie *Lonesome Dove*. We've finished the first part, *Comanche Moon*. It's become our routine. Since the episode with his daughter, he's been more attentive. *Bless his tainted heart!*

Daniel insists on holding me close to him. He leans in closer. I smell his breath on my cheek. Before getting into bed, he even removes his pants and shirt, but he's an empty suit. I remember the plans we made, the enticing future. My heart remembers the love I once had for him. Obsessed with the picture-perfect life he painted, I persevered, grasping for the brass ring and getting thin air.

The slightest enjoyable moment ended with a condition, a conflict, or something material he needed, something to stress me out. Talk of love, a future of happiness in each other's lives, died, replaced with a steady diet of tolerance until all I feel is disdain.

A part of me will always love Daniel — or at least, his illusion. But it's too late. When I look into his eyes, there's no connection. I wish he were different with all my heart, but I've given him enough chances. There is no cure for what he is. If I were willing, he would continue to manipulate and exploit me. That's his nature. He's toxic—all lies, deceit, and unfilled promises.

⌒⌘⌒

Daniel hasn't replaced the decanter for the brewer yet. I have to boil water to make coffee. You'd think he'd buy a new coffee pot with all his money. The refrigerator is noticeably bare. His wallet closed a few weeks after I arrived. I'm eager to get back to my apartment. I packed yesterday to avoid a scene. My bags are already in the car. Although I'm relieved to be leaving, I'm a little melancholy. I guess it's normal. I've adjusted to his life, albeit dysfunctional, and now I'm ending something familiar.

Although I'm resolved not to spend the rest of my life with Daniel, there are days when I can't breathe. Perhaps it would be easier to stay. I could try to delude myself into thinking we can fix our relationship and retire together on a boat in Aruba as planned, but I know better. I've told myself those lies for too long — lies that led me to pain and despair. Daniel would continue the charade until the end of time. Once, I even told him he was a life sentence. Change is hard, but it's time I make a new choice. It's time to leave. My life will never get better if I stay. The sooner I accept it, the sooner I'll heal.

While he's in the shower, I make one more trip to the attic and then pack the last of my things in the car.

He looks a little lost when he comes down the stairs.

"I don't understand why you're going back to Florida," he says.

"What difference does it make? You work all day. I sit around here twiddling my thumbs."

"You haven't given it a chance. I wish you would stick it out until the spring, Babe."

"I can't do that, Daniel. We've been through this. I don't belong here."

"How long do you plan to be gone for?" he asks.

"I'm not sure," I say.

"If you take a plane, I'll pay half," he offers.

Daniel's not going to make this easy.

I almost want to laugh. Why? Is it his fake generosity, or does he think his half-assed offer will tempt me? I'm not sure.

"Thanks, Daniel, but I'll need my car. Besides, Ripley's never traveled on a plane."

"They'll stick him in the cargo bay!" Daniel's laugh trails off. Although he doesn't acknowledge it, I think he senses the finality of my departure.

The sky looks bruised — all purple and black. It's as raw as my emotions. I couldn't do this if Daniel suddenly declared his love for me.

"Be careful on the road. I think it's going to rain." He kisses me on the cheek, confirming I'm doing the right thing.

Keeping sight of him through my side-view mirror, I watch him retreat into his house. I drive past the lake, where we sometimes sat under the trees and drank coffee. Then the liquor store where the owner and I had become good friends, and then the post office where I picked up my mail. I'll never travel this road again. This is his town, the place where *he* belongs.

My car points south, taking me away from Daniel and the life I've lived for the past three years. The last time we parted, I clung to the illusion that we would see each other again. An overwhelming sense of sadness grips me. My memories are reluctant to let go, but it's time to mourn a relationship that was never real.

A familiar love song comes on the radio. I don't need reminding of what I never had, so I turn it off. The melody in my head remains. My questions will never get logical answers. I need to accept that, but my heart is not in sync with my brain.

Even though I left him, part of me still loves Daniel.

I'm Done

I will soar into the sky
Not knowing where I'll go
Will not look away or back
My dignity I'll show

My Florida world is still here, just the way I left it. The sun is shining. I want to smile, but I can't. I never thought I would end this way.

The phone rings — Daniel. My heart thumps wildly, and that old familiar feeling floods back. The addiction is still there — I miss the sound of his voice. It's my drug of choice. It hypnotizes me into thinking all is well for a moment, but it isn't long until I need another fix. Should I answer? If I do, I risk getting entangled again, and I don't want to fall back into his web. Prolonging this dysfunctional relationship would only postpone my agony.

Thank goodness for my cat, Ripley. His reassuring stare tells me I have his unconditional love. If cats could talk, he would have ended this nonsense long ago. He plops down on my bed and keeps me company while I sleep, but my hand drifts, only to find the vacant space. I miss Daniel's arms around me at night, but I don't miss falling in the toilet or waking up to the smell of cigarette smoke at three in the morning.

The silence of dawn makes my gut clench, and a wave of grief washes through me. I always ran to him for comfort when I felt like this, which is crazy because he inspired most of my anxiety.

The phone rings, but the number is unfamiliar. I let it go to voicemail. It's the electric company reminding me that the bill is late. Oh, shit! I forgot all about that. I send him a text.

"Call the electric company and transfer to your name."

That gets his attention.

My cell phone rings. "Florence. I won't have money until payday. Stop pressuring me."

The phone goes dead.

⚬⚬⚬

Three days come and go. It's a battle of wills, but this time, I win.

My phone chimes.

"What's up?"

I stare at the cold and emotionless message like a knife stabbing my heart.

What did I expect? "I miss you," and "I wish you didn't leave." Every word out of his mouth would be a lie.

Another text from Daniel.

"Bad girl! Have you stopped speaking to me?"

It takes every bit of my strength, but I don't respond.

"r u ok. Just reply yes or no. u have me concerned."

I can sense his panic — his loss of control.

The temptation is strong to ask if he's paid the electric bill, but I resist. Even if he did, I can no longer use money as an excuse to stay connected.

It's time for NO CONTACT! No Contact. Those words stir dread and anxiety.

No contact is necessary to stop the abuse, like when I stopped smoking cold turkey. There were days I felt strong, and others when I dragged forward, wondering if it was worth the discomfort. I need to weather this storm until I'm free from a crippling habit and able to move on to a healthy life.

If I'm really going to go no contact, I can't contact him in any form—no more text, phone, or email, including social media.

I know the risk. If I give in, there'll be no going back.

The blogging community suggests I block his contact information altogether, but I'm not ready for that. Part of me wants to know his reaction.

My determination is fierce. I will not call Daniel. Instead, I read the cheating emails that he wrote to other women. I remind myself that he never loved me and vow not to answer if he calls.

The average attempt at No Contact is about seven times. Will I be resilient enough?

I look out at the night sky. The moon's full round face shines toward the earth, and a nearby planet flickers. Taking one last look, I close the blinds and pick up my phone.

With my heart in my mouth, I send Daniel a text. *"I'm done!"*

For a brief moment, a wave of relief washes over me. Daniel's gone—forever! I feel another panic attack coming on. I just shot myself in the foot and blew the chance of getting any money back.

After a year of "a-ha" moments, I never thought it would come down to two simple words. "I'm done!" Like a light switch, I shut down Daniel's power and broke the last connection.

The minute I sent the text, my anxiety rose. Was I too harsh? I'm finding it hard to breathe.

No Contact

Up I fly with bated breath
Afraid of what I'll find
Further from your life
No longer intertwined

As expected, my phone rings every two minutes, but I don't answer. I let the phone go to voicemail. Not that Daniel leaves a message. He stopped that years ago. As if by not leaving his voice on my phone, he doesn't exist. I don't have anything to say to him anyway. What's the use?

He texts. *"Not cool on your part. We can't talk about this?"*

No doubt, he would hear the pain in my voice. I won't give him the satisfaction of knowing he's torn my heart inside out.

Another text. *"So, X-mas is off, I take it?"*

He's trying to tempt me with a holiday vacation we had discussed. The vacation I never bought into because I know him so well. I'm surprised he hasn't mentioned the boat. That carrot kept me holding on longer than I should have.

Another text. *"What about our plans to retire and live on a boat?"*

I knew he would eventually use my dream of living on the ocean. Well, that boat won't float.

Another text. *"Are you going to answer?"*

I wish I could, Daniel, but it wouldn't change a thing. You never loved me. I was just a meal ticket. I don't want your apologies—not that you would offer them.

Another text. "Okay, you're out of hand for no reason. I'm calling you in thirty minutes. If you don't answer, I will take it deeply. I will never speak to you again... AND I MEAN IT."

His lack of affection is blatant. In the past, his words would have struck me to the core, but now, I'm numb. I've crossed the line from wanting his love to accepting he is incapable of love.

Thirty minutes tick by, then my phone rings. If I engage Daniel, he will twist my words, and we'll end up in a no-win battle.

Another text. *"Okay... thanks. I don't know why you ended this way, but I will respect your way of handling it. I won't contact or be contacted by you again. I wish you the best, always. I will add. You have made me very sad, and I will never forget how you handled yourself."*

Stinger!

Am I a bad person? If so, I'm about to get worse. I called the electric company and scheduled a shut-off date.

He sends another text, giving me just enough time to think about the consequences of my actions.

"I'm not mad anymore. Can't we be friends?"

Ahh, he's offering the friendship card and glossing over everything he has done to hurt me. I'd feel obligated to free him of all responsibility as a friend. No thanks!

Daniel is grabbing for straws. Freud calls it narcissistic injury. By ending the relationship, I've pointed out that he's not as special as he believed. He doesn't miss me, just the power he had over me. I'm sure I damaged his ego.

Another text. *"Hey, Darlin… u can say hi… now and then."* Attached is a picture of his two daughters huddled together, looking sad. It wrenches my heart, although I know it's posed. I wonder what they think of their father exploiting them this way. I don't respond.

Daniel takes another approach. *"Hey! You're not even going to say hello… what's up with that… if you met someone, it's okay. I won't be offended."*

Of course not. That would give Daniel the perfect out and allow him to play the victim with someone new. Instead of wondering what he did to make me leave, he'd tell people I was nuts or mentally unstable. I can imagine the stories he's telling. Daniel's good at playing the victim. I'm sure he'll play it for a while.

Oh, poor Daniel!

Is this his attempt at being magnanimous?

The phone rings. Daniel's testing my resolve once more. I pass, but I can't get him out of my mind.

Even though I'm the one who ended the relationship, I'm feeling the sting. The knot in my throat tightens.

The finality of no contact is like an empty void, quickly filled with withdrawal symptoms and self-doubt.

There are days I feel lucky to be rid of him and nights when I cry myself to sleep. Seeking comfort from the sociopath survival website, I reach out for words of wisdom.

Florence: I've gone no contact, and it hurts. I'm trying to be strong, endure the pain, and remember he does not love me.

Valerie: I went No Contact three years ago - not easy, but I had to save myself & life is so much better now. Yes, it does hurt & will for a while. Keep making lists of all the bad things you've left behind & all the good things that you will have in your life going No Contact. Keep busy. Make new friends. Pamper yourself. Reach out if you need a friend. I went No Contact three years ago - not easy, but I had to save myself & life is so much better now. Remember, you deserve better. {{hugs}}

Tina: Hang in there, Florence; you can do this, Girl! It does get better, and you will get stronger! WE ARE ALL HERE FOR YOU, FLORENCE!

Lisa: Just like crack, they are (well, I've never actually been on crack, but you know what I mean). We have all been there, and it sucks!

Florence: This is day two. I've never been on crack, but I have a new understanding if this is what it feels like. I will NOT call him. Dear God, give me strength. I'm in a tug-o-war.

Traci: Day two? Oh, my. That sucks. I remember day two. That was just over a year ago for me. The thing that sticks out the most is the loneliness. Even though his contact was hurtful and exhausting, it was constant.

Silva: One thing I believe to be true. When trying to give up something, replacing it with something else is important, and I don't mean something similar! Replace it with something positive and good for you. Friends, cooking, traveling, even writing, anything that is wholesome and distracts your mind from what you are suffering. Good luck! I am sending positive thoughts.

Nathalia: No contact will heal you. Repeat that to yourself."

Amy: Redirect your nervous energy into doing kind things for yourself. Go to a movie, take a bubble bath, or have coffee with friends. Stay busy. Stay active. Above all, stay the course! It's worth it, I promise.

Caroline: Remember, you have been his pawn in his emotional games. This is the only way to say you don't want to play. You are no longer his victim. You are taking back your life. You are giving yourself the respect & caring that he never gave you. Once the pain diminishes, the sun will come out. You will find a whole new world out there, and that life is so much sweeter. You go, girl! Hugs.

Words of Wisdom

A million tears will flow
From my eyes today
I do not try to stop them
They wash my hurt away

Daniel sends a text. *"Florence, you upset me. Saying, 'I'm done,' sounds like you just finished a meal. What's that all about?"*

There's no turning back for me. I have nothing to say to him.

He sends another text. *"Now, I see your true colors. After everything I've done for you! I can't believe you're treating me this way."*

It figures Daniel would deflect blame and accuse me. Everything he's done for me? True colors?

I'm not supposed to break the No Contact Rule, but I'm furious. I fire off a response.

"What did you ever do for me? If anyone showed their true colors, it was you. You tricked me into loving you and then took advantage of my feelings. I let you move in with me and expected nothing but love and companionship. Instead, you used me until I was broke. Then when nothing was left, you went home. You weren't man enough to tell me it was over, so you strung me along. Now, you left me to deal with the boat. The boat you wanted so badly and let sink. On top of that, I'm in debt, but I don't expect you will man-up to pay me. It's funny how you can twist things around to

suit your needs. Well, count me out. I don't even care about the money at this point."

My finger hovers over the send button, but instead, I click delete. Even though it would give me great pleasure to tell him what I think of him, what good will it do? No, I won't give him the chance to twist the truth.

Being free of Daniel should be a blessing but cutting myself off from him is so final. It's past the time he usually reaches out to say good morning. There's a painful knot in my stomach. My withdrawal symptoms are at their peak. I'm so used to living on crumbs I even miss his calls. I start to hyperventilate as anxiety takes over. He's been like Prozac. As soon as he called, I'd scrape myself off the floor.

No contact only works when I'm feeling strong. Today, I don't. I'm screaming out for a fix, but if I break down and call him, I'll feed my addiction and continue my dependency on Daniel.

He doesn't love me! Why can't I get it through my thick head? Actually, my head knows. It's my heart that betrays me.

❧

Daniel's power will be shut off today. Part of me feels guilty that he won't have electricity in the middle of winter. Should I warn him? I'm not sure I could live with myself if all his pipes burst. I'm about to break the No Contact Rule, but my conscience rules. I send him a text.

"Daniel, the electricity will be turned off today. Please transfer the account into your name."

The sound of my phone sends panic snaking down to the small of my spine. My cell phone is blowing up with calls from Daniel. I don't dare answer, knowing he's on the warpath.

He sends a text. *"Call me right now!"*

Another text. *"That's so fucked up shutting down the electricity.*

His mask is slipping. He's starting to freak out.

Another text. *Don't ever try to contact me – ever."*

Poof! I'm nothing.

I let Daniel have another bullet to shoot at me y breaking no contact—just in case he missed the first time. Did I think he'd appreciate my warning? All it did was to give him permission to abuse me more.

Vomit rushes up to lick the base of my throat. I swallow hard, forcing it back down. Any confidence I had is fading, but Daniel is still lurking in the shadows of my subconscious. I wake up in the night, longing for someone's arms around me. *Oh, Daniel! If only you were the man, you said you were. You gave your love, then took it away …Why?*

I quiet my brain with self-soothing techniques. When that doesn't work, I abandon my bed. Thank goodness, even in the middle of the night, someone's online to console me.

Florence: I was so tempted to call him today. It took everything I had not to call. I feel sick.

Kate: Florence, you will get through this. Keep reminding yourself of all the bad stuff. Write it down and keep reading it over and over. That helped me. He will never change. Don't waste any more of yourself on him. I regret thirteen wasted years.

Rachel: Give him nothing. With every text you even read, he still has you and has a chance to suck you back in...."

Florence: "I envy your strength. I won't call him, but if he calls again, it will take an act of God for me not to answer. I guess it's another Advil pm night.

Kate: Well done on not giving in. It's better for you. He will only hurt you again. I hope you sleep well. Here's to another day of no contact tomorrow. X.

Rachel: Just remember — every time you even look in their direction, it feeds their ego and makes them more powerful. And every time you respond, it gives them the go-ahead to contact you again. They will lie, deceive and bait you to respond, but the only way you can truly vanquish their abuse from your life is to ignore them so damn hard that they doubt their own existence.

Florence: It's only been four days, and I doubt myself. I'm feeling queasy. When will the pain go away?

Kate: Feeling sick is normal; it's part of the withdrawal. You are doing great. Stay strong.

Rachel: I am nine months out; the first few months were incredibly hard, as your brain doesn't switch off from the mind games, emotional abuse, and confusion.

Florence: I want to tell him what I think about him. I need closure.

Rachel: Unfortunately, no one ever really gets closure with their ex Narc. It may make you feel better telling him he is a worthless piece of garbage, but he won't believe you! No matter what he has done or how bad he has treated you. He will never take responsibility.

❧

It's too early to drink, but to take my mind off Daniel, I pour myself a glass of wine and grab something to read from my bookshelf. Sandwiched between the pages is a post-it note. "GOOD MORNING SUNSHINE" is printed in capital letters. I crumble it into a ball and throw it in the trash.

Tears run down the crease of my nose. Unable to concentrate on reading, I put the book back on the shelf and log on to my computer. I keep glancing at the trashcan. Finally, I dig the note out, unravel it, and stick it back between the pages of the book. When I return to my computer, there's an email from Terry, the woman from California.

"I don't know how you got my email, but I have to warn you. Daniel Weaver is a crook. He cheated me in business and had an affair with my au pair. He's not a good man. I suggest you stay clear of him."

Her email confirms what I suspected all along. I'm not the first. Daniel's left a trail of broken hearts and empty wallets.

There's also another email from Daniel. *"I'm heading down to Florida to check on a boat."*

I'm scared he will be scratching at my door for a moment, but there's no chance of that. No, it's another ploy, but it won't work. He had plenty of chances.

Daniel must have smelled my weakness like a wolf closing in on his prey.

When I told Daniel, "I'm done!" He didn't see it coming. Nice, sweet Florence would never break up so abruptly and on a text, no less.

There was a time when I would sit and cry over the words he texted me when we first met. Yes, a text was more appropriate. Game over, I win…except, I don't feel like a winner. I'll never get closure. Daniel will never take accountability for the money he borrowed. He will never settle the debt. In his mind, my actions voided any obligation on his part. That's something I must accept. Yet, in the end, I pulled the rug out from under him. There's satisfaction in that. No, I won't get closure, but neither will he.

Filled with self-doubt, I'm still crutching on the narcissist victim website.

Florence: I don't know what day it is on no contact, but the pain is still lurking under the surface. I can go for hours, and then, bam! Emptiness hits me. Was I wrong to end it in a text?

Rachel: You have come so far! Those feelings will be with you for a while, hon. You need to find something to keep you busy to help you through. There is no turning back now, as you would have to start all over again.

Florence: I'm almost through another day. He hasn't tried to contact me again. I can't believe it. I have that achy sad feeling in the pit of my stomach, but I hope that will subside.

Rachel: I fully understand that you are sad, but you already know in your heart that as long as you stay with this man, your heart will ache. He will never treat anyone decently for any length of time, and he *cannot* be fixed. You are doing what is best for you.

Caroline: No contact is hard; it sets them off because they have no control. They hate that. But stick it out, Flo. It eventually gives you your life back.

Rachel: You will go through the motions. Unfortunately, they do your head in. Generally, after leaving an abusive relationship, you will feel loss, anxiety, sometimes fear, most definitely confusion, and even grief. People with this disorder don't experience emotions like others. They can only pretend. Change your mobile number; get rid of him for good.

Silva: They will sometimes go a long while without contact, and then wham! Out of the blue, you will hear from them six months or two years later when you aren't prepared. Stay vigilant.

⁓

The physical and emotional toll of detoxing is hard. Whenever I think I'm over the anxiety attacks—they sneak up on me.

I want to shut off my brain. If I can sleep all night, I'll be one day ahead and hopefully stronger tomorrow.

He has no idea of the agony I'm going through. No Contact gives me that comfort. Although I'm not responding, I should block his number. No Contact means no communication at all, but I'm mired in dysfunctional behavioral patterns. By leaving the door open for him to call, text, or email, there was a sliver of a chance — that *what if.*

The longer I'm away from Daniel, the easier it should get. Yet triggers seem everywhere — the wind in the trees, the clouds in the sky, the scent of spring. Even walking through certain chain stores inspires sadness. I'm back on the victim blog.

Florence: Why can't I get him out of my head?

Rachel: They are masters at manipulation; they mold their masks to be exactly what we want. Then they love-bomb. By the time the mask falls off, we are in too deep, and that's when the discarding, cheating, and confusion start.

Dixie: Block and then delete his number. It's like putting your hand into a blender - it hurts YOU! It's so hard. But the relief, when they are gone far, outweighs any 'good' feeling you thought they ever gave you! It will take everything you have and more - but you have what it takes, one minute at a time if you can't manage a day.

Kate: "Block him on email now too ...you will feel guilty because you can feel emotions. He can't! He has no feelings. It's all fake. He only cares about his own self-serving needs. Don't fall for it, hon. Keep being strong. You are doing so, so, well and dumping by text is the only way to do it; otherwise, they draw you back in and then spit you back out and break you all over."

Rachel: It is like mind madness. They chip away at us piece by piece to create the "addiction!" The best thing you can do for yourself is eliminate ALL forms of possible communication.

Replaced

The winds of winter are upon us
I feel his cold caress
The birds fly south above us
A chill of emptiness

Time is a vacuum of loneliness as I push forward from one day to the next, hoping the pain will lessen. It's disappointing. I had hoped that I would heal faster. It's been a little over three months since No Contact and a long journey to recovery — two steps forward and one back. An occasional trigger could send me crashing back into the past. The people closest to me don't want to hear about my pain anymore. I have to suck it up. They don't understand it will take one to two years to get myself back in a good place. Sometimes, I wish they could read the blogs and websites about surviving relationships with narcissists and sociopaths. Then they would understand — this is not an ordinary breakup.

In the middle of the night, the sound of a semi-truck passing by my window sends me back to Daniel's room. I open my eyes to find I'm in my own bed. It's unnerving how scents and sounds work their way into my brain and wring it out like an old washcloth. Haunted by Daniel, I'm tossing and turning, his voice in my head. Memories pull me into that dark hole of despair. I wonder if this is a post-traumatic stress disorder. Please, God, make it stop!

Memories hijack my emotions. I'm having flashes of longing that send me right back where I started. Looking over my shoulder is not a good idea, but I'm powerless. At a weak moment, I succumb to the tears and log on to Daniel's social media page. My replacement smiles at me, long brown hair flowing down her back in curls and the innocent look of twenty fewer years' experience. I peer into her carefully made-up eyes and see my reflection. Needy and romantic, ready to give up everything for love. I should feel bad for his new victim. She'll give her heart, and he'll crush it. It's like losing your virginity. You can't get it back.

Daniel cleans up good! He must have presented himself flawlessly. Why else would such a young woman be attracted to a sixty-one-year-old man? And what about his problem? Has he had a miraculous recovery? Or does this girl appeal to his libido?

Why does she deserve his affection? Experts say sociopaths cannot bond and are not capable of attachment. It's no comfort. I'm sure he'll dish out the good stuff on fine chinaware, no less.

The feeling of rejection is devastating. If Daniel doesn't want me, will anyone? Reeling from the fact that I loved this man who ground me into the dirt, I'm left to pick up the pieces of my shattered self-esteem while he rides off into the sunset.

Why is it men can get away with anything? Steal your love, time, and money, then end the relationship by saying it just didn't work out.

Apparently, other women are willing to cut Daniel a break. They'll believe his lies and blame the victim without knowing the whole story.

By looking at his Facebook page, I broke No Contact. It serves me right. Needing strength, I log in to my support blog.

Florence: Daniel has a new girlfriend. I'm not sure how I feel about it. My sentiments are all over the map. On the one hand, I feel devalued, as if I never existed. On the other, I feel bad for her. She's being swept away on a fool's journey.

Rachel: Just remember, he is incapable of change. He's disordered, so everything he touches will eventually turn into shit.

Florence: This is true, but it hurts. I'm consumed with venom and want to warn her that she's dating a sociopath.

Rachel: You can tell her he has a mental health problem, but she'll never believe you. With every conversation, with every explanation, you will waste your breath.

⁂

Today the air is crisp and clean, reminding me of a spring morning at Daniel's house when we sat outside and sipped our coffee. I imagine him sitting with her, laughing and joking like we did. It makes me sick to think he's focusing his energies on making her *like* him.

Daniel divulged secrets about his dysfunctional childhood and stories about his ex-girlfriends to stir up my empathy when we first met. I'm sure he's added me to the list of women who wronged him. I wonder if it ever crawls across his warped mind that he owes me money. I need advice.

Florence: It's been over three months since I committed to NO CONTACT with the sociopath. Part of the reason I didn't let go sooner was that he owed me a lot of money. Recently, I found a promissory note for a portion. I had him notarize it the first time he borrowed money from me, back when I had a few functioning brain cells. I'm sure he forgot that he signed it or chose to. Should I send him a copy of the promissory note in an email?

Marie: It doesn't matter if you were to send him a copy of that note or not. He STILL isn't going to pay you ...you will just be opening another gaping wound and starting your recovery all over again.

Florence: I knew he wouldn't pay me back, but how he got away with it gnaws at me. Teflon! Nothing ever sticks to this guy.

Marie: Florence, I understand what you are saying, but if I can just squeeze this by you. What I suspect you are doing is slipping into your head. I know the game as well as you do. You are on the detox train. That's a tough ride. You may or may not be aware of it, but in these relationships, it is similar to being chemically dependent, just like an illegal drug. That dopamine is very addictive. I suspect your brain registered this 'find' as a way to get some 'drugs.' I bet right now. Your heart is racing, your mind ticking, right? Been there, done that. HANDS OFF THE DRUG Dealer! Get off the drugs – shut it down!

Rachel: Flo, you've come so far. It's important that you stay NO CONTACT, hon. I would get legal advice. Marie is right; he isn't going to pay it back unless he is legally forced, OR there is something in it for him ...Please! Do not sacrifice yourself and another day of your sanity by contacting him one-on-one, on any level.

Clara: Florence, you have friends here who love and care for you. You absolutely have this. I have lost everything from my narc and a lot of money. I have written it off. I now see it as a small price to pay for freedom.

Florence: You are right, of course. I had a rough week. I guess I'm just looking for a way to hurt him as much as he hurt me. It would have no other effect than to ruin his day. I'll get back on track.

Marie: Yay, you! I always say – 'Hold my hand — we'll get through this together.' So, you just hang on, sister!

Plenty of Fish

I truly did believe
Our love would never die
But time has chipped away
And I do not know why

It's comforting to have good friends who know what I'm going through and care about me. Face-to-face combat with Daniel would be unpleasant. His mask is off! I can imagine the hatred seething through him.

No Contact is all about getting my power back. It takes practice, but I'm getting better at it. The more I read about Daniel's disorder, the harder it is to focus on my own healing. The only way to move forward is not to let him abuse me anymore, which means I must stop looking back. It doesn't matter what he does or with whom he's doing it. The door is closed. I have to stop checking to see if it's locked. I'll never see Daniel again. I'm trying to cope with the sadness, injustice, fear, and anger, but my grief is the hardest to bear.

I've been going to my group anxiety meetings, and I'm actually in a better state of awareness. I've stopped hyperventilating, but sometimes my mind drifts to the past.

My tears are drying, but the only way I'll get through to the other end is to make new memories, which means dating. I've lost my faith in men.

Like Alice in Wonderland, I didn't know what was up or down and fell down the rabbit hole. Daniel surrounded me with lies and diversions until I was caught in a maze of confusion. Emotionally invested, I held onto the hope he might come to his senses. I convinced myself that Daniel loved me, and I accepted his abuse. I'd like to think he cared at some level. After all, my self-worth is at stake. It's partly my fault. I knew what he was waiting for; the possibility that I would come into money. We both knew I was an easy mark.

Daniel strangled my life force until I wasn't sure who I was. My fragile self-esteem kept me on the verge of tears as he wove his lies and abuse. After extensive research and conversations on numerous support blogs, I feel strong enough to rebuild my self-esteem. With the help of other survivors, I'm learning that my worth had nothing to do with his discarding of my love. He's a sociopath. I am not to blame. I am not unlovable. I did not deserve this.

It's hard for people to understand the devastation he caused to my life. He held all the pieces and dictated every aspect of our life, from when we ate or drank coffee to what movie we would watch when we went to bed. Unaware of his emotional manipulation, I moved along his game board with minimal opposition.

For a long time, I believed it was easier to remain silent. But it fueled his control. I see it clearly now. Daniel is a predator. He's no better than a common criminal is. Only he goes unpunished for his crimes. He as well as ripped me off the street and kept me, prisoner, in his basement. The chains were unlocked, and I could have walked away, but fear and need are invisible shackles. They can keep someone captive. I was brainwashed — a hostage.

The support I get from my anxiety group is an enormous help. Still, until I heal the psychological wounds that compelled me to remain in this dysfunctional dance, I could spend the rest of my life bitter from the injustice of it all. I'll never get those years back. There is no cure for his mental condition. A psychological parasite, he carries the same inner demons, regardless of what holiday he has booked or what younger woman he may be entertaining. He will be who he is.

❧

It's Friday night. Feeling rejected and duped, I'm close to a meltdown. If I could just get the nerve to go out on a Friday night — maybe go to a club and listen to music. I might even meet someone else who could make me forget. I snap out of the gloom and reactivate my membership on Plenty of Fish. Eight out of ten men there are most likely like Daniel, but there is a saying — to get over one man — you need to get with another. At first, I list my actual age, but the men who reach out to me are appalling. They all look so old. I am too, but I'm in decent shape. I'm uncomfortable about it, but I lower the age range to five years younger. Does that make me a cougar?

Bingo! The field of prospects widens. One is especially intriguing. His name is Robert. He lives on a boat—not a rowboat or a speedboat, but a sailboat, a big one. He's smiling in his profile picture as he pours a drink for himself and two friends on the deck. I agree to meet him, but I have no expectations. The most I can hope for is a night out and to forget Daniel for a few hours.

I meet Robert for dinner. The evening is pleasant enough as I stare across the table, trying to decide if I could be with this man. By the end of the meal, I'm a little more comfortable until he walks me to my car. Robert's hand brushes mine and clasps it in his as if we're already in a relationship. I know I'm not ready, and his contact scares me. I stare up at the night sky and comment on its beauty.

Once we get to my car, Robert tries to kiss me, but I pull away. He droops with disappointment, but he's a gentleman and waits for me to get into my car.

I'm not sure how to rebuild my life or how to face my insecurities. Perhaps it's time to see a private therapist.

Post-Traumatic

Parting from the one you love
No one could ever win
Linger do the memories
Of things that could have been

A perky young woman from the mental health clinic leads me into a small room with dim lighting. Sitting behind a desk is a man in his early seventies. He's slight in stature and soft-spoken. I don't think he will understand my situation, but I sit in the chair across from him and take a deep breath.

He scans the paperwork and smiles. "May I call you Florence?"

I nod, wringing my hands, which remain frozen on my lap.

"My name is Dr. Gerard. I'm a part-time therapist here. I was retired, but it didn't sit well with me, so I've returned to offer my services. I see on your chart that you suffer from anxiety and depression."

"Yes. I was in a relationship with a guy I had known from high school for almost five years. At first, I thought he loved me, but he was just using me for my money. I cut myself off from him six months ago. It took everything I had to break it off, but it still hurts." Tears spill from my eyes.

"I see." He hands me a box of Kleenex. The sight of the white fluffy tissues opens the floodgates.

"I've been so upset. I know I did the right thing, but sometimes I can't sleep. I think I have post-traumatic stress disorder."

Dr. Gerald looks at me over his spectacles and narrows his eyes.

"It is possible you have codependent tendencies, but I doubt you have PTSD."

He pulls a book off his shelf and thumbs through until he comes to the page he wants. "Post-Traumatic Stress Disorder is a serious affliction that happens to people in violent situations. The events repeat time and again, keeping the person in a perpetual cycle of terror."

"Isn't emotional trauma just as hurtful?" I ask.

"Yes, but emotional trauma can be overcome. It takes time to rebuild your self-esteem. The first step is recognizing your problem. I'd say you're moderately depressed."

"Sometimes, I can't breathe, although it's gotten better since I left Daniel."

"Have you ever heard of Cognitive Dissonance?"

"No."

"It's mental stress experienced by individuals who have conflicting beliefs or are confronted by things that are contradictory to their values. For example, your behavior was to stay in the relationship, even though you knew you could get hurt. Cognitive Dissonance occurred because his behavior and your beliefs were not in harmony. You weren't willing to establish healthy boundaries, so you hung in there, hoping things would change and compromising your self-worth."

"Daniel tricked me—always trying to make me think our relationship was normal—that he was normal. I wanted to believe it, but in reality, I didn't feel loved. Once I discovered he was a sociopath, everything became clearer, but my anxiety increased. I began to have panic attacks."

"That's because you were trying to balance the truth about Daniel with your once trusting spirit."

"When we first met, he joked about being vague as if it was an attribute! Thinking I could handle it, I maneuvered through the relationship, walking on eggshells so his mask would never slip. I was sleepwalking through my life. That's what the past few years with Daniel have felt like. In a state of denial, I went about my daily activities, unable to snap myself into consciousness."

"It may seem easier to avoid a confrontation by going along with someone or something you don't agree with, but in the end, you end up hurting yourself."

"I let Daniel use me."

"Hmm. Didn't you get something from the relationship?"

"I didn't want to be alone. Daniel didn't show affection, but he was there."

"He filled a need for you to have someone in your life even if he wasn't onboard one-hundred percent."

"I guess he did. I never thought about it that way."

"It's all in the way you look at it. Have you ever heard of cognitive behavior therapy?"

"Yes. The therapist in my anxiety group always talks about it and gives us worksheets. I think it means changing the way you think about things. Like the glass half full instead of half empty."

"Exactly. Cognitive behavior therapy focuses on changing the patterns of thinking and behavior and attitudes to deal with emotional problems."

"You're not going to tell me to think positive, are you?"

"We'll discuss Cognitive Behavior Therapy at your next session."

❧

Dr. Gerald says I don't have Post-traumatic Stress Disorder because I was not a victim of violence, but a recent post on *ANA, After Narcissist Abuse's* website sums it up. Psychic trauma is just as shattering, inside and out.

I guess Dr. Gerard isn't aware of this. I'm trying hard to process the trauma but am unsure what the rules are; my defense mechanisms make it difficult to function. Why did I allow myself to be victimized? Am I weak? Needy? Stupid?

Someone once told me, "First you are a victim, then you are a volunteer," but I didn't choose to be lied to, cheated on, used, and discarded.

My perception of the world and people has changed. I've reached a heightened sense of vulnerability. Everyone looks like a sociopath or may have ulterior motives.

I experience a fresh wound every time my memories take over, leaving me empty and unsure of whom to trust.

ANA refers to this as "the 'walking dead' effect." I wonder if the ladies on my support blog agree.

Florence: I saw a shrink yesterday. He said I was moderately depressed. Also said, I didn't have PTSD, only symptoms. Go figure!

Amy: It's an echo of past pain. I have this too, and PTSD sucks. It was in letting go of wanting and needing the validation of vindication that I started to find my peace. You know what they say, "living well is the best revenge."

Monique: I suffered for years, even when I was still with my ex-narc. I would wake up screaming and didn't know why. I now know my very soul was screaming that he was killing me. I was so disconnected from all the gaslighting and manipulative mind games. I denied my intuition over and over again. Now I'm practicing meditation, self-loving, and positive thinking.

Cognitive Behavior

Heart in pain and stomach knots
Desire not to eat
Body yearns for rest
But doesn't welcome sleep

I'm not confident in the efficacy of Cognitive Behavior Therapy. It sounds too familiar. Like when Daniel accused me of being negative.

This is my second therapy session. Dr. Gerald appears and leads me back to his office. The scent of lavender emits from a small-lit candle on his bookshelf. It's supposed to be comforting, but I hate the smell of lavender. I say nothing, which is typical of me. I don't want to hurt his feelings, you know.

"How are you this week?" he asks.

"I haven't gone out much, which suits me fine. My misery doesn't want company. I can't deal with people lately. I've been hitting the wine."

His face is riddled with concern, and I quickly add, "But only a glass or two at dinner."

There! The wrinkles in his forehead relax. I do hit that bottle if I can't sleep at night, but I rationalize it's better than taking pills.

He smiles. "So, the last time you were here, we discussed Cognitive Behavior Therapy. It's used to help treat a wide range of issues, including relationship problems, drug and alcohol abuse, anxiety, and depression."

"Is it going to make me forget Daniel?"

"No, but it will help you develop a new strategy for tackling the destructive effects of how you think of him."

"That's a hard one. I've never had closure. Nothing I went through counted...."

"You knew the cost, yet you kept paying," he says."

I nodded and looked down. "Yes, I feel so pathetic. I'm carrying an enormous amount of shame—shame for believing in a man everyone tried to warn me about. I let him con me."

"Don't be so hard on yourself, Florence. You did finally leave. Together we'll develop a set of strategies that you can apply whenever you feel overwhelmed."

"Are you going to train my brain?"

"Yes, through a combination of Psychotherapy, which examines the personal meaning we place on things, and Behavioral Therapy, the relationship between our problems, behavior, and thoughts. These patterns begin in childhood."

"I was shy, growing up... and sad, but basically, I had a normal family."

"So, you had a healthy childhood?"

"I didn't say that. My father was an alcoholic. He wasn't pleasant when he got drunk, but he wasn't physically abusive. Most of the time, he took it out on my mother, not me."

"How did that affect you?"

"Well, I felt bad for my mother, but there wasn't much I could do for her."

"How did *you* deal with your father?"

"I avoided him as much as possible and tried to stay under his radar. The slightest noise or disruption sent him into a tizzy, and he'd yell."

"How did that make you feel?"

"Like I needed to be good, so he'd like me."

"Ahh! So, you reasoned how to get the response that you wanted. You had an internal dialogue going on in your mind. My father's angry. He doesn't love me. But what if you thought — Dad is having a bad day today. It may have nothing to do with me. Then, you wouldn't feel bad at all."

"What does this have to do with Daniel?"

"The links between thoughts and feelings are important," he says. "You were conditioned at an early age to blame yourself when things go wrong and feel the need to fix them."

"It didn't always work, but I never stopped trying. Daniel, on the other hand, didn't care. I resented him for that, but I never showed it. Instead, I pretended that it didn't matter."

"That's normal," he says. "With any situation where one person gives more than the other, resentment moves in when there is no appreciation."

"After everything Daniel did to me, he gets to move on while I deal with the loss. Did he ever care about me? I feel worthless." Tears spring from my eyes.

"What we ignore continues. Have you ever heard of the author Elisabeth Kubler-Ross? She wrote a book called *The Five Stages of Loss and Grief.* Typically, there are five responses to loss, denial, anger, bargaining, depression, and acceptance. He jots it down and hands me the sheet.

"Aren't you angry at Daniel?"

"Yes, but I never expressed anger. I was afraid of what he would do if I called him on it. If anything, I was careful not to seem angry or demanding."

"Anger is one of the five steps of grieving. It's essential to healing. According to her book, we don't enter and leave each stage in a linear fashion, and sometimes we get stuck. We may feel one, then another, and back again to the first one."

"I'm angrier with myself," I say, "but stupidity makes me swallow it."

"I think you're trapped in that cycle, Florence, but you haven't reached the acceptance stage."

"We were so in love in the beginning. Then the sexual intimacy stopped. Every time I tried to put my finger on the problem, he'd distract me or minimize my feelings. For a long time, I was stuck in the denial stage. I stopped talking about it."

"Denial doesn't mean you didn't know there was a problem. It's just a grace period. Elizabeth Kubler-Ross explains it as nature's way of letting in only as much as we can handle."

"That makes sense. Even though I didn't voice my concerns, I started to question the validity of our relationship. It put me on the road to survival."

"Not everyone goes through all of the stages in the prescribed order, but until you're willing to feel your anger, it won't dissipate and heal."

"All my life, I've feared a confrontation," I say. "I don't like it if someone is mad at me."

"It's easier to suppress anger because just beneath the surface is pain."

"I didn't want to hear Daniel say he didn't love me, so I avoided arguments." I look down at the list of stages. "I don't understand the third stage, bargaining. Daniel was uncompromising. There was no bargaining with him."

"No, but you did bargain with yourself. Otherwise, you might not have accepted the dysfunction in your relationship."

"I thought I could hold onto him if I made excuses. I guess that's a form of bargaining."

"You probably told yourself that if you did a, b, or c, things would go back to how they were when you first met."

"Yes, he had me convinced that as soon as he was back on his feet financially, our lives would get better, but after a while, the 'what ifs' turned into 'if onlys.' I kept thinking I could have done something differently."

"Bargaining caused you to find fault in yourself instead of the reality that no matter what you tried, the relationship would never return to the way it was."

"I couldn't deal with the pain. At that point, I would have done anything to hold onto Daniel."

"So, you remained in the past and negotiated your way out of the hurt you felt from his lack of affection."

"It was very depressing, but I couldn't show *that* emotion either. Along with any talk of feelings, Daniel saw it as a sign of weakness."

"Now that you have left Daniel, you are free to feel that emotion."

"I've never been one to pull the covers over my head and give up," I say. "It wasn't until I attended one of the group anxiety sessions that depression hit me, and it hit hard. I walked around in a daze for a week. Luckily, I pulled myself out of it. The sadness does return from time to time, but I fight the urge to withdraw from life."

"Depression isn't a sign of mental illness, Florence. It's a response to your loss and a necessary step in the process of healing. Like I said before, I think you are going through the circle of emotions and not getting to the acceptance stage."

"I don't know if I'll ever accept what happened to me."

"Acceptance doesn't mean you're all right with what happened to you. It's about accepting the reality that the relationship is over and your life is changed. You can't replace what you've lost, but you can make new meaningful relationships," he says and scribbles an address on a pad.

"There's a codependency support group that meets weekly and can help you."

Stages of Anger

Dreams and goals that disappear
Invade your mind and soul
A melancholy bittersweet
Of things, you'll never know

I feed Ripley and dress for my eight o'clock Zumba class. It's seven-thirty, the time Daniel used to call. Even after months of No Contact, my mind floats back to him. The all-consuming urge to hear his voice is gone. So, why can't I cut the cord? I imagine him comfy with his new woman. He's a physiological rapist, yet he repeats the same patterns with someone new while I fall apart at the seams. It's not fair. I need comfy.

My mangled heartthrobs are like an open wound. I try to ignore the inner critic, saying no one will ever want me. I don't want to be alone.

I want to meet someone without a lot of emotional baggage — someone I can connect to below a superficial level, but that won't happen unless I conquer my fear of being hurt again. Maybe I'll give the dating site Plenty of Fish another shot. There's a man who has shown interest in me more than once. I replied to his last message and agreed to meet him for dinner.

❧

Arriving at the designated restaurant early, the waitress seats me, and I order a glass of wine. I check out everyone who comes through the door, comparing him to the picture Marcus posted. Finally, he arrives. Sporting a black leather motorcycle jacket and a blue bandana that sweeps his curly blond hair into a ponytail, he's not at all what I expected. He smiles as he makes his way to the table.

"Hi, I'm Marcus." He gives me a hug and stands back. "Wow. You're prettier than your profile picture. Have you been here long?"

"No, I just got here," I say.

The waitress comes to the table, takes his drink order, and we study the menu.

"Geez. This place is expensive."

He scans the list to find the least expensive item on the menu.

"We'll have the burgers," he tells the waitress.

Great! We're in an expensive steakhouse, and he orders two burgers. Determined to push past it, I ask about his recent move to the area.

"I left New Jersey three weeks ago. My wife is giving me a hard time."

"You're married?"

"Technically, but we haven't been together in two years."

Oh great! Cheap and married!

"She's trying to force me to pay child support, but I quit my job." He gives me a sinister smile. "She can't get blood out of a turnip."

Another deadbeat, Dad!

The food comes to the table, and Marcus lifts the bun.

"Excuse me, Miss," he says, calling her back. "This burger is overcooked. I'm not paying for something that isn't edible."

I want to apologize for his rudeness, but I'm just as stunned as she is.

"My burger is fine," I say.

Two hours crawl by like an eternity. The food goes down in clumps. I want to go home. Finally, the bill comes. I watch him do the math — twice.

Marcus walks me to my car. "When can I see you again?" he asks.

"I'll have to let you know. Uh, I have a lot of work coming up this week."

"Well, call me," he says and closes in for a hug and plants his lips on mine. Panicked, I pull away. He turns to leave, but not before I see the disappointment in his eyes. As he drives off, my mind is reeling. Rushing home, I throw myself on the bed and cry. *Why? Why didn't Daniel love me?*

My cat is meowing and nudging me. I'm not sure if Ripley is upset that I'm crying or if he wants to eat. He follows me into the kitchen. I open a can of cat food for him and pour myself a glass of wine. I know there is someone on my blog to listen to my woes, and I log on to my computer.

Florence: Oh, God. I went on a date. I thought a new memory would help erase the sociopath. It only made things worse. All I want to do is drink wine and cry.

Lisa: We're entitled to have a pity party when our hopes are dashed a bit. But then go to sleep. Wake up and take a fresh look at where your journey is leading you. It's surprising how clear the path becomes in moments like this.

Florence: It was awful. We didn't connect, and it was very awkward. I guess I'm not ready.

Lisa: Dating in 2015! If you're not afraid of STDs, you're scared of sociopaths, narcissists, murderers, rapists, and creepy weirdos. Please take the time to heal. Find yourself and gain strength before heading back into the jungle world of dating.

❧

According to Martha Stout, author of *The Sociopath Next Door,* only four percent of the population is sociopathic, so why do I feel surrounded.

Anxious to see Dr. Gerard, I arrive at the center twenty minutes early, and I'm forced to wring my hands in the waiting area. Finally, he pops his head out and calls me back to his office.

"I think I'm in the anger stage of grief," I say before I even take a seat. "Isn't that the fourth stage?"

Dr. Gerard leans back in his chair and ponders my question.

"The stages of grief are responses to feelings," he says. "They could surface at any time and in no particular order."

"Well, lately, I feel even more abandoned by Daniel. I have the urge to strike out and hurt him for ruining my life."

"How do you hope to achieve that?"

"Daniel's guitar is tucked away under my bed. I thought about selling it to pay my credit card bill that he ran up. I also have seven pieces of his artwork."

"I guess you have a right to keep it as collateral."

"But it's not mine to sell — is it?"

"You said he owes you a lot of money."

"Yes, but somehow it doesn't feel right. I should send Daniel a copy of the promissory note that he signed. Not that I have any illusions of getting my money, but it would be nice to ruin his day."

"Anger can be an anchor to your feelings of abandonment," he says. "It gives you the strength to push through your pain and get past it, but not if you use it as a weapon. Life will continue to give us lessons until we learn, grow, and move past them."

Dr. Gerard says thoughts can be changed and that the very things we fear keep repeating themselves if we continue to focus on them and give them power. I have moments of self-doubt, but they are only thoughts. I'm luckier than most. I managed to escape while some people are strung along forever. The worst is over, except for Christmas, making me a little apprehensive. I log on to my blog for moral support.

Florence: The holiday's coming like a freight train, and I'm a little unsteady. Christmas music makes me melancholy, and being alone makes it worse. How will I ever get through the holidays?

Lisa: You can do this! You will be so glad when you do. Just think. When the New Year starts! And a better year lies ahead for you!

<u>Florence:</u> I know you're right. Daniel wasn't into the holidays. He always found a reason to be unhappy and made sure I was too. If I cry, it will be on my terms.

<u>Rachel:</u> "I'm so incredibly proud of you, Flo. Once you start letting go is when life starts to get beautiful again."

Joe Dial

I need a life-long partner
I want to find true love
He is out there somewhere
The one that I speak of

After my last attempt at dating, I didn't think I'd ever want to see another man. So, I was surprised when I received a text from Robert, whom I had dinner with last year. Although I'd had a lovely evening, I ran like a scared rabbit when he tried to kiss me.

"Have you met the man of your dreams yet?" he asks.

I have to laugh. Robert has no idea what I've gone through this past year.

"No. Not yet," I respond.

"Well, as I remember, the only time we've sat and talked face-to-face was last April."

"Yes...I'm sorry. It takes me a long time to feel comfortable. I take things slowly...."

"I think it's fair to say we're taking it slow. So, how is beautiful Florence doing these days? Still in Florida? If you would be interested in meeting again, just let me know. It's up to you. I'm hoping you might drive more south one of these days."

"I may visit that area next week to see my mother. Maybe I'll stop and meet you for coffee as I pass Palm Beach."

"Please let me know when and where. Perhaps the stars will be in alignment!"

Hmm. As I recall, Robert was very sweet and not bad-looking. I just wasn't ready then. I wasn't enthusiastic about a long-distance romance. Now it doesn't matter. What if he tries to kiss me again?

Oh, stop it, Florence. What's the big deal?

⤞⤝

My confidence is shaky, but I'm ready to meet Robert again. Daniel's constant belittling made me question my self-worth. He criticized everything about me, from my appearance and abilities to my very existence. He even went so far as to tell me I wasn't Italian and wasn't a true New Yorker as I had moved to Florida. Seeking validation, I jumped through his hoops, only to feel degraded. It was all part of the sociopath's game to devalue and deflate my self-esteem. Now that I am free from Daniel, my true essence has a chance to rebuild.

My cell phone rings.

"Hi, Robert. I'm almost at your exit."

"I'm sorry, Florence. Something came up. I won't be able to meet with you this morning."

Disappointed, old familiar voices come back to haunt me.

"No worries," I say. "I'll go on to my mom's house. Maybe another time."

"How about this evening? We can meet for dinner."

Hmm. Maybe I reacted too fast. You would think I'd learn to stay out of other people's heads.

"That would be nice," I say. "I can meet you on my way home."

"Great. What do you like? Chinese, Italian, French?"

"Anything is fine. You decide."

"Okay, French, it is. I'll make a reservation for six o'clock and text you the address."

Now I'm on cloud nine. My mother picks up on it right away. "You look happy, Florence. I'm so glad. I've worried about you."

"Yes, I've been a little down since I broke up with Daniel, but I'm feeling much better."

"He wasn't right for you, Florence."

"I know, but that didn't make it easier."

"Are we going out for lunch?" My sister says as she bounds down the stairs.

"Of course." I smile and hug her. "Let's have Chinese food. It's light, and I don't want to overeat. I have a dinner date."

"Oh?" She laughs. "Do tell!"

"It's that guy I met last year. I thought I blew it, but he contacted me again."

"Well, be careful, Florence. You tend to get attached too easily, and you can't afford to make the same mistake twice."

"Yes, Mom… I know."

She's deflated my balloon a little, but it's still floating.

The sun is shining, not a cloud in the sky. Could this day get any better?

My phone chimes at four o'clock with a text. *"Six p.m. at Le Bistro."*

Two more hours and I'll see Robert. Last time, I didn't get a good look at him because it was dark in the restaurant. A little older than me, he wasn't very tall and was packing an extra pound or two, but he had smiling eyes. I imagine they must be blue. Keeping an eye on the clock, I can't stop smiling.

Palm Beach Gardens isn't far. I find *Le Bistro* with ease. I'm early as usual. I park my car and follow the sound of carousel music to the inner circle of restaurants. The horses go up and down with happy children on their backs. I take a seat on a nearby bench. Aromas from nearby restaurants mingle in the air, creating a smorgasbord of mouthwatering sensations.

Surrounded by high-end boutiques, I watch shoppers laden with packages. I've always known that some people live like this but are far removed from me. Engrossed in the splendor of the lifestyle, I don't notice Robert until he's by my side. He's grown a beard and looks very dashing. I stare into his soulful eyes, reaffirming they are smiling like they did last year.

He hugs me. "I'm so glad you decided to meet me for dinner."

"So am I. This is a great place."

"Come!" He takes my arm. "This is one of my favorite restaurants. You're going to love it."

Robert orders a bottle of wine while I look over the menu.

"The scallops look good," I say.

"Excellent choice!"

The time flies by quickly. I don't want it to end, but it's getting late. Robert asks the waiter to re-cork the wine, and we walk out to the parking lot.

"Do you have to rush off, Florence? I want to show you my boat. The marina is just around the corner."

"Well...."

He laughs at my caution. "I won't keep you if you want to leave."

"All right, but I can't stay long."

"Great. Let's take my car. Yours will be safe here."

He opens the passenger door for me and gives me a gentle kiss. I instinctively pull away.

Robert smiles. "I forgot how shy you are. No worries." He slides into the driver's seat and heads toward the marina.

At the entrance, he punches a code, and the gates open to a magical world of boats and restaurants. As we drive around the curve, lights twinkle in the palm trees, making it look like a winter holiday wonderland even though it's spring. He parks in front of a large sailboat. "Here, she is!"

"Wow!" I've seen boats like this before but never had the opportunity to board one. My heart is racing as we step onto the dock. Intracoastal water slaps against the hull, but the boat isn't affected. It remains stationary.

Robert helps me step into the boat. We descend the stairs to a cozy kitchen area.

"Would you like another glass of wine?" he asks.

"Yes, but only one. I have a long drive home."

After a tour and a glass of wine, he says. "I guess I'd better let you go," but he stops before we go up the ladder.

"I have something for you."

He scans through his bookshelf and pulls out a book. "Remember, I told you about this book, *The Joe Dial*.

"Yes, the book about givers and takers. You said the author is your friend."

"I want you to have it. Then you can let me know what you think next time we meet," Robert says with a smile.

Next time? Oh yes, I'm sure there will be *a next time*.

Robert drives me back to my car. This time, when he kisses me, I don't pull away.

Along the way home, my phone chimes with a text. *"Do I have to wait a year to see you again? (And kiss you again?)"*

I smile. *"We'll see,"* I text back.

Gypsy

I know that he is out there
Could pass him on the street
I hope that I will recognize
My soul mate when we meet

I plan to see Robert the following week after visiting with my mother. He had mentioned staying overnight on his boat. It's tempting, but I'm not sure I'll feel that comfortable with him yet. Just in case, I pack an overnight bag.

My family keeps me longer than expected, and I get stuck in bumper-to-bumper traffic. My nerves frayed by the time I step out of my car. My legs are wobbly as I board his boat and descend the stairs to the main cabin. He wraps his arms around my waist and kisses me. It feels good, and I want more, but this time, he pulls away.

"I made us a reservation at one of the marina restaurants. It's a beautiful night. We can walk."

The boat is rocking, and he guides me up the stairs in front of him as I struggle to keep my balance. Once on solid ground, we stroll hand in hand like two seasoned lovers. I almost have to pinch myself. The staff at the restaurant knows him and seats us far enough from the band so we can talk. Robert orders a bottle of wine and suggests some things from the menu. He orders an array of appetizers to sample the delicacies they offer. It's more food than I can eat in a week, and my eyes widen.

"We can take the leftovers with us and eat them for breakfast," he says.

Hmm. "Assuming I'll be here for breakfast."

He smiles.

The restaurant buzzes with affluence and prestige. The band rolls into a slow romantic song, and Robert gets up.

"Would you like to dance?"

"Eh... I don't...." HE GRABS MY HAND before I could finish and leads me onto the dance floor. With his arms tight around my waist, he holds me in his eyes as we move together in a sensual rhythmic melody. I feel more comfortable by the second song and don't object when his hand inches toward my butt.

"A thong?" he asks.

I smile shyly and wrap my arms around his neck, drawing him closer. By the time the music ends, I'm more comfortable.

"I have more wine at my place," he whispers.

Under a starlit sky, we walk arm in arm from the restaurant. Robert pours us more wine back on the boat and sits next to me on the couch. His intense stare melts my inhibitions as he cradles my face lovingly in his hands and kisses me. Looking for proof that I'm still a desirable woman, I swing my leg over his and give in to the passion. I'm unsure if it's the wine or his kisses, but my head is spinning. I'm not thinking straight.

"I hope I'll be able to drive home," I say, but we both know I'll be spending the night.

Robert takes my hand, and I follow him to the aft stateroom. I want to feel his body next to me tonight, and the fact that we're on a boat makes it much better. I disrobe, except for my thong, and slip under the sheets.

"Watch your head on the overhang," he warns and slides in next to me. As he devours me in kisses, I float away in a fantasy dream.

"It's been a while since I've been sexually active. I'm more sensual than sexual."

Sensing my reluctance, Robert stops.

"I'm not going to make love to you tonight, Florence. I don't think you're ready for a new relationship, and I don't want to hurt you."

Disappointed, I nod. My desire to be close to someone is stronger than my desire to have sex. "I need to be in your arms tonight," I say.

"And you shall." He kisses me again. "I may change my mind in the middle of the night, though. I'm just warning you."

Feeling the effects of the wine, I lay my head on his shoulder and close my eyes. In the middle of the night, I wake. Robert is on the other side of the bed. No *comfy* here!

⁓

Robert's asleep next to me. I don't know if I should get up or lie there. I move to put on my clothes.

"Wait," he says in a sleepy voice. "I'll get dressed and walk you out."

He gets up and puts on his pants. "Would you like some coffee before you leave?"

"Coffee would be great."

I brush my teeth while he's busy in the kitchen.

Robert pours coffee, and I sit at the small booth waiting for him to join me. We sip from mugs decorated with little white sailboats without speaking.

"I have a headache from the wine," he says.

"I'm sorry."

"There's nothing for you to be sorry about." He laughs. "If anything, it's me who's sorry. I had a beautiful woman in my bed last night, and I fell asleep."

"Maybe next time," I say.

"You know, Florence. I'm going back north next month. I'm a gypsy. Usually, I'm attracted to strong women. You're a sweet girl. I don't want to hurt you."

He places our empty coffee mugs in the sink and slips on his sandals. "Don't forget your food from last night."

I don't really want it but take it anyway and make my way up the stairs — probably for the last time.

Robert gives me a tentative kiss on the lips, and I drive off, leaving him on the dock. He said he liked strong women. The comment went over my head and flew around. Now that it has landed, I ponder his remark.

I think he's confusing aggression with strength. After everything that I've been through, I am strong! He doesn't know me.

Why did I think I had a chance at love? Why am I attracted to the same kind of men over and over? Men who make me compete for their affections. It's a game and one that I usually lose. I feel like crying, but my tears have been spent crying over Daniel. Robert lives on a mega sailboat in one of the most prestigious marinas in Florida. Any presentable man with a bank account will have women all over him. He can choose from younger women all day long. They may be shallow, but youth will have its way, and there's no competing with that. I'm not sure I want to, so I'll walk away with my battered pride.

The truth is, he may not have been the right man for me. Yet, I was ready to ignore my boundaries and let him claim me out of need. I'm so anxious to get to the acceptance stage of my recovery that I reached out to anyone. Now I see that I can't do that until I've worked through my grief.

Survivor

The venom that was left behind
Will surely drain away
You will live once more
To love another day

When someone hurts your body, you tend to try to get away. Psychological abuse is different. The emotional abuse Daniel inflicted hurt me physically, perhaps worse. Day after day, he undermined my opinions and perceptions of the world. This constant beatdown eroded my self-esteem, leaving me confused, off-balance, and emotionally drained. He'd turn on the charm if I tried to pull away and expertly divert my feelings. I gave him the benefit of the doubt and ignored the nagging voice inside me. My persistence in maintaining the relationship made me crazy. I couldn't let go, even if it meant living in limbo.

Daniel's financial abuse was blatant. At first, I believed I could stay one step ahead of him, but my savings slowly trickled away. As my account dipped from 30K to 20K to 10K, I struggled to hold on, but he stepped over every line I drew in the sand. Fearing judgment and criticism, I chose my words carefully to avoid confrontation.

It was all typical of a narcissist sociopath. After reading Dr. Rosenberg's article, I understand what happened to me, and I don't feel stupid.

At first, having no closure was impossible to accept. By cutting off all communication with Daniel, I was acknowledging the relationship was over. Still, it turned out to be a catalyst. I'm working to understand the dynamics that led me to where I am today. Slowly, I'm learning to forgive myself for falling prey. I've blamed my problems on him, but I'm as much at fault. If I'd set better boundaries, he couldn't have used me. Beyond that, I'm beginning to forgive Daniel too.

At first, I was indignant. *Why should I bear the onus of forgiveness? I'm the one who was injured. It was my blood that was spilled.*

It took some time to realize we were each a prisoner in our relationship. I took on his financial problems without realizing their effect on our relationship. The more I loaned him, the less affection he had for me. Maybe he felt less of a man for taking it — or he lost respect for me when I couldn't refuse.

I've finally reached the fifth stage of grief, acceptance. I can't be angry with Daniel anymore. I'm more accepting of what I went through and ready to leave it in the past. Letting go of my anger was the last obstacle.

The scar on my heart is like an ugly garment in the back of my closet. It's always there, but I don't have to wear it.

Since I decided to save myself, I no longer have to assume responsibility for keeping Daniel's financial boat afloat. Still, I don't regret taking responsibility for the mess he wanted to leave behind. I don't know what I would have done if it weren't for Chuck offering to help me with my boat. He understands what *Call it a Day* meant to me and how much hard work I poured into that boat. He found a buyer for me. After paying to lift the boat and have the engines "pickled," I'm walking away with thirteen hundred dollars.

Daniel and I could have lived on that boat and enjoyed our golden years at sea. My dream of living on a boat will have to wait. Some might think it's presumptuous, but the fantasy keeps me focused. For now, I'm doing all right on terrafirma.

Most victims of sociopaths say it takes a year or two to get over most of the pain. I'm having more good days than bad, but sometimes I slide into sadness. Daniel crawls through my mind like an uninvited guest at unpredictable times. I still experience a dull ache in stores and restaurants that we frequented. I can't even go to McDonald's for coffee anymore.

For a while, I worried that Daniel had destroyed my ability to trust and love. However, my desire to find someone is getting stronger every day. Thanks to Robert, I've broken through the fear of dating. At times, I still stumble, but I've become aware of red flags and discard potential problem relationships when something doesn't feel right.

In the past, rushing into relationships caused me to completely miss or ignore the warning signs. Now, I detour before I get too involved. It's harder to make mistakes when you know which direction you want your life to go.

Fear has been the motor that drove me rather than the search for the promise of something greater. The desire to avoid pain has ruled my life, but no more. I'm working on stronger boundaries, making me more assertive. I no longer tolerate people who discount my value as a woman.

Self-esteem has to do with resilience. I'm taking baby steps—I'm crawling, but I have tenacity. Someone once told me that. Isn't it strange how a small comment like that can be a lifeline? It keeps me moving forward. Sharing my experience with others who are going through the misfortune of a fraudulent love affair helps me. After two years of research, I've become an advocate for other women to help them through the psychological minefields associated with narcissists. If I can ease the pain of one victim or spur them onto the journey of discovering their self-worth, then what I went through has value. In that way, I hope to find my closure.

I've been through a grievous ordeal. There were times I didn't think I'd live through it. I've escaped finding my peace, while Daniel's persona will always be camouflaged in lies. He'll never know "normal."

Victory is mine, complete with a better sense of who I am and how I want to live my life. And that makes me a survivor!

Florence: "Okay! It's been eight months, No Contact. I'm limping toward the finish line. Thanks for all the support, especially you, Rachel. I don't know if I could have gotten this far without all of you.

Rachel: Most welcome, hon. You are doing an awesome job, Flo. I plan to educate and support as many people as I can. Unfortunately, I have had an abundance of experience with narcissistic shitheads, but my strategy is to turn that experience into a positive by helping others. I truly believe that no contact is the only way.

Diana: "It was never real. It was just an illusion. They are predators, manipulators, and completely self-serving. The best advice is to view the relationship as a bad nightmare. So, it's daytime now. Forget the darkness."

⁓⟁⁓

Lying on the beach under my umbrella, I watch the puffy white clouds sail by and listen to the sounds of the waves crashing. A man is by the shore with his fishing pole and a bucket of fish. I watch him cast and wish I had remembered my pole. I hear that Pompano is running, and it's my favorite fish. There's a small boat on the horizon. Usually, that gives me a melancholy feeling, but I'm light as a feather as I breathe in the salty air. I close my eyes, letting the breeze take me into a peaceful slumber.

The man fishing walks up respectfully close to my blanket and coughs.

"Sorry to bother you, ma'am. I left my cell phone in the car. Do you know what time it is?"

I smile and look at my watch. "It's a little past noon."

"That's a nice Rolex," he says, but isn't it a little big for you?"

I laugh. "Yes, but it has sentimental value."

"Oh. Well, thank you!" He walks back to the shore."

My cell phone rings, but I don't recognize the caller.

"Hi, my name is David. Chuck gave me your number. I hope you don't mind that I'm calling. I wanted to tell you. I love your boat."

"It's your boat now."

"Chuck speaks very highly of you," he says. "I can't wait to meet you."

"What did he tell you?"

"That you had a dream to live on the boat. Chuck told me how much work you did."

"Yes, it was unfortunate when it sunk. Do you think you can restore it?"

"Definitely. I'm working on it every day. Maybe once it's finished, you can come and see it."

"I'd like that. Do you have a name for the boat?"

"Yes, I call her Florence… Florence of the Sea!"

Thank You for Reading Entangled
Please post a review on Amazon.com and
Friend Florence St. John on Facebook

Parting from the one you love
No one could ever win
Linger do the memories
Of things that could have been

Heart in pain and stomach knots
Desire not to eat
Body yearns for rest
But doesn't welcome sleep

Dreams and goals that disappear
Invade your mind and soul
A melancholy bittersweet
Of things, you'll never know

You long to see your lover's face
And crave to hear his voice
To hold him in your empty arms
You cannot change the course

The warmth of breath upon your neck
The touch of his caress
You feel the bite and cry in pain
A sense of emptiness

A serpent's sting, it hurts so much
You think that you will die
But time will heal all wounds
You know that you must try

The venom that was left behind
Will surely drain away
You will live once more
To love another day

The concept of a Sociopath is often confusing to most people. I struggled with the term as I wrote this book and debated if narcissist was a more correct term. Through my research, I've found that there are only slight differences. Although all sociopaths exhibit narcissistic behaviors, not all narcissists are sociopaths. According to Medcare Public, the following signs will indicate you are dealing with a sociopath:

http://my.medicarepublic.com/sociopaths-ten-tell-tale-signs

The sociopath's most deadly weapon is the charm offensive – but beware—it's superficial charm and lacks an atom of sincerity. Sociopaths are accomplished actors. Smooth, engaging, charming, flattering, a sociopath will never be tongue-tied or embarrassed. They are fond of quoting from movies or books – this is because, despite their manipulative skills, they never have an original thought of their own. As charming as they are, they also have a need to be respected, even adored, by others. Some stoop to hints of the way they were [supposedly] abused at the hands of others, spinning dreadful tales of their own imaginary traumatic experiences. This is guaranteed to elicit sympathy and, therefore, assistance from the uninitiated.

An over-inflated sense of self-worth. Sociopaths believe they are superior human beings, on a higher plan than others, often portraying themselves as having some deep intelligence, pretending to possess some great insight others lack. Some of them even pretend to have qualifications – a phony Ph.D. is a common one – bought from a dodgy online American pseudo-university or college. Nonetheless, they feign modesty, admitting to being 'a bit of a nerd (or geek) really' or appear to sublimate themselves to [pretended] spirituality. They have cottoned on to the fact that humility is a powerful tool.

Prone to boredom. They have a need to be constantly stimulated, yet they rarely engage in long-term hobbies or pastimes. They have an inability to hold down long-term relationships, referring to their latest conquests as 'Brazilian Beauties' or the like. This is because, despite their apparent charm, they are shallow human beings with nothing to add to the collective knowledge of humanity.

Pathological liars. Sociopaths are deceptive and dishonest, and they can lie to your face with heartfelt sincerity – and to prove their point, they will win your confidence by displaying a genuine faux interest in you; they will laugh at all your jokes and appear to feel your pain. They will agree with everything you say.

Master manipulators. They will say and do anything to deceive and cheat others. This is their one true hobby, and their skill has been honed to perfection, the result of years of practice. They are adept in enlisting the sympathy of others, to whom they will be the very embodiment of goodness itself.

Often, they will play the part of the victim to gain the sympathy of people they wish to recruit to their particular cause. They are incredibly talented when it comes to garnering support from others; playing the victim is a common ruse de guerre.

Lack of remorse. Sociopaths have no sense of the suffering of their victims. On the contrary, they enjoy the suffering of their victims. To them, this sort of domination is better than sex. Often, it's payback for all the times they were frustrated or snubbed in childhood. Their victim is often a substitute for the one who abused them when they were children.

Limited range of feelings. Don't expect them to express any emotion other than happiness or sadness. There *is* nothing in between. Everyone they meet is either 'wonder-filled' or 'low class' unless, of course, they can be used. Yes, Sociopaths use people and throw them away like Kleenex.

Callousness. Sociopaths are cold and contemptuous of others. This is an emotion (or lack of emotion) they are skilled at concealing; the pretense of the caring humanist butter-wouldn't-melt persona is kept up at all times – even to the person they are busy destroying – and that's part of the fun!

Parasitic lifestyle. Sociopaths are often financially dependent on others. They trade off time and 'caring' for financial security, and they will very soon know more about your finances than you do yourself.

Can't control their behavior. When challenged, sociopaths get angry. This is the only real emotion they are capable of experiencing. Sometimes they get their lawyers to bury you under an avalanche of litigation. Or they will refuse to let you see your children – this is a common lever and again, something that gives them huge, orgasmic pleasure. In cases where they have been found out, you run a very high risk of becoming their new hobby, and they will involve themselves in that bordering on obsession.

Codependency: Don't Dance

The inherently dysfunctional "codependency dance" requires two opposite but balanced partners: a pleasing, giving codependent and the needy, controlling narcissist. Like a champion dance partnership, the dancing roles are perfectly matched: the leader needs the follower, and vice versa. Or in other words, the giver-taker dance role combination enables the two to dance effortlessly and flawlessly.

Typically, codependents give of themselves much more than their partners give in return. As "generous" but bitter dance partners, they find themselves perpetually stuck on the dance floor, always waiting for the "next song," at which time they naively hope their partner will finally understand their needs. Sadly, it never happens.

Codependents, by nature, are giving, sacrificing, and consumed with the needs and desires of others. As natural followers in the "dance," they are passive and accommodating to their partners. Although narcissists are typically selfish, self-centered, and controlling, when paired with a codependent, they are enabled to become champion dancers. As natural leaders and choreographers of the dance, their ambitions are focused only on fulfilling their needs and desires while ignoring the same for their partner.

Codependents experience their narcissistic dance partner as deeply appealing, especially because of their boldness, charm, confidence, and domineering personality. Narcissists are delighted with their partner choice as they find someone who exudes patience, deference, and a yearning to help them find greatness and recognition. With this pair-up, the dance sizzles with excitement – at least initially.

Narcissistic dancers control or lead the dance routine because they are naturally and predictably attracted to partners who lack self-worth and confidence and have low self-esteem. With such a well-matched companion, they can control both the dancer and the dance. Similar to their codependent partner, this dancer is also deeply attracted to a lover who feels familiar to them: someone who lets them lead the dance while, at the same time, allowing them to feel in command, competent, and appreciated. The narcissist dancer is most comfortable when encouraged or allowed to dance boldly and decisively while garnering attention and praise from others.

Having little to no previous experience with mutually and reciprocally affirming dancers, codependents anxiously reject invitations by healthier individuals. Without self-esteem or feelings of personal power, they are afraid to dance with a mutually-giving and unconditionally loving partner. Dancing with such a person would feel confusing, uncomfortable, and awkward.

When a codependent and narcissist meet each other, the dance unfolds flawlessly. The narcissist effortlessly maintains the lead while the codependent automatically and willingly follows. Their roles seem natural because they have been practicing them their whole lives. The dance is perfectly coordinated: the pleasing partner naturally and reflexively gives up their power, and the needy partner thrives on power and control. Both feel like they have practiced this dance their whole life. No one gets their toes stepped on!

The magnetic-like attraction force that brings codependent and narcissist dancers together (and keeps them together) paves the way for a dancing experience that is explosively pleasurable while feeling strangely familiar. To illustrate, the selfish and controlling narcissist effortlessly leads the dance while the codependent intuitively and reflexively predicts and follow his moves. One was "born" to lead, while the other was to follow. As well-matched and exquisitely coordinated dancing partners, the dancing experience is euphorically exciting and deeply satisfying.

The accommodating dancer confuses caretaking and sacrifice with loyalty and love. And why should they think otherwise, as this has been their lifelong experience in relationships? Although proud and boastful of their unwavering loyalty and dedication, they feel unappreciated and used. This codependent dancer yearns to be loved and cherished, but because of her dance partner, her dreams will never come to fruition. With the heartbreak of unfulfilled dreams, codependents silently and bitterly swallow their unhappiness while dancing furiously toward the finals of the dance competition.

The codependent is convinced that she will never find a dance partner who will love her for who she is, as opposed to what she can do for them. Over time, they are essentially stuck in a pattern of giving and sacrificing without possibly ever receiving the same from their partner. They, however, pretend to enjoy the dance while harboring deeper feelings of anger, resentment, and sadness. Over time, their low self-esteem and pessimism deepen, which later morph into feelings of hopelessness. But they continue to dance, not for the joy of it, but because dancing with a narcissist is familiar and natural for them.

Since familiarity breeds security, the meaning of love for the codependent dancer is distorted into exciting but dysfunctional dips, twists, and turns. Just because the blue ribbons and trophies accumulate, love, respect, and thoughtfulness often do not follow. Such familiarity creates the paradox of the dance: remaining secure with what you know but what doesn't feel good versus risking the unknown so that a relationship with a loving and respectful partner can be an actuality.

After many "songs," the codependent's enchanting dream-like dance experience predictably transforms into drama, conflict, and feeling trapped. Even with her dance partner's selfish, controlling and antagonistic nature, she dares not stop dancing. Despite feeling deeply unhappy, she remains committed to her partner while helping him achieve his glorious dancing ambitions. For most codependent dancers, remaining with the narcissistic partner is preferable to being on the sidelines, where they predictably feel worthless and lonely. To the codependent, loneliness is a toxic and unbearable experience.

Sadly, codependent dancers were taught the codependent/narcissist dance routine early in their lives. Hence, their dancing choices are connected to their unconscious motivation to find a person who is familiar – someone who reminds them of their parents, who abandoned, neglected, and/or abused them when they were a child. Their fear of being alone, their compulsion to control and fix at any cost, and their comfort in their role as the martyr who is endlessly devoted and patient, are a direct result of attachment trauma that they experienced at the hands of their own narcissistic parent.

Codependents cannot bear a prolonged period off the dance floor because of the wave of self-doubt and loneliness that predictably follows. Being alone is the equivalent of feeling lonely, and loneliness is an excruciating, debilitating experience for codependent dancers. Like withdrawal from drug addiction, they are unwilling to cope with the resulting deep and throbbing pain of loneliness and feelings of worthlessness, which is indicative of the childhood trauma they endured.

Although codependents dream of dancing with an unconditionally loving and affirming partner, they submit to their dysfunctional destiny. Until they decide to heal the psychological wounds that ultimately compel them to dance with their narcissistic dance partners, they will be destined to maintain the unsatisfying and potentially dangerous steady beat and rhythm of their dysfunctional dance.

Through psychotherapy and, perhaps, a 12-step recovery program, codependents can begin to fulfill their dream to dance the grand dance of love, reciprocity, and mutuality. Through a challenging and, at times, heartbreaking journey, codependents have an opportunity to heal the childhood trauma at the root of their codependency.

Ultimately, the recovering codependent's healing and transformative journey will result in deep and profound feelings of self-respect and self-love. They will have learned that the true measure of their value is determined by who they are, not what they do. Such will lead them into the arms of someone willing and capable of sharing the lead, communicating their movements, and pursuing a mutually loving rhythmic dance.

****

Ross Rosenberg, LCPC, CADC, CSAT
Author of **<u>The Human Magnet Syndrome: Why We Love People Who Hurt Us</u>**
Clinical Care Consultants Owner
Advanced Clinical Trainers Owner
Psychotherapist, Author & Professional Trainer
3325 N. Arlington Heights Rd., Ste 400B
Arlington Heights, IL 60004

Suggested Reading

Signs of a Sociopath are Big Time Scary
Tanya J. Peterson
https://www.healthyplace.com/personality-disorders/sociopath/signs-of-a-sociopath-are-big-time-scary/

How to Spot a Sociopath
M.E. Thomas
https://www.psychologytoday.com/articles/201305/how-spot-sociopath

Your Conscience, the Sociopath's Weapon of Choice
Marisa Mauro Psy.D.
https://www.psychologytoday.com/blog/take-all-prisoners/200912/your-conscience-the-sociopaths-weapon-choice

How to Spot a Narcissist
Scott Barry Kaufman, Ph.D.
https://www.psychologytoday.com/articles/201107/how-spot-narcissist

Four Steps to Leave a Narcissist
Judith Orloff M.D.
https://www.psychologytoday.com/blog/emotional-freedo